Falling Star

Also bv Lillian O'Donnell

NO BUSINESS BEING A COP
AFTERSHOCK
LEISURE DYING
THE BABY MERCHANTS
DIAL 577 R-A-P-E
DON'T WEAR YOUR WEDDING RING
THE PHONE CALLS
DIVE INTO DARKNESS
THE FACE OF THE CRIME
THE TACHI TREE
THE SLEEPING BEAUTY MURDERS
THE BABES IN THE WOODS
DEATH OF A PLAYER
MURDER UNDER THE SUN
DEATH SCHUSS
DEATH BLANKS THE SCREEN
DEATH ON THE GRASS

Falling Star

Lillian O'Donnell

G. P. PUTNAM'S SONS
NEW YORK

Library of Congress Cataloging in Publication Data

O'Donnell, Lillian.
  Falling star.

  I. Title.
PZ4.0254Fal 1979 [PS3565.D59] 813'.5'4 79-11060
ISBN 0-399-12407-1

Printed in the United States of America

Falling Star

1

He would not be back tonight; she was sure of it, yet she couldn't sleep. Julia Schuyler lay in her sweat-soaked bed listening while she waited for the booze and the tranquilizers to take effect.

She had learned through countless such hours to identify the sounds of night. They were many and varied for this was not a quiet part of the city. "The Tenderloin," it had been called in the bad old days at the turn of century, dubbed so by the venal police captain who, newly assigned to the sector, said, "I've had the chuck; now I'm going to get me some of the tenderloin." It had been squalid and dangerous then, and it hadn't changed. Its denizens came out after dark, their pale skins taking on the bluish tinge of the vapor lamps, the greenish or reddish glow of neon signs over porno houses, bars, massage parlors the way their more fortunate brethren absorbed the rays of the Miami sun. At dawn they crept back to dingy tenement rooms to fall into sodden sleep. Julia Schuyler

7

catalogued their comings and goings the way some people counted sheep. These hot July nights with the windows wide open—nobody around there had air conditioning—it was easier than usual.

Tonight, however, Julia Schuyler wasn't interested in what was going on down in the street. Huddled in the dark, her flimsy nightgown soggy and plastered to her bruised body, she listened only for familiar footsteps. Sweat soaked her black hair and trickled down to mix with the blood from the cut on her left cheek. The tiny, airless room was rank with sweat—the aftermath of what had happened and the fear of what still might come. She closed her eyes, which were just about swollen shut anyway, so she could concentrate harder.

From the way the boards creaked she could tell whether it was Petersen in 4A staggering home, a bum looking for a flop, or an addict prowling for an easy "break and enter." She could interpret the moans of lovers on the landing, of the prostie steering a john upstairs, or of one of Petersen's brats getting smacked by his Ma. She recognized and ignored their cries just as she supposed they recognized and ignored hers. Like the rest of the tenants, Julia Schuyler didn't give a damn for what went on outside her own flimsy door.

He would not be back tonight.

Of course, she could call the police. She knew where that would get her. Nowhere. They were on the man's side every time. She'd seen the cops bound into the building on that kind of complaint. She remembered that poor wisp of a woman with the four slobbering brats calling in after Petersen had broken her arm for her. A piece of the bone was sticking out, but the husband claimed she'd slipped and fallen. Oh, they'd called the ambulance all right, and while she was being strapped into the stretcher, Julia had heard one of the cops whisper to the other:

"Maybe if I beat up on my old lady she'd act right."

They had laughed together.

Of course, she wasn't Helga Petersen, your ordinary household drudge; she was Julia Schuyler, star of stage, screen, and TV since the age of fourteen. If she went to the precinct and swore out a warrant, they couldn't ignore her. But that didn't mean they'd believe her. She could take her clothes off and show her bruises, and he'd say somebody else beat her up, or maybe he'd just give them the wink, the sad shake of the head and whisper: "She's always falling down." They'd take his word in the same way they took the word of that lout upstairs, all the more so in her case because even cops read the scandal sheets and they'd know her reputation.

So she drank. Nothing wrong with liquor. Drugs now, that was something else. Certainly, you couldn't mix the two; her psychiatrist had warned her so she was always careful with the tranquilizers. But alcohol—some doctors recommended it for relaxation of tension. The bible mentioned it as one of the benefits of man. Her father had been a heavy drinker and he had also been the most magnificent actor of his time. John Malcolm Schuyler had no equal, then or now. The tragedy of John Malcolm was that he had lost control, had let the booze destroy first his professional judgment, then his liver. He'd appeared in a series of execrable vehicles with his current mistress as co-star. He'd made himself a laughingstock. But that was at the end, the very end. Julia was forewarned. It wouldn't happen to her.

. Suddenly the bed started to rock; her gorge rose; she couldn't control it. She turned over and heaved.

She didn't give a damn whether the police went for her story or not, Julia thought when the retching finally subsided, leaving her spent, gasping, and filthy. She was Julia Schuyler; her name had been up in lights, in headlines, her picture on front pages and magazine covers, and the story would be picked up. Reporters would jump on it. It would hit every paper in New York and L.A. The tabloids, God! The tabloids would have a field day with it.

She could see the black scare headlines, the garish pictures of herself—at her worst naturally; they'd find a
bleary shot taken at some bash where she'd had a few too
many. She wasn't going to subject herself to that! Julia
Schuyler, a has-been at thirty-one, could handle contempt, but she couldn't bear pity.

Footsteps on the stairs. She tensed. The tread was even,
not favoring the right, without that slight halt as the
weight shifted. Not him. She was sure. Almost sure. She
hadn't really been paying attention. Oh God! she
thought, not again, not tonight. She couldn't take any
more. She pulled herself up against the headboard as she
heard the key inserted into the lock, turned, and the door
opened. Slipping out of bed, she stumbled to the bureau
and grabbed the heavy, cast-iron frying pan she'd put
there.

The lights went on in the living room. She screamed.

"Julia, it's only me. It's all right, Julia. It's all right."

Her knees wobbled. She managed a smile. "Did you
bring anything to drink?"

He held out a brown paper bag. The shape left no doubt
there was a bottle inside.

"You're a sweetheart." Julia Schuyler smiled and let
the frying pan fall to the floor.

The two cops were parked halfway down Forty-fifth
Street between Eighth and Ninth Avenues. All four windows of the patrol car were rolled down in the hope of
sucking in a breeze. There was none. Raymond Emmenecher, the senior of the team, held the steaming container of coffee in his hands and wondered why in hell
he'd sent Pace around for it. The stuff was too hot to
drink and by the time it cooled it wouldn't be fit to drink.
A glance at his partner, alternately blowing and sipping,
blowing and sipping, made Emmenecher clench his teeth
on a new wave of irritation. He had sent Pace for the
coffee to get rid of him, to enjoy a few moments of
blessed peace. The guy was driving him nuts.

10

Attilio Pace was blissfully unaware of the effect he had on Em. He was twenty-three, a victim of the first wave of firings due to budget cuts and had only just been rehired. Recently married, with a new house and a new baby, Pace couldn't afford another period of unemployment; all he wanted to do was please. He was always on the lookout for ways to entrench his position. He had it figured that if he could make that new grade, patrolman first class, his chance of surviving the new cutbacks, whenever they came, would be enhanced. The rank was similar to detective but without the gold shield. It was a merit promotion, and in theory you didn't need either a rabbi to push for you or a sensational bust to make it; still, you had to attract attention somehow. He figured the Times Square area should offer opportunity and when he heard that scream coming from a building across the street he thought he had it. He jumped, sloshing the scalding coffee on his own hand and over Ray Emmenecher's right knee.

"Christ! Watch what you're doing!" Emmenecher snarled as the stain spread. "I just had these pants cleaned. Hell!"

On one squad or another—Narco, Vice, Pickpocket, Pimp—Ray Emmenecher had worked the area in plain clothes for seven years. Suddenly, on the whim of the latest P.C., who wanted to emphasize "visible presence," he, along with a lot of others, was back "in the bag" as the cops called having to put on the uniform again. He hated it. Driving around in the damn car was like being shut off from the real world of the street. He was removed from the contacts, both civilian and criminal, he had so laboriously built up. Worse, if anything could be worse, he was being saddled with greenhorn partners, one after the other. As soon as he got one broken in to his reasonable satisfaction, they moved the guy on.

Pace stared in dismay at the damage he'd done to his partner's uniform. "Jeez, I'm real sorry, Em. That scream . . ."

"Relax, relax. That scream wasn't nothing more than a family argument or somebody on a bad trip. You'll hear a lot worse before you're through. This ain't a quiet neighborhood."

"Sure." Pace was ashamed of having overreacted. Still, he hadn't wanted to miss out on anything big.

"Will you please grab those paper towels and wipe up this mess?" Emmenecher indicated the brown puddle on the seat between them.

Pace complied with alacrity. He had the kind of watery eyes that seemed constantly on the verge of tears, never more so than now. "She sounded like she was getting raped."

"In this neighborhood?" Emmenecher snorted. "Forget it. We're supposed to be looking for kid prosties, remember? We're supposed to be making friends with them and gaining their confidence, saving them from the clutches of their pimps so they can be rehabilitated and sent back home to their mommies and daddies." He stared morosely at the damp patch on his knee. "Baby-sitters, that's what we've become. Goddamned baby-sitters."

Julia Schuyler didn't get out of the sack and on her feet till two-thirty the next afternoon. She made it to the kitchen and found one last can of beer in the refrigerator. It helped. At least it got her as far as the bathroom where one look in the mirror at her bloated face almost sobered her. But she'd seen that face in the mirror too often lately to be really disturbed. She hardly remembered what she used to look like, say . . . three months ago, six months ago. If she happened to run across a photograph of herself taken just that short while back before she'd broken up with Alfred, she was surprised at how pretty she'd been. Not beautiful. Julia Schuyler had never been beautiful—her face was square rather than the classic oval and her nose a trifle long like her father's—but her brown eyes were fine and her skin, in the pictures at least, clear and

12

unlined, though that was partly due to the retoucher's skill. Yet no retoucher could put the brightness in her eyes nor impart the spirit implicit in the way she held her head. She had looked, Julia thought, not innocent—when had she ever been innocent—but unscathed. Even so recently. If she happened to catch herself on the late show, that took her even farther back and it was like watching a stranger. She cried then with self-pity. Where had it all gone? It was her birthright to be a star. What had gone wrong?

Slowly, Julia applied makeup. It didn't help much; her hand wasn't steady enough to do a good job. What she needed was another beer. She'd throw something on and go over to the deli for it; Tony was a good guy, he'd put it on the tab. After that she'd really fix herself up and go and see. . . .

She stopped and stared at herself. What was she, crazy? Julia Schuyler didn't gussy herself up like a raw kid for her first audition. Julia Schuyler didn't go begging. She called people; she told them what she wanted and they went and did it for her.

"Sue me for nonsupport?" Alfred Cassel repeated, stunned. "Is this some kind of new trick?"

William Zipprodt shook his head.

Cassel stared at Julia Schuyler's emissary in disbelief; then he threw his dark, handsome head back and laughed. It was a bitter laugh and forced, but Cassel was, after all, an actor and an exceptionally good one. After a while the laughter came more easily till the rolling gusts were almost genuine, till his narrow face, romantically pale with thin, sculptured features, high brow balanced by sensuously full lips, became red and rubbery with merriment, till his slim, elegant figure was wracked with laughter and he started to choke.

William Zipprodt, Billy Zip for short, was not overly impressed, or at least he was impressed only by the tech-

13

nique. He remembered that Cassel and Julia had once played a laughing scene in a show—what was the name? He couldn't remember; it hadn't lasted, but the laughter in the scene had built in just this way and ended in choking tears, too.

"She means it," Billy Zip said.

Cassel let the tears subside. He groaned. "I am supporting her to the best of my ability. I'm turning over every spare cent I have. Don't let this fool you." A sweeping gesture encompassed the living room of the relatively modest suite which was prestigious only for being in the Algonquin Hotel. "I'm living on credit. And I'm not indulging myself, either. You tell Julia. I need this setup for business. I've got my producer coming up here, my director. They bring prospective backers. What are backers going to think of the man being sold to them as a big star, a big box-office attraction, if they find him holed up in a furnished room?"

"I understand."

"Of course you do, Billy; any sensible person would, which naturally eliminates Julia. Still, she's been the route herself; she ought to remember."

Billy Zip flushed in embarrassment. Though he had a certain elegance and considered himself cosmopolitan, Billy at forty-six still nurtured the illusions of his youth regarding the great or near great of the theatre. He was devoted to both Julia Schuyler and Alfred Cassel, had served them in one guise or another for over ten years. Their talent and flamboyance fed a need in him which he had been forced to stifle when he faced the reality that he wasn't going to make it as a stage designer. He found a niche for himself as a stage manager, the executive officer, so to speak, of a theatrical production, the one who implemented what others conceived, the liaison between crew and cast. As such Billy Zip was competent, even skilled; he dealt with inferiors and equals energetically and efficiently. It was only in the presence of the stars

14

that he became humble. When Julia Schuyler and Alfred Cassel separated, he had been deeply torn, but finally loyalty to Julia won out. She was the weaker; she needed him. To have Julia Schuyler, daughter of the great John Malcolm Schuyler, dependent on him fed his ego. Still, it was hard to take her side against Cassel. Billy's jowls quivered. His eyes were anxious behind their tinted glasses.

Cassel put a hand on his shoulder. "Don't take it so hard, Billy. This is just a ploy. What Julia wants is for me to drop the divorce. She's trying to make me nervous. You tell her that if she sues she won't get anything, and she'll ruin any prospect of ever getting anything. What good is it going to do her to ruin my reputation? Nonsupport, that's a lousy label to pin on a man. It could cost me the show, and then where would either one of us be?"

"I've already told her that."

"Tell her again."

"I will."

"And don't worry. Julia has no more intention of dunning me before the play opens than any of my other creditors and for the same reason: the well is dry now, but it may be overflowing later."

The two men were silent for a moment, sharing concern for the woman each loved in his own way.

"How is Julia?" Cassel asked quietly. "What's she doing with herself these days?"

"Waiting for the phone to ring."

Cassel sighed. "Drinking?"

Zipprodt nodded.

"I wish she'd get off the sauce."

"Maybe if you went to see her, talked to her . . ." Zipprodt suggested.

"I lived with the woman for six years and I couldn't straighten her out," Cassel muttered.

"I mean about this nonsupport business. I think all Julia really wants is to know that you haven't forgotten

15

her, that you still care. I honestly think that if you go over there . . ."

"Maybe." Cassel nodded as though to himself. "Maybe I will go over there and try to talk some sense into her. It's worth a try." He slapped a hand on the stage manager's shoulder and steered him to the door.

As soon as Zipprodt was gone, Alfred Cassel sprang to his telephone. When it was picked up at the other end, his tone became elaborately casual, as it had been with his visitor.

"Oscar? How are you? How are you feeling? Good, that's good. I was wondering, have you heard from Julia lately?"

"Yes, I have," Oscar Brumleve replied. "In fact, I've been meaning to call you." He paused. "She wants to sue you."

Cassel groaned. "Then it's true. Billy just told me. You talked her out of it, of course."

"I'm sorry, Alfred," the lawyer replied. "I tried. I told her that a suit like that would be seriously damaging to your career. I also pointed out that it would be defeating her own interests. But you know Julia. At the moment what she wants is to hurt you, even if it means your losing the show. Later on she'll be sorry, naturally."

"Naturally." Cassel echoed bitterly, a vise tightening across his chest. "What are you going to do?"

"What can I do? If I don't go ahead, she'll get somebody else, some shyster who won't give a damn about either one of you. But don't worry. It's just a question of going through the motions. She'll drop it before it gets to court."

"Meantime she'll ruin me!" Cassel cried. "You can't do this to me, Oscar. You can't file this charge. For one thing, it's false and you know it. I'm giving her every cent I can spare."

"Do you have canceled checks?"

"I've been giving her cash."

"That wasn't very smart."

16

"Hell! I didn't expect to have to prove it!" Cassel groaned. "Oscar, you can't do this to me. I'm your client, too. You can't represent us both."

"I'm aware of that."

"You're dumping me?"

"You must have realized that if Julia agreed to bring action for divorce I'd be representing her."

"That's different."

"She was my client first," Brumleve pointed out. "And her father before her."

"It doesn't matter who's right?"

"John Malcolm Schuyler was my client before Julia was born."

Cassel did not like being reminded of his wife's father. Once he had admired Schuyler—the actor, not the man—had even emulated his style, for Alfred Cassel was basically a classical actor. He had dreamed of playing the great Shakespearean roles and what finer model could he have had than Schuyler? In many ways, Cassel was much like him. He had the elegance, the flair, the voice. He supposed—hell, he knew—that was what had attracted Julia to him. And he to her, he admitted. To have John Malcolm Schuyler's daughter rate him in the same category as her father was the supreme compliment. He had married Julia thinking they could help each other, only to discover that where it had taken John Malcolm sixty-two years of licentious living to destroy his talent along with himself, Julia was likely to do it in half the time. Cassel was not going to let her drag him down with her.

Though he was talking on the telephone with no one in the room to observe, Alfred Cassel drew himself erect and placed his right foot at an angle to his left, slanting his body as though posing for the photographers. "You need publicity, Oscar? Business slow? Looking for new clients?"

"I didn't expect that from you, Alfred," Brumleve sighed.

The lawyer was retired, had been for several years. He

was also a very sick man. Everyone knew it. "I'm sorry, Oscar. It was a cheap shot," Cassel apologized.

"I'm sorry, too. I wouldn't do this for anyone but Julia."

"Sure. Do me one favor, Oscar? Hold off for a few days? Give me a chance to talk to her, to try to reason with her. Do that much for me?"

"Of course. You know what I think? I think she just wants you to give up on the divorce. Maybe if you move back in with her? Maybe that's what she's after."

Now it was Cassel who sighed. "We both know what she's after and we both know I can't give it to her. I wouldn't if I could."

2

It was a decent middle-class neighborhood, a pocket of the old ways and the old morality. Situated just across the Queensboro Bridge from Manhattan, it was bordered on one side by the Pennsylvania Railroad yards and on the other by acres and acres of graves. The house had been the end house in a row of neat, red-brick, one-family dwellings identical as paper cutouts that stretched block after tree-lined block. It had had a lovingly tended garden with the standard patch of front lawn individualized by a family of gaily painted plastic ducks perpetually waddling across it. The house was now a gutted, blackened shell, a rotted tooth in the otherwise gleaming row. The garden, flooded by water and smothered in chemicals, had become first a swamp, now, after being trampled and baked by the ninety-degree heat, resembled a lumpy pie-crust. The plastic ducks, melted down, were somewhere inside.

Bare-legged, bare-armed, red-gold hair twisted into a

19

knot and pinned on top of her head, wearing a faded denim sundress, Mici Anhalt picked her way through the debris. Tall, slim, and agile, Mici with her arms outstretched as she carefully placed one foot in front of the other looked like a child balancing on an imaginary line on the sidewalk. A gust of hot wind threatened to blow her off. It came from across the polluted waters of the East River and bore no relief, but rather noxious fumes from the city and more heat. This was no day to be examining an arson site, Mici Anhalt thought, her blue eyes tearing. This was a day to be home in Greenwich, sitting on the shady back porch looking across the field to the apple orchard, listening to the soothing midday hum of the cicadas. Maybe she'd go up this weekend. It wasn't so much the oppressive heat that Mici wanted to escape but the nagging, niggling stresses that had been building up in her work for . . . longer than she cared to admit.

Even in a job one loved—and Mici loved her job—there were bound to be difficulties from time to time, she thought as she sat down to rest on what had once been the front stoop of the burned dwelling but was now a fragment of broken steps leading nowhere. There had been misunderstandings, disagreements with colleagues before, but they'd never lasted.What troubled Mici Anhalt now was a change in the atmosphere, a barrier between herself and the other investigators. It wasn't because she was the only woman on the staff. She didn't know what it was. She had countered by being friendlier and it hadn't worked. Mici was puzzled.

Maria Ilona Anhalt was not used to being rebuffed. She liked most people and expected to be liked in return. Even her nickname, Mici, the Hungarian spelling for Mitzi, was an endearment meaning "honey" or "darling." She was extraordinarily pretty, in fact striking, with that tall, fine figure and that mass of red-gold hair. Her skin was clear and unfreckled, exceptional for a redhead, and her light-blue eyes had a way of turning pale

20

under stress until they became almost colorless—translucent. Mici Anhalt was thirty-three, but she seemed younger because of her energy. In fact, it was her spirit that pulled it all together: her enthusiasm for whatever she happened to be doing and her complete absorption in whomever she happened to be dealing with. When Mici Anhalt talked to you, you were the focus of her attention completely and without outside distractions. It was devilishly flattering, and completely sincere.

Mici came from a closely knit family. Her grandfather, Laszlo, had escaped from the Communist revolution in Hungary after World War I and on arriving in his new country immediately bought the house in Greenwich where her father, Paul, grew up and married and where she had been born. She was used to loving and being loved, which wasn't to say that she wasn't tough. She wouldn't have survived in the world of professional ballet otherwise. But after two years with the Joffrey, Mici Anhalt found herself oddly restless, and when the company went to Seattle that second summer she joined the ranks of volunteers for Kennedy during his presidential campaign. There had been plenty of competition there, too, but she'd taken her knocks and given as good as she got. As a member of the Attorney General's staff during John Kennedy's term, she'd learned about the wheeling and dealing, the *quid pro quo* of politics. After Robert Kennedy was assassinated, she returned to New York but not to the ballet—she'd progressed beyond that limited sphere. Mici had become dedicated to criminal justice. She got a job with the Vera Institute and was assigned to the Victim/Witness Assistance Program. It opened her eyes to the victim's plight.

With all the current concern for the rights of the criminal, Mici soon realized that the rights of the victim were all but forgotten. Time after time, the criminal was back out on the street while the victim still lay in the hospital; often the criminal was out repeating his crimes while his

21

first victim still struggled to pay the medical bills. Ostensibly, the awesome forces of law and order were arrayed behind the victim. In essence, he was alone. Once the criminal was caught, nobody paid any attention to the victim. He was abandoned to his pain and his sorrow and the ugly memories that would be part of his life forever.

Mici moved over to the New York State Crime Victims Compensation Board where some attempt was being made to help the victim of crime financially and medically. First, of course, those needs had to be assessed. Mici's job, often referred to as social worker, was actually similar to that of an insurance investigator. Usually it was enough to confirm the identity of the victim-claimant through a birth certificate, a marriage license, and the like; to check his financial status, his insurance coverage, extent of injury, and extent of his medical policies. But if there was any uncertainty regarding the claim, Mici Anhalt didn't quit till her client got every benefit available to him under the law. That was why she was out here now in the midday heat examining the burned remains of Karl Spychalski's house. The unemployed ironworker was one of the borderline cases. If there was any evidence in his favor that had been overlooked by the police and the regular insurance investigator, Mici intended to find it.

Wiping the film of sweat from her face with a tissue from the straw satchel she carried, Mici got up and resumed her examination of the area.

As many slum landlords knew, and others were rapidly learning, it wasn't easy to determine the cause of a fire. A bomb might leave evidence, but matches thrown on a trash heap or an old sofa doused with kerosene went up in flames along with everything else. What could Mici expect to find that the Arson-Explosion Squad or the Fire Marshal had not found before her? Or the agent for the company that carried the insurance on Karl Spychalski's house? None of them had been able to make a determination as to the origin of the fire, yet Mici Anhalt went on looking.

"You there! You! What do you think you're doing?"

Startled, Mici looked around. She couldn't see anybody.

"You. I'm talking to you. That's private property. You're trespassing."

A slight, frail figure appeared from behind the vacant house next door. She was old, at least eighty, Mici thought. Her hair was snow-white, a halo of sparse curls through which the sun shone, unmercifully revealing portions of pink scalp. Her skin was crazed like fine china, and she was dressed like a girl in pale-blue cotton sprinkled with rosebuds, white stockings, and white shoes. She had a cane but didn't use it to pick her way across the uneven terrain; in fact, her step was so light she seemed to float over the ruts and fissures. A ghost at midday, Mici thought and smiled.

"You've got a tongue in your head, haven't you?" The voice was high and feisty.

"You must be Mrs. Feirick."

"Never mind who I am. Who are you?"

"I'm Mici Anhalt, Mrs. Feirick. I'm an investigator for the Crime Victims Compensation Board. I rang your doorbell just a while ago." She had rung all the doorbells on both sides of the street. Only one or two people had answered, though she was certain nearly everyone had been at home.

"I heard you." Marge Feirick tilted her head sideways as though sizing up the interrogator. "I was having my nap."

"I'm sorry I disturbed you."

"I didn't get up, did I?"

"No, ma'am."

"So then you didn't disturb me." This bit of testy logic seemed to give the old lady satisfaction. "Well, what did you want?"

23

"I wanted to ask you about the fire. I wondered whether you saw anyone around the house before it started."

"Did you talk to any of the other people on the block? What did they say?"

"I talked to one or two. Neither of them saw anything or anyone."

"Me neither."

Mici hadn't really expected any other answer, yet she was disappointed. "How about the Geramita boys? Had they been hanging around?"

The old lady jerked her white head toward the silent houses with their shades drawn against the heat. "What did they say?"

"They didn't see the boys."

"Me neither."

"If you don't know anything and you didn't see anything, why did you bother to come out and talk to me?"

"I wanted to see what kind of young woman you were. Now I see that you're no different than the rest of them— no patience and no respect for your elders."

"It's not a matter of respect, Mrs. Feirick. A crime has been . . ." She stopped. She had been about to say that a crime had been committed, but she didn't know that it had. That was what she was trying to determine, whether in fact there had been a crime, whether the fire had been of natural origin or deliberately set. Karl Spychalski had accused a pair of teenage boys, Robert and Damian Geramita, of starting the fire. If the suspects had not been juveniles they would surely have been arrested on probable cause, Mici thought, but probable cause didn't mean a thing where juveniles were concerned. The tragedy was that the children knew they could get away with just about everything, including murder, at least till the age of sixteen.

The Geramita brothers were the local bad boys, hardly in the league with delinquents in other parts of the city— they didn't carry knives, use or deal in drugs—but they

24

showed disturbing tendencies. Many a day when he should have been in school, Robert could be seen weaving down the street obviously drunk; at thirteen, he had already learned that you could get a good high on alcohol and you wouldn't get busted because alcohol was legal. At fifteen, Damian was deflowering girls of eleven and twelve, though he did go outside the neighborhood for them—so far. Combining these hobbies, the boys held liquor and sex parties in the summer in the backyard of the empty house next to the Spychalskis. The parties went on most of the night and into the morning. The sounds not only disturbed Karl Spychalski's sleep, but they embarrassed his wife and frightened his two girls. They were not the kind of sounds he wanted the women of his family to be forced to hear. Against Rose Spychalski's earnest pleading, he called the police and complained, naming names. Two days later every window on the first floor of his house was broken.

Spychalski took matters into his own hands. Though fifty-two, the ironworker was accustomed to handling heavy weights and clambering over steel girders at great heights, and he was still both strong and quick. Dark-haired, with a heavy, black growth of beard which he could never shave really close and bulging biceps in arms and thighs, he was physically intimidating. The boys were gangling youths who had not yet reached their full growth. It was no match. He got them both on the same day, one at a time; he could do that because they went to different schools—one to junior high and the other to high school. All Karl Spychalski had to do was wait for each boy to get off the school bus and then grab him. Each was momentarily stunned, without the wit to run. By the time the boy recovered, the ironworker had pulled him behind some shrubbery, thrown him across one knee, pants shamefully pulled down, and administered a blistering, old-fashioned spanking.

Each boy yelled, of course, and, as soon as he was released, ran. But neither one ever told, not his parents, not his friends. Karl Spychalski had counted on that. He had counted on the boys not confessing the humiliation to anyone but each other.

It would have been better for him if they'd told everybody.

A week later to the day, a neighbor—Mrs. Feirick as it turned out—had spotted the boys lurking around the Spychalski garage. Evidently she hadn't learned yet to fear the young for she came out of her house to scream and shake her cane at them and thus alerted Rose Spychalski who was in her kitchen. Mrs. Spychalski smelled the smoke and saw the flames and was able to call the fire department in time to limit the damage. Again Spychalski refused to listen to his wife's advice. A woman who took her marriage vow of obedience seriously, Rose seldom argued with him and now that he had high blood pressure she almost never disputed with him. Not that she could have stopped Karl; he was determined to bring the Geramita boys to court.

At the hearing the boys' lawyer denied everything, beginning with the backyard parties and responsibility for the broken windows. When Spychalski charged that the fire was retaliation for the spanking he'd administered, the lawyer denied the spanking. He admitted his client's culpability in the fire—could hardly do otherwise since they'd been caught in the act—but dubbed it a childish prank that got out of hand. The judge found in the boys' favor. He reprimanded them and sent them home, and he warned Spychalski to stay away from them.

Indignation sent the ironworker's blood pressure soaring. He had a seizure on the courthouse steps. Medical bills wiped out the last of the Spychalskis' financial reserves. Unemployment benefits were suspended because, being sick, Spychalski was not available for work should work be offered—though for the past seven long months it had not been.

Two weeks after the debilitated and frustrated man

26

was back from the hospital and down at the hiring hall, there was another fire. Rose Spychalski, on her way home from the weekly trip to the supermarket, turned the corner in time to see her house a torch. She also saw her two girls leaning out of the window of their second-story bedroom, screaming. She dropped her groceries and ran.

Once again Spychalski brought charges against Robert and Damian Geramita, but there was nothing to support them, not even the testimony of a Mrs. Feirick. The neighbors weren't talking. Pressed, they admitted to knowing about the backyard parties that took place next door to the Spychalskis but professed to have no idea as to who attended. Regarding this, the most recent and most devastating of the two fires, no one had seen anything, heard anything, knew anything. Who could blame them? They didn't want their houses burned down.

Meanwhile, Rose Spychalski lay at the Jacobi Hospital Burn Care Unit with second- and third-degree burns that would permanently disfigure her face and arms. The two girls, Natalia and Sophia, were dead.

"What I'm trying to do is substantiate Mr. Spychalski's story," Mici explained.

"Are you calling Karl a liar?" Mrs. Feirick demanded. Her frail figure stiffened, her rheumy old eyes challenged. "Karl is a good, decent, hardworking man." Raising her cane, the old lady shook it at the girl as though about to call down a curse on her.

"I believe him, Mrs. Feirick," Mici assured the irate woman. "That's why I'm here, because I believe him. Others don't. What's needed is proof that the fire wasn't just an accident."

"I see."

"The way it stands now it's Mr. Spychalski's word against that of the boys and their parents."

"How about the first fire in the garage? I was a witness to their setting that. I testified."

"Yes, ma'am, I know. I wish your neighbors were as

civic-minded and showed as much courage. Unfortunately, proof that Robert and Damian took part in those backyard parties . . ." Mici paused to choose her words. "As long as no one can definitely place Robert and Damian at those parties, the broken windows afterwards can't be blamed on them. If no broken windows, then no spankings, and the garage fire becomes not a retaliation but an isolated prank to which Mr. Spychalski overreacted. It all hangs on those backyard parties."

"Why didn't you say so? You're not very good at your job, are you, girl?" Mrs. Feirick scolded. "I can tell you about the parties. Orgies for depraved children. Terrible. This is the curse that God has put upon our generation— that our children are monsters. Do you have children?"

"No."

"Then you are blessed."

Mici got her back on the track. "How about the Geramita brothers? Did you actually see them at the parties?"

"I saw and heard them. Many times."

Now we're getting somewhere, Mici thought.

"I could look right into that backyard." By a series of sidesteps in place, she turned her body about forty-five degrees and raised her cane to point in the direction of her own house. It was one block behind the Spychalskis' and raised slightly above theirs on a ground elevation. "I could look right down into that backyard and see everything."

"Uh . . . it would have been nighttime, of course," Mici reminded her. "I suppose they must have had some kind of light—lanterns or a bonfire?"

"I have cat's eyes. I can see in the dark."

Mici let it go; she could check the street lighting, also the almanac for the phase of the moon on the night or nights in question. "It would help Mr. Spychalski if you would make a list of the dates when you saw the boys at those parties and if you would be willing to make a formal statement."

Mrs. Feirick smiled sweetly. "Of course."

Mici was delighted. "That's very good of you."

"It's my duty."

"I wish your neighbors felt that way. Most of them won't even admit they were home the afternoon of the fire."

"I was home," Mrs. Feirick said. "I was upstairs taking my nap when something, I don't know what, woke me. A noise . . . like a dry wind. We don't get that kind of wind here much—rustling, sinister. When I was a girl back in Iowa during the drought, we had winds like that; they burned the crops; they took the topsoil right off the fields, blew it away in clouds. . . ." For a moment she was lost in her recollections; then she shook them off and returned to the present. "As I was saying, I heard this sound, like a sigh, and it woke me. I got out of bed and went to the window. There was a flickering light over at the Spychalskis'. The day was cloudy so I knew it couldn't be a reflection of the sun on a window. It could have been candles, but why would they be burning candles in the middle of the afternoon? Then I saw two figures run out the back door. . . ."

"You actually saw them?" Mici couldn't believe her luck. "Were you able to recognize them?" *Of course not,* Mici silently answered her own question, *if Mrs. Feirick had been able to identify them, she would already have told the police.*

"It spread so fast, so fast. . . ." A wild light flickered in the old woman's eyes much like the flames she had just described. "Are you a Catholic?"

Mici blinked. "Yes."

"According to the faith, a child is supposed to know the difference between good and evil, between right and wrong, at the age of seven. These children won't ever know it; they weren't taught. And that's our fault." She pointed a bony finger. "Yours and mine."

Mici winced. Though she assumed that Mrs. Feirick

was generalizing, she was becoming distinctly uneasy. "Were you actually able to recognize the running figures?"

"I knew who they were—demons spawned in hell."

Mici's heart wasn't in it, but she tried anyway. "I mean, were you able to see their faces well enough so that you could identify them in a court of law?"

"Yes, yes!" The fragile figure shook with almost religious fervor. "Yes," she repeated earnestly.

Mici was somewhat reassured. She took another look at Mrs. Feirick's house up on its rise. From the second story, where she assumed the bedroom to be, Mrs. Feirick would certainly have a clear view into the entire row of backyards, including that of the Spychalskis. If the boys had made their getaway through the kitchen door, they would not have been likely to head for the street but back through one of the side yards and in her direction.

"I saw them, I tell you. I saw them as clearly as I see you."

"Would you be willing to sign a statement to that effect?"

"I've said so, haven't I? Why do you think I'm telling you all this?"

As far as Mici Anhalt was concerned, the return to testiness meant a return to normalcy. She was relieved. Then she was elated. "I wish your neighbors had your courage, Mrs. Feirick."

The old lady smiled sunnily. "I'm not afraid. I'm alone now. If anything happens to me . . . well, I've had a good life and there's no one to mourn me."

The simple statement touched Mici because it was neither maudlin nor an appeal for pity. She did wonder, of course, that none of the various investigators who had covered the neighborhood before her had discovered Marge Feirick and gotten her testimony. Well, maybe she hadn't been home on the particular day, or they hadn't asked the right questions. So she'd struck it lucky; nothing wrong with a little luck once in a while. Only one small point remained to be cleared up.

"About the backyard parties, Mrs. Feirick. Why didn't you call the police and complain the way Mr. Spychalski did?"

For a moment the old lady hesitated; then she smiled a sweet, sad smile. "To protect the girls, to spare them. I was sorry for the little girls. So young. Debauched. I didn't want their shame to be made public."

"Their names wouldn't have been mentioned," Mici explained. "The names of juvenile offenders are never . . ."

"But I was wrong. Wrong!" Marge Feirick cried out as though seized by a spirit, as though testifying at a revival meeting. "And I have been punished. I had no right to make a judgment. *Judgment is mine, sayeth the Lord.* I have been punished. I bear the scars of the fire on my body the same as Rose Spychalski does on hers. I am crippled and bent by the sins I have permitted to flourish around me. Crippled and bent . . ."

She seemed to shrivel; bending down and leaning on her stick, she turned from a sprightly old lady into an old crone. "My bones are broken, my body consumed by the murders, the rapes, the kidnappings. Every day, every day I am tortured. I suffer . . . the pain . . . the pain. . . ."

The nerves at the back of Mici's neck tightened; a cold chill passed over her.

"You call on me, girl, and I'll testify any time to whatever you want . . . whatever. . . ."

Mici backed off, one step and then another. "I will. Yes. I'll be in touch. Thank you, Mrs. Feirick. Thank you . . ."

Backing off and murmuring reassurances, Mici made it to the street where she turned and walked as quickly as she could back to the reality of traffic and elevated trains and the jackhammers of Con Edison repairing underground lines. Just as well that Marge Feirick hadn't been

31

discovered by police or other insurance investigators, she thought. If they ever did interview her, even her testimony about the earlier fire in the garage would become suspect, and Karl Spychalski's hopes of proving arson and pinning it on the Geramita boys would suffer a severe setback.

3

"Nice of you to drop in."

"I'm sorry, Adam. The time just got away from me."

Adam Dowd's homely, pitted face showed his displeasure. "You could call in now and then. Just to let us know you're still on the job. I assume you are still working for us?"

Mici Anhalt flushed. She had hoped to get through the big main room and into her own private office without anyone's noticing. As luck would have it, Supervisor Dowd emerged just as she was scurrying by. Or was it luck? Had Adam been watching for her? If so, he must be very annoyed indeed. Still, it wasn't like him to be sarcastic. Suddenly Mici was aware of the silence around her; nobody was typing or phoning. She sensed that nobody in the row of private offices was doing anything but listening, either. It wasn't like Adam Dowd to make a reprimand in public.

She apologized again. "I'm sorry, sir. I wasn't near a phone."

"Mind telling us where you were?"

Us? Mici stiffened. What was going on? Was she reporting to the whole damn office? "I went to the scene of the Spychalski fire. I interviewed some of the neighbors."

"And?"

She hesitated. She could feel the expectancy as they waited for her answer. Her blue eyes narrowed and turned pale. She tilted her head defiantly. "Nothing, sir. Nothing new." She'd be damned if she'd report her interview with crazy old Mrs. Feirick under these conditions. Besides, what she'd said was true; the interview had no credibility. Mici waited a beat; then, her eyes now faded to a cold translucence, she made a slow sweep of the room establishing contact for a moment with each and every person in it. It was like restarting a clock: all the parts went into motion at once; suddenly everyone had something to do and was very busy doing it. Now Mici turned back to her boss. "If that's all, sir?"

"No, it isn't. Step into my office, please."

Not one head was raised; not one pair of eyes so much as glanced in her direction, but everybody heard. Seething, Mici strode past the supervisor and into his office. She could hardly wait till he followed and closed the door.

"What's going on?" she demanded hotly. "What have I done?"

Despite his concern Adam Dowd could not repress a smile.

"It's got to be more than my being out of touch for a few hours to warrant that harangue out there."

Dowd frowned. "I'm afraid it is."

"What? Would you care to explain?"

With deliberation the supervisor crossed to his desk and sat down. "Clay Marin was in a couple of hours ago. He said he had an appointment with you."

"Damn." Her outrage was stopped in full spate. She flushed. "I forgot all about him. It went clean out of my head. I'm sorry, Adam. I really am."

"I know that Marin isn't one of your favorites." She started to protest, but he waved her to silence. "I don't like him much myself. He's a whiner and a complainer, but he has cause. And anyhow that's not the point. You can't work just with the people you like."

"I know that."

The supervisor clasped his hands over a small but developing paunch and considered the only woman on his investigative staff. He had liked Mici Anhalt from the first moment she had walked into his office for a job interview two years ago on a day in July almost as hot as this one. He remembered it particularly because the air conditioning had broken down and not one of the job applicants had dared refer to it by so much as wiping his brow—till Mici.

"If I'd known you were running a sauna I'd have worn my bathing suit," the good-looking redhead had said.

Dowd had thrown his head back and roared. "I wish you had," he'd retorted.

She came with a good background in criminal justice. She appeared enthusiastic about the concept of victim compensation, and after a check of her credentials he'd hired her. She had fulfilled his expectations. She was dedicated, no clock-watcher, and she had an intuitive feeling for the pattern of a case. He'd encouraged her to think and act independently. Maybe he'd encouraged her too much. To that extent Dowd felt responsible for her present predicament. Adam Dowd was nearing fifty. Big, balding, with that growing paunch and scarred complexion, he was certainly not attractive, but he was a kind man and a fair one and everybody liked him. Yet he was also lonely. His two sons, though unmarried, no longer lived at home. His wife was a secret drinker—though by now she was the only one who considered it a secret. To

35

Dowd, Mici was like a daughter and he'd treated her as such, unconsciously at the beginning. That was part of the problem, too.

The rest of it was Mici herself. Maybe she was too dedicated, too intense for the job. Her exuberance could be either endearing or overwhelming, depending on the point of view. He sighed and leaned forward; she was thirty-three years old and should be able to face reality.

"You can't slough off the dull cases and work only on the ones that appeal to you."

"I honestly forgot about Marin."

Dowd waved that aside. "Wally saw him. The point is that your missing the appointment brought the resentment to a head."

"Resentment?"

"The other investigators feel that you're getting special treatment. They feel you get all the good cases."

"But you assign the cases."

"That's right. I try to match case and investigator. I consider the investigator's special talents. It appears that I have an extra high regard for yours. Perhaps too high."

"That's a lousy charge."

His smile was tight. "I do regard you highly." Dowd sighed again. "Another complaint is that you spend too much time on these special cases and are therefore not carrying a full load. Which in turn means that the others are carrying more than their fair share."

Now she understood the scene he'd played outside. She came forward and took the chair beside his desk. "I'm sorry, Adam. I'll watch myself in the future."

"You step on a lot of toes, Mici. You have very little patience with anybody who thinks or reacts slowly. You don't mean any harm, I know that, but you just forge ahead and they're humiliated. You're too quick mentally. Excellence is more resented than admired."

She felt the warmth as her cheeks flamed again. "I had no idea. I will try to attract less attention. I promise."

Dowd unclasped his hands and drew them across his face in a gesture of weariness and helplessness. "There's more. There's resentment because your claims are approved more often than anybody else's."

"Maybe that's because they're prepared better," Mici snapped indignantly. "Did they ever think of that?"

"The settlements your clients get are big, almost always maximum."

"Come on, Adam! That's really too much. The commissioner makes that decision, for heaven's sake. I have nothing to do with it." She tried a laugh, hoping to get Dowd to join in. When he didn't, she pleaded, "Adam, you can't be taking that part of it seriously?"

"It was Mr. Cornelius who remarked on it."

Mici gaped. The state board was appointed by the Governor and consisted of ten commissioners, two of whom were assigned to the New York City office. One of these was J. Hammond Cornelius. The other was Louis Weyerhauser. All cases handled by the office were divided between them and, based on the reports filed by the investigators in the field, one or the other made the decision as to whether or not the claim should be granted.

"Mr. Cornelius thinks your reports may be slanted in the claimant's favor, unconsciously, of course." Dowd's homely face was graver than ever.

Mici sucked in her breath. "Do you think they are?"

"You're working in a bureaucracy, and unilateral decisions are frowned on. Face it. You've got to go through channels. The ultimate action may be the very one you would have initiated on the spot and it may come hours, days, or weeks later, but it's been sanctioned. That's the game. Those are the rules. You are not in business for yourself. You are not handing out your own money."

"You can't slant figures," Mici retorted hotly. "That's what I report principally. As to circumstances, there are sometimes borderline situations, gray areas that can be interpreted either in the victim's favor or against him.

37

Maybe I do give him the benefit of the doubt, but I thought that was our policy."

It was almost an accusation, and Dowd knew it was as close as she would ever come to one. He acknowledged that he had encouraged her to bend in the victim's favor. "I also told you that we are neither a charity organization nor a social agency. Compassion is a fine thing, but we are dispensing public funds. Now that the victim is being informed of his rights by the police at the time the crime is reported, the claims are pouring in and the money is pouring out. We've got to stick to the rules."

"There are still hardship cases."

"Sure, but it's not up to you to decide which ones."

She had made that judgment many times in the past. "I'm sorry if I've embarrassed you, Adam."

He could not let her take the full blame, for the truth was that she had not made those judgments without his knowledge and approval. "It's not up to me, either."

For a moment their eyes met and the bond between them was as strong as ever.

"I don't want you to be caught in the middle, Adam."

"I won't be, not as long as you watch your step. Okay?"

"Okay." She rose but she was still uneasy. She had the feeling that he hadn't told her everything. 'Adam . . ." She hesitated. A flash of intuition sent a chill through her and brought out goose bumps. "Do you want me to resign?"

"Of course not. Don't be ridiculous. It won't come to that." He answered quickly, too quickly and too heartily.

Oh my God! she thought. It had come to that. It had been discussed. She left the supervisor's office reeling.

Fired? Mici had never considered the possibility. It wasn't fear of not finding another job but fear of having failed, of having been rated inadequate to the job she had. The talk with Adam Dowd had shaken Mici Anhalt on several levels. She didn't know which allegation surprised or hurt the most. Her honesty had never before been questioned. Oh, Mr. Cornelius had admitted that if she was indeed slanting her reports it was done subconsciously—or had he? Could it in reality have been Adam who made that suggestion to the commissioner in order to protect her? And was she going overboard in favor of the claimants? In Mici's opinion, the poor unfortunate who walked through the door marked Crime Victims Compensation Board needed sympathy as much as monetary assistance. Of course, one had to maintain perspective; of course, one couldn't afford to become maudlin. She'd always thought that she had maintained proper balance. As for the attitude of her colleagues, Mici was more disappointed than angry, but she didn't feel like facing them right away. Glazed vision and a low ringing in her ears acted as a protective barrier as she passed along the row of doors to her own office. It was broken by Wally Lischner coming out of his office and colliding with her.

"Oh." She forced her usual bright smile. "Thanks for seeing Clay Marin this afternoon, Wally."

"For you? Any time, sweets."

As usual he leaned too close, almost pushing her into the wall and asphyxiating her with his cologne. Thin, slightly sallow, with medium-long, wavy hair brushed forward into bangs over his eyes, sideburns, and a rather elegant beard, Wally Lischner wasn't bad-looking. If you liked the type. Unfortunately, Mici did not. He went in for the macho bit, wearing everything skintight, shirt open to the waist revealing the gleam of a gold medal amid manly chest hair. In the office he sported a safari-type jacket that just happened to fall open whenever he leaned over one of the secretaries at her desk. They seemed to appreciate it.

When she'd first come to work there, Wally had made a play for Mici so strong and so insistent that she'd thought the only way to deal with it was to agree to go out with him and get it over with. It had been a bad mistake. He'd made a heavy pass, one she'd had more than the usual trouble parrying. The next day at the office had been embarrassing for both of them. They avoided each other, and for a while Mici thought that was the way it was going to be for good. She didn't like that kind of situation, but what could she do? To her relief he got over it. The only thing that Mici could complain of in Wally's treatment of her afterwards was that he was overfriendly, suggesting an intimacy between them that hadn't taken place. There were plenty of times when she'd been on the verge of rebuffing his public advances in a way that would leave no doubt in anyone about her feelings. Somehow she never did.

Mici squirmed as he put his arm against the wall blocking her passage. She choked back the familiar urge to tell him off; of all the times to do it, this would be the worst. "What did Marin want?" she asked instead.

Lischner shrugged. "What does he ever want? To cry on somebody's shoulder."

"I'm sorry you got stuck. If I can ever return the favor . . ." Too late she realized the opening she'd given him.

"You can. Easy." He leered good-naturedly.

She laughed. "Come on, Wally, you know how I feel about office romances."

To her surprise he grinned and dropped his arm. "You can't blame a guy for trying."

For a moment she stared in disbelief, then flashed him a grateful smile. Just as well she hadn't been smart with Wally Lischner, Mici thought as she went on to her office. At the moment, he might be the only friend she had.

4

"My God! She's finally gone and lost her marbles!"
The words were at odds with the presence. Delissa
Grace was a Junoesque figure in her flowing scarlet drap-
eries with the white scarf binding her brow to hold back a
mass of frizzed black hair. She had a broad, pale face with
large, widely spaced, and brilliant eyes, a prominent,
slightly hooked nose, and a high, noble brow—the whole
forming an ample canvas upon which the passions could
be portrayed and transmitted across the footlights.

"You're not going to let her get away with it!" It was a
demand, not a question.

"Calm down, Dee, please. Take it easy." Eyes half
closed, Alfred Cassel lay slouched against the cushions of
a black-velvet sofa positioned in the center of Delissa
Grace's living room so that people could move around it
freely like actors on a stage.

She now stood behind the sofa looking down on Cassel.

"You've got to do something. She could create a very nasty scandal; she's crazy enough. And you could lose the show. Do you realize that you could lose the show?"

At that he opened his eyes and looked up into hers. "I am not going to lose the show—and neither are you," he added pointedly. "She can't make the accusation stick. For one thing, because it's not true and she knows it."

"Fine. She knows it, you know it, I know it, but she can make you look pretty cheap while you're trying to clear yourself." Delissa swept around to the front of the sofa where she could deliver herself directly to his face. "She doesn't even have to take you to court; all she has to do is tell her story to a reporter."

Cassel sighed. How was it that he always got involved with temperamental, overbearing, domineering queen bees who tried to consume their mates? He was himself a mild man, introspective, and above all rational. "If that's what she intended she would have done it without sending a warning through Billy Zip and then Oscar. No. The whole thing is an elaborate form of blackmail."

"For what? What does she want?"

"Ah . . ." he shrugged.

"Does she want you back?" Delissa Grace was very still awaiting his answer.

"We wrote each other off romantically a long time ago. I think she'll take action for the divorce after she's made me squirm a while."

The actress flung herself down beside him, threw her arms around his neck, and kissed him, forcing his head back among the pillows. After a pleasant and relaxing tussle, they leaned against opposite ends of the sofa regarding each other with satisfaction.

"Darling," Delissa cooed, "it's a question of your image. Maybe it wouldn't matter if you were doing character work, but you're a leading man, a romantic leading man. The women in the audience are going to look up on the stage and see you making love to the leading lady and remember that you abandoned your wife and that she had to sue you to get her rent and grocery money."

"Ah, thanks, luv. You've certainly made me feel better."

"I'm trying to make you face reality. Julia can ruin you if she persists."

"All right, all right." He got up and paced. The way they were playing the scene it was his turn. "What do you suggest?"

"Don't ask me. She's your wife."

"She's sick, Dee. She's sick and she's desperate. What she needs to get well. . . . You know what it is as well as I do."

Not a muscle in Delissa Grace's expressive face twitched.

"She's fighting for her life, her professional life—it's one and the same."

"What does she want from you?" The actress asked the question despite herself; her voice quivered as she asked and the quiver was not acting.

"You know damn well what," Cassel replied. "She wants to be in the show. She wants me to ask to have her in it. She wants me to demand that she be in it."

"There's no part for her."

"Of course there is. Yours."

"Mine?" Delissa Grace's emotions followed one another so quickly none lasted long enough to be portrayed. Finally, she began to laugh in broken spurts as though feeling her way in an insufficiently rehearsed scene, then gaining assurance. "Mine! She can't play Teresa. No way. It's ludicrous even to suggest . . ."

"Hold it. Stop right there," Cassel ordered. "Julia Schuyler can play any damn thing she sets her mind to, and don't you ever forget it. She's come a long way from the Hollywood brat she used to be—half Shirley Temple, half Bette Davis. They exploited her too soon, before she was ready. But she's got the talent. It's there."

"She got it from her father."

"Okay. It's got to come from somewhere. Where do you think you got yours? All talent is inherited."

"My people weren't actors. I had to claw and scratch for every damn job I got."

"Maybe Julia would have been better off if she'd had to do the same."

Delissa Grace, born Demetria Garrity of a Greek mother and an Irish father, had been performing since the age of fourteen. Starting as a member of the chorus with a local Greek troupe doing the classics of Aeschylus and Aristophanes, she made the transition to the American theatre via readings, avant-garde experiments in back rooms and lofts, off-off Broadway, road shows, and stock. She had climbed virtually line by line to this opportunity of playing the lead role opposite Alfred Cassel. When *Of Light and Dark* opened, she confidently expected that the critics would exclaim that a new star had burst upon the Broadway scene overnight, not knowing or caring what had gone before. She resented Julia Schuyler, not because of her talent and her acquired skills but because Julia Schuyler had thrown away the opportunities Delissa Grace had had to scrabble for. It was a matter of pride with Delissa that she had never used her sex to get a job. When she took a lover, it was because her passion had been aroused. If, on occasion, the lover was also able to assist her in her career—that was fortuitous coincidence.

"Julia could play the pants off that part," Cassel told her with uncompromising candor. "It would be a different interpretation from yours certainly, but just as valid." He thought about it, envisioned what Julia would bring to the role. "It would have certain underlying values . . . nuances . . ."

"Terrific! Marvelous!" Delissa Grace rose majestically. "She'd give a typical Schuyler performance laced with 'intuitive insights' and 'garnished with pyrotechnics.'" Derisively she quoted some of Julia's best reviews, then

44

added, "If you managed to get her through rehearsals and to the stage on opening night. Assuming you did, she'd give you a triumph, but what would happen the second night? And the night after that for six nights every week and two matinees?"

"That's why you've got the job, dear, and she hasn't."

It was what she'd been waiting to hear, of course, and she calmed instantly. "So what are you going to do?"

"Nothing. Aside from your part in the show, I've got nothing she wants."

"Talk to her. Reason with her. Point out to her that if she accuses you of nonsupport you can accuse her right back of being an alcoholic and drinking up whatever you give her."

"You don't mean that."

"I don't mean for you actually to do it, no. Of course, you're not going to do that any more than she's going to take you to court. It's just tit for tat. Threat and counter-threat."

"Pretty spectacle."

"She started it."

For some reason he didn't himself understand, the mild, introspective, and rational man suddenly exploded. "Shut up, Dee! Will you just please shut up! God damn it, shut up!"

"Billy! Billy Zip!"

Mici sprang from her chair and went running to him. They threw their arms around each other and kissed. Then, at arms' length, each examined the other in mutual delight.

"Billy, it's so good to see you."

"You look exactly the same, darling," he told her. "Not a year older, only prettier—if that's possible."

"You haven't changed either." He hadn't, Mici thought. As natty and stylishly turned out as ever in this season's latest, an impractical, cream-colored, linen suit.

45

His hairline had receded, or was that a wiglet he was wearing? It wasn't till she looked closely that she noticed the fretwork of fine lines behind the rose-tinted glasses and at the corners of his smiling mouth.

"I've put on weight," he murmured deprecatingly.

"Who hasn't?" she grinned. "But what's this 'Mr. Zipprodt' bit? When the girl brought your name in, it took me a minute to figure out who was here."

"I'm so impressed with your position, darling. I was trying to live up to it." He smiled back fondly.

"Billy, Billy, you're so good for my ego; you have no idea . . ." She waved him to a chair and then took her own place. "So how are you? What's new? Are you working?"

"You could call it that."

"What are you doing—designing the decor for massage parlors?" she teased.

"Nothing so exciting. I'm stage manager for daytime TV. I've got two soap operas—'Storm of Life' and 'The World We Live In.'"

"But that's marvelous, Billy! Terrific! Do you like it?"

"It's not exactly the fulfillment of my ambitions, but . . . yes, I like it all right. It's steady. It's nice to know there's a paycheck coming in every week." He paused. "I guess you're crazy about your job?"

She shrugged. "Nothing's perfect. So what can I do for you, Mr. Zipprodt? I don't suppose you came down here for a social call. By the way, how did you find me?"

"You remember Julia Schuyler?"

"Who could forget Julia?"

"Julia read about you in the papers, about some case you were prominent in where you helped clear a woman of murder."

"That was a while ago."

"You've turned into a real hotshot investigator, Julia says. She's very impressed."

"That's nice to know. As I recall, she didn't think

46

much of me as a dancer. And she was right." Mici grinned to alleviate the stage manager's embarrassment.

Billy Zip had been an assistant stage manager for the Joffrey Ballet Company when Mici was dancing minor roles. He'd aspired to be a scenic designer but got sidetracked. During the run at the Civic Opera House in Chicago, they were next door to Julia Schuyler at the Civic Theatre in *A Streetcar Named Desire*. Mici remembered that she'd thought Cassel miscast in the Brando role, too civilized, too sensitive, but Julia had been absolutely magnificent as Blanche. The stage doors of the two theatres were adjacent, and actors and dancers encountered each other coming and going. There were cast parties; they met at after-the-show hangouts. It wouldn't have happened in New York. Neither Billy Zip nor Mici Anhalt would have met Julia Schuyler or moved in her social circle, but it was different on the road. A company on tour is usually the only show in town. Hitting a city like Chicago, able to support several shows, was like coming back from exile. The casts fraternized, stars and bit players; even when they didn't like each other, the actors mixed and were friendly. Having met Julia Schuyler, Billy was instantly smitten. Julia and Alfred Cassel weren't married then. Mici didn't recall to whom Julia had been married at the time, if anybody. At any rate, she was sure that Billy would have been content to worship the star from afar, but Julia had encouraged him. Whether she'd used Billy to stir Cassel's ardor or whether she was just flattered by his adulation—for he was personable, intelligent, and did have a rather shy charm—Julia and Billy were an item during that Chicago season. When the time came for the Joffrey to move on to the next stand, Billy quit and stayed behind. In due course, Julia got him a job with *Streetcar*, and from then on he worked in every show she did. Unfortunately, they weren't many and the "rest" periods between grew longer and longer. Even after their romance—if there had actually been one—faded and

47

Julia married Cassel, Billy stuck with her. He was her unpaid secretary, companion, errand boy. He saw to it that there was food in the house and even cooked it. He nursed her when she needed nursing. He'd finally had to go out and get himself a real job, but evidently he was still in touch.

"How is Julia these days?" Mici asked. "I don't hear anything about her."

"She's bad, Mici. Terrible."

"I'm sorry. I did hear that Alfred has a new show."

"They're separated."

"Again?"

"This time it's for keeps. You have no idea what they went through. Neither one of them could get work for . . . oh, a couple of years. They sold everything they had—the car, that went first, then the co-op. They moved into a friend's apartment, which was all right, a decent place, but when they couldn't pay the rent he had to ask them to leave. After that they went from one furnished dump to another. It would break your heart. They got down to the clothes on their backs, just about. The furs, the jewels? Forget it—sold or in hock. They never stopped fighting, blaming each other." He shook his head. "They were dragging each other down."

"I'm sorry."

Zipprodt peered at her through the upper half of his tinted bifocals. "So darling, that's why I'm here. I came to ask you to help Julia. Please, for God's sake, help her."

She was completely taken aback. "Billy! What can I do?"

"That's your job, isn't it? To help people? To help the victims of crime?"

"Julia's the victim of a crime? What crime?"

"Assault. He came around and beat her up."

"Who?"

"Alfred."

Mici gasped. "I don't believe it."

48

"It's true. I saw the bruises."

"Did she say he was responsible?"

"No," Zipprodt admitted, "but it had to be him. I'm not saying she didn't provoke him but . . . Actually, I blame myself. Julia sent me over to see Alfred and to tell him that she needed more money and that if he didn't provide it she would sue for nonsupport. He was very upset, naturally. He claimed he was already giving her every cent he could spare. I suggested he go over and talk with her. In fact, I urged him to go over and see her, reason with her. He said he would. So I suppose one thing led to another and he lost control. Alfred has a temper. Most people don't realize it, but he can get violent."

"I know that they're both highly charged, emotional people, but . . ." Mici shook her head. She tried to forget that these were people she liked and even respected. "Has she had medical attention?"

"I don't think so."

"She ought to see a doctor. How about the police? Has she reported the beating? She should do that, Billy. She should do it within forty-eight hours of the alleged assault."

"Alleged?"

"Manner of speaking, Billy."

"I don't think Julia wants to go to the police."

"It's up to her, of course, but in any case I'm afraid that there's nothing this agency can do. It's a family matter and we can't touch it."

"If she'd been mugged on the street, then could you help her?"

"Yes."

"If she weren't married to Alfred, if they were just living together, then you'd pay?"

"It's not that simple, Billy."

"Sure it is. Sure it is. The present morality is a joke. On the one hand, society looks down on 'cohabitation' and on the other, rewards it. Don't tell me I'm wrong. Two

49

singles living together pay less taxes than a married couple. Senior citizens lose part of their social security if they remarry, and here's a situation where a woman has suffered bodily harm and your wonderful agency refuses even to consider her case because the assailant happens to be her husband." He finished on a rasping note of indignation.

"Don't lay it on me, Billy Zip. I don't make the rules." Mici's indignation matched his.

"From you I expected a little compassion, a little sympathy. . . ." he raged.

"I have all the feeling in the world for Julia Schuyler," she shouted back, then paused, and when she resumed it was with a touch of irony. "Only yesterday my supervisor called me on the carpet for having too much compassion."

"Maybe I should have come over yesterday." William Zipprodt got up and started for the door.

"Billy, come back. Please, come back and listen to me."

He did stop but remained where he was. "She needs help. She's run out of things to sell and friends to mooch off. I give her what I can, but I've got to live, too." He took a breath. "She's even trying to write a book. It's pitiful to see her commercializing her own degradation."

"Is there any interest?"

"In her own story? There have been too many like it. In what she has to say about her father . . . possibly. John Malcolm Schuyler has been gone nine years, but he still pulls the old magic. Of course, nobody's going to give her any kind of advance until she can show something on paper. I'm trying to help her but . . ." He sighed. "She won't work on any kind of regular schedule. She gets muddled, contradicts herself, can't seem to keep her facts straight."

"I suppose her unemployment insurance has long since run out. How about welfare?"

50

"You want Julia Schuyler to go on welfare?" The stage manager was outraged.

"You came to me and I'm doing the best I can."

"Which is nothing."

"Because there is nothing I can do. I just wish there were."

He stared at her for a long moment. "She's terrified, Mici. She can't sleep at night, she's so scared."

"Of Alfred?"

Once again Zipprodt headed for the door. "Thanks. Thanks for your time."

"Tell her to go to the police," Mici entreated. "Even though he's her husband, she can swear out a complaint. They'll arrest him and put him in jail. The law was passed last September."

"She'd never do that."

"All right then. Let her apply to Family Court for an order of protection. It would enjoin Alfred to stay away from her. If he disobeyed, then he'd be arrested."

"Well, maybe if you explained it to her . . ."

"Me? Billy, I haven't seen Julia in . . . I don't know how many years. I can't just walk in on her and bring up this kind of subject."

"Yes you can. She's expecting you."

"Julia is?"

"Tonight. She sent me to get you."

"She sent you? I—I can't see her tonight." She succumbed without realizing it.

"Tomorrow night then."

"Tomorrow's Friday. I'm going home for the weekend," she protested weakly. "I'd planned to leave right after work."

"Take a later train. You can do that much, can't you?"

The rain started just after 6 P.M. on Friday night. According to the weather bureau, it would do little to alleviate the heat that continued to rise by a few degrees each day, but at least there would be a temporary respite. As far as Officers Ray Emmenecher and Attilio Pace were concerned, it meant that there were fewer people on the street and therefore less work for them. The girls lounged in doorways, but the johns weren't out. Emmenecher half dozed behind the wheel of the parked patrol car. Even Pace was bored.

"It's sure quiet," he complained.

"Mm . . ."

"It's the quietest night we've had. At least since I've been on the job."

"You don't like it?"

"It makes the time go faster when there's action."

Emmenecher didn't bother to comment.

"You think it would be okay for me to go around the corner and get a hamburger?" Pace asked out of restlessness.

"Why not?"

"You want one?"

"Okay." Em didn't want one any more than his partner did; it just offered a break in the monotony. "Medium with plenty of catsup."

Pace had one foot outside the car door and on the pavement when a shrill scream froze him and galvanized Emmenecher into sitting up straight. After the initial split second of paralysis, the two men looked at each other, each with his hand on his gun.

"What was that?" Pace whispered.

"Shut up," the older man snarled.

They listened hard, but the scream was not repeated. They watched. No one came out of any of the buildings within their range of vision. Suddenly, preceded only by a hiss that was like the rushing of a train through a tunnel, the light rain turned into a downpour.

Ray Emmenecher rolled up his window.

Pace hesitated; then he pulled in his foot and shut his door. "Shouldn't we do something?"

"What?"

"Find out where it came from?"

"How?"

Pace thought about it. They couldn't ring every door-bell of every apartment in every building. They couldn't check every bar and massage parlor. Unless somebody called 911, and people in that neighborhood weren't inclined to call the police over every scream in the night, there was really nothing they could do. Reluctantly, he rolled his window up too, though he left it open just a bit at the top in case there should be another scream. . . .

"I thought you were going to get us hamburgers?"

"You don't expect me to go out in that, do you, for Chrissake!" Pace was so frustrated he forgot to be humble.

Emmenecher's shaggy eyebrows shot up.

Both men automatically checked their watches. It was 11:12 P.M.

5

They might not have found her as soon as Monday if her windows hadn't been shut against the rain and the temperature hadn't soared above ninety-five for the third straight day. The sickly odor seeped through the loose frame of the kitchen window into the courtyard where it mixed with all the other noxious fumes from all the apartment and restaurant kitchens, the overflowing garbage cans, the rat and human feces. It filled the apartment; then oozing from under the front door like a viscous liquid, it evaporated back into poison gas that contaminated the second-floor hall and filled the entire stairwell. Inured as they were to the stinks of summer, the tenants passing up and down ignored it. When it was no longer possible to do so, they began to whisper among themselves. On Monday shortly before noon, the tenant of the third-floor front, Bettedene Barber—also known as Barbi or Barbidoll—feeling queasy anyway after a big weekend, nearly gagged on the stench on her way downstairs. But it was the ringing of the telephone inside the apartment from which the foulness emanated, a ringing insistent and somehow desolate, that decided her. When it stopped, unanswered, she went looking for the super.

"I didn't smell a thing," Eddie Manzor insisted.

"How the hell could you? You haven't been in the building in a week."

"I've got other buildings to look after, you know. You got a complaint, you know what you can do with it."

"And I'm doing it," the teenage blonde shot back. "I'm telling you. The smell is sickening."

"Bad for business?" Eddie Manzor leered. He was a slovenly man of indefinable age. Never clean, never shaven, always tired, he shuffled from one tenement to another doing little more than hauling out the garbage; even that he couldn't manage, leaving a trail of spillage in the halls. He knew that none of his various employers was likely to check on him. If any one of them did, for the money he was getting Manzor could tell him to stick it.

Bettedene Barber didn't rise to the bait. In her abbreviated version of the doll's outfit with her cluster of golden curls falling around her shoulders, she was sexy and childish at the same time. At the moment, with her heavily made-up face puckered and her black-mascaraed eyes filled, the childishness predominated. "I'm telling you, Eddie, something's dead in there."

"What do you want me to do?"

"You've got a passkey. Open the door."

What Eddie Manzor did, reluctantly, was to call the police.

A patrolman cleared the way through the ogling crowd for Detective Donald Swell, Homicide Third Division, and he made his way walking jauntily on the balls of his feet like a fighter warming up in his corner of the ring. The people were everywhere—on the sidewalks, in the doorways, on the fire escapes. He ignored them. As far as

Detective Donald Swell was concerned, this was your typical crime-scene turnout, a little extra heavy because this was a hot summer's day and nobody in this neighborhood had much to do anyway. The local toughs had congregated right at the top of the stoop blocking the entrance to the building, but at a look from Swell they parted—sullenly, but they parted.

The odor of decomposition hit him as soon as he got inside. Swell merely wrinkled his nose and started up the stairs lightly at a half run, noting with satisfaction that he wasn't even breathing hard when he got to the top. That daily jogging sure paid off.

Inside the apartment was your typical homicide scene, Swell thought—ordered confusion, each man doing his thing with complete disregard for anyone else. Nobody so much as looked up at his entrance, but that didn't bother Donald. He might be only a dick three, but the information these hotshots were laboriously collecting would feed through him and he'd decide what was important and what was not. They were the experts, but he was the boss; he was carrying the case.

At thirty-five, Donald Swell had been a detective third grade for four years, two of them working out of Homicide. He liked the job, the guys, the feeling of belonging. It was like the army except that there was more freedom and one could act independently—within limits. The limits didn't bother Donald. He was a pragmatist; in fact, unconsciously, he found reassurance in the rules. He didn't dwell on the horrors with which he came into daily contact; he'd made his accommodation—they were part of the human condition. Take this room. One look sufficed—the threadbare carpet, dirty, cracked walls, cheap furniture; he'd seen a hundred like it. Unfortunately, the victim required more than a cursory glance. She was on the floor lying across the threshold between living room and kitchen, head in the living room. She lay on her left side, knees partially drawn up as though bunched over her wound. Her back was toward him, so the detective took a couple of steps forward to look more closely, but her hands were clutched over the injury. Her head was down, chin on chest, and her dark hair had fallen forward masking her face, which was probably just as well. The gases inside the body had caused her chest to bloat and burst the white cotton shirt she'd been wearing. If the same had happened to her face, which probably it had, then she would be unrecognizable, eyes bulging, tongue protruding, and the usual mess exuding from nose and mouth. Donald Swell swallowed the bile that rose up to the back of his tongue.

"Officer," he called to the uniformed cop at the door. "I'm Homicide. What've you got?"

Joe Camby, one of the two radio-car patrolmen who'd answered the call put in by Manzor, pulled out his notebook. "Name of the victim is Julia Schuyler." He paused. As the name didn't seem to make an impression, he added diffidently, not wanting to appear snobbish, "She was an actress, sir."

"Yeah? What kind of an actress?"

"Legitimate theatre, sir, though she did appear in some motion pictures years ago."

"Yeah?" Swell was not into the legitimate theatre, or ballet, or any longhair stuff. He wasn't much into movies either unless there was plenty of action involved.

Camby on the other hand was a culture freak. He decided to take one more chance. "Her father was John Malcolm Schuyler."

"Yeah?" Even Donald Swell had heard of him. "So go on, what else?"

"The super called in on a complaint from one of the tenants about the smell. We told him to use his passkey and let us in. The tenant who complained, a Miss Bettedene Barber, is waiting upstairs in her apartment, 3A.

The super, Eddie Manzor, is in the hall. My partner's with him and some of the other tenants."

"Any of them notice anything? Have anything to say?" Dumb question; these people made it a way of life *not* to notice anything, but if they were unfortunate enough to do so kept it to themselves. Swell had asked because it was routine.

Officer Camby answered and did so earnestly for the same reason. "No, sir."

"Okay, thanks." Swell prided himself on being courteous to lower-ranking men, but he hadn't taken the trouble to note the officer's name prominently pinned to the front of his blouse. If he should need to get back to him, what the hell, he'd find him.

"Hi, Doc." Swell moved on and greeted the assistant chief medical examiner. "You got an estimate how long she's been dead?"

"You should know better than to ask," Herman Childs grunted without looking up.

He did know better, but again it was routine. "Can't you give me any idea, Doc? A ball-park figure? Unofficially."

The exchange was choreographed down to the grunts and gestures. Childs, a twenty-year veteran, had been in line for the chief's job when the chief retired. He'd taken the exam along with the only other two forensic men qualified and then had sweated out the appointment. With each passing day, week, month, the threshold of his irritability was lowered. It took six months for a decision to be reached and Childs lost out. By then the strain had left permanent scars on his face and temper. "In this heat, with the windows shut tight . . ." He cast a glance at the kitchen window. "What the hell, we had to open it. You'll have to take my word that everything was closed when we came in."

"Hey, Doc!" Swell smiled and spread out his hands in a gesture which said that Childs's word was good with him for just about anything. Actually, as there was no discernible movement of air in the apartment, the detective wouldn't have noticed that the window was in fact open if the ME hadn't called attention to it. However, Childs was on the defensive and Donald hurried to take advantage. "So, taking into consideration the heat and humidity, the position of the body, the type and size of the wound, the amount of clothing she was wearing . . ." He listed it all just to let Doc know he wasn't a complete ignoramus.

"I'd say she'd been dead two to three days. Closer to three." Childs made a grudging estimate.

"How was she killed?"

"Stabbed in the heart. Her assailant was facing her. The weapon was some kind of carving knife, very big and very sharp. Apparently the killer took it with him."

"Yeah?"

"It's not around, is it? I don't see it, do you? So unless the killer washed it and wiped it and put it neatly back in a drawer . . ." He shrugged. "You want to take a look?"

"You're kidding, huh, Doc?"

"I never kid," Childs replied.

Swell hesitated. His eyes swept the small kitchen perfunctorily but took note of the empty bottle of Dewar's on the counter. Good brand, he thought. Then, just to be on the safe side, he went through the drawers. "There's no kind of carving knife around," he said.

"Really?" Childs grunted.

Swell still wasn't sure whether he'd been had. He tried to reassert himself as an expert. "If the attack was frontal, then she would have made some kind of attempt to defend herself, wouldn't she? There would have been a struggle, right?"

"Yes," Childs admitted. "There are bruises, but under these conditions it's pretty hard to say exactly when they were inflicted. We'll have to see."

"There could be skin particles from the perpetrator under her fingernails, huh, Doc? Traces of his blood and like that. So you'll let me know, right, Doc? First chance." Considering that he had evened the score, Swell thought it was time to get out. "Where's the officer who caught the squeal?" he boomed.

Camby stuck his head in from the hall.

"How about those witnesses?" Swell demanded. "Where are they?"

Camby forebore to remind the detective that he'd already been informed of their whereabouts. "Waiting for you, sir."

"Fine, fine. I'll see the super first."

Camby hesitated and Swell realized why; the place was swarming with technicians and cluttered with their equipment. "In the bedroom, of course. I'll talk to him in the bedroom." Swell sauntered off as though that had been his intention from the first.

The sagging bed took up most of the space; pushed up against one wall, it left barely room enough to get to the closet. It was covered by a chenille bedspread and apparently had not been slept in. The room was so small that the only other piece of furniture, a scarred bureau, partially blocked the single dirty window. Julia Schuyler couldn't have been much if she had lived like this, Swell mused. The father now, John Malcolm Schuyler, his name was legend. He'd come from a long line of distinguished actors—father, mother, uncles, aunts—but John Malcolm had been the brightest star of them all. He'd also become a hopeless alcoholic. He'd drink anything he could get his hands on, including—once when he'd been out at sea on a private yacht for the express purpose of drying out—the alcohol used to heat his wife's curling iron. Donald ranked actors in two categories: those who made it and those who didn't. The former he regarded as superior human beings, the latter as bums too lazy to go out and get regular work. It looked as if Julia Schuyler had been one of the bums.

Swell sat down on the edge of the bed because there wasn't anywhere else. "You the super?" he asked the bleary-eyed, unshaven man in soiled work clothes who presented himself at the door.

"Yes, sir."

"Well, what are you waiting for? Come on in. What's your name?"

"Manzor. Eddie Manzor." He crept in along the wall.

"Well, Mr. Manzor, how come it took you so long to call us?"

Manzor flinched. "Uh . . . well, you see . . ."

"According to the officer, you called only because one of your tenants insisted. How's that?"

Manzor was defensive. "I didn't know she was dead. I mean, how could I know?"

"She's been dead for close to three days, Mr. Manzor." Swell's tone was cutting. "You've got a nose, haven't you? Just like Miss Barber upstairs?" He hadn't needed to consult his notes for the name; Donald Swell remembered what he needed to remember. "So why did you wait? Why did Miss Barber have to go looking for you?"

"I don't live in the building."

"This is Monday. Don't you come around on Mondays anyway to put out the garbage?"

Manzor looked down at his matted, stained shoes. "I was here. But I didn't come upstairs. They're supposed to bring their garbage down to the back door for me to put out. I mean, this ain't the Ritz."

"You don't say? When was the last time you saw Miss Schuyler alive?"

"I don't know." Manzor shrugged, but the look Swell shot him made him add quickly, "I don't remember."

"When was the last time you were in this apartment? Come on, Mr. Manzor. I asked you a question."

"I was never in here. Never."

Swell looked his disbelief. "You never came in here to fix anything? She never called you to repair a leaky faucet, or unstick a window, or any damn thing?"

"Oh, you mean like that? Well, sure, naturally."

"How did you think I meant?"

"Her bathroom sink got clogged once. Hair balled up in the drain. I warned her about that. Dirty habit."

"When? When did you clean the bathroom sink?"

"Uh . . . maybe a week ago?"

"Are you asking me?"

"No. It was a week ago."

"You're sure? You remember now?"

"Yes, sir. I remember."

"Good. Was she alone?"

Too late Manzor saw the trap. The sweat stood out on his grimy forehead. "Yeah."

"What are you so nervous about?"

"I'm not nervous. Why should I be nervous?"

"That's what I was wondering," Swell replied blandly. "If nothing happened."

Manzor raised his squinty eyes up to the ceiling but found no help there. "She invited me to have a drink with her, but I said no. I know better than to get involved with a lush. No. No. I didn't mean that. I swear I didn't. What I meant . . . she was a nice woman, a lady—when she was sober. But she's been real lonely since her husband walked out and ready to grab out for anybody . . . Oh, God!" He realized, again too late, that he was making the situation worse.

"When did her husband leave?"

"Four, five months ago? I don't know. I mean, after a while I just kind of realized he wasn't around any more. He's an actor too, Alfred Cassel. Maybe you heard of him?" Manzor was eager now, eager to talk as long as it wasn't about himself. In fact, in order to divert attention from himself, the super was anxious to tell everything he

62

knew or had ever heard—just as Swell had intended. "He's been in the movies and on TV, and I hear he's gonna star in a big, new Broadway show. According to Ms. Schuyler, she threw him out on account of he had a girl friend. I guess she was sorry when she found out he had this good job. I guess she tried to get him back, but it was no go."

"How do you know that?"

"I seen him coming out of the building a couple of times. What was he doing here if not visiting her?"

"How do you figure it was no go?"

The super shrugged. "He didn't move back in, did he? Besides, every time he showed up, the next couple of days she was really knocking back the booze." This time he anticipated the question. "I could tell from the trash— the empties. You can tell a lot from people's trash," he went on. "Like Ms. Schuyler and Mr. Cassel—used to be Chivas Regal empties I found in their can; then it went down to house brands in quarts and half gallons; now it's mostly beer cans. Or was," he corrected himself.

"So when was the last time you saw Alfred Cassel?"

Manzor considered. "Thursday for sure."

"What do you mean—for sure?"

"I spoke to him on Thursday, but on Friday . . . It was a lousy night. I'd had a few at the corner bar and when I come home I thought I spotted him coming into the building. I thought it was him, but like I say . . . I'd had a few."

The ME estimated she'd been dead close to three days. Swell did some mental figuring. "What time Friday?"

"I couldn't tell you."

"Try."

Manzor shook his head. "Eleven? A little before, a little after." Swell's look scared the hapless man into the ultimate sacrifice. "If you want, I'll ask the wife what time I got home. She'll remember, believe me."

63

"I'll ask her myself," Swell told him. *I'll also ask the bartender what time you left, Buster, and if there's a gap—God help you!* the detective thought, but spoke with deceptive mildness. "This man you saw entering the building—what made you think it was Cassel?"

"The raincoat. Cassel had this raincoat, black with a cape around the shoulders. How many of those do you see around?"

"Policemen have them," Swell observed.

"No, no. I mean, those are like a rubber material; this was more like cloth. It didn't shine."

Swell nodded. "Was the rent getting paid?"

"Sooner or later."

"Who paid? Her or him?"

"How should I know?" Thinking he was off the hook, Manzor reverted to his normal truculence.

"She didn't mention it?" Swell asked pleasantly. "What did you talk about while you were drinking together?"

"We weren't drinking together! Never. I swear." The sweat glistened in the creases of his dirty face and his whole body gave off a smell so rank it was noticeable even in that fetid atmosphere. "Listen, I'm a married man. I've got a kid. I know better than to . . ." He stopped, grimaced, groaned, and gave up. "Okay. All right. So I had a beer with her. One beer, once. I felt sorry for her and I had a beer with her and I let her tell me all about how big she used to be in the business, the jobs her agent was lining up for her, the book she was writing. But she was dreamin'. All she wanted was for somebody to listen."

"Where's Cassel now?"

Instinct prompted a flip reply, but Manzor caught himself. "I don't know, Officer." He waited and watched anxiously as the detective got up and began poking through the bureau drawers, examining the closet which was half empty. "Say, uh, Officer . . ." Manzor cleared his throat. "You through with me? Can I go now?"

Swell turned as though he'd forgotten all about the super. "Oh, sure. Go ahead. And say, thanks for your help, Mr. Manzor." He was breezy and friendly and sent Manzor off in a state of bewilderment.

On the shelf above the clothes rod of Julia Schuyler's closet were a couple of good-quality but badly worn handbags. By hefting each one, Swell determined which had been in current use. The contents were the usual wallet with a couple of dollars in it, credit cards, driver's license but no vehicle registration, and a checkbook showing a balance of eleven dollars and two cents. There was also a small, red-leather address book. Swell flipped through it cursorily. A name caught his eye, then another. He took the book over to the window as though the bit of extra light would make a difference.

A big grin transformed Detective Donald Swell's tough-guy face into that of a happy schoolboy. Names, names, names he recognized! Big important names of famous people in show business, sports, the jet set. God! The only one missing was Jackie Onassis.

He'd hit it lucky—at last. You needed the breaks to get ahead in the police department the same as anywhere else. He'd had his share; he couldn't deny it. The first had come when he'd been in the force only three years. He'd been parked in his radio car across from the New York Medical Center—his partner was making a pit stop—when he noticed a couple of orderlies strolling out of the main building. It was January and a real cold day and they weren't wearing coats. That made him suspicious. They sauntered down the U-shaped drive to the street awful slow for guys without coats, he'd thought, and then he heard the faint sound of the alarm. They heard it too and made a run for it, but he collared one of them. The other was picked up in due course through his buddy's turning state evidence. The haul was over $200,000 worth of drugs which they'd hidden in special holders taped under their shirts. That was what had kept them warm. The bust had put Donald into plain clothes.

Two years later he was once again in the right place at the right time. He and his partner walked in on a robbery in progress in a liquor store. It'd looked like a one-man job, and they'd disarmed the perpetrator and were cuffing him when his accomplice came up from behind the counter. Swell spotted him and fired first. Damn near killed the guy, but probably saved his partner's life, not to mention his own and that of the proprietor. That got him the gold shield. The PC himself pinned it on Donald. He was a hero—for a couple of days, anyway.

That had been four years ago. For four long years he'd been stuck in his present grade doing the most routine kind of leg work. When he thought back to the two incidents, which he did more and more often lately, Donald was honest enough to admit that he'd acted more out of instinct than bravery. He wondered whether he'd act so quickly now if the opportunity arose. He was older and smarter. He'd weigh the consequences—the mandatory Internal Affairs investigation into any shooting by a police officer, possible charges by the perpetrator, the reactions of bystanders which could be ugly—and the moment would pass him by. But there was no instant stress in this particular situation.

The little red book in his hands, Detective Third Grade Donald Swell stared out the unwashed window at the other unwashed windows overlooking the steamy courtyard. Brown eyes narrowed, pudgy face puckered, Swell considered how best to make use of the case that had been handed to him. Though herself a has-been, as her father's daughter Julia Schuyler had publicity value which was much enhanced by the circles in which she'd moved—never mind how long ago. As for Alfred Cassel, if he had been on TV and was now due to star in a new

66

Broadway show, then the case would hit the headlines for sure. And if Swell could break the case, it could mean making second grade.

The grin returned, very broad, turning him back into the chubby schoolboy. Depending on who the killer turned out to be—maybe he could make first grade! Donald Swell daydreamed.

6

On Sunday night Mici Anhalt returned from her weekend at home. She was much calmer. She'd decided that she had overreacted to Adam's lecture, but that he too had overreacted to the situation because he was tired, overworked, and dragged out by the heat. She admitted that she did have a tendency to slough off the dull, routine cases, to neglect paperwork, and to crow over her successes. In the future she would allot equal time and attention to all and maintain a low profile with her colleagues. As for Julia Schuyler, the image of the actress had haunted Mici through most of the weekend. Though forewarned, she hadn't been prepared for the squalor in which she found Julia living or for her emotional state. Regardless of Adam's recent strictures, nothing could be done for Julia under the program. The truth was that nothing could be done for Julia except by Julia herself. Mici kept thinking of the once glamorous actress as she had left her on Friday—asleep on that hard, sleazy couch, mouth open and snoring like a day laborer—and she couldn't shake off a sense of responsibility toward her.

Several times on Monday morning Mici reached for the telephone to call Julia but it was always too early—Julia Schuyler wouldn't be fit to talk till at least noon. Not that Mici had anything special to say; she just felt the need to contact the actress once more and to make sure she understood the options that were available to her. At noon, while the number was ringing, Clay Marin appeared on the threshold of Mici's office. She had to put the receiver down. The blind man's visits always tried her patience. Today, his arrival would put her recent good resolutions to the test.

Dowd's secretary, Mrs. Jarrett, had escorted the blind man this far. Though she knew that he couldn't see it, Mici forced a bright smile and ran over to take him from Fran and guide him the short distance to the chair beside her desk. With a sweep of his cane that stopped just short of hitting her, he made his own way. Mici jumped aside but didn't say anything. She was sure he'd done it on purpose. She was glad that his mobility was improving; too bad the same couldn't be said for his disposition. She stifled a sigh and spoke with that false, loud cheeriness reserved for invalids.

"It's good to see you, Mr. Marin. You're looking fine, just fine." He wasn't. He was badly shaved, wearing a rumpled suit, a stained tie, mismatched socks. It was his way of pointing up his affliction. There had been a time, she well remembered, when Clay Marin had done everything possible to hide it.

"You stood me up last Wednesday," he accused.

Apparently he was in an exceptionally sour mood, even for him. "I'm sorry about that, Mr. Marin. It couldn't be helped."

"Do you realize the effort I have to make to get here?"

"Yes, I certainly do, and I'm really very sorry . . ."

"I depend on the charity of neighbors to bring me. My

69

wife, what the hell does she care? She can't be bothered. We don't sleep together any more, did you know that? Sleep together? Hell, we hardly talk any more."

"I was at fault on Wednesday, Mr. Marin, completely at fault. Please forgive me."

"Nobody had any idea where you were," he whined. "Nobody had any idea when you'd be back. I didn't know whether I should wait around for you or what."

Mici was getting tired of apologizing. "I understand that Mr. Lischner took care of you."

"Mr. Lischner was very sympathetic, but what could he do? He didn't have access to the recent medical reports. He went through your desk, but he couldn't find them."

Mici frowned. Wally sympathetic? That wasn't his style with clients. Wally going through her desk? She didn't like that. She didn't like his telling Marin that he couldn't find the reports; they were right there in the bottom drawer. Why had he lied? Unless it was a way of getting rid of Marin. That was it, of course. Unfortunately, she couldn't do the same.

"He didn't know where to look," she offered as cheerfully as she could. "But here they are. If you'll just give me a moment to look them over once more . . ."

She felt sorry for Clay Marin. One year and four months ago he had interrupted a rape. Coming home at dusk, he had parked his car in his own driveway on Dartmouth Street in Forest Hills, got out, and was just approaching his front door when he heard a woman screaming. The screams came from an empty lot at the corner. Marin—in his early forties but in excellent physical condition from daily workouts at the prestigious West Side Tennis Club further down the street—ran to investigate. The trees, one of the beauties of the privileged "Gardens" enclave, were in full leaf, further cutting down the light from the street lamps, replicas of old-fashioned gaslights which gave almost as poor illumination as the originals.

70

Marin could barely make out shapes down among the tall grasses at the back of the lot.

The woman screamed again and then she began to sob and whimper. "No, no . . . please . . . oh please . . ."

For a moment, Marin froze. He didn't know what he faced. Was the assailant armed? Did he have a gun or a knife? Was he young, old, big, strong? There were apartment buildings across the street overlooking the lot; had anyone there called the police? When would the police arrive? Meanwhile his eyes adjusted to the shadows and he could make out an amorphous mass writhing and heaving on the ground.

"Say, you! What are you doing? Let her go! Let that woman go!"

The movement stopped; the mass separated into two parts, and the rapist rose from his victim to look around. Surprised and encouraged and sure now that the man was not armed, Marin pushed through the dew-heavy grass, lunged, and grabbed the assailant by the shirt collar.

"Run!" he yelled to the woman. "Run! Get the police!"

In the effort to pull loose, the attacker turned and for a couple of seconds he and Marin were face to face. Then the attacker, younger and stronger and more desperate, literally tore free and fled, leaving Marin with the ripped shirt collar in his hand.

Later that night a suspect was apprehended. The victim was willing to press charges, not always the case in such crimes, but she had not seen her assailant clearly and could not make a positive identification. But Marin could.

Clay Marin had a strong sense of duty and of confidence in ultimate justice. He was further motivated by the fact that the victim turned out to be the nineteen-year-old daughter of a neighbor. All this combined to make him an excellent witness. He picked the suspect out of the lineup without indecision of any kind and agreed to testify at the trial. Both the police and the

71

prosecutor were delighted. Marin was a hero at home, at his club, throughout the neighborhood. And when the story appeared in the newspapers, his name and address were given.

The threats began: letters, phone calls, a dead cat thrown on the doorstep. His children—Rosalie, twelve, and Kenny, six, cried; his wife was frightened; but Clay Marin refused to be intimidated. As the time of the trial drew near, the harassment stopped abruptly.

"They know they can't scare me," Marin told his wife smugly, and Sandra Marin smiled and prayed to God that he was right.

On the night before he was due to testify, with the children sleeping soundly upstairs, he and Sandra were watching the late news before turning in. Each was thinking that by that time the next night the ordeal would be over, the suspect convicted and behind bars for good—well, for several years at least. Then the front doorbell rang. Marin, assuming it was one of the patrol officers assigned to keep a special eye on the house, got up automatically to answer. Sandra Marin stayed where she was, expecting to hear only a murmur of voices as her husband and the cop exchanged good nights. What she heard was her husband's shriek of pain. She got up and ran out to the hall in time to see him stagger back from the door, hands clutching at his eyes.

"Water! Water! Get me some water!"

Clay Marin did not appear in court the next day to make the identification: you can't identify somebody you can't see. The acid thrown in his face had blinded him.

Early medical opinions were cautious. There was hope; he could distinguish light from dark. There was hope. Wait and see. That was all they could say. Or would.

Mici had handled the case from the start and she remembered Clay Marin when he first came in—an angry, proud man, determined to beat the disability and to punish the criminal who had caused it. His claim was approved under the Good Samaritan provision. In case of death this would have meant larger benefits for the surviving family but in Marin's situation entitled him to reimbursement for loss of earning power for a longer than usual period. All the victims who qualified were entitled to unlimited medical assistance. Every possible avenue of treatment was investigated for Marin and passed on to J. Hammond Cornelius with Mici's and Dowd's recommendation for approval. In each instance, Cornelius had given his final okay.

As the months passed and the medical reports turned pessimistic, Marin turned bitter. Who could blame him? But the more that was done for him, the less he did for himself. He had started eager to become self-sufficient and taken mobility training at the Lighthouse for the Blind. The board okayed the purchase of a C5 Laser cane at a cost of $2,000, instead of the usual, conventional cane. In this costlier device, the laser beam is converted into sound of varying pitch by which the user can judge the relative height and distance of the obstacle in his path. It gives protection to the entire body, where other devices—the sonic glasses, for instance—cover only the area above the waist. According to his instructor, Marin had learned to handle his cane proficiently, yet, so far as anybody at the board offices knew, he seldom used it except when he came in to recite his woes and ask for more benefits. He was a salesman of commercial real estate and the company for which he'd worked offered him his old job back, reasoning that most of the properties had been listed before Marin's blindness and that he could be briefed on any new ones. According to Marin, to show what he couldn't see would be playing on the clients' pity. He refused. He also refused vocational training, claiming that the jobs available were menial and beneath his talents.

He was getting to be a pain.

Psychiatric treatment was arranged for him. It didn't help. The deterioration, physical and psychological, accelerated. It was downhill all the way.

Having started by admiring him, Mici now dreaded Clay Marin's visits. Everybody in the office did. As Adam had said, he was a whiner and a complainer, but nobody would turn his back on Clay Marin.

Privately, Mici thought he would adjust to his disability if he weren't still hoping to regain his sight. For a while he had been able to perceive shapes, and the Eye Research Institute of the Retina Foundation in Boston had advised patience in the hope that nature would do her own healing. For a period that appeared to be happening. But the improvement had only been minor, followed by further deterioration.

Marin had heard of a new surgical procedure to replace the vitreous, jelly-like filling of the eyeball, and he was convinced this would restore his sight. Of course, he was sent for examination to the specialist who had developed the procedure. It was that specialist's report which Mici was now reviewing. Finished, she looked up to meet the dark glasses through which her client could not see.

"Did Dr. Harden discuss his conclusion with you?"

"He told me he didn't believe that a vitrectomy could help me."

"That's what he says in his report. I'm sorry, Mr. Marin."

"He said I could always get another opinion."

"Dr. Louis Harden is the authority on the subject. I doubt that another opinion would contradict his."

"I want it. I'm entitled to it."

"I understand how you feel, Mr. Marin but . . ."

"The hell you do! You haven't the faintest idea of how I feel or what my life has become!"

"You're right, of course," Mici admitted. "At the same time . . ."

"I want another opinion! I demand it!" He was shaking

74

with rage and frustration. His long, dour face contorted; sweat glistened amid the stubble on his chin.

"I'll put through your request, Mr. Marin." Mici hesitated. In the past Marin had been handled too carefully, shielded too much, given false hope. She decided to be frank with him. "But under the circumstances I don't think the request will be granted." She waited for the outburst.

He took it quietly. In fact, he took it very well. "You've always been honest with me, Miss Anhalt. I appreciate that."

Surprise, what a surprise! "Thank you."

"I know you want to help me."

"I do, Mr. Marin."

"Well then, what could be simpler than to say that Dr. Harden has suggested another opinion?"

"But what about the report?"

"You could hold that back."

Slowly she shook her head. Remembering that he couldn't see, she murmured, "I'm sorry, no. I can't do that."

"You mean you won't."

"All right, I won't. It wouldn't do you any good. The second man might discuss the matter with Dr. Harden and the whole thing would come out."

"Not if you explain the situation to him."

Tired of his importuning, Mici cut Marin short. "Forget it, Mr. Marin. I'll put through your request along with Dr. Harden's report in the usual way."

"You women are all alike. All alike. You're sweet, willing to help as long as it's done your way, your way. Well, I don't need you and I don't need her. Forget it." Shaking, he got to his feet and, using his cane, expertly pointed himself toward the door.

Automatically Mici rose and went around to put a hand on his arm.

He shook her off. "I can find my own way."

75

He could and did, leaving Mici's office and heading through the big main room toward the exit while the various secretaries and clerks stopped to watch in amazement.

So, Mici thought, what Clay Spoiled Rotten Marin needed was not sympathy but a kick in the pants.

Suddenly she thought of Julia Schuyler. A swift kick wouldn't do her any harm either. But not on the telephone. The best thing would be to run up there. It shouldn't take too long. Mici grabbed her handbag, threw a light jacket over her arm in case she happened to get an air-conditioned subway car—what a hope—and sped out of her office.

"Leaving early?"

Wally Lischner just happened to look up as she passed his open door.

She paused guiltily and glanced at her watch. "Going out for a late lunch."

"Sure."

Their eyes met. He winked. "I'll cover for you."

"Thanks," she smiled. *Nuts,* she murmured under her breath.

By the time Mici Anhalt got uptown the block of Forty-fifth between Eighth and Ninth Avenues was pretty nearly back to normal. The official cars were gone. No one stopped her from entering the building. It wasn't until she climbed to the second floor that she spotted the uniformed officer, and the vague dread she'd been suppressing since Friday night rose up to choke her.

"What happened?"

"Homicide, ma'am."

"Who? Who was killed?"

"The woman who lived in this apartment, ma'am."

God! Ice-cold sweat broke out all over her body. "When? When did it happen?"

76

"I don't know, ma'am. I don't know anything about it."

If he did, he wouldn't tell her. "I'd like to talk to the person in charge."

"There's nobody here, ma'am. They're all gone." Because she seemed genuinely distressed, he added, "You could try the precinct, ma'am. Midtown South; that's 357 West 35th Street. Talk to the desk sergeant, ma'am."

"That's being handled by the Third Homicide Division, ma'am," the desk sergeant informed Mici. "If you want to leave your name I'll see to it that . . . ."

Mici had a good idea what leaving her name would mean; a couple of days from now, a week from now, when he had nothing better to do, some detective on the fringes of the case would get around to calling her. She was jittery; she felt like pounding on the sergeant's desk and it took considerable effort to smile sweetly instead. "If you could just tell me who's in charge of the case, Sergeant. I need to talk to him. The victim was a friend . . ." Her voice broke. It wasn't put on. All Mici was doing that she wouldn't ordinarily do was let her feelings show.

Sergeant Eugene Crance, faithful husband, devoted father, dedicated deep-sea fisherman, still appreciated a pretty woman and not many like this redhead walked up to his desk. Procedure was to take her name and pass it on but . . . what the hell! Unaware that he was licking his lips, Crance reached for the telephone.

"This is Sergeant Crance at Midtown South . . . oh, is that you, Vito? How are the blues running? . . . Way out there, huh? Yeah, I'm going to try to make it on Wednesday. Say, who's carrying the Schuyler homicide? . . . Today on Forty-fifth, that's the one, right. . . ." He covered the mouthpiece and spoke to Mici. "He's checking. . . . Yeah, Vito? Okay. Thanks,

77

pal." Feeling Mici's eyes on him, he added, "Is he there now? . . . So when's he coming in? I've got a witness here with important information. . . . Sure, I'll tell her." Crance hung up, pushed the piece of paper on which he'd written over to Mici. "You want Detective Swell. He's off duty; you should call in the morning. I've put the number down."

Mici sighed. "Thanks, Sergeant."

Crance watched the sway of her hips as she headed for the door; then he noticed the slouch of her shoulders.

"Miss?" He beckoned her back. "No guy on a hot homicide is going home at the end of his shift—not if he knows what's good for him." He winked.

Maybe Detective Donald Swell knew better than to quit at the end of his tour, but wherever he was and whatever he was doing nobody in the squad room on East 51st Street knew anything about it. Mici decided there was no point in going back to her office. She could only hope that nobody besides Wally had noticed that she was gone. She had the uneasy feeling that if he tried to cover for her, Wally would only succeed in making matters worse. She wished now that she'd challenged his offer. Hell! The damage was done; she might as well sit it out here.

Every time anybody new walked through the door, Mici looked up hopefully, but it was never the man she wanted. By eight, too dispirited to be hungry, she gave up. She wrote a note and asked one of the detectives, the one with the black patent-leather hair who had been making a play for her between phone calls and trips to the cooler, to put it on Swell's desk. On her way out, she also left her name with the desk sergeant downstairs. Then she bought all the late papers at the stand outside the subway and started reading them on the ride uptown.

Donald Swell had more urgent things to do than hang

78

around the squad room. He had important people to see, the first being the victim's estranged husband.

As soon as he walked into the actor's suite, Swell sensed that the scare technique he had used on Eddie Manzor was not going to serve. The actor puzzled the detective. Economically, Swell knew that Alfred Cassel was in bad shape, worse off than the detective himself, that the suite in the old-fashioned but prestigious hotel had to be all front. So the respectful routine was inappropriate. But socially, Cassel was way up there in a stratum Swell could never hope to reach. Therefore the buddy-buddy bit wasn't right, either. What was left? Man-to-man, Swell decided; he'd adopt the forthright, straight-from-the-shoulder approach.

But Cassel was a better actor than the detective; the skill of the professional all but swamped the amateur. Swell arrived before the news of Julia Schuyler's death hit the radio or the newspapers; Cassel received it with a convincing demonstration of shock and sorrow.

"When?" he asked. "When did it happen?"

"It's hard to say. She wasn't discovered till this morning, and several matters have to be taken into consideration in estimating how long . . ."

"Ahh . . ." Cassel looked sick. He turned aside for a few moments, and when he faced the detective again he was at least three shades paler. "Have you any idea who did it?"

"I was hoping you might have, sir." Swell frowned; he hadn't meant to add the sir.

Cassel shook his head. "We weren't living together. Well, you know that. In fact, I wanted a divorce which she refused to give me. I might as well tell you; you'll find out soon enough. I called her, wrote her, I asked mutual friends to intercede, but she was obdurate." He paused, apparently lost in a reverie. With a slight start, he came out of it and observed. "You don't kill a woman be-

79

cause she won't give you a divorce, not in our day, anyway. There is someone else, a lady I would like to marry
but . . . if we can't . . . that's no big thing nowadays,
either. And, of course, we can now, can't we?" The performance was disarming, as intended. "Julia was bad-
mouthing me around town; you'll find that out too. But
in this business if you went around killing everybody
who took a crack at you, you wouldn't have any friends
left."

"When did you last see Miss Schuyler?"

The slightest hesitation, the first touch of uncertainty
was in his reply. "Thursday, I think. Yes, last Thursday.
Frankly, it was an unpleasant meeting. I didn't want to
go, but I was strongly urged by several friends to try to
reason with her. Of course, I should have known better.
Nobody can ever—could ever—reason with Julia even
when she was sober, and last Thursday she was very, very
drunk. It ended in a yelling match and Julia always won
those. I guess the whole house must have heard us."

Which is why you're so forthcoming, Buster, Swell
thought. "Would you mind accounting for your time over
the weekend, Mr. Cassel? Say from Friday noon to Sunday night? Just routine."

"Is that when she was killed?"

"As I told you, sir, we don't know for sure."

Cassel sighed. "I spent the weekend with the lady I
mentioned."

"Her name, please."

"Miss Grace. Delissa Grace."

Dutifully, Swell wrote it down. "You were together the
whole time?"

"Just about."

Swell let it go. This was a preliminary interrogation.
He'd be back.

Delissa Grace was one gorgeous doll, Donald thought

as he looked her over with great appreciation. Unfortunately, the macho approach didn't impress the lady. She kept her cool and backed her boyfriend right down the line. According to her, the only time they were apart during the whole weekend was when one or the other of them went to the john.

Swell wasn't discouraged, not at all. In fact, he was elated. These people were a whole new breed to him, a challenge. Everything was proceeding satisfactorily. Julia Schuyler's death made a bigger splash in the papers than Swell had anticipated, in fact bigger than he had dared to hope. Either hard news was scarce or Schuyler had been a real star. Just as the publicity was dying out, the autopsy report was ready. According to the report, there was a heavy percentage of alcohol in the dead actress's blood. There were indications that she'd been severely beaten sometime before her death and also that she'd had sexual intercourse just prior to the stabbing. Zoom! The coverage shot right up again.

As it turned out, the case got *too* big, from Swell's point of view. The brass began to take an interest, and as they did, naturally, so did Swell's lieut and his captain. The whole thing was too rich for a mere dick three. Swell was eased out. Oh sure, technically Donald Swell was still carrying—that was procedure—but it was the big guys who gave out the progress reports, stood in front of the TV news cameras squinting in the glare of the spotlight, got their pictures on page two or three of the dailies—page one was reserved for crime bosses and theatrical personalities. A task force of twenty men was thrown in to canvass the neighborhood in which Schuyler had lived the last months of her life, and Swell was one of the troops. Specifically, he was to interrogate the tenants of her building. He was okay for that, but not for celebrities. Donald Swell saw his big chance slipping away and he didn't know what to do about it.

He'd gotten the message from the desk sergeant that a woman had been around to see him regarding the Schuyler case. M. Anhalt. The name didn't mean anything, but he knew enough to check Julia's little red book. Not listed. Forget it. By the time Donald sat down at his desk, Mici's note put there by her detective admirer was down at the bottom of the pile Donald swept aside as he prepared to write his report.

7

For forty minutes in the morning usually starting around eleven—beginning later and lasting for a shorter duration during the winter—the sun found its way between two buildings to the east and entered the window of Bettedene Barber's kitchen. This morning there were about ten minutes to go before it disappeared behind the water tower two blocks to the west when Mici Anhalt rang the doorbell.

By permitting him to think he was making headway, Mici had prevailed on her friend at the Third Division to divulge that Detective Swell would be at the Schuyler address for most of the day conducting interrogations. It was forty-eight hours since the discovery of Julia's abused and partially decomposed body and one hundred and eight hours or four and a half days since the earliest estimate of the time of her death.

"I'm sorry to bother you," Mici apologized to the wispy

teenager with the dark circles under her eyes. "I'm looking for Detective Swell. Is he here?"

The girl nodded. "Somebody for you," she called and stepped back so Mici could pass.

Mici entered through a dingy, dark living room into the sunny kitchen, its tenement rawness camouflaged by checked-gingham curtains, scalloped edging on the shelves, decals of fruits and animals on the walls. The cheap pots hanging over the stove had been burnished bright, the antiquated refrigerator sprayed a daffodil yellow.

Swell, jacket off, tie loosened, and collar opened, was sitting at the kitchen table having a beer. "Who wants me?"

"My name is Anhalt."

He frowned. He remembered. "Oh yeah, M. Anhalt. You left a message."

The sun hit Mici like a spotlight, highlighting her red-gold hair so that it threw off rainbow sparks. Her tanned arms and shoulders, covered with a thin film of sweat from the exertion of climbing three flights in the heat, looked as though she'd just put on suntan oil. She was wearing a loose but clingy cotton knit, and every curve of her knockout figure was delineated. Swell put the beer can down, got to his feet, and took a step towards her. Looking into her clear blue eyes, he sucked in his breath. He didn't miss the fine lines around the eyes nor at the corners of her nice, wide mouth. He judged that M. Anhalt was in her early thirties, a little mature for his taste but by no means over the hill. What the hell! Like the ad said: *you're not getting older, darling; you're getting better.* He buttoned his collar and pulled up the knot of his tie.

"Sorry I didn't have a chance to get back to you." He started to put on his jacket but decided that was overdoing it.

"I left several messages."

"I've had my hands full."

"I can see that." She glanced at the beer can on the table.

"What can I do for you, Miss Anhalt?"

Mici had taken her own inventory of Swell and formed her own opinion. Donald Swell was flashy, overconfident, overweight, but—with his rumpled sandy hair, boyish yet rugged face, and blue eyes—not unattractive. Not that it mattered; she wasn't here either to put him down or to try to make points with him. "I have what may be important information about Julia Schuyler. I saw her on Friday night. She told me something which may or may not be true, but which I feel I must pass on."

"Where did you see Miss Schuyler?"

"Here. That is, downstairs in her apartment."

"What time?"

"I came a little after seven-thirty P.M. and left by eight."

Swell's eyes narrowed; his lips formed a silent whistle.

"You could be the last person to have seen her alive."

Mici waited till they were alone.

"Except for the killer," she said, correcting the detective's statement.

The sun had passed on and in shadow the little kitchen looked sad despite its cheery decor. Bettedene Barber had not taken kindly to being sent out of her own home, but Swell had handed her a couple of dollars and told her to go out and buy herself lunch. Barbidoll had already eaten but knew when to do a cop a favor.

Mici, resenting Swell's arrogance toward the girl, was testy. "I may have been the last person to see Julia alive except for the killer."

"Of course, sure, that's what I meant."

"Thank you." She frowned. What she had to say was a heavy weight on her conscience, and she was treading cautiously. "Do you have a suspect?"

"Now Miss Anhalt, you came to tell me something, remember?" Donald was almost coy. "You say you visited Miss Schuyler on Friday night and were with her for half an hour. How was she when you left?"

"Sleeping."

"Sleeping?"

"All right, passed out."

"Ah . . ." He nodded. "And you walked out and left her like that?"

"What else could I do? You've got to understand that it wasn't the first time I'd seen Julia drunk and passed out. She was liable to get that way at any time. At a party. She'd just lie down on the floor and go to sleep and people would just step around her, over her if necessary."

"This wasn't a party, was it?"

"No."

"You just walked out and left her?"

"I had a train to catch. I was going away for the weekend."

"Sure. You were in a hurry."

"Look," Mici pointed a finger at him and was mortified to note that it was trembling and she couldn't make it stop. She clenched her fist and put it down into her lap. "Don't you try to lay any guilt trip on me, Detective Swell."

"You've already done that yourself, lady."

"When I left Julia Schuyler, she was sleeping as peacefully as a baby. I expected she'd wake up in a couple of hours and probably start drinking again. The same as all the other times."

"So you left her alone with the door unlocked."

Mici was genuinely shocked. "Are you telling me that somebody just happened to try her door, found it unlocked, walked in, and killed her? A stranger?"

Swell hesitated. He had her on the defensive. He could hit hard, make her feel responsible for leaving that door unlocked, and maybe break her. Swell was shrewd and he sensed two things about Mici Anhalt: one, that kind of

86

attack could have the opposite effect and cause her to clam up; two, she was a friend of the dead woman and might prove useful if he had her on his side. Besides, she was the type of witness it would be fun to cozy up to.

"Why don't you just tell me what happened, Miss Anhalt?" He offered an engaging smile.

"That was the original idea," she reminded him, then mused ruefully that she wasn't used to being on this end of an interrogation. So she smiled back. "I was a dancer at one time, and I knew Julia Schuyler from my show-business days. I hadn't seen her in . . . oh, seven or eight years. Thursday afternoon a mutual friend, William Zipprodt, came to my office. Julia sent him to say she wanted me to help her."

"Why didn't she call you herself?"

Mici shrugged. "Julia never did anything herself that she could get someone else to do for her."

Swell's eyebrows went up. "What did she want?"

"Money. Financial help. She knew that I work for the Crime Victims Compensation Board, and she wanted to file a claim."

"She was a victim of a crime? What crime?" Another hit, Swell thought. This was his case, no doubt about it.

"Assault."

Swell's excitement mounted; he was going to get the answer the autopsy had not been able to supply—how long before death the bruises had been inflicted. "When? When was she assaulted?"

"She didn't say. She had all kinds of marks on her arms and legs. They were various shades, as though the results of several beatings."

Swell was disappointed. "Did she file a complaint?"

"No."

"Why the hell not?" He was almost personally affronted.

"She didn't think the police would do anything for her."

"Why should she think that?" he demanded, and then

he got it. All at once he got the whole picture. "Who did she say did it to her?"

"Her husband."

"Ah ha." A tight, smug smile was in direct contrast to the caution with which he spoke. "Alfred Cassel moved out four months ago."

"He still had a key and showed up whenever he felt like it."

Still playing devil's advocate, Swell continued his objections. "The way I heard it, Cassel's got himself somebody new—his leading lady."

"I'm telling you what Julia told me; I'm not saying I believe it."

Swell didn't like that. "Go on."

"That's all, really, I urged her to file a complaint, but she said the police didn't consider wife-beating a crime."

"There's a new law . . ."

"I'm familiar with it. I told her about it. She didn't want to go that route. She didn't want to humiliate herself."

"So what did you do? Did you agree to file a claim for her?"

"How could I? We don't cover crimes within the family, not to the third order on consanguinity," she quoted with some asperity; he should have known.

"Yeah, well listen, don't feel bad. We've all got to say no sometime." He put a hand on her shoulder. "Hey, you want some coffee? I could fix us some." He looked around vaguely.

Mici shook her head. "All I could advise her to do was to go to Family Court and seek an Order of Protection. She turned that down, too. So then all I could do was tell her to change the lock on her door." Mici bit her lip.

"Don't blame yourself, Miss Anhalt. I can certainly understand how troubled you've been about this, but actually your being there on the night she was murdered was just a coincidence." While he was offering solace, Swell

88

was inwardly exulting. A battered-wife case involving show-business personalities. Terrific! And he was right in the thick of it. The thing was to play it cool with the chick. He had to handle the redhead just right; she wasn't exactly hostile, but . . . call it reluctant. "You've shown integrity coming forward like this, Miss Anhalt, and I'm very sorry that I put you to so much trouble in finding me."

"That's okay."

"So let's just review what we've got. Julia Schuyler asked you to come to see her, and in the course of the conversation she accused her estranged husband, Alfred Cassel, of beating her."

"That's what she said."

"I understand. Now, I get the impression that this was something new. In other words, that he hadn't been in the habit of beating her while they were living together."

"Never. I never heard of it. Nobody ever heard of it. There was no indication of such a thing."

"Hm." Swell pursed his lips. "If it's in a man's character to commit this kind of violence, he doesn't wait long to start."

He was perceptive, Mici thought, and for the first time during the interview she felt a surge of optimism.

"I gather the marriage was tempestuous," Swell continued. "Yet Cassel only got violent after the separation. Why? Did she say why he suddenly started to beat her?"

"No."

Swell moistened his lips and thrust them forward while he thought. "The divorce. He wanted a divorce and she wouldn't give it to him. He came over to plead with her and ended up losing his temper."

"I could see that happening once," Mici agreed. "Not more than once. Not time after time."

"Describe the bruises."

Mici sighed. "As I told you, some seemed more recent than others. Some were turning yellow, and some were black and red. She had one big, ugly, black mark on her upper right arm, as though she'd raised that arm to shield her face and he'd grabbed it and tried to pull it away."

The detective had a list of the salient facts of the autopsy, among them the type and location of the various bruises. "How about her face? Was it badly marked?"

"There was a cut on her left cheek and her lower lip was swollen. Those marks didn't seem as recent as the one on her arm."

"How about her eyes?"

"Nothing wrong with either one of her eyes."

"You're sure?"

"Absolutely."

According to the autopsy findings, the victim's right eye had been blackened long enough before death to be distinguishable in spite of the postmortem bloat. He underscored the word *eye* in his notes and put a big question mark beside it. "So you advised Miss Schuyler to swear out a warrant against Cassel, but she refused, even though you explained to her that the new law was supportive of the claims of battered wives."

Mici nodded.

"Was she afraid that swearing out a warrant would affect his earning power, or was she afraid he'd come back and give her a worse beating?"

"I don't know."

"You must have formed an impression." he suggested, still handling her carefully.

"She was pretty well loaded by then. I have to take that into account."

"You mean she'd been drinking through the interview?"

"Steadily. Opening one can of beer after another."

"Beer?"

"That's right. That's one of the reasons I didn't worry too much about leaving her. I figured since it was only beer she'd been drinking that she'd come out of it in a couple of hours at the most."

"Unfortunately, she'd also had a few belts of scotch, but of course you couldn't know that. Or maybe," he mused aloud, "maybe she had the scotch later."

"No, no to both. She didn't have any hard liquor in the house. She told me. She offered me a drink when I first arrived and apologized that it had to be beer as that was all she had. She said she wasn't drinking anything else because she was trying to cut down, but we both knew it was because she couldn't afford anything else."

"According to the autopsy report, there was a heavy concentration of scotch whiskey in her blood." Swell scowled. According to the super, there hadn't been anything but beer empties in Schuyler's trash recently, which supported the redhead's evidence. "So where did she get the booze?" he asked aloud. "According to you, she wasn't in any shape to go out for it, and she didn't have the money to pay for it, either. She had no credit, not in any of the local taverns or liquor stores; I checked that. So somebody had to bring it to her."

"Not Alfred. Alfred would never bring Julia anything to drink; he'd spent too many years and worked too hard trying to get her off the sauce."

"That was before he'd given up on her, while he was still trying to salvage their marriage and their careers. Now she was proving hard to shake, and maybe he saw the booze as a way to get rid of her."

"I knew it!" Mici exclaimed. "I knew this would happen."

"What?" The outburst surprised Swell.

"You're taking Alfred's guilt for granted. The husband did it. Right? I know; I know the figures: sixty-five percent of all homicides are committed by a member of the victim's immediate family. What percentage of those are committed by the husband or wife? Never mind, it doesn't matter. What does matter is that those are the cases the police solve. The others are *mysteries*. How many mysteries a year do you solve, Detective Swell?"

"Hey, wait a minute . . ."

"Mighty few. Why? Because you don't pursue the mysteries. It's so much easier to rack up a good score in the husband or wife cases."

"Hold it. Just hold it . . ."

"The person who beat Julia wasn't necessarily the one who killed her. Did you ever think of that?"

"As a matter of fact . . ."

"She didn't die as a result of the beating, did she? She wasn't hit in such a way that she fell and suffered a fatal injury. No. She was stabbed, a different method entirely. To me it suggests different attacks by different persons."

Swell was impressed by her logic, but he had no intention of letting her know it. "So! The husband walks in, knocks her around, walks out again. The next guy walks in, boozes her up, and sticks a knife in her heart. With which one did she have intercourse?" He paused. "I guess you read about that in the papers?"

"Why does it have to be either one?"

"You're suggesting a third party? She sure was a busy lady."

"And you don't like that because it makes it tough for you."

"If true, it would."

The ready answer and the grin that went with it were disarming. "I'm sorry," Mici sighed. "I've been uptight about this. In spite of everything, I liked Julia Schuyler and I admire Alfred Cassel." She got up. "That's all I came to say. If you need me for anything more, you've got my number on those messages on your desk."

"Miss Anhalt?" He called her back from the door. "Can I ask you something? Every one of those messages was signed M. Anhalt. What does the M. stand for?"

"Mici."

"So, Mici, do you have a boyfriend?"

Her blue eyes widened. "Yes, I do."

"Steady?"

"More or less."

"That means less."

"How about you? Do you have a girlfriend?"

"Nope."

"Why is that?"

"Can't find anybody who'll have me."

"Really?"

"Can I call you for dinner sometime?"

Mici took a breath and looked straight at him. "I don't think you're going to want to, not when you find out where I'm going right after I leave here."

He waited.

"I'm going to see Alfred Cassel. I'm going to tell him everything I've told you. It's only fair."

"You're a private citizen, you can do what you want. What's that got to do with having dinner?"

"I swear to God I never laid a hand on her."

Alfred Cassel reacted to the accusation with a mixture of sadness and indignation. He got up out of his chair and immediately regretted it; his right knee started to jerk spasmodically and he couldn't make it stop. It was like one of his rare, but nightmarish attacks of stage fright. The knee was merely the prelude of worse to follow—a tremor that would creep upward and possess the rest of his body, freeze his vocal chords, and culminate in a disorientation that would wipe out every line and bit of business laboriously worked out and learned and repeated during four weeks of rehearsal. Unconsciously, Cassel turned away from Mici Anhalt as though he were indeed on the stage and the young woman—whom he had known as a dancer and was now some kind of investigator—were the audience from which he was trying to hide his affliction.

"I swear that I never laid a hand on her," he repeated. "I knew that she was circulating some wild rumors about me, but this . . . this is ridiculous. Well, no, I don't mean ridiculous, of course not." At this point, the actor was more concerned with controlling himself as an instrument than in refuting his dead wife's charges. "I just wish you'd come to me before the police," he said.

"I couldn't."

"No, I suppose not. Actually, I have to thank you for coming at all. I hope that means you don't really believe that I hurt Julia."

"She showed me the bruises."

"You'd seen her with bruises before."

"Not like these."

The actor's knee began to twitch again. "If she'd been drinking heavily as you say . . ."

"I don't think she could have gotten those bruises from falling down drunk. And according to the autopsy, she had a black eye. I don't see how she could get that accidentally."

Cassel's pale face looked as though all the blood had been drained out of it; his full, sensuous lips were blue to match the thick vein pulsing at his temple. A vise of fear tightened across his chest as the full force of his peril hit him. The accusation in itself was ugly enough and since the accuser was in her grave there was no possibility of retraction, but the fact that it could lead to a charge of murder shocked him out of his fantasy world. The knee stopped jerking; the sweat on his body dried.

"I need a drink. How about you?"

Mici nodded gratefully. The two interviews had both depressed and depleted her.

When he fixed the drinks, Cassel came over and sat down beside Mici. "Even in the old days, when things were going well, Julia had those drinking bouts and got herself knocked up."

"She never blamed anybody then. Why should she now?"

His reply was short and bitter. "Blackmail."

Mici just looked at him.

"I wanted a divorce. She wanted the lead in my new

94

show. Of course, I couldn't trade. So then she called Oscar Brumleve and accused me of nonsupport and ordered him to take me to court. Well, that didn't get her the part, either. So I suppose accusing me of wife-beating was the next step."

"But why go through me? Why not go to the police?"

"And land me in jail? I might lose the show then, and if I did I couldn't help her even if I wanted to. I'm afraid she tried to use you, Mici, just as she did me."

"I turned her down. I told her I couldn't file a claim for her."

"Dear girl." Cassel gave her an avuncular smile which managed, nevertheless, to convey plenty of sex appeal. "She was just using you to get the message through to me."

"She didn't ask me to talk to you."

"She wouldn't be that obvious. She'd have waited a few days; then if you didn't make the move on your own she'd have given you another little goose. Be honest, hadn't it occurred to you to get in touch with me?"

Mici frowned. "It seems so devious . . ."

"Ah well, she was devious, our Julia." Cassel sighed. "I don't know, maybe she did think she could get money through you—though she wasn't all that hard up. She didn't have to stay in that fleabag. I gave her enough to get out; it's not my fault if she drank it up instead. I did my best for her and I would have gone on doing my best for her. I would never have abandoned her. Never. That's the truth, and she knew it."

The actor's face softened. "When I first met Julia Schuyler, she had all the promise of her heritage, her youth, and her desire. She was a rising star, going up fast, too fast. They were exploiting her out in Hollywood, putting her into parts for which she wasn't ready, but she didn't know it. I was making a picture with her; we had scenes together, and it struck me right away that she wasn't getting any direction, any help from anybody. At

95

first I figured she didn't want it, then that they thought she didn't need it. But she did. She had inherited some of John Malcolm's talent, but not his greatness. She tried so hard to imitate him instead of trying to create her own style, to find her own truth. I don't know where I got the nerve—maybe it was selfishness because I wasn't getting anything from her and my own work was suffering as a result—but I offered her a few suggestions. She was pathetically grateful and eager and willing to try them. They helped some, but she gave me too much credit. She thought of me as a Svengali. Oh, she improved, but not to the extent she'd expected and so in the long run she was more disheartened. She turned down the light, easy roles for which she was suited and took on—well, Hedda, for God's sake! Fell on her face, of course." His smile had long since vanished. "And the Medea—that was a disaster that nearly drove *me* to drink."

He finished what was left in his glass, got up, but didn't appear to want a refill. "We produced the Medea ourselves and it wiped us out financially. Worse, it destroyed what was left of Julia's confidence. I understood what she was going through. John Malcolm Schuyler had been an idol of mine, too, at one time, and I'd patterned myself on his grandiose, swashbuckling, larger-than-life delivery. I went around dressed in somber suits, wore my hair long when it wasn't in fashion, and listened to the sound of my own voice till I realized it wasn't right for me. But Julia refused to learn. When she couldn't match John Malcolm on the stage, she set out to do it in real life."

"She was his daughter."

"True." Cassel nodded. "But she couldn't even destroy herself with his style. It took Schuyler years of profligate living to die. He played out his tragedy as he had played out his triumphs—in the grand manner, on private yachts belonging to Greek tycoons, in Beverly Hills mansions with the jet set for his audience. Julia went fast; she went in squalor, and she went alone. In the end, she blamed me."

Mici thought back to that final visit with the murdered actress and remembered that there had been little rancor in Julia's accusation of her estranged husband. In fact, Julia had been almost tender when she spoke of him. If Mici hadn't been so shocked by the nature of the charge, she would have been more sensitive at the time.

"No, she didn't blame you."

"We didn't have a marriage; we had a professional alliance," Cassel continued. "Each failed the other. I didn't bring out her talent, and being married to her didn't automatically make my name a household word. She didn't refuse me the divorce because she loved me, but because I was finally and at last on my way up and she had to hang on to my coattails. I understood that. I would have helped her if I could, but the producers wouldn't touch her. Who could blame them? Ultimately, she would have agreed to the divorce, and I would have been able to do something for her in some other show or movie or something. She knew that. There was no real antagonism between us. It was all an act on her part."

And how much of this was an act on his part? Mici wondered. How much was he selling her? How much was he selling himself?

"I'm sorry that I had to go to the police," she said.

"You did what you had to do."

"Will you postpone the opening?"

He was amazed that she should ask. "Our out-of-town bookings are set. We've got a Broadway house. We might not get another till the end of the season. That wouldn't be fair to the cast or to the backers. And what good would it do?"

"Have you any idea who killed her?"

"I haven't slept asking myself that question. Julia wasn't a bad person. In spite of her tantrums, her drinking, she never hurt anybody. On the contrary, she tried to help whenever she could. You know that."

"Yes."

"Everybody wanted something from her. Everybody used her."

Mici knew he was including himself. "Except Billy Zip," she noted.

"Maybe." The actor paused for a few moments. "The only thing I can think of is that some psycho broke in and attacked her. She tried to defend herself, but she was too weak and boozed up. So he killed her. It happens. My God! Nowadays it happens all the time. Not two weeks ago there was a woman up in the Bronx, eighty-five years old, stripped and beaten to death." He covered his face with his hands, and his hands were trembling.

Mici trembled, too. She had just about succeeded in convincing herself that Julia's death was the result of what she was and how she'd lived, and now Cassel had reawakened her sense of guilt for having left Julia sleeping behind an unlocked door.

Assume, she said to herself, walking the tawdry streets of Times Square after she left Cassel's suite at the Algonquin, that some creep sheltering from the storm entered the building and tried the doors till he found one that was open and slipped inside. Julia awakens; she's groggy, half conscious; she screams. He beats her, assaults her sexually, kills her. Maybe the creep had the knife on him and so he took it away with him. But how about the booze? No way some creep trying doors in a storm would have a bottle of expensive scotch with him and then share it with his victim prior to the attack. No way.

So it had not been a crime of opportunity. Mici felt tremendous relief. Passing the pocket park between Forty-fifth and Forty-sixth Streets just off Sixth Avenue, she went in to sit down. Thank God! she thought. Not till that moment when she was free of it did she realize how heavy a burden of guilt she'd been carrying. The liquor was the key, she thought. Someone had brought Julia Schuyler the scotch—not a friend, no friend would bring her booze. . . . Hold it. Wrong. This friend had brought the scotch knowing the effect it would have on her. Purposely.

It could also have been somebody from the neighborhood, a casual acquaintance, somebody Julia had talked to in a bar, a pickup. Maybe he'd come looking for her with his bottle of scotch and she welcomed him and drank his scotch and then repulsed him. He was drunk himself and angry at being denied. He beat her up first, then killed her.

Though she'd taunted Detective Swell for looking for the easy solution, Mici couldn't blame him if he shied from this one. To find a killer with so little prior connection to the victim was one of the toughest jobs in a criminal investigation. In this instance, the problem was made more difficult by the uncertainty regarding the time of death. If the time of death could be narrowed down somehow . . .

8

Mici called Donald Swell to tell him about the patrol car she'd noticed on the block near Julia's house the night of the murder. She mentioned that the car was there when she went in and still there when she came out. True, that was only a period of half an hour. Still, if that was a regular post, the officers might have noted the comings and goings from Julia's building unaware of the significance of what they'd seen.

Donald wasn't impressed, but he said he'd look into it.

He only did it because he'd covered every other possible angle and had nowhere else to go. There was no difficulty in locating the two men who had been on duty that night in that location. When he learned that Raymond Emmenecher and Attilio Pace had heard a scream late Friday night, Swell blew his stack. Not because they hadn't gotten out of the car to investigate. It had been a lousy night; they were on another job; there had been one

100

single scream and no way for them to know where it came from. Their rationale for doing nothing held as far as he was concerned. If Donald had been sitting in the squad car himself that night, he would have reacted in the same way. What teed him off was that they hadn't reported it later.

"You must have heard about the homicide? Read about it in the papers, maybe?" Donald was heavy on the sarcasm. Sure, he knew why they hadn't come forward, scared of getting blasted. Well, now they'd get it worse from him, the lieut, maybe even from the captain. "I hope you noted the time at least."

"Look, sir, what's unusual in one neighborhood is just background noise in another." Emmenecher strove to justify their apparent lack of concern.

But Attilio Pace had his notebook out and was clearing his throat. "Yes, sir, yes, sir, I made a note. It was 11:12, exactly 11:12 P.M. when the scream occurred."

Emmenecher looked the way he felt—sour. After all these years, he thought, to get hung up on a lousy thing like this. And the twerp wasn't helping; he gritted his teeth and glared at his partner. "What were we supposed to do, sir? Go ringing doorbells in every building?"

"It was 11:12 exactly," Pace repeated, waiting for a word of commendation.

Swell ignored him. "You should have reported it," he berated Emmenecher who was the senior man. "How do you think it looks getting the information through a civilian?"

That was neither accurate nor fair, and Emmenecher wasn't taking it. "If we reported every scream . . ."

"Nothing moved on the whole block, Detective Swell." Pace was still seeking favor. "We were there another fifteen minutes, sir. It was a regular cloudburst and nobody came out of any of the buildings."

"What does that prove?" Swell demanded.

"I don't know, sir." Pace was finally squelched.

"We don't know that the scream was from your homicide victim, sir," Emmenecher pointed out.

"Yeah, yeah, yeah." Swell waved them off and slumped low into his chair. Emmenecher was right, of course. He'd already interrogated everybody in the damned building and nobody had mentioned any scream. Maybe now that he had a specific time to home in on . . . He reached for his hat and jacket. It was better than sitting around on his butt.

Three hours later, jacket and tie dragging in one hand, collar wilted, shirt plastered to his back, Swell returned to the squad room. You could get more cooperation from inmates of a deaf-and-dumb institution, he thought, than those damn tenants. That kid prostie on the third floor, she knew something for sure. He should have brought her in, sweated her. So, it wasn't too late to go back and get her.

"Say, Don," Reiseberg at the next desk looked up. "La-Rock wants you. Now."

"Yeah?"

Swell had no idea why the lieut wanted him, but he wasn't worried. Actually, he was glad of the summons. He was now convinced that the scream heard by the two patrol cops at 11:12 had actually come from the Schuyler apartment. The woman two floors up in 4A had admitted hearing a scream, but she thought it wasn't anything out of the ordinary. Of course, she'd had her TV on. The kid prostie, one floor closer, had absolutely denied hearing anything. To Donald's way of thinking, that made it more interesting than if they'd both agreed. So while Swell didn't exactly swagger into Lieutenant John La-Rock's office, he pranced lightly, weight forward, confidence high. He was going in with what could turn out to be a significant break in the case—the time of the attack. Never mind how he'd got it.

"Where the hell have you been?" LaRock blasted him before he was through the door.

At forty-eight, a high-school football player who hadn't made it in college, gone to fat and given to double-breasted suits that emphasized his girth, John Willard LaRock could pass for the typical middle-echelon executive who had risen as far as he ever would in the company and knew it. All LaRock was interested in now was in keeping what he had. It wasn't so bad: a nice house in Massapequa five minutes from the town beach; two cars; a satisfactory marriage. How many could say that? All provided by his job, a job with dignity and authority. True, compared with the real brass up at the top he wasn't much and sometimes, as now, the pressure came down pretty heavy. Still, he had men under him on whom he could unload.

"What the hell do you think you're doing?" LaRock demanded.

Swell didn't get a chance to speak, not that he would have known what to say, before getting hit with the next barrage.

"What do you know about this?" LaRock snatched up a late edition of the *News* and an early edition of the *Post*, waving each briefly in front of Swell so that he had only a glimpse of the black scare headlines. A glimpse was more than enough.

COPS IGNORE DYING WOMAN'S SCREAM
COOPING COPS COLD TO CRY FOR HELP

A cramp knotted Swell's intestines. It was all he could do to keep from doubling over. "I was just coming to tell you about it, Lieutenant."

"Oh, you were, were you? Isn't that nice? Thank you, Detective Swell. Thank you so much."

Bad, this was real bad, Swell thought. "What I mean, sir, is that I was following up the lead before bothering

103

you in case it should turn out . . . uh . . ." The corner of his mouth developed a nervous tick. "Uh . . . in case it didn't amount to anything."

"How considerate."

Paralyzed except for the humiliating, betraying tick, it took what seemed an interminable period but was actually only a couple of seconds for the reason for the lieut's ire to filter through to Donald. "Oh, my God! No, sir, it wasn't me. I didn't release it to the press. My God, Lieutenant, I wouldn't do a thing like that."

"Then who did?"

"I don't know. I haven't the vaguest idea." The lieut was waiting and he had to come up with something. "Maybe Emmenecher or Pace?"

LaRock snatched up the *National Enquirer* and read with dripping bitterness: "COPS STAY COZY IN PATROL CAR WHILE WOMAN FIGHTS FOR LIFE. You think they gave that out?"

"No, sir."

The lietuenant continued to read. "This reporter learned today that Detective Third Grade Donald Swell who is carrying the Schuyler case has been canvassing all officers on patrol in the Times Square area on the night of the murder. He discovered that two men assisting the Pimp and Prostitution Squad were staked out on the very block of the tenement in which the homicide occurred."

"I didn't give out that story."

"Story! What story?" LaRock's voice vibrated with indignation. "There is no story. Officers Emmenecher and Pace are a lot smarter than you, Detective Third Grade Swell. They didn't report anything because nothing happened. On Friday night at 11:12 some woman somewhere in the neighborhood screamed—once. So what? You've made the whole uniformed division look like shit, Swell, and the bureau like a bunch of morons."

This was not the moment to discuss his latest canvass

of the tenants. "It wasn't me, sir. I didn't leak the sto . . . the information."

"Then who did?"

They were back to that. At least the initial shock had worn off and Donald's mind was beginning to function again. Reporters were in and out of the station house day and night; they hung around the sergeant's desk, the corridors, the squad rooms picking up snatches of conversation and they were expert at piecing the parts together. That was probably how they'd got hold of this, but it would not satisfy LaRock, not in his present mood. Swell took a breath. "Actually, Lieutenant, I got the tip about Emmenecher and Pace being parked on the block from a witness. She spotted the squad car on the night of the crime."

"What witness?"

"Miss Anhalt. The woman from the Crime Victims Compensation Board. The one who was with Julia Schuyler on Friday night and who claims that Schuyler accused her husband of beating her up."

"Oh, that one. Uh huh. You think she could have tipped the reporters?"

Swell hesitated, but not for long. It couldn't hurt Mici Anhalt. How could it hurt her? Probably she'd never even find out. He cleared his throat. "Who else?"

LaRock considered then discarded it. "Her name wasn't even mentioned in the stories."

"Well . . ." Swell hedged. "She wouldn't have done it for the publicity. She wants to see justice done—she says. She thinks that Cassel is innocent but that we're not giving him a fair shake."

"But she's the one who put the finger on him."

"That's probably why she feels responsible."

"Amateurs," the lieutenant grunted. "They screw up every time." Swell knew he was off the hook.

* * *

"There's good news and there's bad news," Adam Dowd told Mici.

It was the sixth day of the heat wave and, though the air conditioning was on full, the torpor that lay over the city affected them both physically and in spirit. There was tension left over from their last meeting and so they looked each other over warily.

Mici was depressed because she knew that she had not made the change in attitude which she'd tacitly promised. At this point, she wasn't sure she could. In essence, what Dowd wanted was for her to process claims without getting emotionally involved, by simply totting up the figures like an accountant. It wasn't the job she'd signed on for, and if that was what it had become then she wasn't sure she wanted to continue with it. She liked and respected Adam Dowd, had had a good rapport with him in the past, and knew he'd had the same concept of the program that she did. That he was now asking her to turn her back on their ideals and behave like a bureaucrat had to mean that he was himself under pressure.

On his part, Dowd was depressed because he was about to hand an investigator he regarded highly a heavy disappointment, and he wasn't sure how she would take it.

"It's about the Spychalski claim," he began.

"Oh?" Her eyebrows went up. "Let me guess. The Geramita boys were cleared of the arson charges."

"Right."

"Well, we expected that, didn't we? I don't suppose any of the neighbors came forward? Too scared."

"There was one old lady, a Mrs. Feirick. She claimed she saw the boys prowling around the house a short time before the fire started."

"But they wrote her off."

Dowd didn't ask how she knew. "The attorney for the boys got Mrs. Feirick started on the subject of religion."

Mici sighed. "I don't know how much of what she babbles she really believes and how much is for effect. Either way, I realize it doesn't enhance her credibility as a witness. What's the good news?"

"The arson investigators have come to the conclusion that the fire was deliberately set."

"Great!" A big smile replaced Mici's frown. "So now we can go ahead and process the claim. Poor Mr. Spychalski and his wife need all the help they can get. The cost of medical care . . ."

"Not so fast; you haven't heard it all," Dowd interrupted Mici's euphoric prattling. "Since the fire was of deliberate origin and since the Geramita boys have been exonerated, the insurance company is holding up payment on Mr. Spychalski's policy."

"Why?"

"Karl Spychalski is the most likely suspect to have set the fire, isn't he?"

"No. Absolutely not." Mici hotly defended her client. "Anyhow, Karl Spychalski has an alibi. He was down at the hiring hall at the time."

"No, he wasn't." Dowd's homely, pitted face was grave. "He reported early in the morning, but he left before lunch and didn't go back."

Mici was stunned. "I don't believe it. There's some mistake. His two girls were killed in that fire. His wife nearly died trying to save them. She's burned over sixty percent of her body. She's in excruciating pain . . ."

"The house was supposed to have been empty at the time. The two kids should have been in school and Rose Spychalski usually went to the market for the week's shopping on Wednesday afternoon."

"No, no," Mici muttered doggedly. "Karl Spychalski loved that house. It represented the security he'd built for himself and his family. It wasn't just a place to live. You have to understand how Europeans feel about the land . . ."

"He was also unemployed, with benefits running out and no job in sight. The insurance money could keep him going a long time."

"Naturally that's the view the insurance company would take; that way they don't have to pay off," Mici argued. "What we're concerned about is whether or not there was arson. Okay, the police now say yes, there was. Mrs. Spychalski and the two girls were victims. That's it. It doesn't matter who set the fire."

"Unless it was Spychalski."

"Can anybody prove he did it? Can anybody place him at the scene?" Dowd shook his head. "I thought a man was supposed to be innocent till proved guilty."

"We're not throwing out the claim."

"Just filing it," Mici commented bitterly.

"I feel just as sorry for the Spychalskis as you do, but rules are rules. We have only so much money at our disposal and it has to go to those whose claims are unclouded."

Mici was silent.

"All the man has to do is say where he was at the time of the fire and he's in the clear; the insurance company pays off; we process the claim."

"He won't say?"

"He insists he was at the hiring hall."

"Nuts." Mici got up. "I'll talk to him."

"I did not kill my children. I did not burn my wife. I did not destroy my home and everything that I love. It was those boys."

"Forget about them, Mr. Spychalski," Mici advised, keeping her manner brisk and impersonal. "They have been exonerated. It doesn't matter who set the fire as long as it wasn't you."

"Doesn't matter!" Spychalski, a burly man accustomed to hard labor and danger, had wasted physically in the past months as a result of loss of courage and pride, but at this moment rage sustained him. Anger struggled with sorrow and the result was tears that welled in his deep-set, tired eyes. "Nobody came forward at the trial. Nobody was willing to speak for us against those boys except one crazy old woman."

"I know how you feel, Mr. Spychalski . . ."

"It matters to me!"

"What matters is for the insurance company to pay your claim and for the Compensation Board to approve medical care for your wife."

"They will pay. They must. They cannot prove I did this terrible thing. They cannot prove it because I am innocent. So in the end they must pay."

He sounded very sure. "Maybe," Mici said. "But it will take a very long time. You could shorten that time if you'll just say where you were the afternoon of the fire."

"I was at the hiring hall."

"The men say no. They say you left before lunch and did not return."

"I brought my lunch and I had it there as always. They're mixed up. Or maybe the insurance company is paying them to lie."

"You don't really believe that, Mr. Spychalski."

He turned aside and shrugged.

"Wherever you were, whatever you were doing that Wednesday afternoon at two-thirty, nobody is going to blame you. If you were having a few drinks in a bar, or you were out at the ball game to forget your troubles for a few hours, nobody is going to hold it against you." Mici was watching him carefully. In profile his expression remained set; only dried streaks on his sunken cheeks were reminders that he had very recently been weeping.

She had to tread carefully, but she couldn't leave any possibility unexplored. "Even if you were with someone . . . If that person were to step forward . . . I'm sure it wouldn't be necessary for Mrs. Spychalski to know."

She expected Spychalski to rail at her, to order her out, but he didn't deign to answer. He simply stood in the cramped, hot living room of the apartment where they were staying with his wife's relatives and looked out the window over the low roofs of the other row houses toward the big gas tanks in the distance. There was nothing for Mici to do but to leave.

She had shown him the way, she thought, as the subway hurtled its noisy way back to Manhattan. Now it was up to him. One thing, a bitter smile twisted her soft, full lips, nobody could say her cases were gaining automatic approval now. The Spychalski claim would be set aside indefinitely. The Marin benefits were drawing to an end. She thought again of the blind man's suggestion that she suppress Dr. Harden's report. Maybe she should have agreed and given him one more chance? No, of course not! She was not the arbiter of the fate of every man and woman who walked into her office and sat down at her desk. Her job was to investigate and write a report. Dispositions were made by others.

For once the lithe ex-dancer didn't sprint up the stairs to the second floor but waited sedately for the elevator. She squeezed in, wriggled out, and stopped short when she opened the door of the reception room to find Detective Swell comfortably sprawled on the blue-tweed settee.

"Hi." He unfolded himself and rose to greet her.

"What are you doing here?"

"I came to take you to lunch."

"Oh? I've already had lunch. I'm sorry." That wasn't true, but Mici was neither hungry nor in the mood for conversational sparring. "Thanks anyway."

"Dinner then."

She hesitated. "What's up?"

"Nothing's up." He stepped in close. "I just want to see you."

About to answer, she was suddenly aware that they

110

were being observed. She moved back. "I'm sorry if I got those two officers in trouble. Or you."

He shrugged. "What trouble? The press exaggerates everything. The lieut knows that. He didn't pay any attention."

"I'm glad. So does that mean you've been able to fix the time of death?"

"Hey! First we've got to prove that what those two cops heard was in fact Julia Schuyler screaming. So far we haven't been able to do that."

"I see."

"But your buddy, Cassel, is in the clear. His girlfriend backs up his alibi." He moved in again, closer. "So . . . about dinner. I'll pick you up at seven. Be ready."

"For what?"

"That's up to you, babe."

9

Why had Donald Swell gone out of his way to inform her that Cassel had an alibi? Swell seemed so easygoing, without professional jealousy, but Mici knew he looked out for number one. He could have called her for a date for lunch or dinner but had appeared in person instead. She was convinced that he had come specifically to tell her about Cassel and to observe her reaction. Also, there was the business about the alleged dying scream. There'd been plenty of flak over the police reaction, or rather lack of it. Donald had been too casual. It didn't ring true. Maybe he didn't want her meddling any more. Maybe he thought that if he offered her assurance that Cassel was no longer under suspicion she'd lose interest.

It had the opposite effect.

Flashing her credentials, which most people considered on a par with a police card, and which certainly was not the case, Mici Anhalt had no trouble getting the address she wanted from Actors' Equity Association. As she'd expected, it wasn't far outside the theatrical hub and she treated herself to a taxi ride over to the old-fashioned but well-maintained building on Fifty-fifth Street across from the City Center.

Delissa Grace was as impressed with Miss Anhalt's ID as the people at the actors' union. Usually Mici took care to point out that answers were purely voluntary. This time she didn't. She let Delissa Grace take a good look at her card and draw her own conclusions.

The actress scanned it quickly but thoroughly, as she would a script before an audition, to assess what was in it for her and what she could make of it.

"I've already spoken with Alfred," Mici prompted.

Delissa Grace hesitated before picking up the cue. "Yes, I know." Now she was committed to playing the scene a certain way.

Mici was glad; it saved trouble. "Then you know that I used to be in the theater myself and that I knew both Alfred and Julia."

"He told me."

She presented a striking figure with that wild mass of tightly curled ringlets in a dark cloud around her head, hazel eyes flashing, creamy, flawless skin, and lips that were a lustrous maroon without the aid of lipstick. She didn't need the drama of the dark-green velvet caftan trimmed in gold and the row of gold bracelets on her right arm. She was about the same age as Julia had been, but she was just reaching her peak.

"Did Alfred tell you what we talked about?" Mici asked.

"He said that Julia had accused him of beating her. That was a lie! They fought like cat and dog; they screamed and yelled at each other, but there was never any physical violence. Never. He never laid a hand on her. He couldn't. Alfred isn't that kind of person."

"I was repeating what Julia told me. I had to make a statement to the police and sign it. If they decide to re-

113

gard what Julia said as a dying declaration, it would carry a lot of weight."

"Since she wasn't dying at the time and she didn't expect to die, how can it be a dying declaration?" Delissa Grace was very sure on this point.

"I see you've had legal advice."

"That's just common sense."

"Nevertheless, an accusation like that can be damning."

"What can we do? We can't accuse a dead woman of deliberately lying. We can't malign her character, but we can't let her destroy us either."

"Have you any idea who might have killed her?"

"No." Delissa Grace raised a slender hand to her forehead as though to wipe away a headache; her bracelets made a jangling accompaniment to the gesture. "Who would want to hurt Julia? I mean, why? Those wild stories she made up, they were embarrassing but nobody took them seriously. At least not while she was alive. Now that she's dead—they're damning, as you say. You can see that as far as Alfred and I are concerned, it would be better if she were still alive."

Shrewd, Mici thought, but was it sincere?

"Julia was finished. She'd had everything and thrown it away. You couldn't help but feel sorry for her," Delissa Grace observed.

"Did you feel sorry for her?"

Up to now the performance had been a tightly woven skein of fact and expediency, now Delissa Grace permitted herself one moment of raw truth. "She brought it on herself."

"You mean her death?"

"I mean everything. How much longer could she have lasted the way she was going?"

"And how did Julia feel about you?"

The actress assayed a wry smile. "You couldn't expect her to love me. I've got the part she wanted and that

114

could have meant a comeback for her, except that she couldn't possibly have handled it."

"And her husband. You've got him, too."

"She'd thrown Alfred away along with everything else long before I came on the scene."

"So then why did she refuse the divorce?"

"General orneriness. To bleed us for as much and as long as she could."

"Bleed?"

"I don't know about your financial situation, Miss Anhalt, but for me ten thousand dollars is a lot of money. That's what she wanted to agree to the divorce. Oh, she didn't ask Alfred for it; she knew he couldn't get it. But I've managed to put a little something aside, and she knew it and she wanted it. Well, I wasn't about to let her clean me out so I stalled. I gave her a few hundred every now and then to keep her quiet."

Mici caught it immediately. She looked hard at the beautiful woman. "Keep her quiet about what?"

Too late Delissa Grace realized the slip. "To keep her from bad-mouthing Alfred."

"What did she know about you?"

"Nothing. It's a manner of speaking, for God's sake. I paid her so she'd stop bugging Alfred."

"What did she know about Alfred?"

The actress reached for a cigarette from a sterling-silver box on the cocktail table. She lit it with a trembling hand, then with an effort thrust herself forward and out of the depths of the black-velvet sofa and began circling around it.

"You said Julia's stories were wild and couldn't hurt him," Mici reminded her.

"That's right. We just didn't want that kind of publicity."

"What kind?"

"That Alfred wasn't contributing to her support, that he was beating her . . ."

115

"She hadn't actually circulated those stories?"

"She was threatening to."

"And so you paid her to keep quiet. Blackmail. That's what it amounts to, Miss Grace. And it makes you a suspect as well as Alfred."

"Alfred and I were together the whole weekend. Whether Julia was killed Friday, Saturday, or Sunday, we were never out of each other's sight."

"That doesn't eliminate either one of you; it makes you accomplices."

"No. Neither one of us killed her, singly or together." Her eyes glowed with intensity, her soft voice that could carry up to the second balcony without aid of a microphone quivered. "There's no way you or anybody else can prove we did."

"Why were you paying her?"

"I told you."

"It's not good enough."

"That's all I'm going to say."

"Then I'll ask Alfred." Mici picked up her handbag, slung it over her shoulder, rose, and started for the door. It seemed as if Delissa Grace would let her go, then at the very last moment she called out.

"Alfred doesn't know. He doesn't know I was paying Julia off."

Mici turned.

"When I first started out, when I was making the transition from the Greek theater to the American stage I had a . . . friend. He was a big shot in organized crime. I didn't know. I was young. He told me he was in the construction business. I didn't question it. They got him for tax evasion, what else? He's in the federal penitentiary. Julia threatened to make a big thing out of it. My friend wouldn't have appreciated that."

"But if he's in jail . . ."

"You don't understand. My friend put up some money for the show." She paused, sighed. "He put up all of it."

116

"You mean he would have pulled out?"

"No, no." Delissa Grace shook her head violently, the dark frizzed hair flying. "Alfred would. If he thought the backing was for me and not for him . . ."

Her lovely, unlined face twisted; her eyes darkened. She was speechlessly pleading with Mici to keep her secret and she wasn't acting; the pleading was intense and real. At last Mici understood. It wasn't the play and her co-starring role that Delissa Grace was worried about. She hadn't been paying Julia to keep the secret from the public, but from Alfred. She loved Alfred. It wasn't the show she was afraid to lose, she couldn't lose that, but she might lose the man.

"How did you make the payments? In cash?"

"Of course,"

"So that between you and Alfred . . ." Mici began and then remembered someone else. "Billy Zip! Billy says that he was giving Julia whatever money he could spare. Between the three of you, she wasn't so hard up after all. Obviously she didn't spend the money on herself. So where was it going?"

Delissa Grace shrugged. "She drank it up."

Not if she was drinking beer, Mici thought. Drugs? There'd been no traces in the autopsy—the papers would have made headlines out of that, and the police would be tracing the drug connection. "Gambling?" she asked.

"Who knows?"

Mici recalled the days in Chicago when Julia had been comparatively affluent. She'd thrown her money around but she hadn't gambled. At the local Variety Club there'd been all kinds of slot machines rigged to give favorable odds to the performers who frequented the place but, as far as Mici knew, Julia had never put so much as a quarter into one of them. Still, people change. "Was there anyone else Julia could have been hitting for money?" She asked simply because she didn't know what else to ask.

"Oscar Brumleve maybe, her lawyer. He's pretty

strapped himself, I hear, but he would have helped her somehow. It's amazing what people were willing to do for Julia. They loved her and forgave her no matter what. I don't know what she had."

Mici got up.

"You're not going to the police, are you? It's not going to help them to know about the play, I mean about the backing for the play."

Mici hesitated; she hadn't thought that far ahead.

"If they examine my bank account, of course, they'll discover the withdrawals and want an explanation, but why should they examine my bank account?"

"You had a strong motive for killing Julia Schuyler."

"No, I didn't. Her hold on me would last only till the show opened. It wouldn't have mattered after that. Alfred is sure to be a hit. If he finds out about the backing then, well, he'll have his pride and self-confidence and he'll forgive me."

"Well . . ."

"Please. We're going into rehearsal next week, Next week. It's taken months of preparation, of delays and disappointments to get to this point. You've been a performer yourself, Miss Anhalt, you know what's involved. If you could just wait a little while . . .

Maybe the blackmail wouldn't have worked on Delissa Grace once the show opened, Mici thought, but then Julia could have increased the pressure on Alfred. Was Delissa Grace smart enough to have foreseen that? Had she asked her "friend" to have it taken care of?

Mici made up her mind. "I won't go to the police unless I have to. I'm not working for them. I'm working for Julia. I owe her."

Donald Swell surprised Mici. He'd discarded his FBI suit and looked very relaxed in a summer-weight navy blazer and cream slacks. He also turned down the cus-

118

tomary drink before leaving, explaining that he'd made reservations at a restaurant out on the Island and that they ought to get started.

"I figured it would do us both good to get out of town for a few hours."

It was nice, Mici thought as they drove along, windows down to let in the cool night breezes, the conversation skipping lightly through the list—opera, theater, sports, both active and spectator—to discover mutual interest. She relaxed and began to enjoy herself.

The restaurant was a revelation, not merely for itself but that it should be Donald's choice. It was on the outskirts of the town of Roslyn, a white frame house much like Mici's home, with plenty of ground around it. They parked under fine old trees and went around to the back to a garden with perhaps a dozen tables lit by flickering candlelight. Swell ordered drinks and then the consultation about dinner began; no menu was ever presented but Donald did not appear to require one. He knew the house specialties and in fact seemed knowledgeable about fine cuisine. Mici had liked Donald but with reservations, the main one being not that he lacked refinement but that he was proud of it, so she was impressed by this new aspect. When the meal was ready, they went indoors to a small room accommodating only three tables so that there would be little distraction from the proper appreciation of the food set before them. It was superb. In fact, Mici willingly admitted that she was not qualified to fully appreciate its excellence.

It was midnight by the time they were back at Mici's door. Again Swell surprised her; he declined the invitation to come in for a nightcap. Oh, there was the customary goodnight kiss, and very nice, too—friendly but with enough intensity to suggest more was available if she were so inclined. What he was telling her was that he was secure enough to play by her rules. She liked that. Inter-

119

esting man, Mici decided as she stepped inside her apartment, brash but with a certain style. She was looking forward to the next encounter.

She always left a light burning in the living room visible from the street so that the apartment would appear occupied—an ordinary protection against burglary. Passing through with barely a glance, Mici now turned that light off and entered the bedroom which was dark. Here she now turned on the bedside lamp and the air conditioner, then closed the door to keep the cold air in. Pulling off her dress, she started for the closet to hang it up. For some reason, she stopped to listen. There was nothing to hear but the hum of the machine working extra hard to lower the temperature. Otherwise the room was silent. Unusually so, Mici thought. In fact, the whole building, even the street, seemed unnaturally quiet. Well, a lot of people were away at this time of year, she reasoned, but could not shake her sense of unease. Holding her dress in her hands, Mici stood clad in bra and panties in the middle of her bedroom, her skin prickling as though someone watched.

Women who lived alone sometimes became neurotic. They put all kinds of locks on their doors; they kept their shades drawn, they imagined someone watching their comings and goings, even that their phone was being tapped. But Mici liked living alone. She drew strength from it. Her apartment was sleek, functional, and modern—the image of herself she wanted to present to the world. It was unthinkable that she could be afraid here, unthinkable that she should feel threatened.

But she did. Her heartbeat accelerated; her breath came in short, shallow gasps. Ridiculous! There couldn't be anybody in the apartment. The door had been locked until she handed Donald the key and he unlocked it. Striding purposefully to the closet, she flung it open. Empty of course. Laughing at herself, she hung up her dress. Nevertheless, before entering the bathroom she turned on the

120

light. There wasn't anybody there either. Yet the feeling persisted. She took her nightgown off the hook on the back of the door, but instead of putting it on she stared at the closed door to the living room.

Obviously she wasn't going to get any sleep till she went out there and had a thorough look around. If there had been a burglar, say in the kitchen, he'd had plenty of time to get out by now. She hoped he'd taken advantage of it. She was sure he had; still, she hesitated. What she needed was some kind of weapon. What? There were no fire tongs or heavy-based statuettes handy. Her eyes swept the room and rested on the small chintz-covered dressing table. There were scissors in the drawer. Nail scissors, small but sharp.

At the last moment before opening the door and stepping into the living room, Mici remembered to turn out the bedroom light. God! The light would have made her a perfect target. She inched the door open and peered out. As she did so, she had a mental image of herself, scissors clenched in her hand, cowering. She was disgusted. Flinging the door wide open, she turned on the overhead lights and marched boldly forward. There was nobody there. She took a quick look into the kitchen. No one. She checked the front door and it was locked as she had left it. What in heaven's name was the matter with her? She turned every light off again, marched back to her bedroom, closed the door as before, and got ready for bed.

She hadn't been in bed long before she sensed that her bedroom door was opening. Not again, she said to herself, not again. She stiffened under the covers. She heard a step, definitely, no imagination. Before she could decide whether she should open her eyes and throw back the covers and make a run for it, or keep them shut and pretend to be asleep and let him take whatever he'd come for and go away, he was on top of her. In a single move he had one hand over her mouth, the other in her hair holding her head back against the pillow, and he was straddling her. She opened her eyes and looked into his. In the faint light from the street she could make out a ski mask.

"Don't fight." The mask muffled his voice. "Make it easy on yourself." He gave her hair a sharp, warning yank before letting it go so he could reach down to raise her nightgown. He did not take the hand away from her mouth.

Easy! Mici thought. *No way I'm going to make this easy for you, mister!*

Keeping her strong dancer's legs together, she tried to kick upward like a fish swimming. She squirmed under him; she heaved. No good. In fact, it was adding to his excitement and that she didn't need. She thought of grabbing his hair, but the knitted helmet prevented that. There was nothing she could get hold of, no part of him she could bite or scratch or gouge. She gasped for air. Her sobs of fear and anger were thrust back down into her throat by the hand over her mouth. But she wouldn't give in. Arms flailing wildly in the attempt to push him off, an elbow struck the edge of the bedside table. The pain shot up through her arm setting off a tingle of nerves. The scissors. She hadn't put the scissors back in the drawer. They were there on the bedside table. Her groping fingers found them and closed on them. For a moment Mici stopped struggling and lay still, frightened at what she was about to do. She had never purposely injured anyone. If she attacked this man it had to be done forcefully. She had to wound him seriously or it would be useless, worse than useless, for unless he was badly hurt he'd take the weapon away from her. He might even turn it against her.

Drawing as much breath as she could with him on top of her and her mouth and nostrils partially blocked, Mici raised her arm over the middle of his back, held it poised for a moment, then plunged the scissors down full force. She was surprised at how easily they entered the flesh, surprised and even a little relieved.

122

Then he screamed. It was the worst scream that Mici had ever heard. After the scream, he went limp, lay still on top of her. Had she killed him? Oh, God, not with those little scissors?

"Pull the goddamned thing out," he muttered. "Pull it out." She was so relieved that he was alive that she did as he ordered.

They remained as they were; he resting, she not daring to move. Suddenly he shifted, rolled off her, and was on his feet running across the room and out the door. Before her muscles could relax, she heard the front door slam shut.

It was a long time before Mici was able to swing her legs over the side of the bed and sit up, and longer before she turned on the light. The scissors were still in her hand and she examined them as one might an object completely unfamiliar. The closed points were stained with blood about an inch up. She'd had the feeling of plunging them deeper than that. Thank God she hadn't! A drop or two of blood had dripped on the carpet as he ran and the bedclothes were rumpled; otherwise there appeared to be no trace of what had happened, or nearly happened. Then Mici looked down at herself. There was a white, scummy stain down the front of her nightgown.

She wanted to throw up.

The first thing she did when she could control her nausea was to pad out to the front door, turn the bolt, and put the chain back on. After that she went into the kitchen. There was a fire escape outside. The top half of the window was kept partially open to accommodate a ventilating fan. There was enough space between the fan and the window frame for a hand to reach in and raise the lower half. She pushed the top of the window up and locked the catch. She would never leave it down again.

Then, though she hadn't been raped, Mici Anhalt did what a great many rape victims instinctively do. She took off the soiled garment she was wearing, threw it into the laundry hamper, got under the hottest shower she could tolerate, and just stood there till her skin felt raw. After that she put on a clean gown, changed the bedclothes, and finally, exhausted, lay down between the clean sheets.

Not till then did she let herself cry. She wept quietly into the pillow till she finally fell asleep.

10

Mici awoke at first light. For a few moments she lay warm and groggy as though she'd taken a couple of sleeping pills that hadn't quite worn off. Then, with a jolt, she remembered. Waves of nausea washed over her anew. She kept very, very still till they passed. Her instinct was to put the whole thing out of her mind, forget it ever happened. That, she knew, was a typical reaction of women who had gone through a similar experience.

Mici Anhalt was neither a virgin nor promiscuous. She had what she considered a healthy enjoyment of sex, but she did not lightly enter into a sexual relationship; there had to be an emotional commitment on both sides. She was, therefore, shocked at the way the incident had traumatized her. After all, nothing had actually happened; she had neither been sexually molested nor physically injured. Yet she felt degraded. It was only six but she couldn't stay in bed. She got up, took another shower, and changed the bed linen a second time. She fixed herself coffee and forced herself to eat at least a bowl of cereal in the hot, stuffy kitchen sitting at the table in front of the closed window. All the while as she tried to follow her usual routine, Mici Anhalt knew that she had to go to the police.

She searched for excuses not to go. To start with, she couldn't provide any kind of description of the man who had attacked her. She had only a fleeting glimpse of him as he ran from the room and had been too agitated to note height or general build. The knitted helmet had had a slit in it for his eyes only so that she hadn't been able to tell the color of his hair or the shape of his nose, or even recognize his voice. Yet she must report the incident. The other tenants had a right to know that an intruder had gained admittance and how it had been done. She might not be able to give a description, but she had inflicted an injury and the nature of that injury might serve to identify him at some future time when he attacked someone else. There was even the possibility that he had gone to some hospital emergency room for treatment. In that case there would be a record, and he could be traced right now. For the sake of other future victims, she had to go to the police.

She dressed slowly, but at last was ready. Calling the office offered a further brief postponement. The switchboard wasn't open yet so she dialed Adam's direct line, and he answered as she had known he would. She told him only that she'd surprised a man in her apartment but that she'd been able to drive him off.

"You're all right? He didn't harm you? You're sure you're all right?"

"I gave worse than I got." She managed a chuckle and it made her feel better. "I'm going over to the precinct to report it."

"You didn't report it last night?"

"No." She didn't elaborate. "I'll probably be late for work."

126

Dowd sensed she was holding something back, but he would not force a confidence. "Take your time. Take the day off. It'll do you good, Mici."

"No, thanks, Adam. I'd just as soon come in."

"Whatever you want." His concern was a palpable vibration over the line. "If there's anything I can do . . . You want me to come over to the station house with you?"

She was touched and grateful. "No, no thanks, Adam. There's nothing to it. I'll be fine."

But it wasn't easy. It wasn't easy sitting on the other side of the desk being the victim. Mici had not before fully appreciated a woman's reluctance to report this particular type of crime. And it would have been a lot worse if she'd actually been raped. At least she was spared the medical examination and the recounting of each intimate detail. Even so, the procedure took up most of the morning, and when she was through Mici felt spent, as though she were recuperating from an illness. Adam had suggested she take the day off and she decided to take him up on it. She went back home. Before going upstairs, she got the mail out of her box. Nothing important—a couple of bills, a couple of ads, and a plain white envelope without name or address, just her apartment number. Obviously it had been hand-delivered. Holding it, Mici had the same kind of presentiment, the same sense of menace she'd felt the night before when she entered her apartment. Her hands trembled as she opened the envelope and pulled out a single sheet of paper.

"Mind your own business or you won't get rid of me next time."

Mici stared at the block letters crudely printed with a felt-tipped pen. *Mind your own business.* What did that refer to? The Schuyler case? Had to be. But who besides Donald knew she was taking an interest? Well, of course, Alfred Cassel and his Delissa. And Billy Zip. But that

127

hadn't been either Alfred or Billy in her bed last night. So who? And why? She didn't know anything. Unless . . . wait a minute. Suppose Delissa's "friend" had ordered it?

But why rape? Or attempted rape?

Whoever it was knew that that particular kind of assault would affect her deeply, that she would feel used and humiliated. But by leaving the note and connecting it to the Schuyler case he had depersonalized the attack. She could now regard it as she might a shot that had missed or any other attempt to frighten her. That she could deal with.

Mici came up out of the subway at Forty-fourth on the corner near the St. James Theatre. She was struck anew at how seedy and run-down the theatrical district looked by daylight. On this overcast afternoon it seemed dingier and sadder than ever. When she was starting her career as a dancer, Mici had answered several calls at the St. James. It had been all glamour then, day and night. There had been a sense of suppressed excitement in walking along those very special side streets among the silent theatres. To be privileged to enter a grimy alley, open the stage door, and go inside if only for a tryout had been thrilling. It hadn't mattered that the theatre was dark and cold, that when you walked down to the apron to give your name you had to squint into the glare of an unshaded pilot light. Now there were porno houses interspersed with the legitimate theatres, amusement arcades, quick food shoppes, cheap bars; once elegant hotels had either been torn down or become SRO, Single Room Occupancy dwellings. Actors looking for work still walked the streets, but they mingled with addicts, pushers, male and female prostitutes. Mici decided she was glad she was out of the business.

Had Julia Schuyler seen the dirt and decay? Mici wondered. She could have lived anywhere else more decently

128

and comfortably, yet this had been her choice. Because it was close to her memories or close to her hopes? Julia had had hopes. She had spoken of them to Mici on the night of her murder. She had spoken of offers, of a comeback. Mici had discounted them as the usual actor's talk. Had it been more?

Climbing the crumbling steps of the brownstone in which Julia Schuyler had died, Mici rang the bell of the only other person who knew about her interest in the case. The answering buzzer released the lock and she entered. Bettedene Barber was leaning out over the railing of the third-floor hallway.

"Who wants me?"

Mici waited till she'd reached the landing and was face to face with the girl. "My name is Mici Anhalt. I was here a couple of days ago to see Detective Swell."

"Oh, sure, I remember."

"I thought, if you don't mind and if you can spare the time, that we might talk."

"What about?"

Mici looked around the dingy hall, then toward the door the blonde teenager had left ajar. "Could we go inside?"

The girl shrugged. "Okay."

There was no sun in the apartment, but the curtains were pulled back from sparkling clean windows and let in plenty of light. There were bright, flowered chintz covers on what was obviously a set of dilapitated furniture; tables were skirted and flounced, pillows abounded. Everything that could be covered and camouflaged was.

"You've done a fine decorating job, Miss Barber."

The thin, sallow face lit up. Seeing her without make-up, wearing jeans and a sloppy shirt, blonde hair tied up in a ponytail, Mici was struck at the girl's youth. She couldn't be more than sixteen at the outside.

"I like to sew."

"You're certainly good at it."

129

"I make all my own clothes. Oh, not what I'm wearing now, my good stuff. I go to all these wholesale outlets where they have remnants. You can get some real nice material for very little money." She pointed with pride to a table in front of the window on which was spread some cream-colored silk which she'd been cutting to pattern. "That's a shirt I'm making for Dominic. He's my old man."

"Lovely."

"Think he'll like it?"

"How could he help it? Tell me, Miss Barber, how long have you been in New York?"

The eager light in her face died. "Why do you want to know?"

Mici instantly realized she'd made a mistake. She shrugged it off. "No reason. Just making conversation."

"You some kind of social worker or something? I'm eighteen years old. I can show you my birth certificate."

"No, no." Mici held up her hand. "I'm not a social worker.

The girl was only partially reassured. "What makes you think I come from out of town?"

"You don't talk like a New Yorker. Your voice is softer, kind of southern. Nice."

"Thank you." She colored shyly. "I've been here for two years. I thought I'd gotten rid of the accent."

Mici didn't believe that she was more than sixteen, so that would have made her fourteen when she started hustling. "Do you like it? New York, I mean."

It's all right. One place is pretty much like another, don't you think? I mean, I don't get to see much of New York, you know? I don't go to the fancy places you read about in the papers. I don't go to the shows; they're just down the street, but I don't get to see them. But who cares? I probably wouldn't like them. I see all the movies I want, and I've got this terrific color TV." She pointed to

130

the big, blank screen in a corner. "Dom's real good to me."

"I'm glad."

"He cares about me. He really does. There's never a day goes by that he doesn't check to see how I'm making out. He spends as much time with me as he can."

"That's good."

"Yes. I'm lucky. There's some girls . . . I could tell you stories . . ." She stopped, wary again. "What do you want anyway?"

Mici took a breath. Why not level? If she wanted this girl to be straight with her, shouldn't she set the example? "Julia Schuyler was an old friend. I visited with her Friday night. She got drunk and passed out, and I left her like that. I feel really bad about it."

The hooker nodded. "I can see that. I can see how it would bug you." She frowned. "You want some coffee?" she asked abruptly.

"Yes." Mici responded quickly and positively. "A cup of coffee would go great." A barrier had been breached.

"It'll only take a couple of minutes to perk. I don't go for the instant."

"Neither do I."

"How about some toast? Cinnamon toast?"

"I haven't had cinnamon toast in years. It would be a treat."

They smiled at each other.

"I'm a good cook, if I say it myself," the girl confided. "When Dom stays over—that's not often because he's so busy. He has . . . so much to do—I fix him a real fine breakfast, homemade pancakes from scratch. He loves them. Come on into the kitchen and sit with me while I fix our snack."

The girl was some housekeeper, Mici thought, as she sat at the table near the window while the ruffled curtains billowed in gusts that foretold a heavy storm. She

131

hadn't properly taken it in when she was here before, but she saw now that, as in the living room, everything had been lovingly camouflaged with paint, paper, or fabric—except the stove; there was nothing that could be done with that relic. "Miss Barber, it's about my friend's murder that I'm here. We all keep to ourselves in New York. We respect our neighbor's privacy because we want him to respect ours. But when somebody's killed, then we have a duty to tell what we know. I'm appealing to you, Miss Barber. . ."

"I don't know who you're talking to when you call me that."

"Barbi . . ."

"Bettedene's my given name. Bette for my aunt and Dene is a family name. Nobody hardly calls me Bettedene any more."

"Bettedene. It's pretty and it suits you. Will you call me Mici?"

"Yes, Mici, and I wish I could help you, but I didn't know Miss Schuyler. I told Detective Swell. We met sometimes on the stairs, going in and out the front door. We'd say hello, nice day, lousy day, and that was it. She wasn't snooty or anything, but, like you said, we respected each other's privacy."

"And her husband?"

"Mr. Cassel?" Her thin, heart-shaped face broke into a real smile. "He was something else! He held the door for me every time and stood aside so I got to go through ahead of him. Once he bowed and kissed my hand. Made me feel like a princess."

"How did he and Miss Schuyler get along?"

"They had plenty of fights. I mean, they were always yelling at each other. You could hear them all over the building, but they weren't the only ones. The woman upstairs with the four kids? When her old man gets a couple of belts in him—watch out!" Bettedene clucked and shook her head.

"Do you think that Alfred Cassel ever beat his wife? Did you ever see any sign that he had beaten her?"

"No, ma'am . . . Mici, I never did."

"When I visited her Friday, she had bruises all over her arms and a cut on her cheek."

"That was after Mr. Cassel had moved out. I thought you meant before."

"I did. But he was still coming to see her occasionally."

"If he didn't beat her while he was living with her, why should he do it after?"

The question had already come up and the answer, of course, was that he was driven to it by Julia's stubborn refusal to give him a divorce. No use going into that with the girl. "About Friday night, Bettedene, did you hear anything—an argument, sounds of a fight—coming from Miss Schuyler's apartment?"

"It was raining and I had the windows shut. I couldn't hear anything. I told Detective Swell."

"Were you alone? I'm not prying, Bettedene," Mici hastened to assure her. "I just thought that maybe . . . if you had a friend here he might have heard . . ."

"I was alone."

"Maybe going in and out of the building you noticed somebody, some man who could have been visiting Julia Schuyler?"

"It was raining. I don't work outdoors in the rain."

Mici flushed. "How about other nights?"

"What other nights?"

Was she being purposely dense? "The other nights she got beaten up. There had to be other nights, Bettedene."

Without the layers of makeup the girl's small brown eyes were undistinguished, but they were completely steady as she fixed them on Mici. "I'm busy nights. That's when I earn my living. I don't have time to snoop."

She was blunt enough now, Mici thought; why had she been almost coy earlier? "Did you see Alfred Cassel in

133

the building and then notice Miss Schuyler with bruises afterwards?"

"No."

"You're answering without thinking, Bettedene."

"I don't have to think, I know. You say Mr. Cassel's been around and I have no reason to doubt you, but I haven't seen him, not once since he moved out."

Might as well drop it, Mici thought, the girl wasn't going to believe anything against Cassel. Her loyalty was as stubborn and unquestioning as a little girl's. What had gone wrong for Bettedene Barber? she wondered. She knew that there were hundreds like her nestled in hutches in the seamy fifteen-block stretch along Eighth Avenue paralleling Times Square. They were recruited in the small towns of middle America, put on buses and shipped like parcels to the big city to be claimed by strangers who turned them into virtual slaves. The stories varied only in detail, with lack of love as perceived by the girl always at the core.

"Coffee and toast's ready, if you still want it." The wispy, blonde teenager sulked beside the stove.

"Of course, I do. No hard feelings, Bettedene?"

"I can't tell you what I don't know."

"I had to ask."

"I guess." Partly mollified, the girl set out the food.

Mici took a bite of the toast. "Delicious." After a satisfying swallow of the coffee, she pronounced it, "Perfect, best I ever had."

Beaming at the praise, Bettedene sat down opposite and they shared the snack in companionable silence.

"I really enjoyed that," Mici said, wiping her mouth and setting the napkin down beside her plate. "Thanks for everything, Bettedene." She hesitated, feeling that somehow she had left some question unasked, some area unexplored. "I agree with you that Alfred Cassel wouldn't have beaten his wife. But she did accuse him of it. Why should she do that?"

"You don't know?"

134

"No. She was getting a fair amount of money every month, but she claimed she was broke. Could she have been gambling? Could some bookie have had her beaten up?"

Bettedene just shook her head.

Mici didn't believe that herself. A bookie would have had it done once, just once would have been enough. Then who? she asked herself. It came with a jolt that all the while she'd been agonizing over why Julia had accused Alfred she'd never asked herself who else it might be. If Cassel hadn't beaten his wife, who had? The killer, of course. Fine. He'd evidently been at it for some time before graduating to murder. Who could it be?

"You honestly mean you don't know?" Bettedene Barber was amazed. "She was covering for her boyfriend."

"Her boyfriend?" Mici repeated stupidly.

"Sure. That explains what she did with her money, doesn't it?"

"You're telling me that Julia Schuyler was keeping a man?"

"No, that's what you're telling me." The girl was almost patronizing. "If a woman really loves a man, she wants to do everything she can for him, give him everything he needs and wants. If it's not enough, what she can do—why, he lets her know it, and if she refuses to understand he has no choice but to beat her up. I've been through it. I know. I had a hard time learning. At first, Dom and me, we were together all the time. It was wonderful, a dream come true. But it couldn't last. He explained to me that we couldn't live without money. When I found out about the other girls I was hysterical. I cried and carried on. He explained to me that much as he loved me, it wouldn't be fair for them to be working and bringing in all the money and for me not to do my share. It took some pretty hard knocks before I got the message. It wasn't that Dom enjoyed beating me, just that I was so dumb, real dumb."

"Are you telling me that Julia Schuyler . . ."

135

"That she went out to turn tricks? No, of course not. Not her. But she was keeping a man and he was beating her, regular."

"Did you ever see him with her? Going in or out of her place?"

"Didn't need to. I saw her the mornings after he'd been with her. A lot of mornings."

Her absolute certainty compelled belief. Thinking back to Julia's behavior that Friday night, Mici had to admit that there had been a certain . . . smugness about her. All the while she was railing against Cassel, she seemed to be hugging a secret to herself. Bemoaning her pain, she'd seemed at the same time to relish it. Mici had noted that and assumed that the actress was anticipating her revenge. Now she wondered if Julia hadn't derived a masochistic pleasure from her lover's violence. Maybe the beatings heightened the sexual satisfaction. Yet for Julia to permit herself to be abused in that way, Julia Schuyler who had once been so proud, who could have had any man . . . Mici sighed.

"It doesn't hurt all that much when you love the man," the hooker explained. "At least you know he cares."

Mici licked her lips nervously. It was too late for Julia, but this girl, this child, could still be helped. "Have you ever thought of going back home, Bettedene?"

"You mean to Richmond? Why should I? Dom doesn't beat me any more. That's over. He's very good to me, I told you."

"But someday, when you get older . . ." Mici couldn't finish.

"I know what you mean. I've thought about it. But that's a long way off. I don't drink or shoot up so I'll keep my looks for a long time." Then, with a smile of real pleasure, she spread out her arms to include the antiquated kitchen and the squalid rooms she'd swaddled in fabric. "I could never have anything as nice as this back home."

136

11

Julia with a lover? Why not? Nothing new in that. Julia had never stayed alone for long. It was Bettedene Barber's paralleling Julia's situation with hers that shocked Mici. But there are many ways a man can exploit a woman without putting her out on the street. At such a low point of her life, Julia would have been easy prey for such a man. It could have been his idea for Julia to contact Mici and ask for benefits. Naturally, he couldn't let her name him as the assailant. The ploy had a double edge: possible monetary gain and the squeeze on Cassel to get him to increase his allowance to Julia.

The murder was certainly a crime of passion, Mici thought. But who was Julia's lover? How could he be found?

Was he someone Julia had known a long time, or someone she'd met recently? More likely the latter and, if so, the meeting could have been casual, perhaps in a bar—Julia was very friendly when she'd had a few. What was needed was a team to canvass the bars in the area. It was a police job, but by the time she got hold of Donald and he went to his lieutenant—forget it. From what she'd heard about John LaRock, the lieut was not likely to throw a task force on the street in response to the theory of a teenage hooker.

So . . . Mici glanced at her watch. Nearly four. She'd been with Bettedene longer than she'd realized, but it was still early for most bars. However, the kind of place Julia would have been frequenting lately opened early in the morning. Down the street, on the corner, was O'Malley's, as good a place to start as any. Placing both hands at the back of her neck, Mici lifted her red-gold hair high and held it there to let the air cool her; then she let it drop and with a toss of her head walked into the dark, dank saloon.

She spent the rest of the afternoon and well into the evening going from one rancid bar to the next, up and down the side streets, along Eighth Avenue: the Red Rose, the Shamrock, the Pub, P.J. McGrath's, P.J. Callaghan's, or just plain P.J.'s. Some were strictly gin mills with paper banners glued across the front window proclaiming the house double-shot special, sawdust on the floor, and the row of regulars on their stools; others had pretensions to style and were decorated in chrome and tinted glass reminiscent of the thirties, but they had the same row of rummies. Mici had no compunction about going into these bars alone; she knew that no one would bother her—these sad men had no interest in women or in anything else but booze. As for the bartenders, at that hour they weren't busy; they welcomed a diversion.

"I'm working on the Schuyler case," Mici would announce and flash her ID.

They'd all heard about the case and no one challenged her right to ask questions. No one really looked at her credentials. New Yorkers were gullible. You could stand

138

on a street corner shaking a can and passersby would drop in contributions without ever asking what it was for.

Though Julia hadn't been around for a while, she was known in several of the bars. She'd made no secret of her identity; not for Julia Schuyler the "I want to be alone" or "I'm entitled to my privacy" routine. Julia let them all know who she was, or had been, and what she intended to be again. They listened till they'd heard all her stories and weren't impressed any more, till she got boring, till she was accepted as part of the scene. Then nobody noticed and nobody remembered Julia picking anybody up or getting picked up.

"She wasn't on the make. She just came in to forget her troubles like they all do."

That was the summation of Joe, the bartender-owner of Joe's Place, which appeared to have been her principal hangout. It was the general opinion and Mici accepted it. Wherever Julia had met her new lover it wasn't in any of these joints, she decided. Though she hadn't really expected to find the man, she had hoped for some clue to his identity and she was disappointed. Yet she had learned something from the past hours' investigation, and that was that the new man in Julia's life had not been a casual pickup. Julia had not been out looking for sex but for sympathy. What type of man could have offered her that? An actor. Julia Schuyler had been married twice, both times to actors. Her romances had been with actors working in her shows, but now that she was out of work why shouldn't she be involved with an actor who was also out of work? The question was how to find him. Go to Actors' Equity again? AFTRA, the Screen Actors' Guild, and check out their rosters of the unemployed? Those unions had more members out of work than working.

Would Billy Zip know? Mici wasn't sure. The stage manager had obviously believed Julia's message that her husband was beating her. He had delivered the message with conviction. However, he might know about a new man in the actress's life without being aware of the depth or quality of the relationship. Mici called the studio and was told that Billy had left for the day. She called his home and got a recorded announcement. She did not leave a message.

It was nearly dark when Mici came out of the phone booth. The lights would be coming on all over the city, but here in the Tenderloin the lights consisted of a kaleidoscope of theater marquees, neon signs, and bright hotel canopies.

A slow smile illumined her face as she watched the magic being turned on. What did actors want more than anything else in the world? To act. What did the deepening dusk mean to an actor? It meant getting ready to come down here, to walk along one of these dirty alleys and enter a stage door, to sit in a bare dressing room, squint into the glare of naked bulbs around an often blurred mirror, and put on makeup. Julia Schuyler had been down and nearly out, but she still had connections in the business. She couldn't get a job herself, but she could have helped her lover get one. By simply picking up a telephone, she could at least have assured him a sympathetic interview or audition with practically anybody casting anything in New York or Hollywood. Mici's smile reached her pale, crystal-clear eyes that mirrored the lights around her. All she had to do was make the rounds of the theatrical offices. It would be like the old days.

She'd tell Adam she needed a rest. She was pretty much turned off by the job anyway, and a few days away from it would do her good. What she did with them was her own business.

In the more than ten years since Mici Anhalt had been a dancer sitting in these same offices, the scene hadn't

140

changed. The faces were the same. At least, they wore the same anxious expression, the false cheeriness, the eagerness to please in spite of rebuff after rebuff. Some had talent, others not—all were treated with contempt, actors being a glut on the market. It was no wonder that when one of them made it he paid back the humiliation with arrogance and outlandish demands. The only thing different now was that Mici was no longer a job applicant and so she got in, where before she would have sat outside with the others.

Every agent, director, and producer was eager to talk. Each wanted to know everything that Mici knew, which was the tip-off that he didn't know anything himself. In the end, each was forced to admit, reluctantly, that Julia Schuyler had not contacted him in her own behalf or anybody else's.

Dead end.

Not quite. She'd forgotten Billy Zip, probably because she didn't have much hope that he'd be forthcoming. Billy would not divulge anything that might be detrimental to Julia. On the other hand, he would surely want to see her murder avenged.

Since "Storm of Life" was televised daily, it was simply a matter of catching Billy after the show went off the air. Seconds after the red warning light over the door of the studio went out, the door opened and the actors started filing toward their dressing rooms; the crew was next, then last, as usual, the stage manager. William Zipprodt came out of studio 2A, shirt-sleeves rolled to the elbow, sweating, carrying a stack of scripts, and looking generally harried behind a pair of clear, horn-rimmed glasses. Mici had to step right into his path to get him to notice her.

"You?" He was surprised, then confused. "What are you doing here?"

"I want to talk to you. Can we go somewhere? It's important."

"I don't know. . . . This is a bad time. I'm sorry, but as soon as everybody's changed we're due upstairs to rehearse tomorrow's episode."

"I just want a few minutes, Billy," she pleaded and didn't move out of his way.

"All right. Come on."

The rehearsal room was like all rehearsal rooms, bare, utilitarian, but for the actors who used it it was the most glamorous of environments—the workshop, the place of creation. Though she was no longer a part of this particular world, Mici felt a twinge of the old, familiar exhilaration. There was the usual large table with a number of folding chairs set up around it where the actors would gather for the first reading. On the floor, purposely bare so that a chalk outline of the setting could be drawn, Mici noted that there were several outlines laid down in vari-colored masking tapes indicating that several shows used the room as permanent rehearsal quarters. The building had once been a stable which had been converted in the early days of television when studio space had been nearly impossible to find. As a result, this room was relatively modern and cleaner than most other such facilities.

Billy Zip dumped his scripts on the table and began to lay out a copy at each place as though he were setting the table for dinner. That done, he went to a stack of folding chairs in one corner and began to set them within the area of the green floor tape; they would represent the various pieces of furniture in the set.

Mici waited for him to finish and give her his attention. He must have done this a thousand times by now, she thought, yet he was being inordinately finicky.

"Who do you think killed Julia?" she asked.

The chair he had been unfolding clattered in his hands. "I thought . . . Alfred." He swallowed, put the chair in place. "Who else?"

"You told the police about Alfred?"

"I had to."

"Yes, so did I."

They both sighed.

"He hasn't been arrested," Mici observed.

"I assume it's a matter of time."

"He has an alibi."

"I know all about his alibi and I don't think much of it," the stage manager snapped. "I don't think much of Delissa Grace's alibi either. I wonder which one is covering for the other?" Now that he'd set the scene and had no further activity to cover his nervousness, William Zipprodt fished into his pocket for cigarettes. "If you want to know what I think, I think they were in it together—to get Julia off their backs."

Mici was silent.

Billy Zip lit up and took a deep drag. "Julia could have had Alfred arrested; you were the one who told us that. With Alfred in jail there'd be no show, or at least no show as far as Delissa Grace was concerned. She was only in it because he wanted her."

"That's not quite true."

Billy Zip blew out a puff of smoke and squinted at her with his sad eyes. "She's strictly no-talent."

For a moment, Mici wondered whether Billy knew about Delissa's friend, the backer of the show. She decided that he didn't, that he was jealous on Julia's behalf. "You think they cold-bloodedly planned it together?"

He turned away.

"Billy dear . . ." Mici followed him and put a hand on his shoulder. "I know you loved Julia and you mourn her and you want to see her avenged. But it won't help to have the wrong man blamed."

"If it's not Alfred, then who?"

Now she could ask the question she had come to ask. "Did Julia have a lover?"

The response was a slow rise of color in the stage manager's sallow, haggard face. "How should I know?"

"You were as close to Julia as anyone could be."

"But I never pried. If she wanted to confide in me, I was there, but I didn't pry or snoop."

"She never mentioned another man?"

"No."

"You didn't suspect there might be another man?"

He hesitated a fraction of a second. "No."

For now that was enough. Mici tried another approach. "Did she tell you what she did with her money? The money you gave her and Alfred gave her and Delissa and God knows who else?"

"What are you talking about?"

"You did tell me that you helped her out from time to time."

"Right. I did."

"You weren't the only one. Alfred was paying her rent and something besides. Delissa was making a contribution."

"How do you know?" Billy Zip croaked.

"They told me and since it strengthens their motive for murder, I believe them."

"Where did the money go?" he cried.

"I was hoping you could tell me."

He shook his head.

"She wasn't exactly living high and she wasn't drinking that much. Was she gambling?"

"I never knew her to gamble."

"Then she was giving it to a man."

The door of the rehearsal room opened, and the actor Mici recognized as the leading man of "Storm of Life" entered, going directly to the table where he took his accustomed place and immersed himself in his copy of the next day's drama. Though she was sure that he wasn't paying any attention to them, Mici drew closer to Billy and lowered her voice. "Isn't it possible that it was this other man who was beating her? Not Alfred?"

144

The stage manager was in a daze. She put a hand on his arm and shook him gently. "Billy, isn't it possible?"

"I don't know." His whole face quivered, his eyes narrowed as though he had just been hit. "I went over one night to work on the book and I found her sitting on the sofa, half drunk, whimpering, her face a bloody mess. My first instinct was to call a doctor, but she wouldn't let me. She screamed at me that she didn't want a doctor. She screamed at me to mind my own business or to get out. Well, what could I do? I cleaned her up the best I could, made sure that there weren't any bones broken but . . . oh my God! You have no idea the state she was in. Anyway, after I was through I tried to call the police, but she wouldn't let me do that either. It finally filtered through to me that this wasn't any ordinary mugging, that someone she knew had done it. I nearly went crazy then. If I could have got my hands on the man, I think I would have killed him. I pleaded with her, I begged her to tell me who it was. No use. I demanded. I threatened. Nothing had any effect. For once in my life I was not going to give in to Julia. For once I was going to have my way. I picked up the phone and dialed 911. That was when she named Alfred."

He was silent for a few moments. "That was almost as big a shock as walking in and finding her like that. I wouldn't have believed it except that she was threatening to sue him for nonsupport. I went to see Alfred about it. It was my idea that he should visit her. He was reluctant; I urged him. And this was the result."

Mici gave him a couple of moments to compose himself. "Alfred might have lost his temper, gone completely out of control—I suppose anything is possible—but Alfred would never, never have got Julia drunk."

"No." William Zipprodt bowed his head. "She lied to me."

"Maybe she was afraid to tell you the truth." Mici

145

didn't believe that. Billy Zip had loved Julia and loyally accepted her marriage to another man, to Cassel, because he believed Cassel was her equal. But how would he have felt about a new lover? One so brutish? Julia had been fond of Billy in her way. Certainly he'd been useful to her over the years. She wouldn't have wanted to lose him. Maybe she had sensed his reluctance to accept the charge against Cassel and had sent him to Mici as a way of reenforcing the accusation. "This man, whoever he was, was in complete control."

The door of the rehearsal room opened again; more actors entered and took their places around the table. There wasn't much time left.

"Did she ever send anybody to you for a job on the show?"

"You mean—him? She wouldn't do that."

"Why not?"

"She wouldn't ask me to give anybody a job unless he had real talent. Julia might have sunk low, but whatever else she did she wouldn't prostitute her professional integrity. Never."

"How do you know he didn't have talent?"

A man Mici had not seen on the show came in. He had an air of authority. "Say, Zip?" he called. "See your friend later and let's get the show on the road, okay?"

From the way Billy jumped, it had to be the director. Mici held his arm for one moment more. "How do you know he didn't have any talent?"

"Because then she would have told everybody about him; she would have touted him to the skies. But she must have been ashamed of him. She lied to me because she was ashamed."

So, Mici thought, an actor but one without special talent. Run-of-the-mill at best. If he was her lover, however, what more natural than that he should ask her to recommend him to her friends? But she refused. He was

146

stunned. They argued. He beat her. But kill her? That was going a bit far. Besides, she was no use to him dead. Mici had already considered the possibility that the murder was not premeditated but committed in the heat of passion, yet the image now taking shape was of a cool and calculating man. He used women. He would not be likely to lose control. Besides, if making love to Julia failed, if beating her didn't get him what he wanted, he had another weapon in his arsenal. He could simply stay away from her. If her addiction to him was strong enough, she would do anything to get him back. She would renounce integrity, accept any humiliation. Mici believed that was what had happened.

She had covered all the agents and directors in New York. Would Julia have used her Hollywood connections for her lover? She could check Julia's old studio—which was it? Or her lawyer. Of course. Oscar Brumleve was a theatrical institution. He would be a more valuable ally to an aspiring actor than any casting director or producer. Brumleve knew everybody, and any favor he asked would not be lightly ignored.

Oscar Brumleve was legend, and so was his apartment at the top of the John Malcolm Schuyler Theatre. The theatre had been dark for several months, but it had a tenant now. As she passed the lobby, Mici noted that there was no one waiting at the box office—an ominous indication that the run was going to be short. She continued past the marquee to a short flight of steps and pressed the bell beside the door. An answering buzz released the lock and she stepped into a small, dingy vestibule where an antiquated elevator stood open. There were two buttons—Up and Down. She pressed the Up. The car shuddered and groaned its way to the top, then halted. The door opened directly into the famous lawyer's office-apartment.

Entering Oscar Brumleve's domain was like stepping

147

back into the days of past theatrical glories. The hallway was long and broad, a gallery in fact, lined on both sides with photographs and portraits of famous clients and settings, playbills, and theatrical mementoes. Unfortunately, the light coming from a skylight in the center was harsh. It revealed the worn spots in the Turkish floor runner, the dents and rust on the suit of armor, and showed that the Jacobean armchairs and the rose tree with its blooms long since turned brown were merely stage props. Everywhere there was the dust of neglect.

"Miss Anhalt?"

A dark-haired young man, pale as though he seldom saw the outdoors, appeared at the end of the corridor. He indicated a pair of double doors. "You can go right in but be brief as possible. He tires easily."

The first thing she saw was not the lawyer but the portrait of his most famous client, John Malcolm Schuyler, for whom Brumleve had built the theatre. It was over the fireplace, the focal point of the room. It showed the actor as Macbeth, hand stretched out, fingers clawing toward the ghostly, non-existent dagger. For a moment Mici stood where she was, transfixed by the painted eyes. She had to shake herself free. She looked around. The room was large, the walls paneled in wood as intricately carved as the chamber of the Knights of the Bath at Windsor Castle. Tall, old-fashioned, glass-doored bookcases were filled with dusty tomes, manuscripts, files, all in haphazard stacks. Twin beams of light passing through a pair of stained-glass windows colored the gloom and created the effect of stage lighting, softening the general shabbiness which in the hallway had been so sadly obvious.

"Well, don't just stand there. Come over here. Come over here where I can get a look at you."

She jumped at the voice. "It's very good of you to see me, Mr. Brumleve," Mici said as she approached the shrunken figure at the desk to the right of the fireplace.

"No, young lady, it's good of you to come. I don't get many visitors nowadays."

Oscar Brumleve was a celebrity. Mici had seen countless pictures of him with countless other celebrities; there were even pictures of him outside in the hall, but if she had met him anywhere else she wouldn't have recognized him. He was a wasted man. He had had, she recalled, an abundant head of hair, but it was thinned now to a few pitiful white tufts. The flesh of his face had been consumed, and the skull showed through prophetically. His eyes were sunk deep in their sockets, but they burned brightly. She had not heard that Brumleve was sick; in fact, she realized that she had not heard about him at all for a very long time and that probably was the reason.

A shaft of light picked up the row of golden statuettes lined up along the front of the desk—awards. She recognized some: the Oscars, of course; the Tonys; a Drama Critics Award; the Valentino, a statuette from the film festival in Bari, Italy. The light bounced from the tarnished metal, streaking the burgundy velvet drapes behind Brumleve's chair. Was there a window back there? Mici frowned because she couldn't quite get the layout of the building clear in her mind.

"You were a dancer, I see."

She started. "How did you know?"

"I recognize a dancer's legs when I see them, particularly if they're as good as yours," Brumleve chuckled. "But you don't dance any more. You haven't in some time."

"I still take classes."

"Not the same. Too bad."

"I wasn't a very good dancer."

"Oh, you were good enough, I'm sure. With your looks you were more than good enough. What happened?"

Mici shrugged. "I didn't care enough. Getting my name up there in lights just didn't seem that important."

149

Oscar Brumleve nodded. "In that case, you did well to get out." He consulted a paper in front of him. "So now you're in Criminal Justice. Quite a switch."

She didn't feel that required comment.

But he did. "Crime Victims Compensation Board. You do good work down there, but don't you find it depressing?"

"Sometimes," she admitted.

The sunken eyes gleamed in the colored light. "But you like it better than dancing."

"It's real."

"Ah." He nodded. "Well, now, what can I do to help you? Which one of your claims am I involved in, eh?" He chortled as though that were a farfetched idea.

Mici had given a great deal of thought to her approach. The mere presentation of credentials would not impress Brumleve; he would know that she had no official standing and that he was under no obligation to tell her anything. She had decided to be honest.

"The Julia Schuyler case."

"You're not working on that. That's police business."

"I have a personal interest. I knew Julia."

"A great many people knew Julia."

"I was with her on Friday night not long before she was killed."

He merely narrowed his eyes slightly. "Have you informed the police?"

"Yes."

"Then you've done all you can and should do. You're a professional. I suggest you let the police do their job as you'd want to be allowed to do yours."

It was exactly the reaction she'd expected. "I would if I thought they were conducting an unbiased investigation, but all they're trying to do is pin the crime on Alfred Cassel."

"That's a serious allegation."

150

"I make it seriously."

"And it matters to you—what happens to Alfred Cassel?"

"Yes, sir. Partly because it's my fault that he's under suspicion, but mainly because I believe that he's innocent. Don't you?"

"I'd like to." The lawyer was thoughtful. "I considered Alfred Cassel decent and honorable. I thought Julia was lucky to get him. Now I'm not so sure. I realize he's been through a trying period and the provocation must have been great. Still, my loyalty has to be to the daughter of my old friend." His eyes went to the towering portrait. "Everything points to Alfred. If it weren't for that alibi, which in my opinion is flimsy, he'd already be in custody."

"So you refuse to help him?"

"He hasn't been arrested." Brumleve raised a skeletal hand, then let it fall limply to the top of the desk. "If he were arrested and charged, I'm not sure he'd want me to represent him. We had a falling-out a short while back."

"Would you help if you could?"

Brumleve considered. "How?"

"By answering some questions."

The thin lips stretched into a taut line that passed for a smile, cracking the flesh around the mouth in the unaccustomed movement. "My dear young lady, the police have been here; they have asked every imaginable question, and I have answered fully and unequivocally."

"I have other questions."

"Indeed? Questions the police didn't think to ask?" He didn't bother to hide either his amusement or disbelief.

"Well, actually only one."

She had piqued his interest. He might not take her seriously, but he was curious. It was enough, Mici thought, and she waited patiently while he studied her anew. She became aware that she was perspiring heavily. Was she

151

that anxious? No, the room was that hot. There was no air conditioning. She realized that the sick old man did not feel the heat, that he required it.

"What's the question?"

"Did Julia send a man to you, an actor, and ask you to help him get a job?"

This time she had to wait even longer, but she knew it was no use adding anything. He would either answer or he would not.

He uttered a long, drawn-out sigh. "Yes."

"Who was he?"

"One question, you said."

She suppressed a surge of excitement. "It's a two-part-er."

"Ah . . . you're a clever girl, very clever. I don't know how you found out about . . . Did Julia tell you? No, of course not, if she had you wouldn't have needed to come to me. Well, what does it matter? She's gone. It's over for her."

"Just his name, Mr. Brumleve."

He didn't hear her; he was away among his memories. "Poor Julia, poor Julia. Everything she touched went bad."

"If you'll just give me his name I won't trouble you . . ."

"Handsome devil, ingratiating, charming when he wanted to be. Of course, he was using her. What could I do? No use telling her, she knew it; she wasn't that much of a fool."

"What did you do? Did you find him a job?"

Brumleve looked at Mici and shifted from the past to the present. "Didn't know what to do with him. Face like a choir boy along with plenty of sex appeal, devastating combination, but froze up in front of an audience. I want-ed to oblige Julia but didn't know what to do with him. Finally got Steinberg-Farber to take him on, use him in their commercials. Only thing he was good for."

"You haven't told me his name, Mr. Brumleve."

"No, and I'm not going to, young lady. I thought . . . I was so sure that Alfred . . . but if there's a doubt . . . I will tell the police. I'll tell them. It's their business." A spasm of pain traveled like a current through his emaciated frame. Sweat broke out all over his gray face and trickled in the deeply grooved lines like fresh rain in dry gutters. With a shaking hand he reached toward the electric bell set in a square, flat box at the desk's corner and pressed. His face a gargoyle mask, the spittle running from a corner of his mouth down to his chin, he collapsed across the desk.

Mici ran to the door, but as she did it opened and the young male secretary came hurrying in with the equipment for a hypodermic injection. With every indication of expertise, he slipped Brumleve's left arm out of his jacket, rolled up the shirt-sleeve, prepared the area, and made the injection.

Mici watched and waited and was relieved to see the lawyer revive.

"You'll have to leave now, miss," the secretary-nurse told her.

"Yes, yes, of course." Mici didn't know what the lawyer's illness was, but he was fighting it and fighting it valiantly. She feared it might be a losing battle. "Just his name, Mr. Brumleve."

His pain-filled eyes met hers and seemed to share her thought. "Kord . . . ," he murmured. "Janos Kord."

12

"Say! That's good work. You're a real pro. I'm impressed." Donald Swell beamed at Mici.

"You don't mind?"

"Why should I mind? You did a great job."

"Well, I thought . . . other times . . . my past experience has been that police officers resent what they call interference."

"That's because they're insecure. I'm not."

Mici's elation at having discovered the identity of Julia's lover was still high. However, she had promised Oscar Brumleve to go to the police and she did agree that it was time for them to take over. So she'd called Donald and Donald had immediately suggested dinner. "Even cops have to eat," he'd pointed out. Now they sat opposite each other in a booth in the back room of a small, pleasant, neighborhood bar and grill near the precinct. Having expected to be chewed out, Mici was both relieved and gratified to be complimented instead.

"You never cease to amaze me, Donald."

He bent slightly, reached under the table, and rested a hand on her knee. "I'll continue to amaze you, if you'll let me."

"I spoke too soon." Laughing, she removed his hand. "What are you going to do?"

He sighed heavily. "Go the route, I guess—send flowers, perfume, call two or three times a day, order a singing telegram, maybe."

She grinned. "You know what I'm talking about."

"Oh, that." Swell shrugged. "The usual. Check out this guy Kord. Find out where he was and what he was doing Friday P.M. and Saturday A.M. around the time we think the murder may have been committed, and . . . like that. Then we'll see."

"Okay."

"I'm not downgrading your accomplishment in tracking this Janos Kord, doll," the detective continued, "but we don't have anything on him yet. Assuming Julia Schuyler had the hots for him, that she was giving him all her money and that in return he was beating the . . . hell . . . out of her, that still doesn't make him a murderer. In fact, it seems to me that it was in his interest to keep her alive."

"You'd think so," Mici agreed. "Obviously what he wanted from Julia was a boost to his career, and she gave it to him by sending him to Brumleve who in turn passed him on to Steinberg-Farber. I understand they put him into a couple of their commercials and that they liked him. Nowadays, that can be a route to the top. So then maybe he figured he didn't need Julia any more."

"Wouldn't killing her be a little drastic? Why not just dump her?"

"Julia wouldn't have been easy to dump."

Swell grunted. "So far it's all conjecture, sweetie pie. Now be honest, isn't it? We can't even prove the relationship."

155

"I wouldn't say that."

"If he chooses to deny it, how are we going to nail him on it?"

"Well, for one thing, the very fact that Julia sent him to Brumleve . . . All right, all right. Somebody in the building had to have seen him with her, going in and out of her place, if not on the night of the murder, other nights," Mici insisted. "You could get a picture of Kord from the advertising agency and show it around."

"I'll do that."

"And what about those two officers in the squad car, what are their names? Emmenecher and Pace. Maybe they'd recognize the picture."

"Don't count on them. They've taken too much flak on this thing already. What they haven't remembered by now is forgotten for good."

Their steaks were served and they ate in silence.

"The weapon never turned up?" Mici asked when they were finishing.

"Nope. Never will either, if you ask me."

"There were no additional clues?"

"No clues period. Zilch. This Kord, if he was having an affair with the lady, was sure discreet. He didn't even keep a razor at her place."

"The autopsy shows that besides being beaten shortly before her death, Julia had had sexual intercourse."

"It doesn't show with whom."

"Kord, who else? Julia had a lot of men in her life, but, like the song, she was always true—to one at a time."

"I don't doubt you."

They continued eating. After the plates were cleared, Mici tried again. "How about fingerprints?"

"The lab came up with a couple of unidentified dabs. Assuming they turn out to be Kord's, there's no way to prove they were made on the night of the murder." Swell reached over and put his hand over hers. "You've done your thing, Red; relax and let me do mine."

156

She nodded.

He patted her hand, then signaled the waiter for the check. "Listen, kid, I've got to run. You stay, take your time, have dessert, whatever." He pushed some crumpled bills at the waiter. "Give the lady anything she wants." He hesitated, considered, made up his mind. "I get off at midnight. How about I drop over to your place?"

"What happened to the flowers and the perfume?"

"This is business. I'm coming to report."

"Oh. Just to report?"

He looked straight down and into her eyes. His tongue flicked lightly out at the corner of his lips and disappeared again. "That'll be up to you, babe."

The phone was ringing.

Mici came to with a start. It took her a couple of minutes to orient herself: she was at home on the living-room couch. It was dark outside; the lamps were lit. Conclusion: she'd fallen asleep waiting for Donald.

The phone went on ringing.

Yawning, making automatic note of the time—11:40—getting up and going into the bedroom to answer were all part of one continuous reflex action.

"Hello?"

"Miss Anhalt? Just a moment, please, Mr. Brumleve calling."

She reached under the shade and turned on the light at her bedside.

"Miss Anhalt? Sorry to disturb you at this hour." The lawyer sounded strong and very alert.

"Perfectly all right."

"I was wondering if you'd taken action on that matter we discussed?"

Mici considered before answering. The time, the very fact of his calling, indicated it was not an idle question. The ambiguity with which he put it suggested he was in a public place. She was mystified. "I took your advice and

157

contacted the police but . . . unofficially." She waited for a comment and, getting none, continued. "I passed the information to a friend, a detective on the Schuyler case. He'll look into it and let us know what he finds out."

The lawyer sighed. "I'm afraid it's too late. Alfred Cassel has been arrested. I'm down here at the precinct now."

"Oh, God! But his alibi . . ."

"They appear to have broken it."

"How?"

"I can't go into it right now."

"I'm so sorry."

"Don't be. Before you came to see me, I believed that Alfred was guilty. Now I not only believe that he's innocent, but I have a basis on which to defend him. What I must know is how far your friend has progressed with his inquiries."

"When was Alfred arrested?"

"A couple of hours ago. I got his call at nine-thirty."

"Well, then, I doubt that my friend could have gotten very far. We had dinner together. He left me at a little before eight."

"Do you think he might have passed the information on? To a superior?"

"I'll find out."

"That would be helpful."

Mici clenched and unclenched her free hand. "Is there anything else I can do?"

"For the moment, no. If something should occur, I'll call."

"Please do that." She let the receiver clatter back onto the cradle. For a few moments Mici just stood where she was, arms folded across her chest, feeling the pounding of her heart, the warmth in her cheeks, giving in to her anger. Her next move was to return to the living room and flip on the television. There would be a news broadcast at

158

midnight. She sat down and waited for it. At about five minutes of the hour, the phone in the bedroom rang again. She ignored it; she didn't even look in its direction, but she counted ten rings before it finally stopped. At midnight precisely it rang again, but the news was on and she watched and listened to that.

When the phone rang the next time, she got up and answered.

"Hey! This is the third time I've called. Where were you? In the shower?"

It was Swell, of course. "No," she answered curtly.

He was puzzled by her tone but chose to ignore it. "Listen, babe, I'm really sorry but I'm going to have to break our date. Business. Something came up. *Capish?*"

"No, I don't."

"Sure you do." He laughed. "I don't punch a time clock. Something comes up, I stick with it and see it through."

"Like what? What came up? Did you make an arrest?" She heard him suck in his breath.

"How did you know? Was it on the news? Already?"

"No, it was not on the news."

"Then how did you know?"

"His lawyer called me. Alfred Cassel's lawyer, Oscar Brumleve, called me. You've heard me speak of him? He called and wanted to know if I'd informed the police about Janos Kord. I told him yes. I told him I had a good friend working on it. I felt like a fool."

"I'm sorry, babe."

"And don't call me babe or kid or sweetie pie. I hate it. You could have told me an arrest was imminent. But no! Great work, you said. You're a real terrific investigator, you said. You let me go on and on and all the time you knew. . . ."

"I didn't. I swear I didn't know."

"You were the one who made the arrest; it was your duty; you explained that to me."

159

"Yeah, sure, all right. It was me, but it wasn't on my own initiative. And I wasn't given advance notice, either. Oh, I knew LaRock had a team working to break Cassel's alibi, but I had no idea how close they were. I didn't find out till I got back from dinner. Then I was just told to tag along with the lieut and we went to the Algonquin. We waited in the lobby, and when an inspector showed up I knew we weren't there for just another interrogation. Sure, I made the collar, but it won't be my picture you'll see in tomorrow's papers."

His bitterness convinced her. "How did they break Cassel's alibi?"

"I can't tell you that, babe . . . sorry, Mici."

She could make a guess. Alfred Cassel and Delissa Grace had been guests at a big movie premiere Friday night and at a party at the Tavern-on-the-Green afterwards. The movie ended at eleven-thirty and everyone headed straight from the theatre uptown to the restaurant. There was only one way that Cassel could have squeezed in a visit to Julia and arrived at the function along with everyone else—to which fact there were countless witnesses.

"He left before the end of the picture, right?"

"Right," Swell replied.

But how had they proved it? Mici wondered. Delissa knew, of course, but she wouldn't tell. "You found the driver who picked Cassel up in front of Julia's place and drove him to the restaurant."

"Not me."

One of LaRock's team, of course. That was what was griping Donald; he had wanted to be the one to break the case. She sympathized. "How could the driver make a positive ID nearly a week later?"

"As soon as he pulled up in front of the Tavern, the driver could tell it was a big celebrity affair and he was naturally curious about his passenger, figured he was a celebrity, too. So he looked him over real close," Swell explained.

As simple as that, Mici thought, feeling a twinge of the detective's frustration. "What does Alfred say?"

"What can he say? He has to admit he was there, but he claims he left Julia alive and kicking."

"Does he say anything about the scream the two officers heard?"

Swell paused a beat. "He says she was drinking beer and she wasn't too coherent. So he tried to take the can away from her and she screamed like a banshee."

Not exactly the death scream described in the newspapers, but a possible explanation, Mici thought, having been in Julia Schuyler's presence when someone was trying to separate her from a drink. "What reason does he give for going to see her?"

"To talk to her, to get her to stop spreading ugly rumors about him. Like that."

He couldn't have picked a worse time, Mici thought. Unless the police could now find someone else who had visited Julia later on . . . But they really had no reason to try.

"What have you done about Janos Kord?" she asked.

"Kord?"

"You haven't done anything at all, have you? You never intended to."

"Now hold it. That's not fair. I didn't have the time. The lieut grabbed me as soon as I walked in the door."

"So what are you going to do?"

"Have a heart, Red . . . Mici? Do you know what's involved in an arrest like Cassel's? Do you know how many hours I'm going to be tied up with the arraignment alone? It could run from twelve to sixteen hours, till tomorrow night, for God's sake!"

"I mean after that."

He groaned. "Listen, I might as well tell you straight.

161

Both the brass and the DA are satisfied they've got the perpetrator. That's it. Case closed. Okay?"

"You mean you're not going to tell them there was another man? You're just going to forget about it?"

"It's not up to me. The case is closed, and I'll be assigned to something else. I'm sorry. I'm as disappointed as you are, believe me. Believe me. I have no choice. I do what I'm told."

"You could tell LaRock."

"It wouldn't do any good. Anyhow, your friend's got a lawyer. Let his lawyer talk to the lieut."

"You just said it wouldn't do any good."

"So then let him hire a private eye."

"That takes money."

Swell sighed lugubriously. "I'll do it. I'll do it. As soon as I've got some free time after I catch up on some sleep, I'll check out your man. Okay, kid?"

"Forget it."

"Ah, come on . . ."

"Forget it. I'll do it myself."

There was a long pause. "Maybe that would be best."

"What?"

Mici was stunned. She had thrown out the challenge impulsively, expecting that he would argue her out of it and end up agreeing to get on the case himself and promptly.

"It would be best," Swell reiterated. "After all, you can go anywhere you want, talk to anybody you want. It's your civil right."

"It is?" She was surprised he'd admit it.

"Sure."

"All right then, I will." She tossed her hair back. "I'll do it myself."

"Fine. And let me know how you make out." He was chuckling as he hung up.

* * *

The next morning Mici had a headache, dry mouth, rubbery legs, and all the signs of a hangover with none of the causatory pleasures to remember. Though the shower helped, she couldn't get down more than a cup of coffee for breakfast. She was due back at work, but she toyed with the idea of calling in sick. She'd never done that before and the fact that she was even considering it dismayed her. She had a good job, a job that basically she liked, and she ought to be glad to be getting back to it. She dumped some cereal into a bowl, poured milk over it, and sat down determined to eat.

The phone rang.

"Mici?"

"Oh, Adam, good morning."

"How are you feeling?"

She'd almost forgotten the reason that he was asking— the attack of the night before last. If she wanted to beg off work one more day, this was her chance. "Fine. I'm just fine, thanks."

"Good. Police come up with anything?"

"Ah . . ." She had to keep reminding herself that he was talking about the attempted rape. "No. I doubt that they will. I didn't give them much to go on."

"You never know. Anyhow, I'm glad you're feeling better. You are coming in this morning?"

"Oh, sure." She made herself sound bright and eager. "What's up?"

"I'll tell you when you get here. Make it as early as you can."

Adam had a new case for her! Mici was sure of it, and she felt a surge of energy, a glow of satisfaction. Nothing like being good at your job and having it acknowledged. She could eat now. Afterwards she dressed quickly and when she checked herself in the mirror decided that she looked better than she had in days, her blue eyes were wide and bright, her red-blonde hair shining. She tossed her head in satisfaction and was humming softly as she closed the apartment door behind her.

She made it to the office by eight-twenty and stopped downstairs to pick up the coffee and jelly doughnuts that had become the traditional early snack when she and Dowd had a meeting. She marched straight into his office and set the paper bag down on a corner of his desk.

"We haven't done this in a long time," she beamed and started to set out the food, napkins, and plastic spoons as though laying out a picnic. Then she sat down in her usual chair. "So?"

Dowd looked tired. There were dark circles under his eyes, and his homely, pockmarked face was drawn. The man had troubles at home. His wife was an alcoholic. God only knew what kind of night he'd had.

The supervisor didn't touch his snack. He kept looking at Mici. "Clay Marin wants you off his case."

Her mouth dropped open.

Then Dowd delivered the second stunner. "He wants Lischner."

A tumult of events and their possible interpretations tumbled through her head. It must go back to the day she'd missed her appointment with Clay Marin and Wally had taken over for her. Wally had probably fed Marin's indignation and sense of rejection, though why he should covet Marin as a client was beyond her—unless it was to denigrate her. Wally was an able investigator in his own right; he shouldn't need to put anybody down. As for Marin, he was an extremely difficult client, but she thought she'd done a good job with him and for him. Evidently she hadn't.

"If that's what Mr. Marin wants. Did he say why?"

Neither one was eating.

"He says you've been taking kickbacks from his doctors."

164

It was so completely unexpected, so baldly false that she couldn't speak.

"Specifically, he claims that you won't put through a request for surgery at the Retina Foundation."

That at least she could deal with. "That's not true. I told Mr. Marin that I would put the request through, but that I would have to append to it Dr. Harden's report advising against the operation."

"Did you put it through?" Dowd asked.

"Not yet. I've been meaning to." At the supervisor's heavy sigh, she hurried on. "It's okay, Adam. Both forms are still in my desk drawer completely filled out, dated, and ready to go."

"No, they're not."

"You looked?"

He nodded. "I had to."

She let that go for the moment to address the more crucial aspect. "They have to be there. Maybe you didn't look in the right place." His expression told her the search had been thorough. "Who could have taken them? And why? Why would anyone . . ." She stopped, closed her eyes for just a moment, and then answered her own question. "Mr. Marin asked me to suppress Dr. Harden's report stating that surgery would be useless, and I refused."

Dowd said nothing.

"Adam, the man has gone through three psychiatrists. He changes doctors like dirty socks."

"He claims that was your doing. He claims he was perfectly satisfied with each one of his physicians, but you moved him because the doctors balked at paying you off."

She passed a hand over her eyes. "I'd like to laugh but I can't." She took her hand away and looked directly at the supervisor. "You don't believe this, Adam, do you?"

"The charge has to be investigated."

"Yes, all right, I understand that. What I'm asking is whether you yourself, personally, believe that I did these things?" She had recovered from her initial shock and confusion and was beginning to fight back. Her eyes blazed as she waited for the man who had taught and befriended her to give his answer.

"No, I don't."

She slumped back into the chair.

"But I can't ignore the charge."

"I don't want you to. Do you think I want to have this kind of suspicion hanging over me? All we have to do is contact the various physicians who treated Marin and . . ."

"Ask them if they paid kickbacks? They'd hardly admit it."

"Well, what am I supposed to do? How can I prove my innocence? I can't believe this is happening to me. I can't. I've done good work here. I have, haven't I?" Again she demanded an answer.

"Yes, you have."

"Yet on the unsupported word of an embittered man . . . Clay Marin hates everybody, resents everybody. He's lost his sight and is on the verge of losing his wife. He's trying to revenge himself on me because I refused to suppress Dr. Harden's report. Can't you see that?"

"Mr. Cornelius doesn't want even the suggestion of impropriety to tarnish the reputation of this office and the program we are administering."

"Clay Marin asked me to suppress a medical report." Mici spaced the words as though Dowd were hard-of-hearing.

"It's your word against his. We'll check with Dr. Harden, of course, and if he did make a negative report on Marin . . . that will certainly help."

"Wonderful."

"In any case, Mr. Cornelius has decided to send Clay Marin to the Retina Foundation. If the doctors there concur that surgery is not indicated, that will be another point for you."

"It should be a point for Dr. Harden," Mici said bitterly. "Never mind, I understand. Either way, Clay Marin wins. It's okay; he's the one who's sick." She got up, recapped her coffee container, put the untouched doughnut back into the brown bag, and reached for Dowd's portion. "Might as well throw this out."

He watched her with growing distress. "I don't think you understand the situation yet."

"Oh?"

"While Mr. Marin's allegations are being investigated . . . " He paused. The color rose in his face. "You're suspended."

There was a roaring in her ears. She felt as though the structure of her days had come crashing down around her, leaving her without purpose, without function.

"What about my current cases?"

"They'll be taken care of."

"You mean parceled out among the staff."

"That's it."

"How about Karl Spychalski? At least let me see him through?"

"The Spychalski case is closed. His claim has been disallowed."

She gasped. "Why?"

"You know why. The fire was of suspicious origin to begin with. It has now definitely been labeled arson. The Geramita brothers are out so that leaves—Spychalski."

"I know all that but . . ."

"He's the logical suspect and as long as he can't or won't offer an alibi . . ." Dowd shrugged. "There's nothing we can do for him."

Suspended! In plain language: dumped, not wanted, out of a job. Mici Anhalt left 270 Broadway in a daze and headed for City Hall park, oblivious of the throngs just going to work or of the traffic as she crossed against the light. Suspended pending investigation! Thanks a lot. Thanks for nothing. If the denials of the doctors allegedly involved were not sufficient, how in the world could she be cleared? The best she could hope for was a grudging "Not proven." That would mean that from here on she would be tainted, mistrusted, given the least sensitive assignments. In essence, she was finished at the Compensation Board. She might as well quit now while it could be done with a semblance of dignity.

The morning sun was already hot on this seventh day of the heat wave as she looked for a place to sit in the shade, but the shady spots were already taken.

Why was she so crazy about the job anyway? There was no future in it. It was a dead-end job. You were an investigator and you stayed an investigator till you were sixty-five or seventy or whatever the retirement age would be when you got to it. The only thing you could hope for in the way of advancement was to become the supervisor, and that meant sitting at a desk and handing out assignments. "Depressing," Oscar Brumleve had characterized it and he was right. Frustrating, too. So why hang on? She could probably get a job with one of the big insurance companies—less headaches and more money. Trouble was, Mici wasn't interested. She was too old to go back to dancing and too out of shape. Classes three nights a week were not enough to keep you in professional condition. Brumleve had said that, too. If she were thrown out of this job, what could she do with her life? At thirty-four, had she already missed the boat?

Mici could have understood an emotional outburst from Clay Marin. If he'd accused her to her face of taking kickbacks, if he'd raved and ranted, she might even have sympathized. But the cold, deliberate, behind-her-back scheming was what appalled her and made her feel so helpless. Of course, it would have been simple enough for Marin to steal the reports in her desk. Her office wasn't

168

locked. All he had to do was announce that he had an appointment, and he would have been left to wait in there for as long as it suited him. Yet somehow Mici didn't think it would have occurred to the blind man to go through her desk. . . .

She stopped short in the middle of the path.

How could the blind man have gone through her desk? How could he have known which documents to take?

If not Marin, then who? The answer was obvious: the man Marin had requested to take over his case—Wally Lischner. Why? Why should Wally do this to her? Surely not because of that one awkward date? Granted it had been worse than awkward—embarrassing for her, humiliating for him. But she thought he'd gotten over it. Evidently he hadn't. Evidently his friendliness had been pretense. Abruptly, Mici turned around and headed back toward Broadway. She was going back to the office. She was going to march straight up to Wally Lischner and accuse him to his face of setting her up.

"Watch out where you're going!"

A nice-looking young man dressed in a neat business suit had slammed into Mici's left shoulder, nearly spinning her around.

"Bitch," he muttered under his breath as he passed.

"Why don't *you* watch?" she was on the verge of calling after him, but the hate she'd glimpsed on his face kept her silent. His entire body was knotted with tension, she thought, as she watched him stride along the crowded, sunlit path. With so much hostility from a stranger, what could she expect from Wally Lischner? Naturally he'd deny her accusation. It would be her word against his, and at the moment her word wasn't worth much. What she had to do was get proof that it was Wally who had destroyed the application to the Retina Foundation and then put Clay Marin up to bringing the charge against her. She didn't know how she was going to accomplish it, but she did know that however satisfying it would be to confront Wally now, Mici would be tipping him off that she'd caught on. Keeping that knowledge from him was the only advantage she had.

Mici Anhalt was something of a fatalist but in the best sense of the word, a believer that time solves many apparently insoluble problems, or at least shows the way to solutions. The problem regarding Wally Lischner was one with which she hoped time would take a hand. Meanwhile, that feeling of emptiness that had come over her when Adam first informed her that she was suspended washed over her again. She felt lost and disoriented, without direction. But she reminded herself that she was also free of all obligations and could do whatever she wanted. For example, she could go and talk to Karl Spychalski and make one more try at getting an alibi out of him.

Then there was Donald. She could hand him a surprise by picking up his challenge. A slight twitch began at the corners of her mouth as she imagined the detective's reaction if she actually did approach Julia's lover. The manner of the approach suddenly occurred to her, and the twitch became a faint smile. It was a natural and what was more could only be handled by a civilian. She grinned broadly.

Why not? Mici tossed her hair back over her shoulders and spotting a food cart bought herself a hot dog, smeared it with mustard, and ate voraciously.

13

The actor emerged from the wings and walked out on the bare stage and down to the apron, peering into the dark house. He was tall, elegantly slim, with wavy blond hair and blue eyes. His lips were full, the lower one glinting sensuously. He squinted against the glare of the pilot light as he tried to locate the person or persons he was addressing. He couldn't and was forced to sacrifice intimacy and announce in a loud voice, "I am Janos Kord. I live at 333 West . . . "

"Thank you, Mr. Kord, we have all your particulars. If you'll just turn to act 2, scene 2 in your script, we'd like you to read the part of Phillip, please."

Eagerly Kord turned his head toward the voice coming from the left rear of the auditorium, at the same time thumbing the manuscript in his hand to find the indicated place. "Phillip. Yes . . . uh, ma'am."

"I'm Miss Anhalt, and you'll get better light if you step upstage, Mr. Kord," Mici called out with professional courtesy and coolness. "Mr. Zipprodt will cue you in. Please begin."

Oscar Brumleve had arranged everything—lent them the theatre, provided the script, one from the pile that every theatrical lawyer, producer, director accumulated. She'd got hold of Billy Zip and he'd agreed to act as stage manager for the audition. Billy had also arranged for other actors to participate to lend authenticity. It was the only aspect of the scheme Mici felt guilty about—raising false hopes in these others.

Billy gave the cue, but Kord didn't pick it up.

"Well, Mr. Kord?" Mici called out with an edge of impatience. "Shall we get started?"

"I'm sorry . . . the light . . . there's so much glare."

"Do you have glasses? Well, use them, Mr. Kord. It's no disgrace to need reading glasses. Use them and let's get on with it, please."

Reluctantly the actor produced the glasses and put them on. They certainly didn't enhance his good looks, Mici thought, and smiled in the darkness.

"What is it now, Mr. Kord?"

"I'm waiting for my cue."

Mici sighed aloud. "Cue him in again, Billy, please."

The reading began. Though Mici was not interested and barely listened, she heard enough to know that it was going badly. Not only had Kord got off on the wrong foot, he was a bad actor. In the middle of a sentence she stopped him, abruptly and unkindly.

"Thank you, Mr. Kord. We'll call you."

His jaw went slack; he stood where he was. It took him a couple of seconds to respond. "But . . . I haven't finished."

"We've heard enough."

"But . . ." He was embarrassed at the poor figure he was cutting and angry at the treatment.

"We're looking for a certain quality, Mr. Kord," Mici

172

told him, and she didn't need to add that he didn't have it. "If you don't mind, there are others waiting."

At that he gave a sardonic bow in her direction. Then he walked off the stage and another actor came on.

To the new man and to the others who followed, Mici listened with real courtesy. She complimented each one and tried to make him feel good about the reading without leading him to expect a job that didn't exist.

"How'd it go?" Billy Zip asked when it was all over and the last applicant had been heard.

Mici nodded. "The way we wanted, I think. Thanks for your help."

"Any time."

The purpose of the audition had been to lay the groundwork for a personal interview. She intended to wait a couple of days and then call Kord. He delighted her by calling her first, and he didn't wait. He called that very night.

"I want to apologize for my ineptness this afternoon," he began, charm oozing over the telephone.

Mici was cool. "How did you get my number?"

"There aren't that many Anhalts in the book; fewer females. I called each one till I got you." He waited for some comment, some recognition of his determination, at least. When it was evident there would be none, Janos Kord tried harder. "I'm notoriously bad at sight reading. . . ."

"A great many fine actors are notoriously bad readers, Mr. Kord. I'm aware of that. As I told you at the theatre, we are looking for a certain quality . . ."

"Please, I had the wrong glasses with me. I could hardly see the page. Nothing but confusion could have come through to you. Let me do it again. I could come to your office, or to your home. I could come tonight if you're not busy."

"That would hardly be fair to the others."

173

"Give me a chance, Miss Anhalt. You won't be sorry, I promise you. Look, I'll read one speech, and if you stop me I won't say a word, I won't argue. I'll leave and I won't bother you again."

"Well . . ."

"That's a promise, Miss Anhalt, on my word of honor."

"All right."

"I'll be there in twenty minutes."

She expected Kord to make it ahead of time and arrive effusive and eager to please. Actually, he was five minutes late and didn't apologize. He did hesitate on the threshold when she opened the door, his blue eyes several shades darker than hers looking her over with appreciation. Then with one of his little bows, very respectful this time, he handed her a bunch of sweetheart roses.

"For interrupting your evening."

"I was just going to wash my hair."

"You have beautiful hair." He was moderating his tactics. "Excuse me for staring, Miss Anhalt, but you saw me at the audition; I didn't see you. I didn't expect you to be either so young or so beautiful." He was gauging her emotional climate.

"Did you bring your glasses?" she asked. "The right glasses?"

It didn't discourage him at all. "I don't need glasses to see you."

"You'll need them for the reading. That is why you came, Mr. Kord, isn't it?"

He made her another bow. "And I do appreciate the opportunity, Miss Anhalt."

"Is Kord your real name?" Mici asked abruptly.

"No, Korda," he replied. "I didn't want to appear to be trading on a famous reputation."

"Typically Magyar."

"It takes one to know one."

If he thought that their common ancestry established a bond between them, he was wrong. Mici was wary of

174

Hungarian men, considered them utterly charming and completely selfish and ruthless—with the exceptions of her father and grandfather, of course.

"As you know, we're looking for an unknown to play the lead in our production. It will be low budget and we can't afford an established star. But we feel the material is strong enough to create a new star. However, we still require an actor with a strong theatrical background. You don't have many credits, Mr. Kord."

Instead of defending himself, instead of producing a string of meaningless and even false credits, Janos Kord counterattacked.

"Then why did you audition me?"

Mici smiled. "I saw a print of a commercial you made for Steinberg-Farber. It suggested possibilities. Also, you were recommended by Oscar Brumleve."

"Ah . . ."

"To whom you were in turn recommended by Julia Schuyler. I thought it an interesting sequence."

"Ah, yes, poor Julia. I'll never forget her."

"You were friends?"

"Good friends, yes. We'd worked together."

"What was the show?"

"*Sweet Bird of Youth.*"

A natural, Mici thought. Julia had always had empathy for a Williams heroine and though too young for this particular role she had tasted the disillusion that the part called for and would have projected the age with a minimum of makeup. As for Kord, his talents might just have stretched to the portrayal of the young lover. "When was this?"

"About four years ago. In summer stock."

"She was married to Cassel at the time, wasn't she?"

"Yes. He directed the show."

And outclassed Kord in every way, Mici thought. "What else? What other show did you do with Miss Schuyler?"

"Just that one, just *Sweet Bird*."

"On a tour of the summer theatres?"

"Just that one week."

"Oh? She didn't carry her leading man with her?"

"Not then. It wasn't in her contract. Later . . . she tried to get me for the part, but I wasn't available."

I'll bet: Mici commented silently. "You must have had further contact with Miss Schuyler for her to send you to Oscar Brumleve." Questions which in another situation might have made him suspicious were natural in the guise of a job interview, and he was eager to answer them.

"We ran into each other on the street. She was looking dejected, lost. Turned out she'd been up for an interview. I was surprised; I didn't think a star of her caliber had to submit to that kind of thing."

"If the part is good enough and the star wants it badly enough . . ." Mici shrugged. "Carol Channing wasn't too proud to audition for *Dolly*, and Angela Lansbury for *Mame*. There are plenty of others and most of them are willing to admit it."

Kord nodded. "Julia didn't say so, but I could see that the interview hadn't gone well. We were standing in front of Sardi's so I invited her in for a drink to cheer her up."

Because he saw a chance to latch on to her.

"She had a hell of a lot more than one. It was embarrassing because I didn't have enough on me to pay the tab." Kord's sensuous lips twisted into a self-deprecating smile. "They know me at Sardi's, of course, and took my check."

They knew Julia and took his check because he was with her. Mici had no doubt that Kord made the check good and so established himself in the famous theatrical hangout.

"I took her home." He looked into Mici's eyes indicat-

176

ing that he had something to confide, then lowered his voice. "I was really horrified to see where she was living. It was no better than a tenement."

"Is that so?"

"I was appalled that Cassel would abandon her in a place like that."

Mici said nothing.

"I didn't like to leave her alone . . . in that condition but . . . there was nothing I could do for her."

He must have been frustrated, Mici thought. Obviously he'd misjudged Julia's capacity and had let her get too drunk. Mici assumed he'd learned just how much would get her to exactly what condition, and had been more careful on subsequent occasions.

"I called the next day to find out if she was all right," Kord went on. "She was very vague about everything, including me." Again that self-deprecating smile intended to engage sympathy, which, surprisingly, it did. "I must say I was annoyed. I'd spent a lot of money on the lady and not even to be remembered . . ." He shrugged.

Mici nodded sympathetically. She sensed that he was skirting the edges of the truth and wondered just how close he'd dare to go.

"A couple of weeks later I heard a show was casting and the director used to be a friend of Julia Schuyler's. I thought, what the hell, she owed me at least an introduction to him. So, as I didn't want to make my pitch over the telephone, I went over there. She couldn't have been nicer. Remembered everything, apologized for crying on my shoulder, and invited me to dinner."

"Did she give you the introduction?"

"Oh, sure, no problem. She was eager to help."

"But you didn't get the part."

"Actually, there was nothing in the show for me."

"I see. How about the Cassel show? Did she recommend you for that?"

177

"Well, they had split up so I didn't like to ask."

"And in any case, you knew Alfred Cassel. You could have gone to him on your own."

"Well, there wasn't anything in that for me, either."

"Too bad. Still, it may turn out to be our good fortune. We'll see, eh?" Mici dangled the bait. Then she withdrew it. "You must have been deeply shocked to learn of Miss Schuyler's murder. To lose such a friend, a friend so willing to help . . ."

"Julia was always generous to actors."

"Do you think that Cassel was actually beating her?" Mici asked abruptly.

"Beating her?" He was startled. Perhaps he'd expected her to ask if he thought Cassel had killed her?

"Yes. You must have noticed the bruises. If you were seeing her recently . . . In view of all the recommendations, including the latest to Brumleve, I assumed you'd been seeing her often."

"Yes, we saw each other, but of course I didn't feel I should mention . . ."

"You surely couldn't ignore her condition." Mici pretended to be shocked.

"Well, no, but . . ."

"Surely you offered your help. As a friend."

"I tried, but she was a very private person. She didn't want to talk about it."

"Too bad you didn't try a little harder."

"Don't think I haven't told myself that a thousand times. Don't think it hasn't cost me sleepless nights."

Mici let out a long, slow sigh. "I just can't understand a woman letting herself be mistreated like that."

"Some derive pleasure from it."

"Julia Schuyler?"

He shrugged.

"I'd call it sexual perversion."

Janos Kord smiled. "There's a lot of that around."

She felt that she had brought him as far as she could on

178

this tack. Time to try another. "When was the last time you saw Julia Schuyler alive?"

A mistake. She knew it instantly. Fear leaped into Kord's blue eyes, followed by suspicion. She tried to make amends. "I'm sorry. It's none of my business. I had no right to ask. I'm sure you've told the police everything that's pertinent, and I'm sure they don't want you discussing it with anyone else."

"As a matter of fact . . ."

"No, no, please. Say no more. I was very indiscreet. Let's get back to business. Do you have a picture?"

"Of course." He handed her the standard eight-by-ten glossy, pulling it out of a manila envelope.

"How about your other credits?"

He rattled off a lot of inflated data: off-Broadway, off-off Broadway, independent films, stock, all tough to check—as she'd expected. He talked commercials and TV appearances. Part of the flim-flam. Mici let him go on till he ran down.

"Certainly, Miss Schuyler must have thought highly of your talents." Mici sweetened the disparagement implied with a smile. She reached for one of the pile of manuscripts she'd set out on the coffee table for the occasion.

Very conscious of the script in her hands, Kord murmured shyly, "I hope you'll think so, too."

She met his gaze, let him beam all the sensuality he could at her, then very deliberately turned him off. "That remains to be seen."

Janos Kord wasn't that easy to turn off. He got up, walked over to her, and sat down beside her on the couch, his shoulder lightly brushing her shoulder, his thigh not quite touching hers. "I'm ready any time," he said, reaching as though to place his hand on her knee but taking the manuscript from her lap instead.

"Will you cue me in, Miss Anhalt?"

Mici didn't realize till then that she'd been holding her breath.

14

Mici decided to go and see Bettedene Barber once more. After all, it was the young hooker who had suggested that Julia Schuyler had a lover. And it was she who had set Mici on the trail of Janos Kord. She'd insisted that she'd never seen him, never had so much as a glimpse of him. Mici had no idea why the girl was so determined to deny ever having set eyes on the man she claimed had been beating Julia, and she hadn't pressed the matter then. But now she had to. She hoped that she had built up the teenager's trust in her.

She rang the doorbell of 3A and the voice that called out was the same as before, light and youthful.

"Door's open. Come on in."

Mici was completely unprepared for what she saw.

"Bettedene! My God, what happened to you?"

Her face was a misshapen assortment of bruises. One eye was ringed black and blue and nearly swollen shut. Both lips were cut. Her jaw was lopsided. Yet Bettedene

Barber sat at her kitchen window calmly sewing a white organdy ruffle to the edge of a baby-blue quilted bedspread.

"Are you all right?" Dumb question, Mici thought. "I mean, nothing's broken? Have you seen a doctor?"

"I'm okay. I don't need a doctor."

Mici wanted to go to her and put an arm around the scrawny shoulders and cry. But something in the girl's manner held her off.

"What happened?"

"He found out. Dominic. My pimp. I guess he was bound to find out sooner or later."

Heretofore she'd referred to him as "my old man." Mici found this dropping of pretense as sad as Bettedene's mauled face.

"I knew he'd beat me if he ever found out, but I didn't figure he'd mark me where it would show. But I should have figured that in a case like this that would be exactly what he would do."

"I don't understand. What did Dominic find out?"

"About my boyfriend. I got me a real boyfriend. He wants to marry me. I've been seeing him up here on my own time, except I don't have any time that's my own," Bettedene qualified.

"But that's wonderful!"

"Not so wonderful. He won't want me now. Allan, that's my friend, he's real straight, got a regular job, lives in Queens. When he sees me like this—he'll know what I am."

"He doesn't know?"

"We never talked about it, but I suppose he had a pretty good idea. Thing is, he could pretend he didn't know. Now . . ." She shrugged.

"He might surprise you," Mici told her. "He might be ready to face the situation and just be waiting for you to let him."

Bettedene shook her head. "It's too late. I've broken it

off. I called him and told him not to come around, that I don't want to see him any more." She continued to sew the pristine white ruffle to the blue quilt.

"You're prejudging him," Mici persisted. "If he cares for you, really cares, Allan won't abandon you. He'll protect you. Why don't you give him a chance?"

Now Bettedene stopped sewing and the tears rolled down her thin, battered face. "Dom said that the next time . . . the next time he'd do a job a plastic surgeon couldn't fix." She burst into sobs.

"Oh, my dear . . ." Mici went to her. She put her arms around the heaving shoulders and felt the sharp bones underneath and stood awhile just holding the trembling girl. When she seemed calm again, Mici made a suggestion. "You could go to the police."

"Are you crazy?" Bettedene shook free. "Dom would kill me."

Mici saw real terror in the young girl's eyes. "There's a shelter just five blocks from here for girls . . ."

"That's the first place Dom would look."

"Let him look. What can he do?"

"Nothing while I'm in there, but I can't stay in there forever and when I come out . . . Forget it, Mici. Forget it. You mean well. You're a real fine lady, but you just don't understand." She picked up her sewing. "What did you want? Why did you come?" As Mici hesitated, Bettedene did the reassuring. "Listen, don't worry about it. It's all part of the game."

"You could go back home. Bettedene, why can't you just go back home?"

"You came about the murder, right? I guess you don't think that Mr. Cassel did it."

Mici sighed. "No, I don't."

"Neither do I. I never thought they'd arrest him. If I'd spoken up, maybe they wouldn't have. I'm real sorry."

This was what she had come for, yet now that the girl

182

was apparently willing, Mici balked. "If it's going to make trouble for you, Bettedene . . ."

"Cat's out of the bag now," she shrugged. "I had Allan here the Friday night and I didn't want Dom to know. Well, now he knows. So anyhow, Allan was here till about one-thirty. When he was ready to leave I went out on the landing to make sure the coast was clear, to make sure Dom didn't have anybody lurking in the halls. Dom sends people to check up, make sure we're not holding out . . . like that. Well, just as I was about to give Allan the high sign, I heard Miss Schuyler's door open and this man just kind of . . . sidled out."

"Could you describe him?"

"I didn't pay any particular attention. As long as it wasn't anybody from Dom, I didn't care. You know?"

Mici groaned. "Try, Bettedene. Please, try."

"Well . . ." She scowled in concentration. "He was blond and tall."

"Did you see his face? Did he happen to look up?"

"Yeah, he did, for a second. I guess he was as anxious to make sure nobody was around as I was."

"Well?"

"He was good-looking. Real good-looking."

Mici stifled her impatience. "You already said he was tall. How about his build? Light? Heavy?"

"I'd say just right. I'm sorry. I really had other things on my mind."

"Sure." Mici refused to give up. "Had you ever seen him coming out of Miss Schuyler's apartment before?" Bettedene shook her head. So, Mici thought, she'd have to try for a direct identification. She took out the eight-by-ten glossy Janos Kord had given her and held it out. "Could this be the man?"

The girl took her time. "Real handsome, isn't he?"

"Is he the man you saw the night of the murder?"

"Could be. Yeah, I guess so."

"Are you sure?"

Bettedene's tongue licked her cut lips. "I guess so."

Not very satisfactory, Mici thought. "Did you hear any sounds from inside the apartment while the door was open? Did Julia call out to say good-bye, anything like that?"

"You're trying to find out if she was still alive when he left? Gee, I didn't hear a thing. Like I told you . . ."

"I know, I know. Let's go back to the man for a minute. Let's try to reconstruct his appearance. How was he dressed?"

The only thing that moved in Bettedene's poor, smashed face were her eyes blinking open and shut while she tried to recall, open and shut like a sleeping doll mauled by a bad-tempered child. "A suit, I suppose," she shrugged. "Nothing flashy or flaky, anyway. Nothing that caught my attention."

"How about a raincoat? It had been raining all night."

"I don't recollect a raincoat. I didn't take notice. I had other things on my mind."

"Well, was he carrying an umbrella? Was he carrying anything? A package of any kind," Mici urged. "A newspaper?"

Slowly the girl shook her head. "I don't think so. I just don't see him with anything in his hands."

It would have to do. Mici took the photograph back. It had not been the proper—certainly not the legal—way to get identification. She should have had a number of photographs and offered them all so that the witness could make a selection. She hadn't had them handy. Anyhow, it didn't matter, it would take a lot more than placing him at the scene to nail Janos Kord for murder. Assuming he were brought to trial and Bettedene agreed to testify, she was less than a reputable witness.

"I don't know if he killed her." Bettedene indicated the shoulder bag in which Mici had stowed Kord's picture.

184

"But he was her lover. Take my word. And he was the one beating up on her. I'll lay you any odds you want."

Mici agreed, but as Bettedene had seen the actor only once, even that couldn't be proved. "I appreciate your trying to help. I wish that . . ." Suddenly she had an idea. "Why don't you come and stay with me for a while?"

The girl was startled. Her face lit up; she even managed a shy, lopsided smile though it must have hurt. "You wouldn't want me."

"Yes, I would. Really. What do you say?"

"That's nice but . . ." She thought a while, then reluctantly shook her head. "It wouldn't work. Not after the first couple of days."

Mici had spoken impulsively and now, already, was beginning to regret it. What Bettedene said was true. She was used to living alone, suiting herself, maintaining her own schedule. A roommate would inevitably disrupt that.

"And where would I go afterwards?" Bettedene asked quietly.

Mici flushed, shamed that she couldn't press the invitation. "Why don't you call Allan? Why don't you give him a chance?"

"You are dumb!" Suddenly the girl screeched; suddenly she lost control. "You are so, so dumb! Don't you get it? So far Dom doesn't know who the man is. He doesn't know Allan's name. I don't want him ever to find out. If Allan sees me like this, he'll go looking for Dom and he's no match for him. He'll get beat up like me—maybe worse."

"I'm sorry." Mici laid her hand over Bettedene's. "I didn't think. I'm sorry."

Bettedene shook if off. "Don't be sorry. Just try to wise up a little."

Mici bit her lip. "You could get out of town, you and Allan together."

"I just told you . . ."

"Yes, all right. Just you then. Alone. I'll lend you money."

"What happens when it runs out?"

"You get a job."

"Yeah. I don't know how to do anything."

"Sure, you do. There are all kinds of jobs for which you could qualify. There's waitress work and sales work and . . ."

"Domestic work." The cut lips curled with disdain.

"Just to start, Bettedene."

"I could have had that kind of work back home. I didn't want it then; I don't want it now. You're wasting your time trying to save me. I don't want to be saved. Bug off, Miss Anhalt, will you?" The girl picked up her sewing. "Just bug off."

Mici dragged along Forty-fifth Street. The heat was just about unsupportable, but that was not what depleted her energies and made her feel so dejected. It seemed that there was no way to prove Janos Kord's involvement with Julia Schuyler, much less pin the murder on him. Assuming Bettedene Barber's shaky identification stood up, which was highly unlikely, it still placed Kord at the scene over two hours after the presumed time of death.

So what was she going to do about Janos Kord? The answer was—nothing. In time he'd get tired of waiting to hear from her about the nonexistent play and call. Then she'd simply tell him the production was off. It had run into snags and was indefinitely postponed. He'd heard that song before; why should he question it? In due course, Cassel would come to trial and she'd be called as a prosecution witness. The DA would dub her "hostile," which would actually serve to give added importance to her reluctant account of Julia's charge that Cassel was the one who was beating her. Brumleve or, if his health did not permit, whoever he engaged to handle the defense

186

would point out the fallacy, but nevertheless the jury would regard that as an accusation from the grave. The defense would argue hearsay and whatever else, but Cassel would be convicted and it would be largely due to her evidence.

Reaching the subway entrance, Mici went underground. It was even hotter. Sweat ran in rivulets all over her body, but at least she was out of the sun. She put a token into the slot and proceeded down the stairs to the uptown platform. Gusts of hot air caused by arriving and departing trains were like gusts from a giant fan.

Well, she thought, maybe Alfred was guilty after all. Maybe Julia hadn't lied. Maybe Janos Kord's relationship with Julia had been platonic.

Not in this world! Mici formed the words silently with her lips. As her train rattled and roared out of the tunnel and pulled up along the platform, she shouted out loud: "Not in this world!"

Nobody heard; nobody even noticed she was yelling.

A kid with a scraggy beard beat her to the only seat. Mici hung onto the strap above his head and thought about Kord sitting beside her on the sofa, script in hand, reading the lines on the page but investing them with a meaning that was wholly personal and directed at her. The man was incapable of any kind of relationship with a woman that didn't involve sex, particularly if that woman might be of use to him. Mici had no doubt that he had been Julia's lover and that he had beaten her and, worse, had been supplying her with liquor. He wouldn't have cared that she was an alcoholic; all Kord would have cared about was what he could get out of her. He hadn't needed to put a knife in her, Mici thought; supplying the booze was another form of murder.

Alfred Cassel said that he had left Julia alive around eleven-twenty and that she had been drinking beer. Kord had come in afterwards, bringing the scotch. Probably he had been trying to wheedle something out of her, more money, another introduction, whatever. She had refused; he had beaten her. This time she had resisted. He had stabbed her.

So what had he done with the knife?

In trying to recreate the moment, to put herself into Kord's skin and react as he might have reacted, Mici was only vaguely aware of her surroundings. She got off at her stop by pure habit and climbed the stairs to the street. She didn't feel the renewed assault of the blazing sun or the windblown grit that stung her eyes.

Okay, she thought, Julia's lying at his feet. He has the knife in his hand and he realizes it has his fingerprints on it. He could wash it and put it back in a drawer. That would take too long; he's too nervous; he wants to get out. Okay. So he takes the knife with him, intending to get rid of it at the first opportunity. Does he just walk out with it in his hand? Hardly. He has to put it in something—a newspaper or a brown bag, if he can find a newspaper or a brown bag.

Mici scowled. Bettedene had said he wasn't carrying anything. She had seemed certain. It was the only thing she'd been certain about.

So, he puts the knife in his pocket: Mici continued her reconstruction. Raincoat pockets would be deep enough to hide even a large carving knife. Assuming that there'd been even one drop of blood left on that knife, there should be traces in the pocket.

A prickling of goose bumps brought Mici back to reality. She had been strolling; now she hurried. She couldn't wait to get home and call Donald. She hoped he wouldn't make a production out of the search, but of course he would. Donald Swell wouldn't do one blessed thing without being sure he was covered in all directions. He wouldn't enter Kord's place without a warrant, and Mici knew that no judge was likely to grant one on the evidence. What evidence?

The evidence she intended to find.

188

So instead of calling the detective when she got home, Mici called Kord's number. It was answered by a recorded announcement informing her that the actor wasn't at home and wouldn't return till eight. Very helpful. The next problem was to gain access. She could present her credentials to the super or claim she was a friend or even a relative from out of town—a cousin. She had a feeling the super might have heard the cousin bit before and decided to try it. She considered carrying a small suitcase to reinforce it but decided it wouldn't be necessary. She was right. All the super needed was one leering, longing look, and then he let her into the apartment.

It wasn't much of a place. Evidently Kord didn't require luxurious surroundings for his conquests, or more likely, his rendezvous took place at the lady's pad. Mici couldn't have cared less. All she was interested in was his clothes closet and that was something else! The man had the best of everything: fine suits stored in individual bags, fine shoes polished and in wooden shoe trees. There were no overcoats—probably stored for the summer—but the raincoat was there. Mici brought it out, hanger and all, and laid it on the bed. She put a hand inside the right pocket. Deep, very deep. She turned it inside out. She peered at it. Nothing that looked like blood, no stain of any kind. Okay, the left. She turned that out. Nothing. No spots, no dust, no lint. God! Had he already sent it out to be cleaned?

It didn't look like it, but how could one be sure? Maybe he had another raincoat? She went back to the closet. No. Maybe he hadn't put the knife in the pocket. Maybe he'd held it inside against his chest. Or stuck it up one sleeve? Quickly, she took the coat off the hanger, turned it inside out, including the sleeves, and went over every inch of the lining.

"Hi, cousin."

She jumped, but before she could turn he had his arms around her waist, hugging her close, head buried in her hair and nuzzling her neck. She was too busy thinking of what she would say to do more than squirm a little; then it occurred to her that squirming was not the optimum reaction. She should cooperate; encouragement gained time.

Finally, of course, he was not content with mere nuzzling. He raised his head and turned her around so that they were face to face.

"Why, Miss Anhalt!" he exclaimed in mock dismay. "The super told me my cousin was here."

"I happened to be passing and I decided, on impulse, to stop by."

"Of course, of course. My dear Miss Anhalt, how charming."

He was smirking at her, smugly licking his chops over the conquest just achieved and the one yet to come. Wondering perhaps how much of the preliminaries she would require, he glanced down at the bed and saw the coat spread out.

Too late Mici realized she should have tried to lead him to the other room. Too late.

"What've you got—some kind of raincoat fetish?"

190

15

Before Mici could answer, and she wasn't very quick because she didn't have an answer ready, Janos Kord noticed that the coat was turned inside out.

"What the hell is going on?"

She still couldn't come up with anything plausible. "Why don't we go into the living room?"

She made a move. He blocked her. "No, you don't. We'll stay right here till you explain, cousin." Taking a look around, Kord now noticed the door of his closet was open. "Why were you going through my things? What are you looking for? What the hell do you want?"

Mici sighed. At least he knew that she hadn't come to jump into bed with him, she thought. "Let's just say I didn't find it and let it go at that."

Once more she tried to get past him and again he stopped her, this time by grasping her right wrist. He pulled her to him in a movement that could have been passionate but had so much force that the pain brought tears to Mici's eyes. His face was near, so near that it filled the entire range of her vision, a close-up on a giant screen into which she felt herself being absorbed.

He shook her. "I want to know what's going on. I don't want to hurt you, cousin." He was still grasping her by the wrist, but now he raised his other hand, and it was all Mici could do to keep from shrinking in anticipation of the blow. Instead of striking, he laid the hand on her cheek, caressing her, and laughed because he knew what she'd expected. "I don't want to hurt you," he repeated, breathing faster. "I would prefer to make love to you. Much prefer it."

She understood that the two would go together, that he was both threatening her with the pain and promising her its pleasure. Janos was arousing himself. And Mici, who up to now had not doubted her control of the situation, shivered and was dismayed to find herself responding.

No, she told herself, no. She felt the warming in her loins. No! Yet she made no move to pull away, staring instead into Kord's deep blue eyes, losing herself in them. She felt her whole being melt, dissolve into his, and she wanted him . . . wanted him. . . . He bent her arm back till she moaned but still did not resist. It was pain and delight as he put his leg between her legs and pushed her back towards the bed. She felt degraded and exalted. She marveled at her own sensations and, in that last sane moment of disbelief of what was happening, she rebelled.

"No!"

With a sudden movement that took Kord off guard because he had thought her compliant, she wrenched her arm out of his grasp and, wriggling free, ran to the far side of the room.

"I'm not Julia Schuyler!"

He gaped at her. Thwarted when he thought that he had conquered, Kord's eyes narrowed. "What's that supposed to mean?"

192

Mici Anhalt was a strong, healthy, young woman, her body fit and agile and kept so by her regular ballet classes. Janos Kord was not much taller or heavier than she, but in a test of strength she knew that she could not match him. She might fight, kick, bite, and scream, but in the end he would prevail. What she was afraid of, still afraid of, was that in the struggle she might let him win. Gritting her teeth, she bit back the last vestiges of the sweet sickness she had briefly tasted, swallowing it like bile. She understood Julia better now. She pitied her, not as someone superior but as a sister.

"What about Julia?" Kord demanded.

She had to get out of there and fast, and the only way was to hit him with the truth.

"Will you let me get my handbag?" She pointed to it on the bed.

With a mock smile of deference, raising his hands as though he were at the point of a gun, Kord took a step back. Quickly Mici got the bag and pulled out her wallet to show him her ID.

"Crime Victims Compensation Board," he read. "You're not a producer?"

"No."

"There's no show? The audition, the theatre, the other actors . . ."

"A setup."

That was all Janos Kord cared about. He turned pale, stared at her transfixed. After moments that seemed to her interminable, his color began to return. She was almost relieved. His lips barely parted to release a slow hiss of air. His tongue darted out and in. He hissed again.

"You bitch," he murmured. "You lying, cheating bitch." He took one step toward her and before she knew what was happening raised his hand and slapped her.

The blow was full force and sent her reeling across the room and against the wall. There was no pleasure in this, none at all and thank God, Mici thought, looking around for something with which to fight back. There was nothing. She'd have to talk her way out.

"Don't you want to know why I went to so much trouble?"

"Oh, yes. And you're going to tell me. Make no mistake."

"I'm not alone in this, you know."

"At the moment you are. All alone with me."

"Oscar Brumleve set it up. It was his idea. He knows that you were Julia's lover and that she was giving you money. He'll show that you had as much motive for killing her as Cassel."

"If she was giving me money, why would I kill her?"

"Passion. You quarreled. You lost control. You don't have very much control, do you, Janos?"

He glared, then laughed. "And you have too much, cousin. A pity. It's all academic, in any case. Cassel was there on that night. I wasn't."

"Oh yes, you were . . . cousin," Mici mimicked. "You were seen leaving Julia's apartment well after Cassel was back at his party and among his friends. Don't bother to deny it. There's a witness."

He stared at her as though he thought that if he looked hard enough he'd be able to tell whether she was bluffing or not. "You can call on all the angels in heaven or devils in hell as witnesses, but I did not kill Julia. She was alive when I left."

"You were the one beating her, not Cassel."

He shrugged.

"Why?"

"She liked it. It turned her on. You understand that, don't you?"

Mici flushed.

"Julia wanted to be dominated. Most women do. In Julia's case, the need was extra strong because of her father. Her father ignored her through her childhood and afterwards. What she was looking for was a father figure

194

and lover combined. For a while Cassel seemed to fill the bill. He was older; he had a touch of John Malcolm's style and talent, but then he walked out on her. Subconsciously, she believed that there was something wrong with her that both the men she'd loved had rejected her. She turned to me. I was her punishment. She needed me."

"And why did you need her?"

"She was royalty, theatrical royalty, and I owned her. I could make her do anything I wanted. Not at first, oh, no. The first time I struck her she threw me out. I had asked her to give me a recommendation to a director friend of hers and she refused. She didn't think I was good enough. In fact, she told me I had no talent, that I was a lousy actor. She laughed. That was when I hit her. I didn't mean to. Actually, I was shocked at having done it. I thought we were finished; I never expected to see her again. I didn't even make any attempt to see her or call her. . . ." He trailed off into silence for a few moments. Then he resumed. "*She* called *me* the very next day, said she'd set up the appointment I wanted for three that afternoon. She said it wasn't up to her to make a judgment on whether I was right for the part when she didn't know what the part was. That was up to the director. She suggested I stop over afterwards and let her know how I'd made out. I arrived with roses and a bottle. We drank, we made love, we argued—I don't remember about what, but she seemed to be trying to provoke me. I held my temper as long as I could; then it came to me that she needed an emotional catharsis and that she actually wanted me to strike her again."

And you obliged, Mici thought, and the pattern of the relationship was set. "What triggered it Friday night? Did you beat her out of habit or did you have a reason? An excuse, at least?"

"I hadn't even planned to see Julia on Friday night. I had another appointment, a business dinner. She called me at the restaurant."

195

"I take it the business was with a lady."

"The producer of the commercial you saw, or said you saw. A genuine producer," he taunted. "The phone was brought to the table and Julia's voice squawked across half the room. It was embarrassing. I took the lady home, but . . . the mood had been broken. The evening was spoiled. So I went to see Julia."

"To punish her," Mici concluded. "Only this time she wasn't in the mood for physical violence. She defended herself. She had a knife. You wrested it from her. There was a struggle and you killed her." She was offering him an out—self-defense.

He ignored it. "No, it wasn't like that. She knew that I'd be coming, that I'd be furious, and she was looking forward to the scene. In fact, she'd set the stage for it. I walked in to find her sitting at the kitchen table scribbling on her dumb book and gnawing on a chicken leg. She had a smug smile on her face because she knew she'd ruined my evening. I knocked the chicken leg right out of her hand but not the smile off her face. Her adrenalin was flowing. She taunted me and screeched at me. The more I slapped her around, the bigger her high. I didn't know what to do to get through to her, to really hurt her. I wanted to make her feel pain. Finally, some instinct made me snatch at those pages she'd been working on, but she sensed what I was about and grabbed them first. We struggled; we fought over those dumb pages. She screamed she'd found a publisher, that they'd taken an option on the book. Well, of course, I didn't believe it. 'Who the hell would pay money for the story of a has-been?' I yelled back. We pulled some more and inevitably the paper tore and we were left standing there with the shreds in our hands and looking at each other. 'The book is about my father, not me,' she said and started to cry. I mean, she cried . . ." He paused as though analyzing it for himself. "She cried like a heartbroken child, gave her-

196

self up to complete despair. I couldn't figure it. I mean, what the hell, it was only a few pages."

"Then what?" Mici asked.

He shrugged. "Then we went to bed."

Mici sighed. "What time did you leave?"

Kord started to answer, then caught himself. "If you have a witness, you already know."

She had to give him that. "Let me ask you this. If you were so angry at Julia, why did you bring the scotch?"

"What scotch? We couldn't afford that kind of booze. And I didn't bring anything that night."

"Are you sure?"

"Yes, I'm sure. Now you owe me some answers. Why do you care? What are you getting out of all this?"

"I'm working for Oscar Brumleve. I've been temporarily laid off my regular job and I need the money."

She was talking his language. "What did you expect to find here? Why were you going through my clothes?"

"I thought there might be bloodstains."

"On my raincoat? I wasn't wearing it. It wasn't raining."

"Yes, it was."

"It hadn't started when I picked up my date at five-thirty, and it had stopped when I went over to Julia's."

It was true the rain hadn't started till about six. As to when it had stopped, she'd been in Connecticut, but she'd check with the weather bureau. "She could have marked you during your fight."

"How?"

"Scratched you or cut you or bitten you."

"Would you like me to take my clothes off?"

"If you don't mind."

He smirked in surprise; then with deliberate slowness, watching her all the while, he complied. Janos Kord was proud of his body and he had a right to be. He was lean, well muscled, with good skin tone.

And there wasn't a mark on him.

What Mici had been looking for was not so much Julia Schuyler's marks on Janos Kord but her own.

He was clean. There was no sign of a wound between his shoulder blades. He was not the man who had attacked her after her date with Donald Swell.

As for the actor, if he'd expected Mici to succumb at the sight of him naked, he was disappointed. It was his back she'd wanted to see and, having made sure that the scars of her scissors were not on him, Mici quickly slipped out the door. Kord let her go. His moment had passed; further pursuit was useless.

Out in the street Mici hailed a cab; she was in no shape to ride the subway. Not till she was home with the apartment door safely shut behind her did the tension snap. Then suddenly her knees wobbled, hot and cold flashes alternated, and she shook all over. A shower and then a cold beer would set her right. But before any of that, before she would even kick off her shoes, she had to call Oscar Brumleve and tell him the good news. Janos Kord had admitted being with Julia well after Cassel was supposed to have murdered her. Cassel was in the clear.

Again she awoke in the dark to the ringing of the telephone. She remembered having a couple of beers and lying down, fully dressed, for a short rest before fixing dinner. She must have fallen asleep. The phone on her bedside table clamored insistently. She fumbled for the receiver.

"Hello?" she murmured in a sleep-hoarse voice.

"You took your time. Did you just walk in?"

"Donald? Is that you, Donald?"

"I want to talk to you. Don't go to bed. I'm coming right over."

The numbers of the digital clock glowed in the dark: 12:51. "Why? What's up? Donald? Donald . . ." He'd

198

hung up. Mici started to laugh. *Don't go to bed.* Kord wouldn't have said that. She turned on the light.

Swell made good time getting there. "What the hell do you think you're doing?" was his greeting as he swept through the door and past her into the living room.

She was too tired to do anything but laugh weakly.

"It's not funny," Swell glared.

"Okay." She shrugged. "I made coffee and sandwiches for us, but I guess you're not interested."

"Well . . . I didn't have any dinner."

"Neither did I. Come on."

She led the way into the kitchen where she sat him at the table while she set out the food and poured the coffee.

"I'm really very disappointed in you, kid." Swell adopted an aggrieved tone. "I trusted you and you let me down. I thought we had a deal."

"What deal? I don't know what you're talking about."

"Come on, babe." He threw both arms out in a dramatic gesture of frustration. "I'm talking about all this investigating you've been doing. Oh, it was okay about the kid hooker; I'd already covered her. But this actor . . . this Kord . . ."

"Wait a minute. Just hold the line. I told you about him and you weren't interested."

"I said I didn't have the time."

"Okay, you didn't have the time. You told me I could go ahead and talk to him. You told me I was a private citizen and I could go anywhere, talk to anybody, ask any questions I wanted. It was my civil right. You as good as urged me to conduct my own investigation."

"Okay, yes, that's right, but . . ."

"You didn't expect me to come up with anything."

"If you did, I expected you to come to me with it."

"Why should I? I'm not working for you."

"Are you working for Brumleve?"

"Of course not, but considering the evidence I turned

up to clear his client I could hardly not tell him, could I?"

"You should have told me first."

"So you could get the credit?"

"To hell with the credit. Don't you understand? You've made the whole squad look like shit. I mean, we had to release Cassel. We've got nothing on Kord. We're left holding the bag and it's empty."

"Sorry about that."

"I thought we were friends."

"So did I." Mici stared at him, her blue eyes growing lighter. "I was wrong."

"No, you weren't."

"You're using me. Or trying to."

"No!" Though his denial was instantaneous, his high color belied it. "I told you the case was officially closed. I told you that anything further that I did would have to be on my own time and that I didn't have any time."

"You told me to go ahead on my own."

"I said I couldn't stop you."

"You wanted me to do your legwork for you."

"No."

"Yes. Oh, yes. You were so understanding all along the line. You didn't mind my horning in on your territory. Secure; you said you were secure. You figured that I was your private pipeline to Julia Schuyler and Alfred Cassel and all their crowd. You figured that if I did come up with any kind of information and passed it on to you, you'd break the case." Mici shook her head dolefully. "Oh, Donald."

"I'm sorry, kid. Things haven't been breaking for me in the last few years. I figured this was a chance to make a big bust."

"I should have known that no pro lets an amateur mess around without a reason. You have a nice line, Donald. I really went for it."

"Ah, now, listen, it wasn't all a line. I like you. I really do. You're a real fine lady."

200

Mici blinked. "Gee, thanks." She smiled ruefully. "You know what? I don't blame you. I just wish you'd told me. If you'd told me straight out what you were after, I would have cooperated."

"You would?"

"Sure. All I'm after is for the real killer to be caught."

The detective's eyes lit up; he sagged with relief. "You're all right, kid. You're all right." He reached for her hand. "So where do we go from here?"

"You don't expect me to go on doing your legwork?"

"Don't put it like that."

"You've got some nerve."

"You've done great work. You're a born investigator."

"Just a minute. Hey, hold it. I had a lead. I followed it to its logical end. Kord is clean. He was Julia's lover, all right. He did beat her. He did visit her the night of the murder and they had intercourse. But he didn't kill her. She was alive when he left."

"You believe that?"

"He could as easily have said she was already dead when he got there. That way nothing would have changed. Cassel would still be in jail, and the police wouldn't be *forced* to look for a new suspect."

"So he's not so smart. He didn't think of it."

"When Kord arrived, she was working on her book and eating a chicken leg. As far as I know, neither of those facts were mentioned in any of the stories about her death. All you have to do is check the autopsy report and find out what the stomach contents . . ."

Swell took a breath. "Chicken. She died maybe an hour after eating chicken."

"That puts the time of death at about two-thirty or three Saturday morning."

"How do you get that?"

"Bettedene Barber saw Kord leaving Julia's place at about one-thirty."

"He could have come back."

"What for? They had a fight; they made it up; that was it for the night. The big question now is what happened to the manuscript."

"What manuscript?"

Mici waggled a finger at him. "Exactly. What manuscript? You didn't find anything that looked like a book manuscript when you searched the place, did you?"

"No."

"But Julia was working on a book about her father. Kord says she'd actually found a publisher."

"Kord again."

"Not just him, Billy Zip, too. He was helping her, transcribing her notes and so on. Check it out with him. The point is that Julia was working on the book when Kord visited her Friday night. They had a fight, and the pages got torn up. He didn't take them. By the time the body was found, they were gone. What happened to them? What happened to the rest of the manuscript?"

"If you ask me it's all part of Kord's alibi. Julia could have eaten the chicken a lot earlier. He saw the leftovers and said that she was eating when he came. Then he threw in the bit about the book just to add to the confusion."

"Kord is out." Mici was emphatic. "You remember the night you took me to dinner out on the island? When you brought me home there was someone in here, waiting."

"How do you mean—waiting?"

"He stayed hidden till I got into bed and put out the light. Then he tried to rape me."

"God! Why didn't you tell me?"

"Nothing happened. I had a small pair of nail scissors handy. I used them."

"All right!" Swell regarded her with admiration. "All right!" he repeated. "Just the same, you should have called me."

"I reported it to the precinct. It was dark and he was wearing a ski mask, so I couldn't give them more than an

202

impression of height and bulk. It never would have occurred to me that there was any connection with Julia's
murder . . ."

"What connection?"

"When I got back I found a note in my mailbox. It had
been hand-delivered. It warned me to lay off."

Swell pushed his chair back and crossed his legs. "You
marked him up pretty good with those scissors?"

"I did."

"How sure are you that Kord isn't scarred?"

"Positive."

Swell didn't ask how she knew.

"If I'd used my head, I would have known right away
that Kord couldn't be the killer." Swell's eyebrows shot
up. "At the time of the attack we didn't even know each
other."

"Correction. You didn't know him." Swell frowned.
"Of course, you weren't that active on the Schuyler case
at the time. What did the note actually say?"

"It said: Mind your own business."

"I think you better look closer to home."

Mici nodded. She was already doing just that.

"And if you get any ideas, you let me know. Don't try
to go after this guy on your own," Swell admonished.
"Let me take care of it. Promise?"

"Sure."

"I mean it, babe. I owe you."

"No, you don't. Forget it."

"Listen, I want to get this guy for you. I want to do it.
So you just let me know anything that occurs to you."

"That's nice and I appreciate it, Donald. I really do."

"That's my girl. Now about Kord, if he's telling the
truth and Julia really did have a publisher, why hasn't the
publisher been cashing in on the publicity?"

"That shouldn't be hard to find out."

Swell grinned. "That's the spirit."

"Me?" Mici gasped. She poked a finger into her own

breast. "You expect me to canvass the publishers? No way."

"Ah, doll, I thought you felt a responsibility to your friend."

"I've discharged that responsibility. Julia did not die because I left her door on the latch. Alfred Cassel is not standing trial because I reported Julia's accusation against him. This real fine lady is out of it."

"But . . ."

"You do it, Detective Swell. Do it yourself. It's your job, not mine."

"Ah, babe . . ." He took her hand; he looked into her eyes.

"Save it. Save it for your girlfriend. Oh, that's right, you told me you have no regular girlfriend. You never did tell me why."

He let go her hand. He swallowed a couple of times. He looked away. "Ah . . ." He cleared his throat. "My wife won't let me."

"You're married?" Mici smiled weakly. "Oh, boy. Oh, Donald. You sure did a number on me. You sure did."

16

Could it have been Karl Spychalski who had tried to rape her?

As she walked down the street of identical, two-family row houses just east of the burned-out property, Mici An-halt worried the question as she had been doing since it first occurred to her. Was it Spychalski who had waited in the darkness of her apartment till she came home, till she got into bed, then hurled himself on her? She could feel again the weight of the stranger's body, his groping hand, his fetid breath mingling with hers, and she shuddered, her skin prickling with revulsion. She had been working on two cases at the time—the ironworker's and Clay Marin's. Contrary to general opinion, the blind do not find it easier than the sighted to maneuver in the dark. They can only find their way in familiar surroundings, having studied and memorized the topography and the obstacles. Clay Marin had never been in Mici's apartment; he would have stumbled, knocked over furniture, and announced his presence long before he ever made it to the bedroom door. It had to be Spychalski.

Having reached the last house on the block, Mici climbed to the second-floor porch entrance and rang the bell marked Havelka. The Spychalskis were staying with Rose's aunt and uncle.

Spychalski himself came to the door. He had aged years in the few days since Mici had last seen him. His craggy face was eroded by grief; his cheeks were sunken; the skin hung loose around his jowls; his eyebrows had turned white. Worst of all, his strong, broad shoulders were stooped in defeat. Mici had never expected this man to give up.

Spychalski did not hide his displeasure at her visit and he would have liked to have kept her from entering, but Mici swept past him before he had a chance to collect himself and deny her admittance. He shut the door and followed her inside but stayed close, ready to let her out as soon as possible.

"I don't know why you're here, Miss Anhalt. My claim has been disallowed. I told you that I am not interested in pursuing the matter."

Even his voice was apathetic.

The voice of her assailant that night, though muffled by the ski mask, had been laced with lust and hate. Mici tried to put the man in front of her now into the mental image of the shadowy figure. There was, of course, only one way she could be sure.

She replied formally, "You need not accept the local board's finding as final, Mr. Spychalski. You have the right to appeal. In which case, your claim will be reviewed by the full board of governors."

A low gurgle turned Mici's attention to the corner of the room where a woman sat beside the window in the only comfortable chair. Rose Spychalski, turning the pages of what appeared to be an old family album, was

206

completely oblivious of Mici Anhalt's presence. Her face was a patchwork of skin grafts of varying shades of lividity. Bandages covered her arms and legs and probably swathed a good portion of her body. She should have remained at the burn center, but Spychalski had insisted on bringing her home and on her further treatment as an outpatient. She gurgled again, and it was hard to tell whether she was expressing mirth or sorrow. Physically, Rose Spychalski appeared to be healing, but mentally she was close to being in a stupor.

Putting her suspicions of the man aside for the moment, Mici concerned herself with the stricken woman. "I'm sure that if you appeal to the full board the decision will be reversed," she told Spychalski. "I'll do everything in my power to help."

"We don't want charity."

"Mr. Spychalski, I believe that your claim is valid and that you should pursue it. Besides, if the negative decision of the local office is reversed by the full board, that in itself will be a strong presumption of innocence. The insurance company might well decide on that basis to pay your claim."

For a moment the hard eyes glinted with hope. Then it was gone. "No."

"But why?" Mici pleaded. "You don't have to do anything. I'll do it all."

"No."

How could he turn it down? Mici was at a loss. Everything had gone wrong for this man in the past couple of years, starting with the loss of his job and culminating in the fire that had destroyed his home, killed his daughters, and apparently—Mici gazed at Rose Spychalski nodding placidly over the pages of the album—destroyed the sanity of his wife. Yet he was still physically strong and mentally tough. He'd have to be for what lay ahead, she thought. She took a slower, more comprehensive look

207

around the cramped living room with its cut-velvet "suite," fringed lamps under plastic covers, porcelain figurines protected by glass domes, and the inevitable battery of faded photographs on the mantel. The Spychalskis were sharing the upper half of the two-family house. Out of regard for Rose's condition, Mici had no doubt that they had been given the master bedroom while the Havelkas made do in what were certainly smaller, cramped quarters.

"You have to be realistic," she told Spychalski. "You'll have to move out to a place of your own soon, and your wife will require medical treatment for a very long time. Psychiatric treatment, too."

"I've got a job."

"Oh? I'm very happy to hear it, but . . . construction jobs don't last forever, as we both know. If the decision on your claim is reversed, at least your wife's medical expenses will be taken care of for as long as necessary."

"There'll be other jobs."

Mici just looked at him.

"If a man is willing, he can find work."

He knew, he must know, what she was after, and still he refused to offer an alibi. Mici thought she understood why he wouldn't tell his whereabouts at the time of the fire. He'd been with another woman. Whether it had been a one-time thing or an ongoing relationship, she thought the ironworker was afraid that the shock would finally destroy his wife. Mici had come to promise him confidentiality, but she could hardly do that in Rose Spychalski's presence. Though she didn't think that Rose was aware of anything going on around her, she had no right to take the risk.

"I have some papers here that I would like to go over with you. Is there some place we could . . ." Her eyes pleaded for a few moments alone.

"I am not interested, Miss Anhalt. I told you before, and I haven't changed my mind and I never will."

208

It couldn't be plainer. She got up. "It's your decision, sir."

She started for the door, but a cry stopped her. It came from the corner where Rose Spychalski sat, a harsh gasp deep down in her throat. She seemed to be trying to speak. Mici and Spychalski hurried to her with one accord, but all she could produce was a series of inarticulate choking sounds.

Her scarred, patchwork face was contorted; she began to heave convulsively. But she was not having a fit, Mici realized as she watched helplessly. Rose Spychalski was sobbing. Her eyes were dry, but she was crying.

Gently, her husband took the album from her nerveless hands and, finding no convenient place to set it, handed it to Mici. Then he lifted the pain-wracked body and, murmuring softly as he might to a child, carried her into the next room.

He kicked the door shut behind him, but Mici could still hear the retching sobs and Spychalski's rough voice in its surprising gentleness.

Had she intimated too much in Rose's presence? Mici wondered. Was it possible the wife knew what her husband had been up to at the time of the fire? And was she torn now between the need to pretend she didn't know and the need to admit that she did so he could exonerate himself from the suspicion of arson?

That was a problem to be resolved between them, Mici decided. The sobs inside the bedroom were subsiding. There was nothing more she could do here, no point in waiting for Spychalski to come out. About to set the album on a table, some instinct made her open it and look inside. She had assumed it to be the Havelka family album with perhaps a few pictures of Rose as a child, of Rose's parents, but as she turned the pages Mici saw only pictures of Rose and Karl.

She sat down in the chair beside the window and started at the beginning.

There were courting pictures, wedding pictures, pictures of what had apparently been the first home, the first baby, the second, the new house, the new car, the girls growing up. It was only half filled. It was the Spychalski family album and the blank pages would remain blank forever. But how had it gotten here to the Havelka home? Rescued from the fire by Rose Spychalski who had not been able to save her own children? There were no traces on the cover or on any of the pages of charring or smoke damage. The book was worn by handling but otherwise in good condition.

The answer was taking shape. It was ugly and infinitely sad. Mici was still sitting by the window, still holding the book, when Spychalski returned.

He had not expected her to be there.

"How is she?" Mici asked.

"Resting. I gave her a tranquilizer. I have made my decision, Miss Anhalt. I thank you for your trouble and your concern, but there is nothing for us to discuss."

She stayed where she was, the open album still on her lap. "I understood that nothing was saved from the fire."

"Nothing was."

She closed the album and put her hand on its cover. "How did this get here?"

He stared at it. He swallowed. His face was granite gray, bleak but determined. It took him a very long time but he found an explanation. "I brought it over . . . before the fire . . . to show relatives. We had relatives coming to visit . . . from Omaha."

"Why not show them the album in your own home?"

"We could not afford to entertain them. They were to come here, so I brought the album here."

"Why didn't you take it back? After your relatives had seen it, why didn't you take it back home again? Your relatives were from—Omaha, did you say?"

"I forgot. Yes, Omaha."

Sadly, Mici watched as he tried to evade the net. "When? When were they here?"

"Ah . . . they didn't come, after all. We had the fire. So naturally it was not a good time for them to come to visit."

"I see." She sighed. "So you brought the album over before your relatives even arrived and left it here. Then there was the fire."

"That's right. Yes. It was preserved by chance. Pure chance. We are fortunate," he said bitterly. "We are fortunate to have this much left of our lives."

"*You* brought it here?"

"Yes."

"Providentially."

"Yes."

No, Mici thought, *not providentially; on purpose.* The album had been brought over here before the fire by the person who had set the fire. To preserve it. Spychalski did not seem like a person who would be so sentimental, but his wife did. Mici thought about the woman sleeping in the next room, ravaged by burns, by the loss of everything she'd held dear in her life, but worst of all ravaged by guilt. Her man had been out of work for over two years. They'd been in dire straits. They would have lost their home anyway when they could no longer meet the mortgage payments. The insurance money could have saved them and even made it possible to build a new home eventually. Probably the earlier garage fire set by the Geramita boys had suggested the plan. She must have reasoned that they would be blamed and that they would get off as they had before when they had actually been responsible. To speculate on what she would have done if the boys hadn't been exonerated was fruitless; that part of the plan had gone as anticipated. The rest had been disaster. Rose Spychalski had chosen a time for the fire when her husband should have been at his hiring hall, the two girls safely at school for a drama-club meeting, and she herself away from the house in the course of her regular routine. She hadn't known till she was a distance from the burning building, till she heard their shrieks from the upstairs bedroom, that the girls had come home early—and that they were trapped. She ran back, but she couldn't save them.

Mici had no idea how Karl Spychalski had found out that his wife had set the fire, but she was certain that he knew. Had Rose babbled in her sleep? Or under the influence of the painkilling drugs? Was that why Spychalski had insisted on getting her home before anyone else made sense of her ravings? At least Mici now understood why he refused to produce an alibi for himself. He never would. As long as suspicion remained directed at him, his wife was safe.

Mici raised her eyes. Of course he wanted the case closed. Naturally he didn't want a review. He didn't want anybody, particularly Mici with her good intentions, meddling. He had broken into her apartment intending to frighten her off, but she had stabbed him with the scissors before he could deliver his message. So then he'd left the note in her mailbox not realizing that there was another case to which it could refer.

Spychalski took a step toward her. His sagging shoulders had squared; his slack jaw was so tight it set the pulse at his temple throbbing; his bloodshot eyes burned fiercely.

Mici got out of the chair and took a step sideways. If she screamed, who would hear?

Not the woman in the bedroom who was locked into a fantasy world. Downstairs? She had no idea whether there was anyone downstairs. In any case, Spychalski could easily stifle her screams with one big hand. She looked around quickly. The ornaments were glass and porcelain which would break and cut superficially. While

212

her eyes darted wildly, he took another step toward her and extended his hands. They could circle her neck and crush it, she thought. She flinched but held her ground.

"It was just chance that the album was preserved." Karl Spychalski's strong hands trembled; they were reaching out not for her throat but to take the book. "It was just chance that I brought it over here," he repeated and his voice broke. He was not threatening. He was pleading, begging for her silence.

Mici hesitated. Spychalski's claim had already been disallowed by the compensation board. The insurance company was not likely to pay off on his policy. So what purpose would be served by charging Rose Spychalski with arson and involuntary manslaughter? She had set the fire that had killed her children. It was their dying screams that she listened to in her near catatonic state, their screams that were shutting out all other voices, all other sounds. Could there be a worse hell for Rose Spychalski? Or for the husband who shared it with her?

Mici put the heavy book into Spychalski's hands.

"Lock it up," she advised. "Or better yet, destroy it."

Mici hadn't needed to look for a possible scar on Spychalski's back. The clue to the man who had assaulted her was in the nature of the attack. Violence obviously was not in the ironworker's character; that was clear in his reaction to her discovery. There was only one other candidate left, and she didn't feel like confronting him on her own. She had to call Donald once more.

"Oh, say, babe . . . I mean Mici. Nice to hear from you. Got over your mad, huh?"

She marveled at his resilience and was at the same time amused. "You wanted to make a deal."

He was instantly on the alert, eager and at the same time wary. "What kind of deal?"

"Oh, well, if you've changed your mind . . ."

"No, no. Keep your shirt on. What's up?"

"First, did you find out who Julia's publisher is?"

"Sure, no sweat, but they don't have the manuscript. Seems all she showed them was a few chapters and an outline. They were interested, but they told her she had to jazz it up, make it more sensational. So she took the thing home with her to work on it. Now, of course, they're eager to get their hands on it."

"They have no idea who might have it?"

"None. They called Brumleve, thinking that since he's the executor of the estate he might know. But he'd never even heard of its existence."

"Well, I've got an idea."

"Where do you think it is?"

"First I want you to do something for me."

"What?"

"Come on, Donald, for once in your life make a commitment on trust."

"It's not that I don't trust you, kid . . ."

"You do realize that whoever has the manuscript is the killer?"

"Probably."

"No probably. There'll be proof."

"How do you mean, there'll be proof?"

"It had stopped raining, you see. I hadn't realized that till Kord mentioned it. Then I called the weather bureau and was told that in mid-Manhattan the rain had stopped completely just before midnight."

"So?"

"So the killer wasn't wearing a raincoat."

"Are you enjoying yourself?" he asked with exasperation.

Mici laughed: then she sighed. "Not really. Billy Zip

was helping Julia with the book, but he considered it therapy for her. I don't think he ever expected that she would find a publisher."

"So? He should have been glad for her. He was her buddy, right?" Swell asked.

"He loved her," Mici replied simply.

17

Activity in the news building was at its height; the last live show of the day, the eleven o'clock report, had yet to go on the air. By contrast, the main building next door was just about shut down and most office and production personnel had long since gone home. Billy Zip, however, had not. He was working on a special, and Mici knew that he would be in the studio till every detail had been checked and double-checked. From the street the brightly lit reception area appeared deserted, but as soon as Mici walked in, guards materialized as though out of nowhere to challenge her. She showed her ID and was allowed to pass through to the elevators.

She rode up to the inevitable and irritating accompaniment of canned music. On the third floor she stepped out into a wide, dimly lit corridor. The doors hissing shut behind her cut off the canned music. Suddenly she missed it. The difference in atmosphere between the offices downstairs and the studios up here was palpable. She found the silence oppressive. Her steps echoed hollowly as she walked along the shadowy hallways cluttered with flats, props, cables, dismantled spotlights, all kind of theatrical paraphernalia. A faint light showed behind the glass insets of the swinging door to studio B. Mici put a hand against the push panel, then hesitated. She was supposed to meet Donald but she had come early—not to put one over on him, not even because she thought she could handle the interrogation better than he, though she believed she could. Actually, Mici Anhalt would have preferred to have no part in the coming confrontation. Billy was an old friend. What had happened between him and Julia had been inevitable, programmed into their relationship from their very first meeting. Mici had arrived before the detective to make the ordeal a little easier for Billy. She considered William Zipprodt as much a victim as Julia Schuyler.

Squaring her shoulders, tossing her loose hair back, Mici gave the door a firm shove and entered the studio.

There was nobody there. The light that she had seen through the glass came from a weak dome fixture. In contrast to the standard stage worklight, this was less garish and hurtful to the eyes. It was also less eerie, producing none of those harsh and mysterious shadows, instead turning the empty studio into nothing more than a prosaic warehouse of unused equipment. The mini sets—the camera requires only that portion of a scene which its lens will encompass and not the complete setting required for the stage—were arranged in the usual pattern on the perimeter with the cameras in the center of the floor, from which position they could swing back and forth, dolly in and out, as the action required. To the left, at the far end of the studio and almost completely hidden by a stack of unused flats, Mici could just glimpse the glass front of the control room. While the show was on the air or being taped, the control room would be dark, lit only by the glow from the bank of monitors inside. Now

217

there should be some light. Mici frowned because she could discern none.

"Hello!" she called. "Billy? Hello!"

There was no answer. Naturally, there wouldn't be; the control room, like the studio, was soundproof, and unless the audio switch was open he couldn't hear her. He couldn't see her either because those flats were in the way. Carefully picking a path between snaking cables, dodging spotlights and cameras, and ducking under booms, Mici reached the center of the floor and stood in what she thought was a narrow sight line to the booth. Now he should be able to see her if he looked. She waited, but nothing happened. Obviously he was too immersed in his work. There was nothing to do but go around to the control room itself. Left or right? She chose left simply because the way seemed a bit clearer. She had just taken the first few steps when the ceiling light went out and she was hit full face by a baby spot that dazzled and momentarily blinded her.

"Billy?" She stopped where she was, blinking. "Billy?" She squinted, then, shielding her eyes, tried to see past the glare. "Turn that thing off, will you, Billy? I have to talk to you." She assumed that now the audio was on.

There was no answer from the control room.

"Let's not play games, Billy. This is important. Either come out here or let me come in there. Okay?"

Still no answer. If he was testing his lighting, then he must surely look up and see her.

"It's about Julia's book, Billy. The publisher wants to go ahead with it, but he doesn't have the manuscript. If you can produce it and show that you were helping Julia with it, you can probably make a very profitable deal. It would mean a lot of money and, what's more, recognition. You deserve it, Billy. After all these years, you really do."

No sound from the control room, none at all. Did he

218

have the audio on? Was he listening? She had no idea. All she knew was that the glare of that spotlight made her feel like an insect under a microscope. Head down, eyes on the floor, Mici shuffled out of its reach. But she had barely savored the relief when it went out and another spotlight came on, pinpointing her again.

"Ah, Billy!" she cried, convinced that he did hear her as plainly as he saw her. "What is this cat-and-mouse bit? You and I go too far back for this kind of thing. We're friends. Either let me in there or you come on out here."

Silence. She took another couple of steps forward, testing, and sure enough the light illuminating the area she'd been standing in went out and a new spot brilliantly lit the area into which she'd moved.

"Okay, Billy. I'll give it to you from here, since that's the way you seem to want it. The publisher is anxious to go ahead with Julia's book. If you can produce the original manuscript and notes, they're prepared to draw up a new contract with you as author." She waited a beat. She hadn't actually spoken to the publisher, but it was a reasonable assumption. "Of course, you don't have to deal with them at all. You can take the material elsewhere. If you have it."

Still no reply, but now Mici thought she detected a low hum which meant an open mike. She intensified her appeal. "I know you didn't approve of Julia's writing the book, but there will undoubtedly be a rash of books about her now, so why not give your version of her life? You've got the inside track, particularly if you can produce her manuscript. You can, can't you, Billy?"

By now she was growing accustomed to the spotlight. It was like being on stage. The audience was out there; you could sense their presence, but you gave a better performance if you tried to forget about them.

"I know that you loved Julia and I know you put up with a lot from her. I know you were deeply dejected when she married Cassel, but you also liked Alfred and respected him and so you could accept the marriage. When they broke up you must have hoped, you must have expected that Julia would finally turn to you.

"But she didn't turn to you. Instead, she took a new lover, a man completely unworthy of her and who treated her shamefully. You were deeply hurt, but she needed you as never before and you remained loyal. Still, it must have been terrible for you, knowing how Janos Kord used Julia and abused her, sucked her dry and degraded her. You tried to help her, to hold her together, to save her pride. You used the book to that purpose. You told me yourself that you didn't have much hope for it, that you were doing it with little expectation that it would amount to anything. Night after night, when you were through here at the studio, you'd go over to her place and pick up her scrawled pages and try to make sense out of them. You pored over them, edited them, typed them."

She paused. Up to now, Mici had been on firm ground, but she was moving into the realm of conjecture, using her instinct. She believed that she could put herself into the skin of these two people because she'd known them and felt affection for them.

"Then one day Julia went out and actually sold the book. But she didn't tell you. How did you find out? Maybe you happened to find the contract among the papers you took home with you. She wasn't exactly orderly, was she? Anyhow, you discoverd that you weren't mentioned in it; no credit was given for your part of the work and certainly no financial consideration, though I'm sure that didn't matter to you. You were deeply hurt. It was the final humiliation, the bottom line to the years of loyalty you'd lavished on Julia Schuyler. You knew that her friends had always looked down on you, considered you Julia's *gofer*; now it seemed that that was her opinion of you, too."

220

Mici was coming to the climax. She believed that she had reached Billy Zip's reason and touched his emotion and that very soon he would admit the truth.

"I know that you never meant to hurt Julia. I know that, after all these years of loving her and serving her, you couldn't deliberately hurt her. I think you were upset and angry and determined to get the recognition you deserved. You went over there and told her you couldn't continue with the book unless you got credit. You threatened to walk out on her. She told you to go ahead; she didn't need you; she could write the book herself. You quarreled. Somehow, she got hold of a knife. She'd been drinking and she didn't know what she was doing. She came at you with the knife. In trying to turn it away from yourself, you turned it on her. It was an accident. Any jury will see that."

The hum of the open mike was clearly audible; now it intensified and became a shrill feedback.

Mici winced till it subsided. "Where is the manuscript, Billy? Julia had it on Friday night. Janos Kord saw it when he was there after midnight. Now it's gone. You have to produce it or your story won't hold up. The manuscript is your defense. You do see that, don't you, Billy?"

A new dread seized her. Suppose while she was talking he'd slipped away to destroy the evidence. "Billy?" she called out. "Billy!" She took several steps forward till once again she was out of the spotlight, in darkness. She waited for another light to blink on and pick her up, but none did.

"Billy! Billy, listen to me. You have got to produce that manuscript. Billy, answer me."

The answer was an explosion. Throwing her arms up around her head, Mici cringed, expecting a rain of plaster and God knew what kind of debris to shower down on her. It took seconds that seemed like minutes to realize that the blast was pure sound—music, if you could call the ear-shattering, magnified discordance music. It was fed from the control room through speakers all around the studio so that it seemed to surround her and at the same time to be directly focused at her.

'Turn it off!" she shrieked.

She couldn't hope to stop it.

Well, at least he was still there, she thought, and he'd given up trying to blind her with those damned spots. So she was finally able to make her way around to the side and up the flight of steps to the control-room door. It was open. She stepped inside. Within the confined space the sound was physically painful. Squinting in the gloom she could just make out the stage manager at the control console. How could he bear the noise? She took a couple of steps toward him, and as her eyes adjusted she saw that he was slumped forward across the counter. On the back of his stark white shirt, a black stain was spreading.

"Billy!" She ran to him.

He didn't stir. His head was nestled in the crook of his left arm and his right arm was stretched out to its limit, fingers clawed, groping among the various switches. *Oh God, my God!* Mici thought. Gently, she turned his head to look into eyes that were wide open, unblinking, pupils dilated. No use. There was nothing to be done. She was too late. She had waited too long.

In a sudden fury of frustration and self-blame, Mici reached across the body, found the master switch, and flipped it. Everything went off—light and sound, inside and out. Then, turning blindly, banging her shins against a filing cabinet, knocking down what sounded like a stack of metal film cans, she blundered out of there. In the corridor she managed to take the wrong turn and went down fire stairs that led directly to the street. Once out, she couldn't get back in again and had to run around to the main entrance. She nearly crashed into Donald coming from the opposite direction.

222

He grabbed her and held her. "Hey, hey. What's the matter? Where are you going?"

"He's dead. He's dead. Billy. Poor Billy. All the time I was out there talking to him, or thought I was talking to him . . . poor Billy Zip—Zipprodt. William Zipprodt," she amended in an attempt to show respect. "Come on." She grabbed the detective by the hand and literally dragged him into the building. As before, guards appeared, startled by Mici's obvious distress, but Swell showed his badge and waved them off. The two of them barely broke stride on the way to the elevators.

On the third floor, Mici took him to the double door of studio B. "Here, I went in here. I thought the audio was open so I was talking to him, but when he didn't answer . . ." Realizing that the place was pitch-dark and Donald didn't know what she was talking about, she took his hand again and led him to the control room by way of the corridor, still dark as she had left it. Feeling her way along the counter, she found the master switch and threw it. The monitors, the studio spots, the sound, everything came on.

Donald jumped.

Mici turned the sound off, then stepped to one side so that he could see the body.

"I was out there," she pointed through the glass, "and he was in here. Every time I moved, one spotlight went out and another came on, following me. Like this." She manipulated various switches, a trial-and-error process but close enough to give the detective the idea. "On and off. On and off. I thought he was baiting me, but he was calling for help." She pointed to the stage manager's outstretched hand. "He was dying. He couldn't reach the audio . . . see. It was just beyond him so he used the lights to attract my attention. I didn't understand. I didn't understand."

"Okay now, kid, take it easy."

223

"He was calling for help."

"Now, babe, you couldn't know that. There was no way you could have known." He patted her shoulder with gruff sympathy. "Listen, how the hell do we get some regular light on in here?"

She pointed to the ordinary light switch just inside the door. After Swell put it on, things seemed more normal, as normal as they could be with a dead man sitting between them. The detective turned his attention to the body, feeling first for the carotid artery, and for one wild moment Mici thought she might have been mistaken, that Billy Zip might still be alive. Then Donald took his hand away.

"How long do you estimate you were out there?"

"Maybe ten minutes. I don't know. It's hard to say."

He scowled. "Why the hell couldn't you have waited for me?"

She glanced at the electric clock on the wall and noted that he had come early, too. "Were you intending to wait for me?" she challenged. "Oh, let's not squabble, Donald. I feel bad enough. The man was dying in here and I stood out there giving a monologue."

Swell sighed. "First things first. I've got to report . . ." He glanced at the row of telephones along the back wall and decided against using one of them. "There must be a booth outside. Come on."

She was glad to get out and quite content to sit in the chair Donald indicated in the hall. She wasn't at all aware of the fact that he had placed her where he could keep an eye on her while he made his call. As she had no basis for comparison, she didn't realize that it was unusually lengthy.

"The lieutenent's coming over himself," he informed her when she came out of the booth. "He wants to talk to you."

"Okay."

"So you just sit there while I go back inside and see if I can locate the manuscript."

"You're wasting your time. Why do you think poor Billy was killed?"

"For the manuscript?"

"What else?"

"According to you, he was the killer."

"I made a mistake. I was wrong about Billy. And believe me, I regret it. I was wrong from the beginning. I see that now."

"Fine."

"Somebody doesn't want that book published and we've got to find out why."

"Okay, you think about it and let me know." Swell started for the control room.

"Do I have to? Wait, I mean."

"You're kidding. You're a witness, for God's sake!"

"I've already told you everything."

"By your own admission, you were alone with the victim for a full ten minutes."

"I was in the studio; he was in the control room. The areas are separate and soundproof. I couldn't see or hear what was going on where he was."

Swell shook his head.

"You can't seriously believe that I . . . Why? What motive could I have? You can't believe it!"

"I guess not."

"You guess not?" she sputtered. "All right, all right. Where's the knife then? You did notice, I suppose, that the murder weapon is missing again? So what did I do with it? How did I get rid of it?"

"Dumped it in the street somewhere. You were out in the street when I ran into you," he reminded her.

"I took the wrong turn down the corridor and I was out on the fire stairs before I realized it, and then I had no choice but to continue on down to the street. I was trying to get back in and notify the guards and call you."

He shrugged.

She clutched her forehead in mock despair. "I can't believe this is happening to me. Would I have made a date to meet you here if I intended to commit murder? I mean, I ask you, does it make sense?"

"Okay, okay. So why don't you just sit here quietly and relax until Lieutenant LaRock arrives and you can tell him the whole thing."

She sighed aggrievedly.

"I'm sorry, kid, that's the way it's got to be."

He lit a cigarette; he paced; he did not go into the control room. Whether Donald agreed with Mici that the manuscript was gone and that Zipprodt had been killed for it, or whether he was afraid to let her out of his sight, he was obviously relieved when the door at the far end of the corridor opened and the first pair of uniformed officers arrived. After a whispered consultation accompanied by significant glances in her direction, the detective finally entered the control room, taking one of the men with him and leaving the other behind with Mici.

To keep an eye on her, she thought, and sat back in the plastic chair to wait.

It distressed her that she'd been so wrong about poor Billy. Her initial error had been in jumping to the conclusion that the murder of Julia Schuyler was a crime of passion. The scene, Julia's past and current history, her emotionalism, all had indicated it. But it was not so, and that error had inevitably led to the next—that the crime was unpremeditated. As for Billy—Mici had never really thought him guilty; she had talked herself into it. She'd misread the clues. No, she corrected herself; she'd let the clues mislead her and in doing so ignored the essential core of the stage manager's character—loyalty. She'd discounted William Zipprodt's years of devotion to Julia Schuyler. So Julia didn't acknowledge his help with the

226

book. Billy wouldn't have cared. He had done and was prepared to do a great deal more for the woman he'd idolized. And Julia knew it. She used him because he allowed himself to be used. But she'd loved him, too.

The crime appeared sloppy and haphazard. It might have been preceded by a quarrel, but it was not a crime of passion. Its motive was neither love nor hatred, but fear. The fear of something in that manuscript. Janos Kord didn't take it; there would have been no point in his mentioning it if he had. Obviously Billy hadn't taken it or he wouldn't be dead.

But if the killer already had the manuscript, why was Billy a threat?

Because he knew what was in it.

Mici sighed. What had Billy said to her that first day in her office? He'd said that it was pitiful to see Julia trying to sell her degradation. He'd said that nobody would care unless she could find an angle for her story. Obviously she had found an angle and Billy knew what it was.

So then why hadn't he been killed right away? Why had the murderer waited so long?

Because the murderer hadn't known that Billy was working on the book with Julia. He'd only recently found out. Mici's heart pounded; her pulse raced. She jumped to her feet and started down the corridor.

"Miss! Miss!" The cop sprinted after her. "I'm sorry, miss, but you're supposed to wait."

She raised her eyebrows at him. "I'm going to the ladies' room."

"Oh. Well, sure." He was young, chubby, and earnest. Evidently Donald had cautioned him severely, for though he stood aside politely to let her pass he kept his eye on Mici till she actually entered the rest room.

She was sure he'd be right there beside the door till she came out. A quick examination of the premises revealed there was no convenient rear exit, no window with a fire escape; in fact, there was no window at all. So now what?

227

It looked as though she had no choice but to wait for the lieutenent and make her case to him.

"The first turn to your left, sir, then left again, and it's the first door to your right, sir."

That was her young guard giving someone directions to the control room.

"Would it be too much trouble, Officer, for you to lead the way?"

"Ah . . ."

The sarcasm of the request was the badge of the authority of the speaker, Mici thought, listening from inside, and the poor rookie was torn between one duty and another.

"Yes, sir, right this way, sir."

The poor guy probably figured he'd be back before she could get out of the john, and he would have been right if she'd gone to the john. Mici grinned, waited till the footsteps faded, then, inching the door open, peered outside. All clear. Avoiding the elevator, she took the stairs and made it down to the main lobby. The guards were all standing around where they could be seen as well as see, but they were watching the parade of police and weren't interested in her. At the reception desk, she helped herself to a page from a memo pad and scribbled a message. Folding it, she handed it to the nearest guard.

"Give this to Detective Swell when he comes down."

It was always a good idea to have a backup.

18

With one or two exceptions, New York—famed for its night life—had become an early town. By ten thirty, eleven for musicals, the legitimate theatres would be empty, their marquees dark, and glamorous Broadway left to the late movie and porno palaces, the shabby bars and girlie joints, and the night prowlers. Mici told the driver to hurry; she had to get to the theatre before the final curtain.

The cab arrived just as the audience was pouring out. Good enough. Mici paid and crossed the sidewalk to mix with the crowd, only she was going the wrong way—in. If anyone should challenge her, she would say she'd forgotten her gloves at her seat, but nobody bothered her as she made her way against the tide into the John Malcolm Schuyler Theatre. She knew that the lawyer would not refuse to see her, but she preferred some element of surprise. She reasoned that the man who had built this theatre and loved it so much that he had an apartment above it would surely have provided private access backstage for himself. That was how she intended to reach him; it shouldn't be hard. Once inside the house, it was simply a matter of whether the connecting door between front and back was at the right or left of the stage. A stream of visitors going back provided the answer. Mici joined them and passed over from the world of watchers to that of pretenders. She found herself on the prompt side—that side from which the stage manager ran the show, where the fly rail and electrician's boards were located. Slipping through the narrow space between the electrical boards, she found what she'd confidently expected to find—a door. Stepping through it, she was in Oscar Brumleve's vestibule with the elevator waiting.

Probably the decrepit car creaked and groaned no more than it had on her initial visit, but tonight to Mici's sensitive ears it seemed to shake the entire building. It seemed impossible that the man up there and whoever might be with him didn't know that someone was coming. When the car shuddered to a stop and she got out, it was a relief to find the long gallery empty and silent.

Bathed in the rose glow of simulated torches at intervals along the wall, the shabby theatrical mementoes seemed almost real—the portraits painted by masters, the papier-mâché masks, rubber daggers, heraldic flags took on substance and grandeur. The oriental runner glowed with color and even felt softer underfoot. It was a stage set waiting for the curtain to rise. Mici crossed quickly and quietly up center and tapped lightly on the door of the lawyer's library-office.

There was no response. She knocked again, waited, then entered.

A green, glass-globed lamp cast a pool of light over the massive desk at one end of the room, glinting off the row of golden statuettes lined up along the front edge. But Brumleve was not at his desk. He was on her right, a hunched figure sitting sideways to a small window and looking down, completely engrossed. Mici frowned. The

230

light coming from the window was too bright to be reflected from the street, and anyhow the window was cut into what she judged to be an inner wall. Of course! It overlooked the stage—a kind of Judas hole. Hadn't David Belasco had one in his quarters? And Daniel Frohman? She'd noted the drawn curtains on her earlier visit; now she knew what was behind them.

"Mr. Brumleve?"

The show was over, but the man looking down remained completely absorbed.

As before, the room was hot and stuffy, without air conditioning, all the windows closed, the one over the stage was not a working window. Sick as he was, Brumleve must find the atmosphere comfortable, but she was already starting to sweat.

"Mr. Brumleve?" She raised her voice.

At last he looked over his shoulder. "Who's that?"

"Mici Anhalt, Mr. Brumleve."

For a moment he scowled; then the scowl cleared. "Oh, yes, I remember you. The girl with the good legs. You used to be a dancer. Yes." He motioned her closer. "Too bad you didn't come a little sooner; you could have watched the play with me. It's quite an experience to see it from up here above the flies. Like watching puppets." He raised his arms, hands arched, fingers tapping the air as though he were manipulating the strings. "I watch every performance, matinees included. That's the only way to keep a company on its toes; I let them know they're being watched."

But it wasn't his play! Mici thought. He hadn't produced it, only rented out the theatre.

"The crew, too—props, juice, grips, you've got to keep an eye on them all. They can get sloppy, put in for overtime to which they're not entitled. Constantly alert, you have to be constantly alert." His voice was thin and querulous.

"I'm sure that's true."

"It certainly is." He was testy as though she were arguing. "Ah there. They've finished striking the set," he announced with satisfaction. "Yes, all right, good time, good time," he murmured, having consulted his watch. "The house should be empty by now. Yes." Again he nodded approvingly, and Mici taking a step forward could look over his shoulder as the curtain was raised on an empty auditorium, the stage lights went out, and the worklight, its single bulb protected by a wire cage, was set on the apron of the bare stage. At the same time, the light coming through the Judas window diminished.

As though that was a signal, Oscar Brumleve rose and started across the room. Mici was shocked at how much he'd regressed in just the few days since she'd first met him. He'd been thin, pitifully thin, but now he was a cadaver. He couldn't seem to straighten up, and he tottered as he moved from his post beside the inner window so that instinctively she moved to offer support. He waved her aside. It took a few moments, but he steadied himself and then walked, slowly but firmly, to his desk where, grasping the arms, he lowered himself carefully into the leather chair.

"What can I do for you, Miss Anhalt?" he asked. The very fact of his presence in the seat of his power, behind that row of golden awards, seemed to act as a restorative. "Anything you want, if I can do it, I will. Just ask. You did me and my client a great favor. We've never properly thanked you."

"There's no need. I'm glad it turned out as it did."

"You're a clever young woman. Both Alfred and I owe you a debt of gratitude. We'd like to repay it."

"There's no debt."

"My dear, you must want something, everybody does. I don't suppose you'd be here otherwise, would you now, my dear? Be honest, eh? Out with it, young lady, out with it." He had become almost unctuous.

"I'm looking for the manuscript."

"What manuscript is that, my dear? I have all kinds."

"Julia Schuyler's book manuscript."

"I didn't know that Julia was writing a book."

Inwardly Mici sighed, partly with relief and partly with regret. "Her editor called you. He thought that, being her executor, you might have it among her effects."

"Oh, yes. Well, that was the first I'd heard that Julia was trying her hand at writing." He dismissed it as beneath notice.

Mici didn't buy it. "I think you've known about that book for some time, Mr. Brumleve. I believe that you were determined it should never be published."

"You're wrong. However, if I had known about the book . . ." He shrugged. "If Julia wanted to do an emotional striptease in public, that was her business. That's the fashion nowadays, to bare all. Why should I care?"

If she knew that, she'd know everything, Mici thought. Never mind, a case could be made without knowing his specific objection to the book.

"You tried to talk Julia out of writing it, but she was determined. Maybe you paid her, I don't know, but obviously when she found a publisher whatever you could give her wouldn't have been enough. On Friday night you went over there to make one more effort to get her to give up the project. It was late, well after one-thirty. It had stopped raining. You brought a bottle of scotch to soften her up. Julia was much easier to deal with when she'd had a few."

He didn't comment. Maybe he was waiting to see what kind of case she had. She didn't mind letting him know.

"You rang her bell. You knew she'd still be up because Julia never went to bed till three or four A.M. So she was up, though she was in bad shape, bruised and half drunk but rational. You gave her the bottle and she had herself a couple more belts; only this time, instead of making her amenable, the drink turned her obstinate. You argued, you pleaded, but the book was her chance to get back into the limelight, to be somebody again. Nothing you could say could stack up against that. She wasn't only determined, she was eager and excited about writing the book, and she kept tossing off the drinks till she finally passed out.

"Well, that was your chance. That was your chance to find the manuscript and get out. You looked everywhere. The drawer of the kitchen table was the last place and by then Julia came to."

Mici paused. The heat of the room was terrible. The sweat poured off her, but Brumleve seemed unaffected. He sat perfectly still in his chair, his eyes fixed intently on her.

"She followed you into the kitchen and demanded the manuscript back. You refused, and she tried to wrest it from you. You struggled, but she was very weak, weaker than you, and suddenly she just gave up. She told you you could have it—burn it, flush it down the toilet, do any damn thing you wanted with it. She'd just write it over. That was when you realized you had to kill her."

Still Brumleve neither moved nor spoke, watching Mici with the same intensity of concentration which he'd earlier expended on the stage below his window. For her part, Mici was drawing from him the kind of electric charge an actor derives from a rapt audience—one mesmerizing the other, each a part of the process of creation.

She took a deep breath. "You were both in the kitchen. Earlier, Julia had cut up one of those deli roasted chickens and the knife was on the drain board. You picked it up. You held it for several moments. For several moments you just stood there with the knife in your hands. Julia didn't move either; she didn't try to get away. She didn't lunge and try to take the knife from you. She didn't even scream because she didn't believe that you would actually use it. You'd known her since she was a child. You had been her father's best friend. You built this theatre to honor John Malcolm Schuyler and to perpetu-

234

ate his memory. How could you injure his only child, his little girl?

"How could you raise that knife high and plunge it into Julia Schuyler's heart?"

Mici could visualize the scene as clearly as though she'd been there. "The knife went in easily, and Julia slid down in a heap at your feet with little more than a sigh of surprise—and disappointment. You panicked. All you wanted at that moment was to get out. You took the knife with you. And, of course, the manuscript."

For one moment Brumleve's eyes left Mici's face and darted to a small picture on the wall, then back again to her. Fast, but not fast enough.

"You should have destroyed it, Mr. Brumleve."

He was silent for a long time. Then, with a deep sigh as though the curtain had been lowered on a particularly affecting scene, Oscar Brumleve stirred, raised his thin hands, and applauded. "Spellbinding, Miss Anhalt. What a performance!"

"What was in that book? What was in it that made you kill Julia?"

The lawyer leaned forward and rested his elbows on the desk. "I assume that you have a reason for coming up here and putting on this show."

"Why?" Mici pressed. "What was she threatening to reveal?"

"What do you want?" he countered. "Money? Fame? Have you decided you want to go back to dancing, after all? Do you want to be in a movie, a Broadway show? Or maybe you're like Julia and you have a friend you want to help. Speak up."

Mici kept to her own script. "When did you find out that Billy Zip was helping Julia with the book? You should have realized that she was in no shape to write it herself, that someone had to be helping her, but you didn't—not till a couple of days ago. Not till the publisher called you in an effort to locate the manuscript. He

235

told you then that he'd checked with her collaborator, Mr. Zipprodt, but that Mr. Zipprodt didn't have it. And now poor Billy is dead, too. Stabbed, like Julia, but in the back. It happened less than an hour ago."

"I'm a sick man, Miss Anhalt, and I'm getting very, very tired. Either tell me what it is you want or go. While you still can."

It was the first hint of a threat, and from a man like Brumleve it was an admission.

"You have no reason to hurt me," Mici said. "I don't know your secret."

"There is no secret. You have no proof of any of these irresponsible allegations."

"The proof does exist though, and it is in your possession. In that safe." Mici indicated the picture toward which the lawyer had surreptitiously glanced a few moments before.

He shrugged. "Very well. I do admit that Julia's manuscript is in there, all three chapters of it which deal with her childhood and are no threat to anyone, believe me. However, my acquisition of it was nothing so dramatic as you've enacted. It was quite prosaically simple. Julia wanted my opinion and offered it to me to read."

"If that's so, why did you tell her publisher you didn't have it?"

"That's my business."

"If Julia gave it to you voluntarily and there's nothing in it that would affect you, then you won't mind my glancing through it, will you? If she gave it to you voluntarily, then there won't be any blood on any of the pages, will there?"

"Blood?"

"From the murder knife. You could hardly carry the knife out in your hand for any passerby to see. You weren't wearing a raincoat because it had stopped raining. The pockets of a regular jacket wouldn't be deep enough. Of course, you could have held it against you un-

236

der your jacket, but that would have been awkward and perhaps you were a bit squeamish about it. It was so much simpler just to roll it up inside the manuscript between the pages. Surely there must have been some blood on the knife and surely the blood will be on the pages. Julia Schuyler's blood."

He was transfixed, hardly breathing. Then suddenly his mouth fell open and his breath began to come in short, shallow gasps. In that hot, airless room, Oscar Brumleve began to shake as though he had an arctic chill, and at the same time sweat oozed out of his pores as he strained to rise from the chair. Either he'd forgotten Mici's presence or assigned to it a lesser priority, but for the moment he had one concern only, one compulsion—to check the manuscript. Somehow he tottered the few steps from the desk to the picture on the wall, pushed it aside to reveal the safe Mici had surmised was there. So anxious was he to get it open that he misdialed twice before he managed it correctly and the door swung open. Cradling the thin sheaf of papers in both hands like the most fragile of treasures, Brumleve stumbled back to his desk near exhaustion.

Hunching forward, he placed the pages directly under the student lamp and turned them over one by one, scrutinizing each meticulously before setting it aside and proceeding to the next. From where she stood, Mici couldn't get a really good look, but she didn't need to. About halfway through he stopped, and the sudden drop of his head told her what she needed to know. Now she could approach and see for herself the spattering of brown spots along the inner edge of the topmost page.

Oscar Brumleve stared for a very long time at those damning spots. Then, as though coming out of a quiet reverie, he shifted in his chair and turned his head sideways to look up at Mici. "You shouldn't have come here alone, Miss Anhalt. That was a bad mistake."

"The police are right behind me."

"So you say." A slight, sardonic smile twisted the bloodless lips as he reached across the desk toward the row of statuettes ranged along the edge and picked up the Valentino, a slim figurine with a heavy base.

"They'll be here before you can get rid of my body," Mici warned.

"The door downstairs is locked."

"I came through the theatre."

"I'll turn the power off. They won't be able to use the elevator."

"They'll come up the fire escape."

"That will be my concern, not yours."

He rose and came around the desk towards her, steps remarkably firm, statuette held tightly in a hand that was completely steady, eyes fixed with purpose. Involuntarily Mici took a step back. Sick, old, and weak, Oscar Brumleve nevertheless had killed twice. True, Julia had been even weaker than he, and Billy Zip taken unawares from behind, but desperation could provide all the strength Brumleve would need to murder again. She must not back off; she must not even flinch. Her fear would fuel his confidence.

"Killing me would serve no purpose," she told him as reasonably as she could in the circumstances. To her surprise, he stopped where he was.

"Right again, Miss Anhalt, killing you would gain me little. I am, one way or another, a dying man."

Slowly, hand trembling as before, he put the statuette down. Mici, too, was shaking—with relief.

Shrunken, the ravages of his illness upon him, Brumleve turned his back on Mici Anhalt and shambled across the dark area beyond his desk to the baronial fireplace and the life-sized portrait hung above it. At the flip of a switch, a soft light illumined the famous face and figure of John Malcolm Schuyler.

"He was the greatest actor in the American theatre," Brumleve proclaimed, gazing up at the deep-set, haunted eyes, the contorted yet noble visage. "He had the sensitivity of a Booth, the flamboyance of a Barrymore, the technique of an Olivier. Offstage, as a lover, he was *nonpareil*. Julia meant to destroy him. For a few dollars of cheap profit, she intended to besmirch his memory."

"How?"

"By claiming that John Malcolm Schuyler—married three times, with a list of conquests to equal Don Juan's, the great lover and sex symbol of his time—was impotent. She would contend that I was his lackey and provided women as window dressing to create the aura of irresistible masculinity that turned him into a matinee idol. That together we cheated the public."

Mici gasped. "But she was his daughter!"

"No, she was not."

Oscar Brumleve heaved a sigh. "While no match for John Malcolm and a great deal more discreet, Julia's mother, Angela Vaughn, had her share of escapades—in part a reaction to John Malcolm's vicissitudes. No matter. Julia was the result of one of Angela's affairs. Of course, the child didn't know and she idolized John Malcolm. Her adulation was flattering but also an annoyance, sometimes even an embarrassment. She had a habit of bursting in on him at any moment, and on one particular occasion she chose a very private moment indeed. Provoked, John Malcolm let the truth slip. Once out, there was no taking it back. So, knowing that she was not biologically his, she set out to prove that artistically she was his child. She wanted to show him and to convince the world that she was his—most of all, she needed to prove it to herself. To his credit, John Malcolm did try to help her, to teach her. He did feel that much responsibility for her, but what he possessed could not be taught and, in any case, he was a poor teacher and not the most patient of men. She was a worse pupil, paralyzed when he uttered a word of advice. The harder she tried, the more severe his criticism and finally his ridicule. That was *his* nature.

Having failed on the stage, she tried to imitate him in life. He told her she didn't have the talent to carry it off. I don't think Julia ever forgave him for that.

"When he died, with the fear of his disapproval removed, Julia did improve. She gained some success. There was hope that she could finally make it in her own right. But either she wasn't quite good enough or her luck ran out, I don't know. It wasn't in the cards. She hit the skids. Well, you know all that."

Mici nodded. "I still don't understand why she'd want to destroy . . ."

"It was all she had left to sell. Not her own story and her own reputation—her father's. I killed her and that poor . . . toady of hers to preserve it." Brumleve looked up into the handsome face, the haunted face of Schuyler in the role of Macbeth. He stared at it for a long time; then as though under its spell he cried out, "I didn't do it for him! I did it for myself!" Brumleve's ravaged features resembled the painted ones, but the horrors he saw were real.

"Everyone accused Julia of trading on John Malcolm's reputation, but she wasn't the only one. I nurtured my career on his talent. What would I have been without him? Because he was my client, others flocked to me. At one time I had just about every major talent under personal management, and producers had to come to me and accept the terms I dictated. I built this theatre and called it the John Malcolm Schuyler Theatre because I didn't have the nerve to call it the Oscar Brumleve. But it was my monument as much as his. It's been losing money for years. At the end of next month, the bank will foreclose, tear it down, and put—God knows what in its place: an office building, a hamburger joint, a garage. When that happens, all that will be left of me will be my association with John Malcolm."

He cast one last look at the portrait; then, as though wrenching himself free of its domination, Brumleve turned and went back to his desk. With infinite weariness he reached for the Valentino and picked it up. For a moment, Mici was afraid that he meant to go for her after all, now that she knew his secret. But he just stood there, hefting the thing thoughtfully in his hand.

"I killed two people to keep a secret that no longer matters. Who cares? Nowadays, who gives a damn?" With a suddenness that took her unawares and a violence that made her gasp, he reared back and hurled the golden statue at the plate glass of the Judas window overlooking the stage below. The glass shattered, and before she could recover, Oscar Brumleve walked the few short paces and stepped through the jagged opening.

His shriek echoed and reechoed in the empty theatre for what seemed an endless time after his body had splattered on the stage six stories below.

Mici remained frozen long after the echoes had stilled. She moved at last, drawn without consciously being aware, to the opening from which a cool draft now wafted clearing the room's fetid atmosphere. Careful to avoid the sharp-edged shards, she leaned out and looked down from above the fly floor, past the old-fashioned festoons of ropes and sandbag counterweights, past the hanging flats for tomorrow's show, down to the floor of the bare stage. Thank God she was too far up to make out anything more than a sprawled outline.

19

From then on, Mici would always associate a hard downpour with that night's lonely wait in the dead lawyer's aerie. It seemed hours that she sat in the long gallery listening to the rain bombarding the skylight till Donald finally showed up, accompanied by Lieutenant LaRock and Captain Schumacher. It was evident that Detective Swell was in trouble. Both officers held him responsible for everything that had gone wrong because of her: for the murderer's having had ample time to get away while she carried on her one-sided conversation with Billy and for the suicide of a very important witness. That was how they insisted on referring to Oscar Brumleve—a witness. Donald defended her as best he could; he was defending himself. When Mici was at last permitted to lead them into the lawyer's office and show them the bloodstained pages of Julia's manuscript, the atmosphere changed considerably.

"The lab will have to analyze this before we can be sure it was Miss Schuyler's blood," LaRock muttered.

"Who else's could it be, sir?" Donald demanded, rising to the occasion. Sensing that he was on top, he went all out. He cited Mici's help and cooperation. She was a personal friend of all those involved, and she had placed herself at the department's disposal. He not only exonerated Mici for leaving the studio and coming over here but hinted she had acted with his full approval. Mici had briefed him on the phone regarding the logic that led to the discovery of the manuscript and the bloodstains, but he couldn't quite bring himself to give her the credit. Thus, he remained modestly silent. LaRock and Schumacher were forced to offer him their congratulations.

Mici bit back a smile. Let Donald make all the Brownie points he wanted; she didn't care. When she was finally released, well after four A.M., she did take him aside to remind him that having kept her part of the bargain she now expected him to keep his. Then she went home to bed.

At nine she awoke long enough to make one phone call to Adam Dowd requesting that the supervisor set up a meeting for the following day with certain specified people. Having made the arrangements, she fell back on the pillow and slept till dinner time. It was still raining. She fixed herself an omelette, ate it, washed up, watched the news on television, and went back to bed. The next morning she felt like a million.

According to the radio, it had gone on raining most of the night. Even now there was a touch of mist in the air, but the forecaster promised it would clear. The temperature had dropped fifteen degrees. The heat wave was broken. Mici called Donald.

His wife answered and told her he'd gone to the precinct. Mici called the precinct. He hadn't come in yet but was expected.

The meeting she'd requested was scheduled for noon. Plenty of time.

She made three more calls to the precinct during the morning, and each message she left was more urgent than the one before. Then, when she couldn't wait any longer, when she had to leave for the office, she convinced herself that Donald had called her there, that there would be a message from him waiting for her. But there wasn't. Fran Jarrett greeted her warmly and informed her that all the people she'd requested to attend had agreed to come, and that the meeting would be held in Mr. Cornelius's office. Mici mumbled her thanks and fled from the curious eyes of Dowd's secretary to her own private office, closed the door, and leaned against it, heart pounding.

What had gone wrong? Why didn't Donald call?

She couldn't sit still. She was up and down and up again. What should she do? How was she going to proceed without having heard from Donald? At five before the hour, just as she was expecting to be summoned into Mr. Cornelius's office—he was a stickler for punctuality—her phone rang. She snatched it up.

"Donald! Oh, thank God! You've had me climbing the walls."

"Gee, I'm sorry, babe. I just this minute got in. I called as soon as I saw your messages."

"So? So? Did you do it?"

"What?"

"What? Donald, please, this is not the time to kid around. My meeting is in four minutes exactly."

"Today! I'm sorry, doll, I didn't realize it was today."

"Sorry? What do you mean, you're sorry? You mean you didn't take care of it?"

"I haven't had a chance."

"Oh, no!" The bottom of Mici's stomach dropped; the bottom dropped out of everything. "We had a deal. I was counting on you."

244

"I'm not welshing. I'm going to take care of it; I just haven't had the time. Listen, while you were in the sack all day yesterday pounding your pillow, I was pounding out reports. I've had a homicide and a suicide to write up. I haven't even had a chance to get out for a bite."

"So how about this morning?"

"Well . . . Jeez . . ."

"Never mind, don't tell me. Why didn't you get somebody else to do it for you?"

"I didn't think you wanted anybody else. I thought you wanted me."

"All I wanted was the information. Just the information. I didn't care who got it or how. I suggested you pick him up for questioning, but it was just a suggestion. I told you that. I left it up to you." She groaned. "That was my mistake. I guess I'll never learn."

"Don't get excited. I promised you and I'm going to deliver."

"Fine. What am I going to tell those people waiting in my boss's office, huh? Come back tomorrow? Next week? Next month? What am I going to tell my boss?"

Swell had never known the redhead to become so distraught. It shamed him. "Listen, I'll come over right away. It shouldn't take me more than . . . twenty minutes . . . or so. You stall them. Of course"—he hedged, he couldn't help himself—"of course, there's no time to get a warrant, but never mind, I'll do my number anyway. Okay? Okay, babe?"

"Forget it." Tears of disappointment and frustration welled up in Mici's eyes. "I'll do it myself," she said and slammed down the receiver.

But how? How was she going to do it?

Magisterially ensconced behind the sleek slab of his desk, Mr. J. Hammond Cornelius peered through square-shaped, black-rimmed glasses that gave distinction to his small, myopic brown eyes. His jutting jaw was set at the angle for reviewing the troops, yet the commissioner had adopted a casual air by slanting his chair sideways, crossing his legs widely to reveal a section of hand-knitted, wildly colored argyle socks, and puffing energetically on his ever-present pipe.

He did not rise when Mici entered—she hardly expected it—but he did remove the pipe and used it to wave her forward.

"Ah, Miss Anhalt. Come in, come in. Sit down."

The geniality was somewhat forced but surely that he had made the effort at all was a good sign? Mici told herself that indeed it was and crossed to the chair he'd indicated, looking around as she did so. They were all present, those she'd asked to attend. Disposed about Mr. Cornelius's office were the Marins, seated side by side on the tufted leather sofa, as well as Adam Dowd and Wally Lischner sunk into the depths of down-cushioned easy chairs. It seemed like a haphazard, informal grouping, but Mici knew that Mr. Cornelius did nothing without planning. As she passed him, Dowd turned his face sideways and winked with the eye his boss couldn't see. Wally Lischner leaned a millimeter forward and mumbled something, hardly moving his lips; it could have been, "Good luck." Clay Marin made no acknowledgement of her presence one way or another, but then he was the adversary. His wife Sandra, a cool, reserved blonde, a Vassar girl trained to understatement in looks and manner, turned away. That, too, was to be expected; Sandra would naturally side with her husband. Mici was sorry because she liked Mrs. Marin; they had the same kind of background and, Mici assumed, the same set of values. At least she'd come, Mici thought, and she hadn't been sure that Mrs. Marin would. She had invited the blind man's wife as added insurance. Now, with Donald having failed her, Sandra Marin was the only leverage she had.

Though Mici was the one who had requested the meeting, it was obvious that Mr. Cornelius intended to conduct it. Mici obediently took the place assigned to her and let him get on with it.

"Now, Mr. Marin," J. Cornelius began in his clipped Harvard accent which with the years grew more clipped and more related to London than to Boston, "I am bound to inform you that the investigation into your allegations against Miss Anhalt has turned up no confirmation whatsoever." Turning to Mici, he intoned with the same pontifical neutrality, "As you are undoubtedly aware, Miss Anhalt, that does not constitute a verdict of not guilty. However, under the circumstances, it would not be fair to penalize you by continuing your suspension. Therefore you are herewith reinstated with all privileges."

He beamed on her. Adam beamed on her. Wally grinned.

"Thank you, sir," Mici replied. "But I don't want my job back."

Consternation. Dismay And from one person in that room the edge of triumph barely showing.

"Not under these circumstances, Mr. Cornelius," Mici continued. "I won't come back unless I'm completely exonerated and restored to your and Mr. Dowd's trust and respect and to that of my colleagues."

"You never lost my trust and respect, Miss Anhalt," Dowd announced with a pomposity equal to his chief's. The looks flashed at him in response from Cornelius and Mici were quite different.

"Thank you, Mr. Dowd," Mici matched the formality. Then she turned again to the commissioner. "I asked for this meeting with the intention of clearing myself. But first I would like to ask Mr. Marin to withdraw his charges."

Everyone looked at the blind man. Clay Marin was well shaved this morning, with accessories matched to his best gray suit, gold cuff links gleaming at his wrists, shoes freshly polished, and yet he managed to look seedy.

"Why should he do that?"

Wally Lischner spoke for Marin. He, too, had dressed for the occasion wearing a straight business suit with proper shirt and discreet tie. His beard was meticulously trimmed. His manner matched his dress: subdued, honestly puzzled.

"Because Mr. Marin has been misrepresenting his situation to us for some time. To all of us," Mici replied. "He has been misleading us on two counts: his medical condition and the situation at home. First, his medical condition. Mr. Marin has become very skilled in the use of his laser cane. I checked that out with his Lighthouse instructor. But Mr. Marin has led us to believe that he was getting around so much better lately not because of his expertise, but due to improved vision. I'm sorry to say that is not the case. According to Dr. Harden's report, of which I have a copy, Mr. Marin's vision has been steadily deteriorating since the original injury." Mici laid the document in front of Cornelius, pausing just long enough for him to glance over it. When he signaled that he had done so, she continued.

"As to his home situation . . ." Mici sighed and turned to Sandra Marin. "I'm afraid that Clay has been saying some very unpleasant things."

"What things?" Sandra Marin asked.

"Miss Anhalt . . ." Dowd shook his head at Mici.

"What things?" Sandra Marin demanded.

"That you're never home."

"That's true enough but . . ."

"I've called several times myself to discuss Clay's treatment with you but have never been able to reach you."

"Yes, all right, but didn't Clay explain . . ."

"He tried to cover for you, naturally. But there came the time when he couldn't. It wasn't easy for your husband to admit that you had turned your back on him, that

248

the house was dirty, the children neglected, that he was the one who had to get them off to school in the morning and fix the evening meal for them when they came home."

Sandra Marin gasped; she tried to speak, but Mici wouldn't let her—not yet.

"It wasn't easy for him to admit that you were having an affair with another man."

Now Mici paused and now that she had her chance, now that everyone waited to hear her side, Sandra Marin appeared incapable of uttering a word. She looked helplessly at her husband, then back to Mici. "I don't believe it," she said at last.

"It's true. We've all heard the story. He has complained to every one of us here in this room, except perhaps Mr. Cornelius."

The blonde shook her head in puzzlement. "Clay . . ." she appealed to the man who sat silent beside her.

Mici came to her aid. "The fact is that you lied, isn't that so, Mr. Marin? Your wife wasn't home because she was working. She has a job. You do get the children off to school and you do fix their meal when they get home because she's at the office earning the money that keeps you all going."

Marin dropped his head.

"Why? Why, Clay?" Sandra Marin asked sadly. "Why did you say a thing like that?"

"I was afraid that if they found out you were working and earning a good salary they'd cut me off."

"Your loss of salary compensation runs a specified period, Mr. Marin. It can be terminated only when you yourself get employment. Weren't you informed?" Cornelius asked sternly.

Marin nodded. "I was afraid . . ."

"You were afraid that if your vision deteriorated to the

point where improvement seemed hopeless, we'd cut off your medical assistance, that we'd give up on you," Mici put in. "We never give up on anyone, Mr. Marin."

"He said you would." The blind man turned his head toward Lischner.

"I did not. I never did." Lischner bristled. "You misunderstood."

"You made it very clear," Marin insisted. "On the day Miss Anhalt missed my appointment, you told me that she had missed it because she was no longer interested in me, because my case was about to be closed out."

"I never said that. Never. It's a lie." Lischner was on his feet and glaring at his accuser. "It's a lie."

"We were in Miss Anhalt's office and you got the records out of her drawer and told me what Dr. Harden had reported. It was the first I knew of it."

"The man's a liar and a cheat." Lischner's cheeks flamed; the neatly trimmed beard served as a catch basin for the sweat pouring off his face. "He's admitted lying about his wife in an attempt to defraud this office. If he can do that, he can certainly . . ."

"You promised me you'd see to it that I got the operation and that all benefits would be extended." Marin's voice topped the investigator's. "You said you'd get rid of Dr. Harden's report, but that I'd have to bring charges against Miss Anhalt."

Lischner's outrage finally drowned him out. "Why should I do such a terrible thing? Against a colleague? Miss Anhalt and I are friends. We've even dated. Isn't that right, Mici? Tell them."

He had given her the opening. "I'm glad you mentioned that, Wally. Yes, it's true. We did go out together. Once. Just once."

"That was your choice. I asked you out again. I asked you over and over and you turned me down. Well, that's another story."

"No, it isn't."

250

But Lischner ignored her and appealed to Cornelius. "It's Mr. Marin's word against mine, sir. He has a reason for lying. I don't."

"You made a heavy play for me." Mici ignored Lischner's appeal to the commissioner. "A very heavy play and I wasn't interested."

He flushed slightly but shrugged it off. "That was your privilege. This isn't the time or the place . . ."

"This is exactly the time and the place."

His color deepened, turned into an ugly, unhealthy purple. Ignoring Marin, he crossed in front of the blind man to confront Mici. "You're cleared. The man has admitted his charges were false. What more do you want?"

"I want you to admit that you put him up to it."

"I didn't," he hissed, his face so close to hers that his spittle sprayed her.

Cornelius cleared his throat. "I think this matter should be discussed . . ."

Neither Mici nor Lischner paid attention; they were bonded to each other in a struggle of wills.

"Okay," Mici said. "Let's talk about our date. You made a heavy pass and you wouldn't take no for an answer. You were very hard to turn off. Did I laugh too much? I'm sorry. I didn't mean to ridicule you. The truth is, I was embarrassed by the display."

He turned livid. He choked and for a moment Mici thought he was going to have some kind of apoplectic attack. He managed to avoid it and appeal again to Cornelius. "Either you order Miss Anhalt to retract . . ."

"One week ago a man broke into my apartment and tried to rape me."

That silenced Lischner. She had everyone's attention completely, and he knew that he could no longer hope to stop her.

"I defended myself by plunging a pair of small scissors into his back, just between the shoulder blades. I told Mr. Dowd about it, and of course I reported it to the police. It was dark in my room and the assailant wore a ski mask so I couldn't give much of a description, but the wound should be sufficient identification. Would you mind removing your jacket and shirt, Wally?"

Wally pulled back as though he feared he would be stripped by force, though no one came near him. He looked to Adam and saw no hope. "I refuse to dignify such a monstrous allegation." He looked to Cornelius and saw distaste. "I was there at her invitation, *her* invitation!" he yelled, his eyes sweeping the room, but each person to whom he appealed looked away till there was only Mici herself.

"You'll never prove otherwise. I could sue you for sticking those scissors into me. I will. I'll charge you with grievous bodily injury . . ."

"Enough!" Roaring, J. Hammond Cornelius got to his feet. "Enough!"

"Nowadays all a woman has to do is scream rape and everybody's on her side," Lischner whined.

"Attempted rape," Mici corrected. "You didn't make it. That's the trouble, isn't it, Wally?"

Her eyes, faded to a platinum sheen, transfixed him.

"That's why you tried to discredit me and get me fired, isn't it? Because you failed and you couldn't bear to have me around as a constant reminder that you'd failed—a second time."

Lischner squirmed but her look held him. He couldn't tear loose; he couldn't speak. A slow flush appeared at the rim of his tight collar and rose till humiliation flamed in his whole face.

And suddenly Mici pitied him. His craven silence was all the admission necessary, she thought, and turned away. No use piling it on.

252

STARDUST

This Large Print Book carries the
Seal of Approval of N.A.V.H.

STARDUST

Shari MacDonald

Thorndike Press • Thorndike, Maine

Most scripture quotations are from: *The Holy Bible, New International Version* (NIV) © 1973, 1984 by International Bible Society, used by permission of Zondervan Publishing House.

Published in 1999 by arrangement with Multnomah Publishers.

Thorndike Large Print ® Christian Fiction Series.

The tree indicium is a trademark of Thorndike Press.

The text of this Large Print edition is unabridged.
Other aspects of the book may vary from the original edition.

Set in 16 pt. Plantin.

Printed in the United States on permanent paper.

Library of Congress Cataloging in Publication Data

MacDonald, Shari.
    Stardust / Shari MacDonald.
      p. cm.
    ISBN 0-7862-1806-1 (lg. print : hc : alk. paper)
    1. Astronomers — New Jersey — Princeton — Fiction.
2. God — Knowableness — Fiction. 3. Large type books.
I. Title.
PS3563.A2887S7 1999
  813'.54—dc21   98-54662

To my brother, Daniel Patrick MacDonald.
For loving the stars and the heavens and
the One who made them . . .
and for loving me.

Thanks for the great memories of
stargazing together when we were kids,
and for having the patience to let your
little sister use *your* telescope (sometimes).
Only for you would
I have braved the flying bats.

Special thanks

To Michael Bakich, Ph.D., for setting me straight on all the things I thought I knew about astronomy, and for helping me out with the countless things I didn't. E-mails even during Christmas vacation? Like God's, your mercies are never ceasing.

To Claire Widmark, for moving to New Jersey and opening my eyes to how beautiful it is, though it doesn't make up for missing you.

To Allen Jones and Beth Reilley for making sure *my* New Jersey sounds like the *real* New Jersey.

To my editor, Traci DePree, for your tremendous help and support.

And to my previous editors, Judith Markham and Gloria Chisholm, because I unbelievably forgot to give public thanks for your wonderful work on my first three books.

The heavens tell of the glory of God and the firmament tells the work of his hands.
PSALM 19:1

Prologue

May 4, 1975

"Look, Mama!" Wide hazel eyes shone bright with hope as the child tipped back her curly, golden head and peered up at the vast New Jersey sky. "It's the first star!" the girl whispered in awe and reached out one red-mittened paw to tug at her mother's sleeve.

Lovingly, Emma wrapped one hand around her daughter's fingers. "I see it, Gilly!" she murmured, throwing a half-hearted glance heavenward but continuing to walk wearily toward the house.

Normally, she might stop for a moment to enjoy the sights, smells, and sounds that were so much a part of the Central New Jersey country experience. But not tonight. It had been a long evening of "networking" with her husband's associates at the university. Joseph had promised they would be home by eight; they hadn't even pulled into the driveway until nine-thirty. If she'd suspected it was going to be more than a

9

simple dinner, and an evening-long affair at that, she would have tried to get a baby-sitter. Amazingly, Gilly had weathered the evening well. Better, in fact, than Emma had. Nevertheless, it was time to get this little girl — and this woman — to bed.

The gloved hand slipped from her grasp as Gillian resolutely planted her feet against the pavement and declared, "I gotta make a wish!" Patiently, Emma Spencer waited as her only child screwed her face up tight and began to whisper in a singsong voice, "Star light, star bright, first start I see tonight, I wish I may, I wish I might, have this wish I wish tonight. I wish . . ." She fell silent then, but her lips continued to move soundlessly.

"Gillian, hurry up," Joseph called out crossly from several feet ahead. He gave his wife a look of disapproval. "You know, you really shouldn't encourage her in these things. She's just going to get her hopes up, thinking her wishes will come true." Without waiting for an answer, he turned and stepped up to the wraparound porch with keys in hand, while Emma stopped and waited for Gilly to finish.

When she opened her eyes again, the little girl's face was shining.

Emma leaned down, with her face close to Gillian's. "What did you wish for, sweetheart?" she asked with a smile and smoothed the fabric of her child's bright red coat.

"Oh no, Mama." Gilly shook her head fiercely. "I can't tell you. Then it won't come true."

The woman's lips twitched in amusement. "Are you sure, honey? I thought that rule was just for blowing out birthday candles."

"We-ell . . ." Gillian eyed her uncertainly. Then, her desire to share the secret overcoming her resolve, she made a decision. "Okay!" she beamed. "I wished for a husban' who will love me," she said confidently. "Like Raggedy Anne has Raggedy Andy, Barbie has Ken . . . and you have Daddy!"

Emma gave her a halfhearted smile. "Well! I'm honored to be in such illustrious company," she said weakly.

Gilly scowled, as if disapproving her mother's choice of big words, but allowed herself to be swept up in a warm, motherly hug.

"That should be an easy wish to make come true," Emma said, holding her tightly. "You're pretty lovable, you know."

"Do you think the stars can hear me when I wish?" Gilly asked, wriggling within her mother's arms.

"I don't know," Emma replied thoughtfully, letting her own gaze drift to the sky overhead. "But my mother — your grandma — always told me that God can."

Gilly searched her mother's face. "Does that mean my wish will come true?" she asked after a moment of careful consideration.

"I don't know," Emma repeated, but her eyes seemed hopeful, too. "I guess we'll just have to wait and see, honey," she said, pressing her lips against her child's soft, fragrant golden hair. "We'll just have to wait and see."

One

To Noon he fell, from Noon to dewy Eve,
A Summer's day; and with the setting Sun
Dropt from the Zenith like a falling Star.
JOHN MILTON, PARADISE LOST

June 19, 1987

From my window I can see him, just sitting there, drinking from a big ol' tumbler of Mom's horrible sun tea. He's at the patio table she bought last summer, the one with the ocean-colored beach umbrella sticking out of the Plexiglass top. Painted butterflies flap across the material, which drapes over his head like a tacky plastic sky. I'd have thought Dad wouldn't be caught dead under anything so froufrou, but I learned a long time ago that he doesn't notice anything he doesn't want to. Not even me.

Yesterday he missed my birthday . . . again. Something about a black hole lecture this time. Isn't that perfect? What I want to know is, what kind of pathetic nerd goes to an astrophysics seminar on June 18, anyway? It's summer vacation, for crying out loud. You'd think these guys would take a break sometimes, but they never do.

Take right now, for instance. He could be off playing golf, like Jenny's father, or setting up a barbecue, if we had one. But what's my dad doing? Waiting around for one of his eager-beaver students from the university. He takes one under his wing every year, and this time he's picked some hot-shot grad student, a math whiz from Idaho. Guys like that are always trying to buddy-up to him. Mom calls it "mentoring." I call it "sucking up." Dad's students know he's friends with important scientists all over the world. They want to milk it for all it's worth. And Dad, he doesn't even see or care that he's being used.

My theory is, he just likes having all these guys around, acting like they worship him. It makes him feel important, though you'd think he would feel important enough already. I don't worship Dad anymore, and he knows it. Not that it mattered when I did. Sometimes I think things would have been different if I'd been a boy, although I'm not sure why. All I know is, Dad somehow makes time for these twerpy little geeks, but he's never, ever had time for me. Not since I was little, anyway. I'm glad I don't worship him. I'd be crazy if I did.

Mom says Dad really loves me, he's just

obsessed with his own little science world, and it's hard for him to see how the things he does affect those of us living in reality. Single-minded, she calls it. Mom's got words for everything. So do I, but I'm not allowed to use them. Mom's very devout. She became a Christian last year, so she's got a lot of rules now about how I'm supposed to behave. I believe in God, too. Sort of. I'm just not all gung ho about it, like Mom is. Most of her rules are okay, though. I mean, I'd never say this to her, but at least she's paying attention to how I live my life, which is a lot more than I can say about Dad.

This year's birthday was better than last year's, though, I have to admit. Dad promised to come to my party, then didn't even show. No Dad, no present. Nada. This year, at least there were a bunch of packages from him. "To Gilly," they said, in Mom's loopy handwriting. "Love, Dad." I'm not dumb — I know Mom bought them. She didn't even try to hide it. But at least she made the effort, so we could all pretend he wanted to be there. That was a relief.

One of the presents, it turned out, was this diary. I think Mom misses being young. Lately, she's been telling me that I'm in the prime of my life. That's why she got me this book, I guess. So I can write down all the

15

*prime stuff that happens to me. Puhlleeeeeze.
Who does she think she's kidding? I can't
think of even one thing that's ever happened
to me that's so exciting I'd want to remember
it forever. Except maybe that time in third
grade when Jamie Kubitz bit my arm, and I
turned around and bit him right back. You
could see teeth marks on his knuckles for
almost a week. That was pretty cool. I think
I'd like to remember that forever. I bet you
Jamie would rather forget.*

*Mom says I should write about me, who I
am, what I think. That seems kinda dumb.
I'm writing this for me, aren't I? Don't I know
who I am? But maybe I'll die, like Anne
Frank. Then I guess I might become famous,
as long as people know who I am and why
they should care about me. So, here goes.*

*I'm Gillian Spencer, fifteen — oops, no, now
I'm sixteen years old. My dad is the very
famous Dr. Joseph Spencer, professor of astrophysics at Princeton University. Mother is
Emma Masterson-Spencer, political speech
writer. If it sounds like it would be cool to have
two famous parents . . . well, it's not. Dad says
that lots of kids would appreciate having distinguished parents. I say, goody for them. The
only advantage I can see is that Mom and
Dad can afford to buy me rad clothes and
stuff, which isn't such an advantage at my*

16

school anyway. Everyone *at Chatsworth has rich parents and expensive clothes. So, really, the only effect my parents' jobs have on me is that they take Mom and Dad away for a few days every month. At least I have our house-keeper, Norrie. I can always count on her to be here. Last summer, one of my aunts was visiting and she called Norrie my* nanny. *Anyone with any sense knows that a fifteen-year-old doesn't need a baby-sitter! Norrie, at least, understood. "Oh no," she shook her gray head and looked at me seriously. "That girl doesn't need a nanny, she needs a friend." Amen to that, sister.*

Not that I don't have friends, mind you. I may not be the most popular girl at Chats-worth, but I have a pretty tight circle of girls I hang with. Some of the teachers think I don't try very hard at my studies, and I guess that's true. Everyone at Chat is just so competitive. I hate it. All the kids have rich, smart parents. Dad says I'll have to try harder if I want to get into a good college. Maybe I'd care about that more if I knew what I wanted to do. Dad's pushing me toward astronomy. Big sur-prise. It's true, I really liked watching the stars with him when I was a kid, but that was a long time ago. Sometimes I still go out and look at the sky, but if Dad sees me, I stop and pretend I'm out picking up my bike or some-

thing. I don't want him to feel too smug. He hasn't got my loyalty. He hasn't earned it.

Speaking of Dad, he's still out there, by the way, and looking pretty ticked. I guess the kid is late. That's something, anyhow. It's good for my father, I think, to have things not go the way he plans every once in a while. That way he knows what it's like. Like this one time —

Oh, wait. Here comes the geek. This should be good. Okay . . . he just poked his bushy brown head in the side gate, and now Dad's waving him in. But . . . you know, the funny thing is, this one doesn't really look like a geek. In fact, he's dressed pretty cool. No dopey little white button-up shirt or polyester pants. Just a navy sweatshirt and jeans. His hair is awfully thick, but it's actually kind of cute. This has gotta be a mistake. He can't be one of Dad's weirdo students. Wait . . . he's starting to turn around now, and . . . oh, my gosh, this one is a babe! And now he's shaking my dad's hand like he knows him, and Dad is smiling and pointing toward the house, and the guy just looked up, and I think he saw me before I could duck, 'cause he smiled real big, right at my window!

Okay, that's it. I've got to go call Jenny! More later . . . Finally, I've got something to write about! Maybe this is going to be a cool summer after all.

"Hey, Bridget! Look at me! I'm Julia Child!" Gleefully, twenty-six-year-old Gillian Spencer raised two eggs high over the kitchen stove — holding one in each hand — and eyed her cast-iron pan, which was already sizzling invitingly. Her hazel eyes danced as she considered the feat she was about to attempt.

"Uhnh," her roommate mumbled non-committally, keeping her brown eyes trained on the newspaper in front of her. "Just make sure you don't drop the eggs on the burner again, please."

Gillian scowled in disappointment but dutifully lowered her arms. "You didn't even bother to look up," she grumbled, throwing a disparaging look at Bridget. "I was going to crack 'em with both hands at once." She narrowed her eyes at a dark spot on one egg shell, shrugged, and dismissed it, having decided it was simply a bit of dried goo that had gotten stuck while in the carton.

From the breakfast nook, tucked into the west corner of the old farmhouse kitchen, Bridget read the paper while nursing a lukewarm cup of coffee. "Yeah, well, I don't stop at the scene of accidents, either." A tiny smile played at the corner of her lips. "There are some things I'd just rather not witness. Like you cooking."

She looked up at Gillian, but Gillian was ignoring her. Having taken Bridget's chastisement to heart, she let her eyes flicker across the sunlit room, looking for a surface other than the pan upon which to crack her eggs. At last her gaze settled back on the edge of the stove. "Ah-ha!" she cried triumphantly.

"Good grief," Bridget said. "What are you doing now?" Then, as realization dawned on her, "Oh no. Gil, wait. Now, don't do that, you'll — !"

"Whoops!" Gilly froze, her hands poised in midair, as two yellow yolks and a clear, gooey mass dribbled down the crack between the battered white stove and the old Amana refrigerator. She chuckled despite herself. Bridget laid the paper down and began to giggle uncontrollably.

"What's going on?" The soft voice of their third roommate, Pam Holzman, could barely be heard over the din of their laughter. Pam padded into the room, wearing her gray cotton pj's and thick, oversized wool socks. "Oh," she said, her bright blue eyes inspecting the mess. "I see

20

Gillian has been cooking again. I thought we made a rule against that." She tucked a strand of her long, black hair behind one ear and began digging in the painted white cupboard for a box of her favorite sugar-coated cereal.

"Well, excuse me for trying to eat something healthy." Gillian sniffed self-righteously, trying to divert the attention from her own faux pas. "At least I'm not scarfing down Sugar-O's, or whatever you call that junk you eat." She wiped egg from her hands with a terry cloth dish towel. Thankfully, she had managed not to spill any on her shirt of lilac-colored linen or on her trim white cotton pants.

Pam yawned and continued her search, undeterred by Gillian's criticism. "Healthy? I don't think so. A little sugar isn't going to clog my arteries," she patiently explained. "Unlike *your* breakfast. I'm surprised at you. You should know better. You're supposed to be a scientist, you know. Doesn't that mean anything nowadays?"

Gillian sighed. "An egg every now and then isn't going to hurt me, and the protein's good for me. Anyway, I *like* real food. I'd never survive on that stuff you eat — which, by the way, isn't as harm-

21

less as you think — or on nothing but coffee, like Bridget."

At the sound of her name, Bridget threw her arms up in the air. "I am *not* going to have this conversation." She shook her head of short chestnut curls. "When we moved in together, we agreed not to mother each other. Remember?" Despite her breakfasts of coffee, Bridget still looked healthy and well-fed but by no means overweight. Actually, she was quite attractive. And even though she hadn't yet met the man of her dreams — though not for lack of trying — her looks had brought her more than a few dates over the years. This morning, Gillian noticed, Bridget looked especially nice, with her cocoa-colored cotton pants and matching short-sleeved cable cardigan bringing out the rich color in her deep, brown eyes.

"Yeah, Gillian. Which means, I'm not going to clean up your mess." Pam stared at the dripping egg goo, which was already beginning to mold itself to the black and white vinyl floor tiles.

"Okay, okay. I get the picture." Gillian rested her hands on her slim hips and regarded the situation with a problem-solver's eye. Then, choosing a plan of action, she leaned forward over the counter, secured the fingers of both hands behind the back corner of the fridge, and began to carefully jog the appliance forward.

"Oh, Gil. You're never going to get it out that way!" Bridget abandoned her newspaper and moved to help her. Within minutes, the two women had pulled it from its corner. As she reclaimed her spot at the breakfast nook, Bridget wiped away a bit of dust that clung to her sleeve.

"Thanks." Gillian went to the sink, retrieved a damp sponge, and set to work. Before long, the spill was gone, the refrigerator back in position, and the egg fiasco nothing more than a memory. "There!" she said, with a little sigh of satisfaction. "Now, let's see . . . let me try this again." But by this time the frying pan was a blackened mess, having burned up the oil coating she had sprayed inside it. "Ugh." She turned off the stove in disgust, grabbed a bowl and spoon, and seated herself at the table next to Pam. "May I?" she said, nodding at the box of frosted oat cereal.

"Hmm." Pam pretended to consider her request. "Are you sure you can *survive* on this stuff?"

"I'm sure," Gillian told her seriously,

refusing to rise to the bait.

"No more mocking my breakfast?" her roommate pressed.

Gillian sighed again. "Oh, all right. If you insist. No more mocking."

"Okay," Pam said cheerfully, pushing the box toward her. "Help yourself."

Gillian grabbed the box, drawing her eyebrows together in consternation as she poured. "Seriously, though, you guys . . . do you really think I'm such a bad cook?"

"What do you mean?" Bridget glanced up from her paper. "Why does it matter what *we* think? The question is, do *you* think you're a bad cook?"

"No-oo," Gillian said uncertainly. "I know I'm kind of disorganized —"

"You mean you cook like the Absent-minded Professor," Pam said helpfully.

"— and I have a tendency toward minor accidents," Gillian continued, ignoring her. "But I think the food winds up tasting okay."

"Well, then. What's the problem?"

"We-ell . . ."

Bridget waved her coffee spoon in the air, and with the expression of a psychiatrist on the verge of a clinical breakthrough said, "Keith hates your cooking. That's it, isn't it?"

Gillian smiled at the reference to her boyfriend. Blond, brilliant, full of smiles . . . No, Keith wasn't her problem. The two of them never fought. Theirs was an easy partnership, one that centered around social functions and mutual cheerleading. He supported her one-hundred percent in her career goals and ambitions, and she supported him. It never occurred to her to criticize him or to challenge him — they didn't have that kind of relationship. Gillian was sure Keith felt the same way.

She shook her head. "Huh-unh. He likes my cooking just fine."

"Well, then . . . ?"

"Oh, it's nothing." Gillian dragged her spoon through her bowl, playing with the floating O's. "Forget it."

"Speaking of Keith, doesn't he come home sometime this week? Aren't you excited about seeing him?" Bridget smiled knowingly, the previous subject already forgotten, and Gillian grinned in return.

Leave it to Bridget to bring the conversation back to romance. Like Gillian, she was a graduate student at Princeton. But unlike Gil, who studied astrophysics, Bridget pursued not science, but Romance Literature. Gillian theorized that at some point, Bridget's studies had seeped into some

25

deeper part of her psyche — there was nothing more interesting to the woman than romance, and nothing she desired more for her own life than love. In some individuals, this characteristic would seem irritating, even pathetic. In Bridget, it was somehow endearing.

"Yes, I'm excited. Of course I am," Gillian told Bridget logically. "He's been away at this legal conference for over a week. I've missed him a lot." She felt a tiny twinge of guilt at the sound of her words. Was that last part a white lie? The truth of the matter was, she had almost been *relieved* to have a week to herself. That didn't mean anything significant, though, she was sure. Lots of couples — *happy* couples — needed to take time for themselves as individuals. Enjoying their time apart didn't mean a thing. She *did* miss Keith . . . sort of. It was always nice to have him around. It was just . . . just that she had been so busy lately. She wasn't quite ready to give up her freedom yet. She'd gotten more done during his absence than she normally did in a month. But, she reminded herself, work wasn't everything.

She had broken up, for one reason or another, with countless men since she had been at Princeton. One guy talked too

26

much, another talked too little. . . . It seemed there was always something that eventually got under her skin and caused her to break up. At this rate, she'd be alone forever. Gillian was determined to hang in there this time.

She would feel more excited, she was sure, once she saw Keith at the airport. He was the nicest guy she had ever dated. She wasn't going to mess this one up, just because there weren't incredible sparks. Sometimes love just wasn't the walk in the park folks expected. Gillian had felt sparks once before, back when she was barely more than a kid, and the feeling hadn't been returned. There wasn't anything very romantic about *that*.

"He's such a *cutie*, Gil. How can you stand it?" Bridget said plaintively, her thoughts clearly still on Keith. "Why can't I ever meet — oh!" She sat up straight. "I almost forgot! Speaking of *cuties*, who's that gorgeous new guy in your department?"

"What new guy?" Gillian lowered her eyes and dug into her bowl of now-soggy oat bits. She knew exactly who Bridget was talking about. How could she *not*? She'd been avoiding him all week.

"Tasty little morsels, aren't they?" Pam

couldn't help but tease. Gillian grimaced but didn't feel much like mocking anymore.

"You know," Bridget said impatiently, ignoring their sparring. "The *new* one. The one without a wedding ring. I saw him yesterday when I dropped off your gym bag. You were at lunch, and I saw him talking with your nerdy boss."

"You mean Ed Cheatham?"

"That's the one. Ed was saying something about finding this guy an office to work in."

Gillian stuck another spoonful of cereal into her mouth and chewed, seizing upon the extra moment to collect her thoughts. *So, Bridget's seen him. I wonder what he looks like now?* After ten years, she was more than a little curious. Not curious enough, though, to stick around the main office where he might run across her. She felt silly avoiding the man. But she'd spent years getting over the crush she'd had on Max Bishop, and she wasn't exactly looking forward to having those old memories come up again. She certainly didn't want *anyone* to know about how pitifully infatuated — and rejected — she had been.

"I have no idea who he is, Bridget," she fibbed.

"Well, do you think you could find out?"

Gillian stared at her. "Why? Are you interested or something?"

"Um, I don't know," her friend backpedaled a bit, her face flushing pink with embarrassment. "I mean, he's cute and everything, but I don't really know hi—"

"Oh, give it up, Bridget. It's too late to play coy now," Pam informed her. "It's *obvious* you like the guy."

"That's not necessarily true." Bridget tried to sound disinterested. "I don't know anything about him. Besides, maybe Gillian's holding out on me. Maybe she knows all about him and is just keeping him for herself."

"Oh, right! That's me. A guy in every port!" Gillian protested, pasting a smile on her face. "No thanks. I've got my hands full already with Keith. You can have the new guy, if you want. I'll see what I can find out about him." Suddenly, Gillie felt sick. She peered into the blue bowl in front of her. *The milk must be bad. I'd better remember to check the date. . . .*

"Thanks, Gil!" Bridget sat back and smiled in relief. "Hey, do you want to forget your gym bag again?" she tried hopefully. "I can bring it by one more time."

"Hmm. Very subtle. I'm sure no one would notice." Gillian said in a weak attempt to tease her. "I think I've got a better idea, though. How about this? You come down and meet me for lunch. I'll arrange to be running late so you can hang around for a few minutes. That way you can meet the guy." She sat back in her chair, her queasiness fading to smugness. *That's it,* she told herself. *Set Max up with Bridget!* It was perfect. After a move like that, no one — not even Gillian, herself — could doubt that she was over him.

"Thanks, Gil. You're the best!" Bridget swallowed the dregs of her cold coffee, made a face, and cleared her things from the table. "Oh, my gosh, look at the time. You want to carpool? I have to go in early today."

"Nah, thanks." Gillian shook her head. "I have no idea how late I'll have to stay tonight. I'll just see you this afternoon."

"Okay."

As the two prepared to head off to the university, Pam grabbed the paper and pawed through the pages, as part of her daily search through the want ads.

"Got any interviews today?" Gillian asked.

"Nope. Still figuring out what I want to do next," Pam said, referring to her recent graduation from Princeton's MBA program.

"Ugh." Bridget eyed Pam with disgust. "I can't *believe* you get to stay home all day."

"Sorry, sweetie!" Pam batted her eyelashes, looking not the least bit apologetic. "I have a feeling you've got a more exciting day ahead, though."

"That's right, Bridget," Gillian agreed, wondering what the day might hold. "You met a cute guy. Who knows? This might turn out to be an interesting summer, after all."

Two

This is the very ecstasy of love.
SHAKESPEARE, *AS YOU LIKE IT* (III, II)

June 25, 1987

I've been spying on this guy for almost a week now. He seemed so great at first, I was sure that there had to be some mistake. So I watched him reeeaaallly carefully. Any minute, I figured, his geek tendencies would begin to show. I looked for pocket protectors, but he carries his pens around in his notebook, just like the rest of us. I checked out the hem of his pants, but they weren't high-waters. He doesn't wear polyester, either. And on his feet he wears regular old athletic shoes, like a normal guy. Is he for real? How'd he end up in one of my dad's classes?

He's come to see my father three times now. During the school year, Dad's grad students don't show their faces so much around the house. But during the summer, Dad likes to make them come here. It's a power thing, I guess. I still don't get to see this one a lot, though. He usually goes straight to Dad's study. If I wasn't watching for him, I'd miss him altogether.

One day I actually gathered up the nerve to ask Dad about him. It was totally under-handed, the way I did it. Quite a work of art, though Mom would never approve. Dad was in his office on Tuesday morning, working on some papers, when I knocked on the door.

I leaned on the doorjamb, all casual-like. "Um . . . some guy called for you this morning, but I forgot to write down the message," I told him. "Sorry."

Dad didn't even look up. "Well, who was it?" he asked.

"I — I don't remember."

"Did you recognize the voice? Was it one of the professors at the university?"

"Nooooo," I said slowly, pretending like I was trying to remember. "He sounded younger than that. Coulda been one of your students. I'm pretty sure I'd recognize the name if I heard it again." Then I set my final trap: "Could be that new guy you're tutoring."

Dad didn't answer at first, and for a sick-ening moment, I was afraid he wasn't going to. Then finally he lifted his head. "What's that?" he asked. "Tutoring? Do you mean Max Bishop?"

I chewed on my thumbnail and played dumb. "I dunno. That doesn't really sound familiar. Are you the advisor for more than one student right now?"

"No, just Max."

"The one who's been coming here to the house?" I must have sounded a little too interested because Dad gave me a funny look right then.

"Yes. Max is the young man who has been coming here. Are you saying that he called?"

"Uh . . . no. I'm sure that wasn't it. Must have been some other guy. I guess he'll call back if it's important. See ya." Then I got out of there as fast as I could.

What's going on with me? I mean, I've noticed guys in my class before. And even though I've never known one I liked that much, I've always kinda enjoyed the idea. But . . . I've never felt anything like this before. No wonder people say that love makes you sick. I'm getting queasy just thinking about it.

Max Bishop . . . Max Bishop . . . Max Bishop. *I like writing the name. I like watching him even better. I've figured out that I have a pretty good line of vision from my bedroom window. Dad's office has a door at the side of the house, and to get to it you have to walk through the backyard. I always liked this before, because if I knew the geeks were coming, it made it easier to avoid them. Now that there aren't any geeks, it's a pain. See, if*

Max had to come to the front door of the house, I could answer it and see him up close. The way it is now, though, at least I get a good look at him when he comes into the yard.

I'm not sure what it is about him that makes him so . . . watchable. Maybe it's the way he moves: all smooth and confident, but full of tension and energy at the same time — like a tiger prowling the desert, looking for his next meal, even though he's not quite ready to eat it. It's not that Max looks uptight. He seems relaxed . . . sort of. His arms swing easily from his shoulders, and he's got a confident, athletic walk that's nothing like the puny little steps my dad's students usually take. But there's a fire in his eyes. I can see it from all the way up here.

One day, my dad was walking Max out to the gate after their session, and they were arguing about something. I remember, I looked down and Max's eyes were just snapping! I've never been able to quite tell what color they are, but at that moment they were bright and black, like the shells of two beetles. His voice was raised in excitement, and he waved his arms like crazy. I wished right then that I had paid more attention when Dad talked at the dinner table about his work. I wanted to know what made this guy feel so passionate. What made him tick. Dad, too. Suddenly, it seemed *really important to understand.*

That was a couple of days ago. But then this morning, it happened. . . . I finally got to talk to Max face-to-face!

He had been in his session with Dad for about a half hour, with another half hour to go. Mom had just called me downstairs to help her peel carrots for dinner. It's Norrie's day off, and Mom hates getting stuck in the kitchen all by herself. So I was down there, peeling and pouting because I wasn't going to get to see Max leave, when Mom realized she didn't have enough potatoes. So I volunteered to run to the store. I figured I was going to miss Max anyway. There wasn't any point in sticking around here.

Mom gave me some money, and I went out to get my bike. All I can say is, thank goodness I got a new one last year. (I'm old enough to get my driver's license now, but Dad hasn't given me permission to drive yet. I think he likes having me stay dependent upon him and Mom. Don't even get me started on that whole issue. . . .) The ugly, babyish, hot pink bike, with its basket and tassels and banana seat, was tucked safely in the back of the garage. I had just climbed on my fire-red ten-speed and turned it toward the road when I heard someone come up behind me and say, "Hey, nice bike."

I looked up, and it was Max! What was he doing out here? I didn't know what to say. How would a girl his age answer a comment like that? I opened my mouth to say something flirty, like, "Thanks. Nice eyes." They were, too. Really intense, this great dark blue. But instead it came out: "Ummmm . . . thanks, I got it for my birthday." Oh no, I thought. Now he's going to ask me how old I am. *And, of course, he did.*

"Seventeen," I lied, then immediately felt guilty. Mom hates it when I stretch the truth. It seemed like an even bigger sin to be lying to him.

"Really?" he said. "You're not Gillian then? Dr. Spencer said he had a daughter who just turned sixteen." Max had me there. He could have been really mean about it, but I'm sure he didn't embarrass me on purpose. At first, I thought he really believed I was someone else. But then I saw the twinkle in his eye, and I realized he knew the truth. He was just making me come clean.

"Oh. Uh, no. That's me. Sorry. I thought you were asking how old I was . . . uh, inside. You know, in my heart. If you want actual calendar years, I'm sixteen." I tried to make a joke of it, but I thought I might choke on my words. The guy caught me lying. I was sure he would give me a look of total disgust. But

37

instead, he actually laughed. I guess he appreciated my talent for making up creative excuses. If only he knew how much practice I've had, maybe it wouldn't have seemed so cute.

"No kidding?" he said. "Hunh. Well, in my heart I think I'm sixteen." That's when I began to melt. "It's a great age. You wear it well," he said. I wasn't sure what he meant by that, but I hoped it was some kind of compliment.

For a moment, neither one of us said anything. Then I couldn't stand it anymore. I had to say something. "What are you doing out here?" I blurted out. Immediately, I wanted to kick myself. I talked like a kid. It sounded like I didn't even want him around. What was wrong with me?

"Your dad got an important call, so I took off early," Max told me. I thought I must look like I was about to fall over, but he didn't even notice that my mind was swirling. "Maybe we'll make up the time next week." He grinned at me. "So, I guess I'll see you?" And then he turned around and walked away, right down the street.

And . . . I know it sounds dopey, but I swear, he took my heart with him. Just like those romance books say. He really did.

"No, no, noooooooooo!" Gillian cried in anguish. "Don't crash, you beast!" she begged the computer, but her words were futile. After an instant-long power surge that sent lines zigzagging across her screen, it was clear that the figures she'd been analyzing for over an hour were gone.

Exhaling slowly, she pulled her long, honey-colored hair back into a makeshift knot and secured it with two pencils. *I should have known better. I should have saved my document.* The thought hadn't even occurred to her, she'd been so engrossed in her work. Most of the computers in the physics department were set up with surge protectors to guard against any power shifts. Unfortunately, her temporary workstation in the break room lacked such a luxury.

Gillian sighed. Sometimes being a grad student was a real pain — she managed to get all the grunt work. For the last couple of weeks, she'd been stuck in the department's only unoccupied space, sorting through stacks of documents that needed analysis. No other office had been available. At least the assignment kept her out of the main office during the week of Max's arrival. But that was the *only* good thing about it. She had been hoping for months that Ed would assign her to some interesting project. All she'd done over the past year was a little bit of number crunching, a lot of paper pushing, and a truckload of filing. Though there weren't any classes this summer, she was to continue working in the department until the fall semester began.

Gillian stared at the empty screen. "Well, that's one hour out of my life I'll never see again." She grumbled and looked at her watch. "Uh-oh. Almost lunch time." She wasn't looking forward to this one bit. At some point, though, she was going to have to face Max. Besides, Bridget was meeting her at one o'clock, and so far Gillian hadn't accomplished any part of her mission. When she had arrived that morning, the "new guy" and Ed had been nowhere to be seen. She'd just have to hope, for Bridget's sake, that at least one of them was back by now.

Thankfully, when she returned to the main office, Ed's in-box was empty — a sure sign that he had recently collected his ever-growing stack of messages. This suspicion was confirmed when she found him in his office, wearing his customary button-up dress shirt, gray slacks, and running shoes. She blinked and tried to ignore the obvious fashion "don't."

"Morning, Gillian." Ed's greeting was polite enough, but he didn't bother to take his feet down from their place of rest on his metal desk. Gillian didn't mind. Ed was a brilliant physicist, even if he lacked the most basic of social skills. She had long ago ceased to take his slights personally. He was rude to every one of the grad students. If it sometimes seemed like he was particularly indifferent to her, she knew this was simply because her eagerness to get rolling on a meaty project could be irritating to even the most gracious of souls.

"Hey, Ed." Gillian glanced at the only other chair in the room — a hard, vinyl-and-metal affair, piled high with textbooks. She didn't feel comfortable moving the stack, and Ed didn't offer, so she remained standing.

"How are those calculations coming?" Ed looked up at her and chewed on the metal end of his pencil. The eraser was already gone. Gillian couldn't help wondering if he had accidentally swallowed it.

She hesitated before answering. "Oh, not so bad, I guess, overall. I'm running behind this morning, though," she finally told him. "The computer crashed for a second, and I lost an hour's worth of work." There, she'd said it. She watched him for a reaction, but, surprisingly, Ed didn't seem as concerned about it as she'd feared.

"Oh, well. You can make it up later," he said easily. "I've got something else I want you to do this afternoon, anyway."

"You do?" Gillian shifted her feet uncomfortably and tried to keep the sound of dread from her voice. What was it this time? Purging the department's files from the 1950s? Inputting a notebook full of someone else's calculations? If *she* was getting the assignment, it couldn't be good. Ed hadn't given her a prime project *yet*.

"That's right." Ed stared at her expectantly, as if waiting for her to sit down and hear the details. Gillian glanced once more at the chair across from him but remained standing. Ed hadn't ever gone out of his way to make things easy for her. She wasn't going to act like an overeager schoolgirl. Manner-impaired or not, if he wanted her to sit down, he could very well make room for her. Finally, his eyes followed hers, and with a look of exasperation, he stood and removed the offending books. "Thanks." Gillian seized the unspoken invitation and took a seat.

"I'm sure you've heard," Ed went on as he settled back into his own chair, "that we have a new research astronomer on board, starting this week." Gillian purposely kept her expression blank. "He's a specialist in quantum cosmology. Now, I know that's your area of interest."

Gillian nodded. It was. Ever since she was a child, she had been intrigued by the night sky — the stars, the planets . . . the asteroids, meteors, and comets. In recent years, her thoughts had turned increasingly to where it had all come from. After centuries of looking to the stars, scientists were now looking farther — and with more accuracy — into the heavens than ever before. Yet with all their scientific advances, there were still an infinite number of questions that remained unanswered. These were the questions that crowded her mind: questions that drove her to the study of quantum field theory, wave function, and the Schroedinger equation of particle mechanics . . . principles of relativity, Hubble's law, and Doppler shifts. Questions that ultimately circled back around to the one key issue: the origin and evolution of the physical universe, which seemingly appeared to have been created from nothing.

". . . but more importantly, that's where you focused your undergraduate and postgrad studies," Ed was saying. "This man has asked for us to assign him an assistant. He specifically requested some-one with an interest and background in the origins of the universe." Gillian's heart began to race as he spoke.

"You know, of course, that there are a number of current-day studies focusing on the first moments after the universe came into existence. So far, we can guess what happened as far back as 10^{-43} seconds after the universe began. The purpose of the study you'll be involved in is to go back even further in time — if it is even pos-sible." Ed licked his lips, as if savoring the juicy project.

"You'll be collecting and analyzing data from other observers who have been working on similar theories. You may even serve as an observer, collecting necessary data — including photometric plots, spec-tral plates, and ccd images — at one of the major observatories. This will add to your workload, of course, but I'm sure you will agree that this opportunity is worth? . . ."

Gillian found her mind wandering as he rambled on about her good fortune. *I can't believe this!* She resisted the urge to hug her knees to her chest like a delighted child. *Finally, a project with some substance! Maybe I'll get to make suggestions, even contribute to the work as a whole.* . . . The fact that she didn't know the full details of the assignment did not concern her. It was a full-fledged research project, and she'd be working directly under? . . .

Max.

Dr. Max Bishop, Ph.D., graduate cum laude from Harvard University, former student at Princeton, where Gillian's father had once been a distinguished professor. Former research astronomer at Rome Astronomical Observatory . . . and former heartthrob to the lovesick teenager Gillian had been.

The horrible truth rang in her mind like a death sentence. What was she thinking? She'd been so caught up in the excitement of getting a real assignment, she'd forgotten for a moment exactly who was in charge of the project. This was terrible! She couldn't work with *Max Bishop!* It had taken her years to make him a part of her past. She certainly didn't want him to become an integral part of her future. . . .

Suddenly, she became aware that Ed was staring at her, apparently waiting for some sort of response.

"What was that?" she asked, feeling her cheeks turn warm. "I'm sorry, Ed, I —"

The man blinked at her, then rolled his eyes heavenward, as if wondering at the wisdom of giving Gillian a key role in such an important project. "I asked if that would be a problem — going down to Palomar Observatory to make some observations in late August. Dr. Bishop may go with you, depending on how your work develops over the next month or so, but I suspect you'll be going alone."

Gillian just stared at him. *A trip to Palomar Observatory? At the university's expense? I must be hearing things. . . .* "No, of course that will be fine." She heard herself speaking, as if in a daze.

"Of course," Ed said dryly. Gillian raised her head and gave him a questioning look, but his face betrayed nothing. Was he laughing at her? Did he suspect that she was hiding something? She couldn't tell. "Well, why don't we go introduce you to Dr. Bishop and get you started? Unless, of course, you were planning on getting yourself some lunch first?" Gillian hesitated. She had planned to finally approach Max this morning; Bridget's request had forced the issue. But now the prospect was not appealing in the least. She was still trying to figure out how to respond when she saw a shadow pass the office entrance. Ed turned in his chair, just as the figure disappeared from view.

"Wait a minute . . . I think that was him." He stood and stuck his head out in the hallway. "Wait up there . . . Max." Ed smiled as the person down the corridor apparently turned to face him. "Say, do you have a second? I'd like to introduce you to your new research assistant."

Gillian felt her body begin to tremble. *Okay, girl. Here we go. The moment you've been dreading. Try not to embarrass yourself.*

Just then, a tall, muscular figure filled the doorway. Gillian stared. Amazingly, unbelievably, there he stood. This man appeared much older than the youthful Max Bishop she had known. Gone was the youthful fervor, but in its place rested an aura of seasoned maturity. When she looked into his brilliant blue eyes, she knew he was the same gorgeous man she had dreamt of so long ago, only better.

Max opened his mouth, then snapped it shut again without speaking. For a moment, there was silence between him and Gillian, as there had been the day they first met. But this time, she could not find the words to fill the empty air. After several long moments, he was the first to speak.

"Is it possible? Can it be . . . *my* little Gilly Spencer?"

Gillian's heart leapt in her chest. Suddenly, it was as if time had not passed. She was a child again. And as if it were yesterday, every fiber of her being remembered how it felt to be his.

Three

Love won't be tampered with,
love won't go away.
Push it to one side
and it creeps to the other.
LOUISE ERDRICH, "THE RELIGIOUS WARS,"
THE BINGO PALACE, 1994

June 30, 1987

This morning, I awoke to the sound of a bird singing right outside my window. I suppose it would be more poetic to say "a lark" or "a robin," rather than just "a bird," but the truth is, I don't know anything about birds since I never paid much attention to them before. Is this a sign that I am, really and truly, falling in love?

Well, whatever *was* singing, *I was all excited because I knew that Max was coming today. The last time he was here, I'd been wearing one of my scrungiest outfits — long cutoffs, beat-up old thongs, and a white T-shirt covered with dust from Mom's potatoes and a bit of brown juice from the potato peelings. I*

49

was Cinderella . . . straight out of the cinders.

This time, I made sure I looked my best. I didn't have a fairy godmother who could transform me completely, but I did have Jenny. I called her first thing this morning, and she came right over to do something with my hair. The last perm I got sort of frizzed it out. The best Jenny could do was French braid it, but it helped a lot just to get it under control. After Jenny was done fixing my hair, I got her to pin it up in back so I didn't look like such a kid. Jenny called me "Swiss Miss" then, but I ignored her. I thought I looked pretty cool.

After Jenny left, I put on my favorite outfit: a pink-and-white jumper Mom bought for me last month. I saw it in a magazine and had to have it. I was a little bit disappointed once I tried it on, though. The model in the magazine filled it out a lot better than I did. But it was still cute, just right for a hot day like today.

Next, I chose my props. One of Mom's chaise lounges, my sunglasses, and a glass of lemonade. That would make me look cool, I thought. Finally, I decided to grab a book from my shelf. What could be more casual than reading in the backyard? I started to grab Northanger Abbey — *I love Jane Austen's ridiculous heroine, Catherine —* but then *thought better of it. In the end, I picked up Dad's copy of* The Odyssey. *I didn't know* anything about the story, but the title sounded pretty sophisticated, anyway.

I got everything set up by a quarter to eleven, and not a moment too soon, 'cause Max was early. I was reading page one of The Odyssey for the fifth time when he came into the yard.

"Hey, Max," I said, looking up and turning to the middle of the book. I tried to sound bored but that was hard to do with him standing in front of me, wearing a navy-colored Princeton sweatshirt that brought out the blue in his eyes.

"Hey, kiddo." He smiled back at me. I felt my heart do a little flip.

I looked down at my watch. "You're early," I told him.

"Am I?" Max sounded surprised. He casually tucked his hands into the back pockets of his jeans. "I was afraid I might be late. I've been walking around this morning, thinking, and I forgot my watch. I have a tendency to lose track of time."

More than anything, I wanted to ask him what he thought about when he walked. But that seemed kind of personal, and I was afraid he might tell me to mind my own business.

"Maybe I'll just sit down and talk with you for a few minutes then, if I'm early. You'll tell me when it's time to go in?" He looked around

51

for someplace to sit, and I wanted to smack myself. How stupid could I be? I'd brought out only one chaise lounge. Now there wasn't anyplace for Max to sit. Of course, that meant he would go inside my Dad's office to wait.

But he didn't. He just looked around, then planted himself on the ground, right by my feet. He looked really cute, sitting there in the thick, green grass. For a minute, I imagined myself as some sort of Egyptian princess on top of my throne, with Max as my adoring slave. But the thought was so ridiculous, I had to bite my lip to keep from laughing.

"So, what do you think of our hero, Odysseus?" he asked me, looking at the book I held in my hands.

"I don't know," I said, then held my breath. That, at least, was an honest statement. I figured I sounded dumb, but Max nodded as if my comment had been truly profound.

"Good idea," he said. "Holding off your judgment until the end."

I never thought I could love anyone so much in my whole life. After that, I wasn't sure what to say. "Nice weather," maybe? Even I knew that was dumb. His studies with Dad seemed like my best bet.

"So . . . how do you like having my dad as your advisor?" I asked. I braced myself for the answer I knew had to be coming. Dad's students *always went on and on about how great he was. I always thought it was pretty nauseating, especially since Dad never showed that side of himself to his own daughter. But Max surprised me.*

"It's incredible, having this opportunity to get extra help in my studies. I want to do the best that I can in my field. This is important to me. Really *important, Gilly," he said. "There's something about astronomy that I find really intriguing. I guess it's just that . . . everyday life is just so sterile, you know? So predictable. We get up in the morning, we go to school — or to work — we eat our breakfast, feed the dog . . . and act like that's all there is. We don't notice that all around us, there are other planets, other galaxies. We don't acknowledge that we're just a tiny part of this incredible universe . . . of a bigger plan. Most days, we don't even look up. . . ."*

I watched him as he spoke, and his eyes lit up with the same fire they'd had in them that day I saw him arguing with Dad.

"Dad doesn't believe there's a bigger plan," I said and took a drink of my lemonade.

Max stopped and looked at me. "I know," he said simply. "What do you think?"

I just blinked at him. I couldn't remember the last time anyone asked me what I *thought. "Well, Mom says that there* is *a God, and that* he's the one in control of the universe."

"I see," said Max. Then he repeated, "What do you think?"

I was quiet for a minute. I wasn't quite sure what to say. "I think I believe in God," I told him finally. "But I believe in science, too. I guess I don't think about it too much because I don't want to have to choose."

Max nodded seriously. "Exactly," he said.

I didn't get it. "Exactly . . . what?" I asked.

Max looked at me thoughtfully. "Has your dad ever mentioned his theory about all things being provable?" I shook my head. Normally, I would have been embarrassed or angry that one of Dad's students knew something about him that I didn't. But this wasn't just any student.

"Well," Max went on, "your father believes that there is a scientific explanation for everything . . . we scientists just have to find it."

Then he went on about how some ancient Greeks thought the earth was the center of the universe, and since they couldn't prove it, they made up a theory and believed it anyway. He was so intense that I let him go on — he's even cuter when he's really into something.

"Don't you see, Gilly?" he said. "It didn't make any sense!"

I just stared at him.

"You mean, because they thought the sun

and the planets circled the earth?" I asked.

"Yes, but it's more than that," he insisted. "They needed a theory to explain why the planets didn't orbit in a perfect circle, so they made one up! They couldn't prove it; they just wanted to believe it. Eventually, though, we were able to prove that the planets travel around the sun. At first people felt threatened by this. The idea that the earth wasn't at the center of the universe challenged their assumptions about the relationship between God and man. But in time, it became clear that everything we've learned about the nature of the universe is consistent with Scripture — and with what we know of God."

Max's eyes got real intense after that. "See, those people had faith, but they didn't have the proof to back it up. But every day, we find more scientific evidence that supports a God-made universe." He looked at me real funny, as if just noticing that I was still there. "Gilly, your father believes that given enough time, man can prove anything that's scientifically true . . . and I agree with him."

"You do?" This surprised me.

"I do. And I'm going to do it, someday."

I was almost afraid to ask. "Going to do what?"

Max leaned forward intently, and I nearly fell off the chaise as I inched forward to hear *what he was going to say. "I believe someone created the universe, Gilly. But I'm not going to just believe it. Someday, I'm going to prove it!"*

As I looked into his bright eyes, I wondered if he could. Mom would have said, no, it wasn't possible, that God's ways aren't ours to know. But Mom has been hardened by years of fighting with Dad over science and religion. Could Max really do what he said he would? I couldn't help but wonder.

And even though I wasn't sure what I thought about God, myself, I couldn't help but hope that he would succeed.

June 14, 1997

Gillian blinked against the fluorescent lighting behind Max's head. For a moment, the room swam, and she found it hard to focus. Could she be imagining things? Was it really him? She blinked hard, clearing her vision, and looked again.

The years had made their mark on Max, that much was certain. But even in the unnatural light he was, indeed, "gorgeous," as Bridget had claimed. Drawing upon her years of scientific training, Gillian turned a careful, observer's eye on him.

Gone was the shaggy brown hair she had once loved and, in its place, a head of closely shorn locks. At one temple, a single, unruly curl poked out like a spring, effectively keeping him from looking *too* professional, yet making him appear even more endearing than when Gilly had first known him. His face was generally as she remembered it, albeit a little older. Tiny laugh lines tickled the corners of his eyes, although he was not laughing now. His skin looked tougher, hardly the same baby-soft skin she remembered from his college days. She knew he wasn't one to waste his time "catching rays." It couldn't be attributed to anything but age. She'd heard about Max's reputation as a prolific writer of scientific papers — it sounded like he worked all the time. Max had never struck her as being a workaholic, but she could see him getting caught up in the subject if it was close to his heart. *Maybe he does look older*, she admitted. *But, still, he wears his age well*. The thought came, unbidden.

The collegiate sweatshirts had been replaced — not by the mandatory white shirt and synthetic-weave slacks worn by most nerdy scientists, Gillian was relieved to see, but by a blue plaid chambray shirt and cream-colored khakis. She almost smiled. Working with Ed had made her almost believe in the scientist stereotype. It was nice to be reminded that some of her future peers had style. Bit by bit, she drank in every detail of his appearance, as if she were starved for it.

Suddenly, Gillian felt very aware of her own body. Her lungs were taking in short, shallow breaths, and she could almost feel the blood coursing warmly through her veins. Seeing Max again was having an even greater effect on her than she had expected it would. But how could she not feel *something* after seeing that compelling face again . . . that strong, tapered nose . . . that masculine chin?

It was Max's eyes, however, that tugged at her heart. Whenever she thought of him — and, although she hated to admit it, she still did from time to time — she remembered the flash those eyes had held. Some people wore their hearts on their sleeves; Gillian had always believed that Max wore his in his eyes. She looked at him intently, fighting the urge to turn away. Kindness and compassion were still there. So was his heart. And suddenly, her own heart seemed to be beating stronger than ever before.

Steadily, Max matched her gaze. For a

moment, he did not speak — whether to give her time to finish her silent assessment, or because he couldn't think of anything to say, Gillian could not tell. Finally, he stepped toward her. Instinctively, nervously, she took a tiny step back. As if to help her catch her balance, Max reached forward and took her two trembling hands into his own.

"The years have been good to you, Gilly," he said quietly but with great feeling.

Gillian cleared her throat and forced a smile. "Always full of compliments, aren't you, Max?" she said, remembering the day they had first met, when he had told her she wore her age well. Then, afraid that her comment sounded barbed, she squeezed his hands enthusiastically before pulling away. Max narrowed his eyes a bit but said nothing.

"Well, here he is, Ed. The very famous *Dr.* Max Bishop!" she said brightly, emphasizing the word *doctor*. She decided it would be best to distance herself from Max as much as possible, although how she was going to do that after being assigned to his project was a question she was not yet prepared to answer.

"I take it you two know each other . . .

uh, pretty well?"

At the look on Ed's face, Gillian had to laugh. Never at his best in social situations, her boss now looked like a trapped animal. Clearly, he did not know what to make of the situation or how he should respond. No doubt Ed thought that the two of them were former lovers or something. For heaven's sake. Nothing could be further from the truth. She might as well put that suspicion to rest, right away . . . and try to collect her dignity — what little dignity she had left where Max was concerned.

"Max was a student of my father's years ago," she said cheerfully, turning to Ed. From the corner of her eye, she could see Max looking at her, but she kept her full attention focused on her boss. "What has it been, Max? Eleven, twelve years?" Finally, she permitted herself a quick peek at him.

"Uh . . . ten, I believe." Max squinted at her curiously, as if trying to read her.

"Ten? Is that all?" She started to act surprised, then decided to abandon her attempt at pretense. "Well, that seems about right, I suppose. Anyway, Max was sort of the older brother I never had. And I suspect I was the little sister he never wanted!" She forced a laugh.

"Oh, I wouldn't say that," Max said in a low voice.

Gillian felt her palms beginning to sweat. "Oh, Max. That's sweet." She tried to meet his gaze but found that she quickly had to turn away. Those eyes . . . they still saw too much. She could tell.

"Anyway, Ed," she continued, "we haven't seen each other in years. This is — this is . . ." She fought for words. "Well, it's quite a shock!" That was certainly no exaggeration.

"Yes, it is," Max agreed, folding his arms across his chest. "Although, it really shouldn't be. I started out at Princeton, even though I later transferred; it's logical that I would come back here someday to continue my research. And you . . . well, it makes sense that you would go to Princeton, too. I imagine your dad insisted."

"You'd better believe it." Gillian laughed, her first spontaneous laugh of the morning. She wiped her sweaty palms against her pant legs.

"Frankly, I'm surprised to find you in this department, though," he said, raising his eyebrows. "I never knew you were so interested in astrophysics."

"Well . . . let's just say it's an interest that developed in the years after I met you,"

Gillian said softly. "My father, and *you*," she admitted, "were so passionate about the subject, I finally decided to figure out for myself what it was all about." It was true. She had resisted her initial interest in astronomy until after Max had left the university and her mother and father had become separated. After those two events, Gillian's fragile trust in other human beings had been seriously undermined. Not knowing who might leave her next, she threw herself into her studies instead of relationships. After Max and her father had left, she clung to astronomy as one final connection to the two men she loved most. Eventually, she got over Max. But her love for the stars remained.

"And what did you discover?" Max asked, taking one step closer to her.

"I discovered . . . that I fell in love," Gillian answered softly, her mind focused on images from the past. In the silence that followed, she noticed Max's questioning look. "With astronomy!" she said quickly, then felt ridiculous about trying to explain. Of course he knew she was talking about her studies! Surely he never would have suspected how she once felt about him. She'd been nothing more than a child. It was nothing but a silly schoolgirl crush. . . .

"Of course you did." Max smiled. "Who wouldn't?" Once again, Gillian remembered how he had responded to her most embarrassing teenage moments, making them seem perfectly natural and putting her completely at ease. Max had always been kind. It was a relief to see that, in this respect at least, he had not changed.

He reached forward and grabbed her clammy hands once again, drawing her arms up in the air at her sides, and bathing her in the warmth of his grin. "Just look at you, Gilly!" he said, employing the childhood name no one else used anymore. "You're all grown up!" His eyes took in the tailored lilac linen shirt, the fitted white slacks, the slim white sandals on her feet. Then his gaze flickered upward to her lightly made-up face, her honey-colored mane, which she had parted down the middle that morning before pulling together in the pencil-twist knot. Finally, Max's eyes came to rest upon her own hazel ones. Sometimes when she was excited, Gillian knew, her eyes had golden flecks in them. Surely those flecks were there now. Did Max notice them?

Suddenly, the absurdity of the thought struck her. What did it matter if Max appreciated her eyes? She had a boyfriend, for goodness sake. She was dating a *very nice man.* A man who cared about her. One who wasn't going to leave her. She had been down this road before with Max . . . thinking about him, dreaming about him, for years after he was gone. She knew what it was like *not* to be loved by Maxwell Bishop. She didn't need to revisit those feelings. Perhaps it wasn't the most comfortable situation in the world, but she would find a way to work with Max without mooning about him or getting too attached to him. He was her new supervisor . . . nothing more. This was no time to get emotionally involved. *You don't need him, Gilly,* she told herself. *You've been over him for a long time now, remember? This is shock you're feeling, nothing more. . . .*

"Yep, I'm all grown up." Gillian spoke cheerfully. "I'm a scientist now, just like you." She pulled away from his gentle grip.

"Married?" Max asked casually.

Gillian swallowed hard against the lump in her throat. "No, but I might as well be! I've been seeing someone for quite a while. We're very happy," she said through stiff lips. "So you see, I *am* all grown up now. I guess I'm not the same little girl you remember," she told Max firmly, more for her own benefit than for his.

64

"I guess not." Max sounded vaguely disappointed, but Gilly guessed that was due to her coolly composed response, and not the fact that she was seeing someone. She knew that Max had always been fond of her. "Brotherly" was an accurate description of how he had felt toward Gillian, she was sure. Perhaps he expected a more enthusiastic welcome? A hug maybe? An "It's good to see you"? Or at the very least, sustained eye contact?

The thought made Gillian feel terrible. Why couldn't she greet Max graciously? He had been nothing but kind to her, as long as she had known him. It wasn't his fault that as a child she had fallen in love with him, only to be left behind. But she couldn't do it. She could not give away too much of herself. His presence alone was disturbing enough. If she looked into his eyes for long, he would see how his unexpected appearance had shaken her. He would know how deeply, how dearly, he had been missed.

"Won't Dad be surprised to hear that I saw you!" she said brightly, keeping a cheerful smile plastered on her face.

"How is your father these days?" Max asked evenly. He continued to watch her every move.

"Oh, he's doing . . . pretty well," Gillian answered slowly. It was hard to respond, with her mouth feeling like cotton. "He moved down to Florida after he retired. Mom moved to D.C. Dad's there now, though, visiting her."

"Your folks split up?" Max didn't look surprised. "I'm so sorry. That . . . that must have been awful for you. And for them."

Gillian nodded. "Yeah, well, a lot of people had been expecting it. Mom and Dad separated for the first time, actually, the year after you left."

This last bit caught him off guard. "I had no idea they were having that much trouble," Max told her, shaking his head. "I'm sorry," he said again, then looked embarrassed that he had repeated himself.

"They've kept in contact, though, over the years. The divorce was never actually finalized. They have most of the same problems they always did, but they're still trying to work things out. That's something. . . ."

"Good for them." Max looked like he wanted to say something, then shut his mouth, as if he could find no further words to offer. It was sad, Gillian thought. They'd never run out of things to say to each other before. But that was a lifetime ago.

"A-*hem*," Ed cleared his throat, and Gillian blushed, having forgotten he was even in the room. Certainly the conversation had pushed the limits of what the socially challenged man could handle.

"Sorry, Ed." She grinned. "Guess you just got a little more information about me and my family than you needed, huh?"

Just then a petite figure appeared in the doorway behind Max, and Gillian heard Bridget's singsong voice ring out. "Hey, Gillian!" she said. "There you are! I've been looking everywhere for you! I thought maybe we could go to — oh, hello!" She smiled brightly, flashing her big brown eyes at Max, then nodding politely at Ed. "I'm Gillian's roommate, Bridget Atwood. She and I were going to grab a bit to eat. Would you two like to join us?"

Gillian blinked. *Whoa. That girl doesn't waste any time.*

Max shook the hand Bridget offered and smiled. "Certainly. I'd be delighted."

"Not me." Ed looked like a cornered animal ready to bolt. "But by all means, you three go. In fact," he glanced at his watch, "you'd better hurry if you don't want to get stuck in the noon rush."

Poor Ed, Gillian thought. *He knows it's too*

late for that. He just wants to get his office back. Taking her cue from Ed, she slipped past Max and worked her way to the door. As she passed, Bridget gave her a conspiratorial smile. Gillian's heart sank. Suddenly the prospect of spending the next hour watching her roommate flirt with Max was more than she could take.

"I'm afraid I'm going to have to bow out, too," she said quickly, trying to sound full of regret. "My computer crashed this morning, and I'm going to have to redo those calculations before I start working on your project," she told Max. "But why don't you two go ahead?"

Max looked confused. Bridget was delighted. Gillian just felt nauseous. But Bridget seized the opening like a seasoned professional, chatting animatedly with Max, slipping one hand casually into the crook of his arm, and leading him out the door toward the university cafeteria.

Gillian watched them go. *Kind of like a lamb to the slaughter,* she thought, cynically. *That poor guy hasn't got a chance.* But despite herself, Gillian couldn't ignore the thought: *If Max is the victim here, how come I'm the one who feels like crying?*

Four

The jealous are troublesome to others,
but a torment to themselves.
WILLIAM PENN,
SOME FRUITS OF SOLITUDE, 1693

July 7, 1987

What a terrible thing it is to love someone! Why
is it that people say love is wonderful? It's not
wonderful at all. It stinks, if you ask me. I'd say
that I'd rather have both ears cut off, but that's
not really true. I don't want to lose my ears. But
I don't want to lose Max, either . . . not that he
was ever mine. Now it looks like he never will
be.
*   All right, let me back up and explain. The*
trouble started this morning, when Dad called
home to say that he had left a big important
folder on the desk in his office, and would
Mom please come bring it to him? The thing
was, Mom had a big important phone call of
her own scheduled for noon, and she couldn't
leave the house. Instead, she asked Norrie to
drive me, so I could take the papers to him.

I didn't mind. I've always liked going to the university. During the school year, it's always full of students rushing off to someplace important — a class or a date, I suppose, and it's so beautiful in the summer, when there are fewer people around to tear up the grass. When I was little, Mom would take me with her to visit Dad, and I would pretend that we were on the grounds of our very own castle. It doesn't especially look like a castle to me anymore, but it did at the time. What can I say? I was a kid.

These days, I like to pretend that I'm one of the students. When I was younger, it was a crazy idea. But now that I'm getting older, it's not so farfetched. I don't get as many people looking at me, like they're thinking, "What are you doing here?" This morning, I figured I'd play "student" again, so I told Norrie she could stay in the car. She didn't mind this, either. It's quite a walk to Dad's office, and if you know Norrie, you'll remember that she isn't exactly a big fan of walking.

So, I grabbed the papers from the front seat, told Norrie I'd be right back, and headed off to the Physics Department. By now it may have occurred to you that there was a possibility of me running into a certain someone. Well, believe me, the thought had crossed my mind, too. I tried to act pretty casual as I looked around the campus. I was almost to the physics building, and just about to give up, when I finally saw him.

There he was: Max Bishop. It felt a bit strange to see him someplace other than my house. I had come to think of him as being my own special property. Usually, I try not to think too much about where he goes when he leaves our house. And I only think about his time with Dad as it relates to developing my understanding of Max's passion for astronomy. But here was the proof. Sure enough, Max exists outside of my world. He has another life. He has his classes. . . .

He has a girlfriend.

I guess I always knew this was a possibility. But seeing for myself that it's true . . . well, that hit me harder than I thought it would.

The thing is, I'm not as deluded as I sound. I know I'm sixteen years old, and Max is, like, what? Twenty-three? It's not that I expect him to love me now. I just wish, somehow, that he could, you know . . . wait. He couldn't ever find someone who would love him as much as I do. I don't think that's scientifically possible. I liked him at first because he's cute. But once I got to know him, I realized that Max is so much more. He's kind and intelligent and passionate about what he believes in. He's really sweet to me . . . much nicer than any of the

71

kids at my school. And he pays more attention to me than my parents ever do. How could I not love him?

But there he was, sitting on a bench next to a girl with long, dark hair and eyes the color of violets. I've read that description in books before, and I thought it was made up. Who on earth has eyes the color of violets? But this girl did. Technically, they were kind of blue, like the dark African kind. But they were like violets, just the same.

I'm not sure how long I stood there, watching them, but it felt like forever. Finally, I opened up Dad's folder, stuck my nose inside, and strolled casually over to where they were at, stopping behind them, just a few feet from where they were sitting. I heard Max's voice first.

"Of course I want to see you tonight, Angela," he was saying. "But I have to study. You know that."

The girl did not look happy, but she batted her eyelashes at him anyway. It looked kind of scary, from where I was at.

"Come on, Max. You know that's not true," she said. "You study every night. You don't have to tonight. You just want to. Admit it: you'd rather study than be with me."

I couldn't believe she was saying this . . . to Max! I've heard of emotional manipulation before, I'd just never seen it in action. My folks aren't so shy; when they're mad at each other, they just come right out and say so. I don't like it that they fight, but at least they fight fair.

I peeked over my folder at Max. Was he going to crumble? It sure looked like he might. Angela had him trapped in her tractor beam. I think he was hypnotized by those eyes. He laid one hand on Angela's bare arm and squeezed it, while leaning over to whisper something into her ear. My stomach flopped. I wanted to squeeze my eyes shut and just disappear. At the very least, I wanted to sneak away. But for some reason, my legs just wouldn't move. I waited to see what the girl was going to do.

Apparently she *was waiting to see what she'd do next, too, because for a minute she didn't say a word. She was looking pretty confused. I guess her temper tantrum wasn't getting her the response she was expecting.*

"Are you saying that you won't *come over to Vicky's with me tonight?" she pouted. What a trooper. She must have thought it was worth one more try.*

"Now, Angela. You know you'll have a great time at Vicky's whether I'm there or not. Half the time you girls just go into a corner and talk about us guys, anyway. Why don't you just do that and pretend that I'm there?"

73

That last bit kind of surprised me. It almost sounded like Max was making fun of her, and that's not like him at all. Maybe he was just getting frustrated. I could see why he would, if that's the kind of pressure he got from Angelllaaaaaa. *Yuk.*

Well, Angela wasn't buying it. "I don't think so, Max. You're going to have to do better than that if you want people to think you care about me. How would it look if I showed up by myself?"

"Angela." Max looked pretty serious now. "That's the point. I don't *care what other people think. I care what* you *and I* think. *Don't you know that you're important to me? Don't you know how much you —"*

My lunch started to come back for a visit. It was time to go, I couldn't listen to any more. Out of some sort of primitive survival instinct, my feet finally started moving. Somehow, they carried me to my dad's office, even though I wasn't really paying attention to where I was going. Dad was kind of grumpy, I guess because it took me so long to get him his precious folder. But once it was in his hands, he was fine again.

Wish I could say the same thing about me.

From her position on the back section of the wraparound porch, Gillian could just make out Cassiopeia's "W" twinkling over the stand of her neighbor's hawthorn trees. Lifting her eyes upward, she quickly picked Ursa Major out of the night sky, then directly overhead, tucked between Boötes the Herdsman and Hercules, she found one of her favorite constellations: the Corona Borealis or, as she had known it as a child, the Northern Crown. Seeing it was like coming upon an old friend.

Gillian drew in a deep breath of fresh, clean country air, wrapped both arms around herself, and sighed deeply. She loved living in Princeton again. It had been easy for her father to convince her that Princeton was the best school. After being dragged off to Washington, D.C., following her parents' initial separation, she had constantly dreamed about coming back. Scenes from her childhood home had haunted her: beautiful Battlefield Park, the towpath leading along Canal Road and the Delaware-Raritan Canal, the marshy remains of what was once Lake Passaic but was now the Great Swamp, the boardwalk at Atlantic City.

The city had made her claustrophobic and homesick, too, for the company of the wildlife she had grown to love: the wood ducks and bitterns, the deer and fox and field mice . . . even the fireflies. *Especially* the fireflies. How was it possible that when people from out of state thought of New Jersey, their thoughts immediately turned to oil refineries and the turnpike, and not the beautiful landscape that had given the Garden State its name? The logic escaped her. People could joke all they wanted about living in *"Joisey,"* but Gillian knew in her heart that it would always be her home.

The old white farmhouse she now lived in was a dream come true as well. After her folks split up, her mom had dragged her from one condo to the next. For years Gilly had dreamed of setting down roots once again. Finally, during her first year of undergrad work at the university, she had moved into this place, which she could truly call home. She'd had several roommates since. So far, Bridget had lasted the longest: eight months, Pam just a little less at six. It was a comfortable enough arrangement. The women all liked one another and joked around quite a bit, though it was clear that each had her own life. It made things easier, there was much less to argue about. Gillian wanted to keep it that way.

With deft movements, she reached down and quickly removed the eyepiece from the telescope she had dragged out of the attic that afternoon, replacing it with one of a higher magnification. In her hand, the first piece felt familiar and comforting. It had been years since she'd used this old 'scope. It was useless in her university studies and horribly outdated, even for amateur use. She had several other telescopes, all of them more powerful and expensive, but this particular refractor had always been her favorite.

She was still messing with the eyepiece when Bridget bounded out onto the porch.

"Gillian Spencer," she cried breathlessly. "You are the *best* roommate in the whole world!" With a happy flounce, she threw herself against the cushions of the porch swing.

"Oh, really?" Gillian tried to sound nonchalant as she finished setting up her telescope.

"Yes, *really!* Taking off like that and leaving me with that guy, Max. *Veeeeery* nice," she said appreciatively. "I thought you didn't know who he was, by the way.

He sure seemed to know a lot about *you*."

"He did?" Gillian's head popped up, as if of its own accord. "Like what?"

"Oh, he knew about your dad, where you lived when you were a kid. Stuff like that."

"Right." Gillian turned back to the 'scope. "He was one of my dad's students."

"That's what he said." Bridget looked at her curiously. "Is something the matter, Gil?"

"No," Gillian said stiffly. "Not at all. Why do you ask?"

"No reason." Bridget shrugged. "Your voice just sounded a little strained." She settled back against her pillows, her concern about Gillian's mood quickly forgotten. "Anyway, I *have* to tell you all about lunch!"

"Do you really?" Gillian mumbled, but quietly so Bridget could not hear her.

Over the next twenty minutes, Gillian was subjected to a running commentary on the details of Bridget's lunch date, including: "Max ordered broccoli at the cafeteria. Can you believe it? Everybody knows better than that!" and, "I know he's a real gentleman, because he didn't ask, 'Are you going to eat that?' and take the leftover food off my plate when I was done." By the time her friend had finally paused to catch her breath, Gillian knew that Max had been in Princeton for nine days, that he had spent the last three years conducting research at an observatory in Rome, and that he had shown more than a passing interest in her relationship with Keith Waterford.

"What did he find so intriguing about my love life?" she mumbled crossly. "I haven't seen the guy in ten years. What business is it of his *who* I date?"

Bridget lifted her shoulders in an almost imperceptible shrug. "I dunno. He just asked what the guy was like, was he good to you, did you love him. You know, stuff like that."

"Well, what did you tell him?" Gillian asked, more sharply than she intended.

Bridget sat up straight and looked at Gillian intently. "What do you think I told him? I told him you were extremely happy. You *are* extremely happy. *Aren't* you?"

"Of course I am."

"Are you sure?"

"Yes, I'm happy. You know I am. Happy, happy, happy."

"Well, you sure don't look it." Bridget stared at her, then asked, "What's going on?"

"It's nothing, Bridget. I —"

"Gillian . . ."

"I said it's nothing. Really!"

"But —"

"Bridget, *stop* it! Just back off!" She practically spat out the words. Bridget's brown eyes opened wide and began to glisten. She stared at Gillian wordlessly. "Oh, Bridget." Gillian sighed. "I'm sorry. I didn't mean that. I just . . ." her voice trailed off. She wished her friend would break in and say, "It's okay. You don't have to explain." But no such offer came.

She tried again. "Look, it's just that . . . well, Max's coming here brought up a lot of old stuff from my childhood, that's all."

Bridget sniffed. "You mean stuff about your parents?" she asked quietly. It was one of the few details of Gillian's personal life that she shared with her roommates. It was pretty much unavoidable. After several months of living together, most roommates eventually asked why her parents rarely called. Gillian usually explained that she didn't have a close relationship with her folks . . . and left it at that.

"Well . . . sort of. But it's more than that. It's —" She stopped, wondering how much she should explain. It wasn't that she didn't trust Bridget to understand her feelings. It was just that Bridget was already

80

emotionally involved as well. Gillian had seen this situation many times in school. It was always difficult when two friends liked the same man, even if one of the crushes was completely in the past — as Gillian's was. She just wanted to handle the situation carefully.

"Do you remember when I told you about a guy I liked when I was a kid?" She seemed to recall a conversation they'd had a while back, in which Bridget had pressured her to explain why she never gave the men she dated a decent chance. Gillian had mumbled something vague about getting burned as a teenager.

Bridget thought for a moment. "It seems like you said there was someone you had a crush on for a long time, but you didn't really go into it."

"Well . . ." Gillian paused. There really wasn't any easy way to say it. "The thing is, the guy was . . . Max."

Bridget's jaw dropped. "Stop it. You're kidding me."

Gillian shook her head. "I wish I were."

"So you're saying that you and Max . . ."

"No. I'm not saying anything about 'me and Max.' It was just me. A one-way crush. Unrequited love." She tried to make it sound melodramatic and funny. But to her own ears, it just sounded pathetic.

"Oh, Gil!" Bridget hopped down off the swing and tried to wrap her arms around her. "How awful! You must have felt —"

"Now, Bridget." Gillian gently untangled herself from her roommate's embrace. "I was just kidding. It wasn't as bad as all that," she protested, even though she knew in her heart that it *was*. "He wasn't my first boyfriend or anything. He was much, much older. A student of my father's. I was just a kid."

"But still —"

" 'But' nothing. It's fine. *I'm* fine." She didn't want anyone's sympathy, least of all Bridget's. Gillian wasn't comfortable letting anyone too close. The last thing she needed was for her roommate to start prying into old feelings from her past, feelings that died long ago.

Bridget looked completely unconvinced. "It's just so *sad*."

"No, it's not." Gillian shook her head firmly. She was starting to get irritated now. "Please, Bridget. Can we just drop it? It happened a long time ago. It brought a lot of memories back for me, seeing Max today. But I've dealt with them, and I'm fine."

"Well . . ." The wheels were turning in

Bridget's head. "Of course you don't want me to see him again. That would be terrible for you."

"I never said that." Gillian swallowed hard, wondering what Bridget meant by "seeing him again."

"But, Gil, we're roommates! You're obviously heartbroken. I can't just —"

"Bridget!" Gillian scowled at her. "I am not 'obviously' *anything*. Could you please stop acting like I'm some kind of precious doll? I'm not going to break — especially over a *man*. And certainly not over a crush I had ten years ago. I went on with my life, remember? For crying out loud, I was just a *kid*. It didn't mean a thing." *Keep telling yourself that,* whispered a tiny voice inside her head. *Maybe one of these days you'll believe it.*

"Does Keith know?" Bridget whispered, as if sharing in a terrible secret.

"Does Keith know *what?*" Now she was really angry. "Bridget, there's nothing going on between Max and me . . . and *there never was*. Do you understand? Nothing. Nada. Zip. Zilch. A big, fat *nothing*." With each word, she made a dramatic karate chop in the air with one hand.

"Gosh, Gillian. You don't have to get so upset." Bridget folded her arms protectively across her chest and sat back down on the swing. "I just don't want my dating Max to come between us."

Gillian's heart sank, but she tried to keep her face expressionless. "So . . . he asked you out, then?" She tried to adjust the eyepiece on her telescope, but her hands were shaking so badly she had to give up and slip them into her pockets. *Stop it, Gil. You're acting like a child again.*

"He said something about going out for coffee together sometime next week," Bridget told her confidently. "I told him he could call me, and he said he would."

"Oh." Gillian sounded relieved, in spite of herself. "Is that all?" As soon as the words were out of her mouth, she knew she had made a terrible error in judgment.

"What do you mean, 'Is that all?' " Bridget bit her lower lip and looked at Gillian, pain clearly visible in her wide brown eyes.

You idiot, Gillian berated herself. *You know she's sensitive. You should have been more careful.* "Oh, Bridget, I'm sorry," she began, reaching out to touch her roommate's sleeve. "I shouldn't have —"

"No!" Bridget interrupted, pulling away sharply. "That's right, you *shouldn't* have. I was trying to be nice, Gillian. I don't care if you *did* like him once. That's no reason to act like he couldn't ever like *me*."

"You're right, it's not. I didn't mean it like that." Gillian suspected that she should stop right there and almost did. But then, she could not resist offering one last bit of advice. "It's just that . . . well, I don't want you to get your hopes up. To get too attached. I've seen him with girls before," she said, remembering Angela . . . and herself. "I know what he's like."

"Oh?" Bridget said suspiciously. "What do you mean?"

"I mean . . ." Gillian looked deep into her friend's eyes, willing her to understand. "Oh, don't take this wrong. Max is a *really* nice guy, and he doesn't mean any harm. It's just that he has a way of . . . of . . . well, of making girls like him more than he likes them."

Bridget pulled back and stared at Gillian as if her hair had turned to snakes. "I can't believe you'd say that to me!" She sounded horrified.

Uh-oh. Gillian knew she had gone too far. "I don't mean that he doesn't like *you*. Wait! Please, listen —"

Bridget jumped down from the swing and ran toward the house, ignoring Gillian's apologies. After reaching out and grabbing the screen door violently with one hand, she turned and called back over one shoulder, "I'm sorry it's so hard for you to believe that Max might like me, Gillian. But I think he does. And I'm sorry, too, if it hurts your feelings, but I *am* going to go out with him — even if you don't believe he likes me enough to ask." With that, she flounced back inside, letting the wood door slam shut behind her.

For several moments, Gillian remained motionless, staring at the spot where her roommate had last stood. How on earth had this happened? The events of the last day seemed like a hazy dream — or, more accurately, a convoluted nightmare.

Finally, she tore her gaze away from the door and plopped herself down on the vacated porch swing. Above her head, the same stars that had comforted her as a child now shone down upon her like great winking eyes.

"I didn't mean it like it sounded," she grumbled. But there was no one there to listen, as usual. If only Keith were here. Normally, she liked the fact that she and Keith led such independent lives. But lately, he hadn't been around much. And even though she didn't feel entirely close to him, having a boyfriend somehow gave

86

her the illusion of feeling connected to *someone*. If he was around, he would tell her that she hadn't done anything to deserve Bridget's wrath. He would support her. If she told him she was having a bad day, he would take her out to dinner, make witty conversation, help take her mind off her troubles.

Gillian found herself looking forward to his return. Things would get back to normal once Keith was home. And that would be happening soon. The thought pleased her. That was it. All she needed was Keith. That was the missing piece. Once he was back, she was sure, everything would be fine.

But that night, as she waited for sleep to overtake her, Gillian's last thoughts were not of her successful lawyer-boyfriend, but of an endearing scientist named Max.

Five

I flee who chases me,
and chase who flees me.
OVID, *THE LOVES*, c. A.D. 88

July 9, 1987

Well, it's official. The "love bug" has struck Princeton. It turns out that Jenny's older sister, Marta, got engaged on the Fourth of July. I think Marta saw it coming, 'cause she's already got her bridesmaids' dresses picked out, and it's only been eight days. I went over to Jenny's house yesterday, and her mother was laying out the pattern. They're hideous: long, Pepto-Bismol pink prom dresses with wine-colored dingle-balls. Jenny even has to wear a pink hairnet with a velvet bow on top. Marta says it's old-fashioned, but I say it's dorky. I think she just wants to make sure she's the prettiest one there.

Sometimes I wonder if I'm ever going to get married. I've always dreamed that I would. I've always wanted to be special to someone, I mean really special, but I never really pictured myself with anyone specific before. If Max asked me, though, I know I'd say yes — after I was older, of course. But I'm not holding my breath. Angela seems to have her claws into him pretty deep.

Angela and Marta aren't the only ones in love. Jenny's been talking about Matt Ross an awful lot lately. He was in her Language Arts class last year, and she's fallen pretty hard. His cousin Chris moved to Princeton last spring, and Jenny thinks he and I would make a cute couple. I don't really know him, he's a whole year older than me. But Jenny said that Matt said that Chris thinks I'm cute. I don't know what I'd do if he asked me to go with him. I mean, I like Max, whether he wants me to or not. But I know I can't wait around for him forever. That's dumb. Mom says I'm too young to go on dates anyway, so I guess it doesn't really matter who wants to go out with me.

The other day, while I was over at Jenny's, Marta came home and was blabbing on and on about her boyfriend, Todd. I asked her what was so special about him. You know, what made her pick him for her husband, out of all those other goofy guys she's dated? It was so weird. . . . She got this funny little look on her face, like no one had ever asked her that before. Finally, she said, "I guess it's that he loves me, and that he's mine."

Jenny and I just looked at each other, but

later we talked about how lame that was. There is no way I'd marry someone just because he wanted to be mine. Ick. Then I started thinking about what I did want in a husband, and I realized I'd never really thought about it before. That's why I've decided to make a list . . . so I know my future husband when I see him. So, here it is:

THINGS I WANT IN A HUSBAND — NON-NEGOTIABLE (Mom and I talked about boys before, and she says it's important to know the difference between negotiable and non-negotiable qualities): intelligent, sweet to me, fun to be with, does well in school, a successful job after we graduate ('cause I plan to have one, too), mature (no spitballs or food fights), nice to kids, and attractive. He and I should also believe the same things about God. My parents argue about that an awful lot. I don't want to be like that when I get married. I suppose that means I should figure out what I think one of these days.

THINGS I WANT IN A HUSBAND — NEGOTIABLE (because I'm mature enough to know that I can't have everything I want): good fashion sense. That's something I can fix. Hey, I never said I was willing to give up a lot.

It's sort of fun to write these things down and think about what it would be like to find someone like that. I have a hard time believing it'll ever happen, though. The guys at school aren't anything like . . . well, they're not anything like Max, who is exactly what I want. This is depressing. What good does it do me to know what I want when I'm never going to get it?

Mom says not to worry about boys, that I've got plenty of time for that. By the time I'm ready to get married, she says, most of the guys I know will be more mature, and I will have met dozens of others besides. I think she meant that to be comforting, but it makes me feel even worse. I'm not real excited about meeting dozens of geeky guys before I find one that's worth keeping. Maybe Mom's right. Maybe I won't be ready for love for a while. It's just hard, seeing Max with that girl, knowing that he's not waiting for me. I wish I was older. I wish I was the kind of girl he wanted to be with. I just wish things were different, *but they're not, and I can't do anything about it!*

I don't want to settle for anyone less than Max. Why doesn't he want to wait for someone who cares about him as much as I do?

June 18, 1997

"Happy birthday to me, happy birthday to *meeeeeee*." Gillian punched haphazardly at the keyboard of her computer. So far, it had been one of the worst birthdays on record . . . and she'd had some real whoppers. This year, she had been completely alone: Keith wouldn't be back until later that night, precluding any chance for a real celebration. Four days after her fight with Bridget, her roommate still wasn't speaking to her. Though Pam had left a gift-wrapped bottle of Gillian's favorite perfume outside her bedroom door that morning, she, too, had been making herself scarce all week — no doubt in an effort to keep herself out of the fray. And, as if things weren't bad enough, Gillian had been working double overtime to get caught up on Max's research.

"Phooey." She blinked at the numbers that danced in front of her eyes. Wearily, she slipped a pair of reading glasses from her head and laid them on the Formica desktop. Then, rubbing one hand absently against her brow, she glanced around the sterile-looking, but functional room. Oh, well. Things could be worse: she could still be at her temporary workstation. Though working with Max *did* present a whole new set of problems, the situation fortunately had its perks as well. Desks in the physics department were available on a first-come, first-served basis. Grad students often had to jockey for work space; from day to day, she had never known where she would be stuck. That was all over, thanks to Max's high-profile project — Ed had managed to snag them two tiny offices in a little-used hallway adjacent to the chem lab.

Gillian consulted the clock on the wall. Seven-fourteen. Keith's flight wasn't scheduled to arrive until 9:50. There wasn't any point in leaving now. Still, she figured, she wasn't going to make any progress if she didn't give her brain some kind of boost. She'd been dragging for the last two hours. Normally, she tried to keep apples or oranges or carrots sticks around. But her mind was so scattered today, she'd left her healthy snacks at home. As a result, she was starving and craving sugar . . . of *any* kind. The more empty and refined, the better.

She was hunched over her purse, desperately digging for loose change to feed the vending machine, when Max walked in.

"Hey, there." He raised one lanky arm in greeting. "Working kind of late, aren't you?"

Gillian bolted upright at the sound of his voice. "Umm. Yeah." She smiled stiffly. "My supervisor is quite a taskmaster." Max met her smile with his own, then looked awkwardly away. She drew in a deep breath. It was still difficult to relax around him. After four days, Max had picked up on her tension and seemed to feel uncomfortable as well. Thankfully, he had his own office and had so far left her pretty much to herself.

"Are you starting to get up to speed on the work we've been doing in Rome?" he asked, flipping through a stack of notebooks piled near the door.

"Yeah. No problem." She nodded enthusiastically. Not only was the research project intriguing, it was *challenging,* which was a pleasant change. Gillian opened her mouth to ask about one particular calculation that had caught her attention, then thought better of it. She and Max would have plenty of opportunities to talk about his findings. Right now, it was late, and with any luck he would leave quickly. She just didn't have the emotional energy to deal with him. Not tonight.

But Max didn't leave. He just stood in the doorway, giving her a funny look.

"What's the matter?" she asked, feeling

suddenly self-conscious. She ran down a mental checklist: Had she forgotten to comb her hair at some point in the day? Was she wearing two different-colored socks? Had something happened to her at dinner? "Oh no!" Her hand flew to her mouth. "There's a piece of lettuce stuck in my teeth, isn't there?"

Max looked taken aback, then his face broke into a wide grin and he began to laugh — a deep, rumbling chuckle that gave Gillian wonderful little chills. "No, no. Nothing like that," he assured her with a sly twist of his lips.

"Then what? What are you looking at?"

"Just . . . you."

"Why? What about me?" Her cheeks were burning up.

"Nothing. It's just that you're . . ."

"Max . . ." She couldn't believe her ears. Was he actually flirting with her?

"— you know, the birthday girl." He grinned again.

"What?" Gillian's face fell. She stared at him, dumbfounded. Max might as well have called her the next Nobel Prize winner. "What are you talking about?"

He just smirked.

"How could you possibly know it's my birthday?"

He looked quite pleased with himself. "Well . . . I was thinking a little while ago about how strange, and . . . well, how *nice* it is, seeing you after all these years. My mind started filling up with all the memories of that summer — including the day I met you, when you told me that you had just turned seventeen."

Gillian felt her cheeks grow hot. "Now, that was a long time ago!" she protested. "You're not going to hold me responsible for what I said as a kid?" The look Max gave her was one of compassion and understanding, and she smiled back at him despite her best intentions not to.

"Of course not. I never held it against you back then, either. I knew you were trying to sound grown-up. Besides, I got you to 'fess up." He grinned. "But that memory made me realize your birthday had to be coming up. I ran up to Ed's office just now. He was still there, so I had him check your student file."

"You did?" Gillian didn't know what else to say. It seemed like a lot of effort for something that shouldn't have mattered to Max at all.

"I did. And I'm lucky, too. If this hadn't hit me until tomorrow, I'd have missed your birthday completely."

"Oh, that's okay." Dismissively, Gillian waved one hand in the air. Things were getting too personal. It was time to put an end to this conversation. She turned away and stashed her purse back under the desk. "You wouldn't be the first one."

"No?" Max looked at her closely. "Well . . . just the same, I'm glad I didn't. 'Cause then I wouldn't have been able to give you these." He reached into his coat pocket and pulled out two cream-filled, chocolate cupcakes, sealed in plastic.

"Junk food!" Gillian exclaimed happily, then jumped up to accept the offered treat. "Where'd these come from?"

"The vending machine, of course. It's the best I could do on such short notice," Max explained. As he placed the package in her hands, his fingers gently brushed against hers. The feeling, warm and gentle, sent a wave of shock through her. For a moment, time remained frozen. The cupcakes blurred before her eyes. It had been a long time since anyone had put any effort into making her birthday special. Gillian smiled as a glimmer of a tear threatened to betray her true feelings. She quickly composed herself. "I'm afraid I don't have any candles," Max said, kindly covering for her emotional reaction. "But you can make a wish anyway, if you want."

Something about the offer made Gillian's stomach muscles constrict. "Uh . . . no, that's okay." She pulled her hands away and quickly wiped her eyes. What could she wish for in front of Max? This was becoming entirely too intimate.

"Are you sure?" Max sounded doubtful. Gillian looked up into his eyes and glimpsed a flicker of sadness in them. He was trying to be kind, and she was giving him the brush off. Again.

She gave him a tiny smile. "I don't need to make a wish, Max. I already got what I wanted."

"You did?" He tilted his head to one side.

"My wish was answered when I got assigned to this research project," she said gratefully. "I've been Ed's clerical slave for the past year, just *dying* to get my hands on some real work! Especially something like this. The data in these files is extraordinary, Max. It looks like you're doing what you've always wanted to do."

"Really?" Max looked at her, question written in his eyes. "And what have I always wanted to do?"

"Explore the origins of the universe."

Max grinned. "That's right. I'd forgotten

that I told you about that."

"So have you done it yet?"

"Done what?"

"Proven that the universe was created by God?"

Max shook his head. "No. I'm afraid it isn't that easy. I had pretty lofty expectations for myself when I was a grad student. I'm not certain that we can *definitively* prove God as Creator. But every day, I am more convinced that scientific evidence points to him."

Gillian regarded him with a serious gaze. "That's what this study is about."

"It is." His eyes searched hers.

"Well, I'm not sure if I share your opinion yet," Gillian admitted. "But I'll admit, I *am* intrigued. And I'm looking forward to assisting you."

Max acknowledged her comments with a nod, then turned back toward the door. Before he left, he turned and gave her a final, searching look. "I appreciate your help, Gilly," he said simply. "It's good to be working with you . . . as a peer. And to finally *know* you as one."

Gillian sat motionless in her chair, trying not to read a deeper meaning into his words.

"And now, I hope you're going home

soon. You must have some kind of birthday celebration planned."

"Mmhmm." She nodded. "Keith's coming home from his legal conference tonight. I'm picking him up at the airport."

"Well, then," Max said seriously. "I guess the research project isn't the only wish that came true for you this week, is it?"

Gillian opened her mouth to speak. But before she could answer, he was gone.

Gillian arrived at the airport, nervous, flustered, and nearly ten minutes late. Well, isn't this a fine welcome home! What on earth is Keith going to think? She'd been so engrossed in her reading, she hadn't even noticed the time. I'll just have to make it up to him, somehow.

When she reached the gate, however, the waiting area was still filled to overflowing with people who had come out to meet their loved ones. Gillian glanced at the airline monitor, picked out Keith's flight information, and groaned. Delayed thirty minutes. Why hadn't she thought to call and verify arrival times before she left?

Her eyes scanned the rows of plastic chairs. Finally she spied an empty spot tucked between an elderly gentleman and a tired-looking woman with two small children. Gillian worked her way through the crowd and slipped into the vacant seat.

She looked down at her oversized shoulder bag in disgust. There was no need to look inside; she knew the contents by heart: one battered make-up purse, a circular brush, a few loose pieces of cinnamon gum, one broken umbrella, a pair of sunglasses, her wallet and checkbook, one Gumby key chain, and a few odd receipts . . . but not a single thing to read. Gillian had left the office in such a rush, it hadn't occurred to her to bring along a stack of files. Who knew the flight would be late? She settled back and wriggled in her hard plastic seat, trying unsuccessfully to get comfortable. There was nothing to do but wait.

Gillian glanced at the man beside her, who gave her a curt nod, then turned abruptly away. She shifted awkwardly and looked in the other direction as the young mother who had been sitting beside her tried desperately to rein in her two wild children. Across the aisle from them, the toddler had approached a man holding a baby and was yelling, "Hi-hi-hi-hi-hi!" while waving one chubby little fist. As the child's mother bent to retrieve him, the older child began to run in circles around the room, ducking in and out of the waiting crowd and crying, "Vrooooooooooom," with his arms stretched out at his sides in a reasonable imitation of an airplane.

Gillian watched with a great deal of amusement and not a little trepidation. Would her own life ever include children? There was a time when she wouldn't have doubted it. Her childhood dreams had included a loving husband, a station wagon, an enormous black lab named Maggie, and a house full of kids.

But somewhere along the line, she had stopped believing in the dream. She still *hoped* she would find someone, settle down, and get married . . . someday. Unfortunately, things never quite worked out in her relationships. Though when she started dating Keith, everyone told her that he was a prize. "Don't give up so easily this time, Gillian," Bridget had urged her. "You're not getting any younger, you know."

Gillian had laughed. "You're crazy. I have all the time in the world to meet someone."

"That's right," Bridget said seriously. "But only if you *try*." Friends like Pam and Bridget sometimes questioned her reasons for breaking up with the guys she occasionally dated. Sometimes they even suggested that she might be avoiding commitment. "You're terrible, Gil. You never even give a guy a chance. Don't be so hard on this one. Keith is a really good guy."

So, "giving it a try" was exactly what she was doing. She didn't feel overwhelmingly attached to him, but they had been dating for only six months. As she watched the woman with her children, Gillian wondered what it would be like to have kids with Keith. She'd never seriously thought about it before. She wasn't even sure she wanted to have children anymore. There was her career to think of. Astronomy was an extremely competitive field. She certainly didn't want to be distracted. On the other hand . . .

She smiled tenderly as the woman scooped up her little "airplane" and planted a kiss on his tiny forehead.

"Vroom! Vroom!" the boy cried happily.

"Vroom to you, too!" his mother said with a patient laugh.

On impulse, Gillian reached into her purse and pulled out her wallet. Flipping through it, she pocketed several ATM receipts, ticket stubs, and empty gum wrappers before finally finding what she was looking for: a photograph of herself standing next to a tall, athletic-looking blond. The corners of her mouth turned up slightly as she studied the image of Keith's smiling face.

Looks could be deceiving, that was for sure. At first glance, her boyfriend appeared more like a typical beach bum than the high-powered lawyer the entire legal community knew him to be. Yet, with his winning smile and competitive spirit, he would be just as at ease spiking a volleyball as he was arguing a case. Keith could fit in, in any crowd. People liked him, and he liked people . . . including Gillian.

That he'd chosen her still surprised her. Keith Waterford could have any woman he wanted. She'd met him at one of the political fund-raisers her mother had made her attend during a visit to D.C. All the women at the gathering had been gossiping about the attractive lawyer who, Gillian was told — as if this were a critical bit of information — was a distant relative of a prominent political family from Massachusetts. At first, Gillian hadn't been interested, even though Keith had paid a considerable bit of attention to her at the fund-raiser. He was thirty-three, quite a bit older than her own twenty-six years. He was the same age as Max, and she was painfully aware of how that had turned out.

When Keith called her the week after the party, however, she decided to reconsider. At twenty-six years old, she still hadn't had a successful long-term relationship. During her high school years, she would eventually find fault with each of the boys who wanted to date her. None of them measured up to the impossible standard she had raised. They weren't smart enough, mature enough, kind enough. In short, they weren't *Max*.

Her parents' breakup hadn't made things any easier, either, although it hadn't really come as a shock. The two were so different, it still amazed her that they had ever fallen in love. Once, as she and her mother were unpacking at their second house in Arlington, Virginia, a teenaged Gillian mustered the courage to ask about her parents' courtship.

Her mother was sorting through a box of comfortable old linens and window treatments from the home their family no longer shared when Gillian asked the question. "Mom . . . what made you fall in love with Dad in the first place?" Her mom, obviously flustered, quickly repacked the box of curtains that would not fit any of the windows in the new house.

"Oh, Gillian," her mom brushed the question aside and kept burrowing in the carton beneath her hands. "That was a long time ago. It's water under the bridge."

"Mom, please." Gillian stood up straight and stared at her. For once, she didn't want to the let the subject go. "I really want to know," she continued earnestly. Emma stopped unpacking, slowly laid down the stack of towels in her arms, and lowered herself onto a stool at the breakfast bar.

"Your father is a brilliant man, Gillian," she said slowly. "You know that, don't you?"

Gillian nodded solemnly, never taking her eyes from her mother's face.

"When I first met him . . . I thought he was everything I wanted in a man: intelligent — no, more than that, he was a *genius*. Powerful, mysterious. Very attractive, too. Best of all, he saw me as a person, not just as a potential wife. He respected my work; he respected *me*. I thought that there wasn't anything we couldn't handle together."

"I don't understand." Gillian dug at the

106

shag carpet with one toe. "What happened, then?"

"Oh, Gilly!" Her mother reached out and took her by the hands, pulling her daughter into her lap. After being dragged away from the home she loved at seventeen-and-a-half, Gillian wasn't much in the mood to be held anymore. But for a moment, she allowed herself the comfort of her mother's arms. "A lot of things happened," Emma carefully explained. "There's a lot more to marriage than what you see on the surface. Your father and I . . . well, we didn't agree about a lot of other things. *Important* things."

Gillian nodded. "Like his working so much, huh? And religion?"

Her mom looked surprised. "Well, that's part of it, yes. You knew that?"

"I knew a lot of things. I heard you and Dad arguing."

"Oh, baby . . ." Emma's face fell, and she held her daughter close. "We didn't mean for you to hear that. We tried to keep our problems to ourselves."

"Well, you didn't do a very good job," Gillian said in a low voice. She didn't intend for her words to sound so mean, but she couldn't help it.

Her mom looked shocked at Gillian's

tone, but she simply nodded. "I'm sorry, Gilly. Your father and I are both sorry. . . ."

"Then, why didn't you make it work? Why didn't you and Dad just tell *each other* you were sorry?"

Emma shook her head. "It's complicated, Gilly."

"But —"

"Now, honey, listen. Do you want to know what happened, or not?"

Gillian clamped her mouth shut and nodded.

Emma took Gilly's hand and squeezed her fingers. "Life isn't easy, Gilly. You need to know that. Things don't always turn out the way you think they will." She thought for a moment. "Everything was fine between your father and me before we got married. But then a lot of things changed. For one thing, after a couple of years, I decided to go back to church. I hadn't thought much about my faith since I was a kid, but it was important to me to rediscover what I believed. I wasn't sure what it meant to follow God, but I committed myself to finding out. Your father . . . well, your father lumps spiritual beliefs in with the supernatural. He won't believe in anything that can't be scientifically proven. It put us on very different spiritual planes, which in turn put a lot of stress on our relationship. It wasn't our only problem. But not sharing this one thing made it even harder to find common ground in other areas." She paused to take a breath.

"After we'd been married for little more than a year, I realized that your father and I had very different expectations for our marriage. One of the reasons he liked my work so much was that he knew it would keep me busy . . . and out of his way while he did his own studies. He really is a genius, Gilly. I haven't always agreed with his conclusions about the nature of the universe, but he's done some incredible research." She paused, deep in thought, then said in a low voice, "His research has always come first."

"Before us." It wasn't a question.

Her mother sighed. "Yes. Before us. It wasn't always that way, but over the years things got increasingly worse. I knew it was hard on you, never seeing your dad. It was hard on me, too. I argued with him about it, but that just made things worse. Over the years, your father began to see me as a nag. Eventually, he stopped loving me."

"Oh." Gillian thought about this for a minute. "Did he stop loving me, too?"

Emma looked at her tenderly, and her eyes welled up with tears. "Oh no, sweetheart! *No.* I promise you, your father loves you the best he knows how."

"Really?" Gilly played with the small emerald ring on her mother's hand, the one Emma had started wearing in place of her wedding band. "Mom, maybe he loves you the best he knows how, too."

"Well," Emma hugged her daughter tight, "maybe that's true. I don't know." The two sat together in silence for several minutes before she spoke again. "Gillian, I'm not saying that separating was the best thing for your father and me to do. The truth is, I don't *know* what's right for us anymore. All I know is, I love you. And I'm trying to do the best I can for us. Can you understand that?"

"Um. I guess."

"Oh, Gilly." Emma gave her one last squeeze. "Just be careful when you get older, okay?" she said wistfully. "Remember, it takes a lot to make a marriage work. It's not all about chemistry and good feelings. I'm not saying you shouldn't marry someone you feel good about. You *have* to feel strongly toward him to love him. But you also have to be sure he's someone you can be with, even through the tough times. You have to be certain that you agree about the most important things in life: like God, and family, and how you are going to love each other . . . and your children. Can you remember that, Gillian — ?"

"Gillian? *Gillian?*"

"What?" Gillian blinked against the bright lights of the airport terminal. Who was shaking her arm? "Mom?" Slowly, the features of the figure beside her began to slip into focus.

"Come on, Sleeping Beauty," a deep voice said with a laugh. "Mom'll take you home."

"Keith?" Gillian shook her head vigorously, trying to clear her confusion. "Oh, my gosh! I just had the weirdest dream."

"Hmm. I guess *so*," Keith said seriously. He took Gillian by the hands and pulled her to her feet. "I can't wait to hear it."

She brushed the wrinkles from her corduroy shirt and wool skirt. "Umm, I don't know, Keith," she said slowly. "I'm not sure I can remember it."

"Sure you can!" He shouldered his carry-on bag and smiled broadly. "Come on. I'll play Dr. Freud, and you can be my patient."

"I don't think so —"

"Aw, come on. It'll be fun, Gillian," he urged.

As they began to wind their way toward baggage claim, Gillian stared sullenly at the carpet beneath her feet. What could she possibly say to him? *"Well, Keith, I was dreaming about this conversation I had with my mom. But it wasn't really a dream. It happened about eight years ago. We were talking about marriage, and love, and what it takes to make things work. And she said —"* No, that would never do. She wasn't ready to talk about marriage and love. Not yet. Not with Keith. "I'm sorry. My mind's kind of foggy," she said stiffly. "How was your flight?"

"Sure, Gillian, changing the subject? . . ." Keith said, a little too cheerfully. "It's okay." He gave her a big smile and turned away. As they walked on together in silence, Gillian felt terrible. She wasn't telling the truth, and she was sure Keith knew it. But thankfully, he wasn't going to push the issue. She fell into step beside him and tucked her hand into the crook of his arm. "Hey, Keith?" She managed a lopsided smile.

"Yeah, Gil?"

"Umm . . . it's good to have you home."

Six

*The relation of faith between subject
and object is unique in every case.
Hundreds may believe, but each has to
believe by himself.*
W. H. AUDEN, "GENIUS AND APOSTLE,"
THE DYER'S HAND, 1962

July 12, 1987

*Before I started kindergarten — back when I
was five or so, I guess — my dad used to take
me out at night to watch the stardust.*

*We didn't go very often, and we couldn't go
just any old time. Only on special nights, when
the sky was clear and the moon was tucked
away behind the Earth's shadow. That's when
it would appear: a ribbon of milky white dust
that stretched high across the heavens.*

*Of course, now I know that what we were
looking at was the Milky Way. But at the
time, it was a magical, unexplainable thing —
this beautiful band of flickering light. Together
we would sit, side-by-side, on nothing but a
blanket of grass, far from the city's lights.*

Sometimes he'd bring a pair of binoculars or even a telescope. But that was later. In the beginning, we used nothing but our eyes.

Mostly we were quiet. But every once in a while, Daddy would point out a sea goat or a centaur or a flying horse and whisper its name in my ear. Those are the only times I can remember Daddy acting like a kid. He seemed in awe then. He wasn't like that at work, behind his telescope, where he tried so hard to be in control. Everything then was about facts and data, radio waves and Hubble's law. Only when we were out, away from the lab, could he seem to really see the stars.

When I got older, it was important to Dad that I know all the statistical facts about the stars: their magnitude and type, color and size. I don't know why. Maybe it was just that I was growing up, and he wanted me to be like him. It wasn't so bad at first. Learning all that stuff was interesting, too. But I liked it better when there was a story behind the stars, when there was something to dream about and not just to know. After a while I got tired of it, and Dad got tired of me. Things weren't the same between us after that.

Last night, I was lying awake, thinking about those stars and wondering if, after all these years, they still looked the same. It's been a long time since I bothered to even look — I *mean* really *look, not as a scientist, but just as a person. The more I thought about it, the more it bothered me. So finally, I decided to go out and see it for myself.*

Sneaking out wasn't hard to do. Dad sleeps like a bear in hibernation, and Mom's away at one of her political bashes. It's a good thing, too, or I never would have gotten out of the house. I didn't go too far, anyway. I couldn't take the car — I don't have my license yet, and I doubt that even Dad would sleep through that *much noise. So I just ran out to the main road and headed down toward the Gillys' field, about half a mile away.*

By the time I got to the meadow, the Gillys' lights were out. No one was up except Elvis the cat, who was prowling the field looking for mice. It wasn't as far from the township lights as the places Dad used to take me as a kid. But at least it was a wide, open space, and I felt really free, for the first time in a long time.

The first thing I noticed out there was how quiet the sky was. I know that's a strange thought, but there you have it. When I look at something really awesome, like the Atlantic Ocean or the Grand Canyon, I always listen to the roar of the waves or the echo of the wind and think about what it sounds like to be so big. But the stars don't make a noise. At least, not one I can hear from here, anyway. Last night, I wished that I could fly up to the stars and just listen. What would I hear up there? Fire crackling on the face of the stars? The sound of wind? Is there wind in space?

Pretty soon, the Gillys' cat came and crawled into my lap, and then it wasn't so quiet anymore. But it was peaceful still, sitting there, looking up at the stars with Elvis on my knees, snoring like an old man.

After a while, I started getting cold. But for some reason, I just couldn't make myself get up. The more I looked into the sky, the more things I noticed — constellations I knew like I knew my own name, and beyond them, an ocean of stars I'd never noticed before. I wondered what made the stars keep moving. Why do the planets follow their orbits? Where did they come from? Where did I come from? And was it the same place? I kept my fingers buried in Elvis's thick fur and tried to imagine what it all meant. Dad seems to have his theories. Mom, too. And Max. Everyone but me.

That thought made me pretty nervous, like I was supposed to know. All of a sudden, the sky seemed a lot bigger . . . and scarier. Mom says a lot of people claim that they're afraid God might not exist, but she believes most of us are really afraid that he does. I think maybe she's *right, because the more I thought about God, the more terrifying he seemed. Mom says that, yeah, he's terrifying, but there's more to it than that. She says that God cares about me, that he sent his son to earth because he loves me. Part of me wants to believe it, but I'm not even sure what it all means.*

Dad says there isn't a God. I used to think he said it just to make Mom mad, but I'm pretty sure it's what he really believes. He likes things that can be explained, and he avoids anything that can't. Like me. Daddy couldn't figure me out. I loved the stars, once. I was good at memorizing all the stuff he told me about them. But one day, I just stopped trying. It wasn't fun for me anymore, and no matter what I said, I couldn't make him understand why. Feelings are funny things, though. They're hard to explain. People aren't so easy to figure out, either. Neither is God, I guess.

I don't know if I have to have all *the answers, like my Dad does. Mom says that it's enough for her to know some of them . . . that it's enough to know that a thing can be true, even if it doesn't have to be . . . and to choose to believe.*

I just don't know yet if it's enough for me.

"Hey, Max. I finished working through these calculations, and I was wondering if you wanted me to —" Gillian broke off at the sight of his shadowed face. Under the cold fluorescent lighting, his skin looked pale and sallow. Large, dark rings encircled his usually bright blue eyes. From behind his desk, he stared, expressionless, through the open window. "Max, what's the matter?" she asked quietly.

"Huh?" He tore his eyes away from the view of the campus and looked at her as if she had spoken Greek. "Oh, Gilly. It's you." His rigid expression softened at the sight of her. "What's that you said?"

"I asked what was bothering you." Gillian tucked her file folder beneath one arm and seated herself across from him. "You look like you haven't slept."

"Oh, I'm fine." He tried to sound confident, but his tone was less than reassuring. Gillian stared at his denim shirt, which looked like it had just been pulled from a tiny corner of his suitcase and could use a good ironing. Not that she was dressed any better. Her white, square-neck tee and celery-green capri pants were flattering, but hardly professional attire. Still, at least she was well groomed. She gave Max a scrutinizing look.

"You don't sound very convincing. Are you sleeping okay, really?"

"Gilly —" Max shook his head.

"I know, I know — you're fine. Sorry." She laid her folder down and raised her suntanned arms in surrender. "None of my business." He didn't have to tell her twice. Gillian didn't appreciate people prying into her affairs. No doubt, Max didn't like it either. With a businesslike nod, she turned back to the matter at hand. "I guess that means you're ready to go over these calcul—"

"Are you happy, Gilly?" Max broke in. She looked up to find him staring again, this time at her. It was more than a little unnerving. Uneasily, she crossed one leg over the other, trying to find a more comfortable position.

"We-ell. Most of the time. As happy as anyone, I suppose," she said slowly. She didn't like the way this conversation was turning. "Why do you ask?"

Max leaned his elbows on the desk and peered at her intently. "No, I mean *really* happy."

Gillian shrugged and tried to look away, but his eyes drew hers like a magnet. He

119

was making her feel like a bug under a microscope. "I guess," she said noncommittally. "I have pretty much everything I want or need, if that's what you mean."

"Well," he said as if considering her answer. "I'm not sure it is."

Gillian tried to read Max's features, but his face was an impenetrable mask. Where was he going with this line of questioning? And what had she done to open herself up to this kind of interrogation, anyway? "What's this about, Max?" A snatch of conversation drifted through her mind. What was it Bridget had said? *He just asked what the guy was like, was he good to you, did you love him. . . ."*

"Max, is this about Keith?" she ventured uneasily. "Are you asking about my relationship with him?"

At that, Max sat up straight. Gillian couldn't help noticing that he appeared more than a little interested at this turn in the conversation. "Actually, I wasn't thinking *specifically* of him. But now that you mention it, how *are* things between you and Keith?"

Disturbed by the intimate question, Gillian rolled her chair back and tried to appear interested in a bookcase filled with technical papers. "Oh, Max. I really don't think this is an appropriate discussion for us to ha—"

"I'm not asking you as your supervisor, Gilly," he said gently but firmly. His eyes sought hers, demanding a response. "I'm asking you as a friend."

"As a friend?" Gillian shifted nervously. She couldn't help but wonder at his motivation. Hadn't they always been friends? Yes, certainly that is what they had been. Nothing more. She had no reason to think he was expressing anything other than a casual interest. "Well, I guess I'd have to say that we're —" She hesitated. How *were* things going between her and her boyfriend? "Yes, Keith and I are doing well. We're compatible. We care about each other. We're headed in the same direction." The sound of her own words made her angry. Why was it so hard to justify her relationship all of a sudden? Why did her response sound so flat? How dare Max ask such a thing in the first place! A trace of irritation crept into her voice. "Does that answer your question?"

At first, Max did not respond. And Gillian's emotions swung from anger to distress. She stared at him nervously. "Max? Come on. What's this all about?"

Max rubbed one rough hand across his

stubbled jawline and let out a deep sigh. "I don't really know how to say this, Gilly. The truth is, you were right. I haven't been sleeping well at all."

Suddenly, any shred of composure she might have retained was in danger of slipping away. Her heart welled up with unwelcome concern. Was Max ill? In trouble? "What's the matter?" she asked anxiously. It was amazing how quickly she had come to care about this man again. It was as if he had never gone away.

He gazed at her with fathomless blue eyes that seemed to pull her into their depths. "Well . . . because I'm —"

Gillian caught her breath. If something terrible were to happen to Max, she didn't know what she'd do.

"— because I'm worried about you."

With a great whoosh, Gillian expelled the lungful of air she'd been holding in. "Me?" She tried to imagine what on earth he could be referring to. "That's ridiculous! Why would you need to worry about me?"

"I'm not totally sure," he said solemnly. "That's what I'm trying to figure out." His eyes furrowed together in an expression of concern, giving him the air of an overprotective older brother. When she was younger, if he had done that, it would have been endearing to Gillian, but the image did not please her any longer.

Gillian met his eyes over the desk. "Max, please. Speak English. I really don't know what you're talking about."

"I don't know. . . ." He shook his head, as if unable to find the words to express himself. "I started worrying the first day I saw you. Don't get me wrong. It was *great* to see you, Gilly. But you seem . . . different, somehow."

By the tone of his voice, Max didn't consider it to be a change for the better. His statement sounded almost like a criticism and Gillian felt deflated. As a teenager, she had dreamed of seeing Max again, of showing him how much she'd grown up, how she'd changed. Now that dream had come true — she *had* grown up and found him again. So what would cause him to act so concerned?

"Different . . . how?" she asked. Her voice was little more than a whisper. It didn't seem possible that after all these years, his opinion would matter so much. But it did.

Max looked confused. "I wish I knew. It's hard to explain," he said uneasily. "I know it's been ten years since we've seen each other. I realize that you've grown up. But you just seem . . ."

"Seem what, Max?"

He spoke slowly, as if the words pained him. "Shut down, I guess. Closed. The Gilly I knew was open and trusting. At least toward me."

Tears threatened to spring from Gillian's eyes, but she fought them back. "The Gilly you knew was a naive child!" She tried to sound tough, but his accusation had wounded her deeply.

His eyes were full of compassion as he gazed deeply into hers. "I'm sorry. It's just that you used to be so happy —"

"Max. I was just a *girl*. Now I'm an adult."

"I think it's more than that." He reached across the desk to touch her fingers, ever so gently. "What happened to you, Gilly?"

Gillian snatched her hand back, as if a snake had bit her. "*Life* happened, Max," she snapped. It wasn't any of his business. Max, her dad . . . more people than she could count, had let her down. Even worse, she'd let other people down, too. Getting close to someone didn't seem worth the risk anymore, but she wasn't about to discuss this with Max. "I wish you wouldn't make me sound like such a basket case," she said, managing to match the cool, controlled tone she had spoken with earlier. "There's nothing wrong with me, really. I'm just not the same Gillian you remember. What's wrong with that?"

"Nothing," Max admitted. "If you're happy."

Gillian frowned. "Again with the 'happy'? Max, believe me. I'm *happy,* okay?"

"Pardon me for saying so, but you don't *look* happy."

Her scowl deepened. "I will *not* pardon you for saying so. And I *am* happy. So there." Gillian knew her words sounded childish, but she could not stop them. They seemed to fly off her tongue of their own accord. She groaned inwardly. No wonder he didn't think she had changed for the better. She was even more immature than the child he once knew.

"If you say so," Max said diplomatically. "I won't argue. But I can't help worrying about how you're dealing with life."

Those were fighting words if she'd ever heard any. Not that Gillian needed any further invitation to fight. The gloves were already on and laced up tight. "Now what is *that* supposed to mean?" she ground out testily.

"Just that . . . well, life is hard, Gilly," he said simply. He rested his hands casually on the desk, his fingers interlocked. He looked more like a salesman trying to sell annuities than a former heartthrob throwing her life into emotional turmoil.

"You think I don't know that?" Her parents had split up when she was a teenager; she'd been dragged from city to city by her politically active mother; at twenty-six years old she'd never had a single long-term relationship . . . and he was trying to tell *her* that life wasn't easy?

"I'm sure you do know it," Max said calmly. "It's just that, I'm afraid you don't have the resources that can help you deal with it."

Gillian blinked. Now he just wasn't making any sense at all. "Resources."

Max grinned sheepishly. "Yeah, resources. There I go, talking like a scientist. I suppose that's because you're a scientist, too. I feel like maybe I can get away with it. But this isn't about facts and figures, Gilly," he said more seriously. "I'm talking about the heart."

Resources. The heart. What on earth was Max getting at? Gillian stared at him blankly.

"I'm not making any sense here, am I?" he said regretfully. "I guess what I'm trying to say is that I care about you. That's why I'm worried. You mentioned last week that you weren't sure you agreed with me about God being the Creator of the universe. Maybe I'm assuming too much here — and please, forgive me if I am — but I'm guessing that means you don't have a relationship with him."

Max's eyes betrayed his sadness, and Gillian squirmed a bit under his gaze.

"I know in my own life, I'd be lost if I didn't have God to turn to when things get tough." He spoke clearly and honestly. "I can't tell you how much it means to me," he said earnestly, "to know that God loves me. That he's with me whenever I struggle to know what to do, what to say." He laughed wryly. "Like now."

Gillian's mind was spinning. A relationship with God? Was he kidding? It had been a long time since anyone other than her mother had suggested she might need such a thing. The prospect was both daunting and confusing. If God was God, then he had the entire universe at his command. What would he want with her? The idea was preposterous.

"Max, even if God exists, I don't think he wants to be bothered with my petty little problems," she said forcefully, but she could not deny the wistful feeling that came with wondering if what he suggested might actually be true.

"Oh, sw—" Max stopped himself. Gillian glanced at him sharply. What was he just going to say? Had he almost called her sweetheart? Impossible. Or was it? But before she could question him, Max had already composed himself and moved on. "I know it's hard to believe. It was hard for me to grasp, too. I still struggle with it from time to time. But honestly, Gilly, he does care. It says so all over the Bible. It's not that he cares about those petty little things, I guess, so much as it is that he cares about us. You and me."

"You, maybe," Gillian allowed reluctantly. How could anyone not care about Max?

"No," Max insisted firmly. "You, too. Here, let me read you something." He reached into an upper desk drawer and pulled out a small, worn leather-covered book which Gillian took to be a Bible. "Here we go. Matthew 28:20: 'Surely I am with you always, to the very end of the age.' And it's not because we deserve it, either. Listen. Romans 5:8: 'But God demonstrates his own love for us in this: While we were still sinners, Christ died for us.' You see, Gilly? It's right here, in black and white."

Gillian stared at her hands as she felt something stirring in her heart. She wanted to believe him, she really did. But, could she face the risk of opening herself up once again? What if it wasn't true? What if God didn't exist? What if he didn't accept her, after all? What if her doubts, her questions, were too much to forgive? Could she survive being left all alone once again?

"God is there for you, Gilly. All you have to do is let him in," Max assured her gently. "Wouldn't it be nice to have someone you could depend on? Someone who would love you and take care of you and be there for you? Always? Just like Jesus said?"

Despite the ninety-degree weather, Gillian felt a sudden chill. Somehow, Max had, with just a few simple sentences, neatly summarized the deepest longings of her heart. How had he known? Nervously, she licked her parched lips.

"That's a nice fairy tale, Max," she said coolly, trying to sound disinterested. But despite herself, Gillian felt a tug at her heart strings. She thought the words would anger him, but Max appeared undisturbed.

"I think it's more than a fairy tale," he

said matter-of-factly. Gillian stood and pushed her chair back roughly, causing it to roll across the smooth office floor and plow into a shelf of books. Max watched with interest as she began to pace. Gillian scrambled for the words to justify her position. "Come on, Max. Be serious. Just what do you expect me to believe?"

"Maybe the evidence?"

"Max, you know there's no solid evidence. You said so yourself."

"I said there was no *definitive* evidence. There's a difference," he argued.

"I've already told you, I don't know what I believe."

"I know. But you could find out." How could he seem so calm when she felt so disturbed?

"Why would I want to, Max? Give me one good reason," she said testily.

Max stood and came to her side. "Peace. Hope. Joy," he said gently, reaching out to take her hand.

Gillian watched his fingers close around hers and felt her fury begin to fade. This time she did not pull away. She should be furious. But Max's words were spoken with such compassion, her anger melted away.

"That's *three* things," Gillian said grumpily, but the words did not sound forceful as she'd intended; they sounded comical.

A hint of a smile tugged at the corners of Max's mouth. "You don't say? And I'm just getting started."

"Okay, Max," she sighed. "I'll admit it. I don't feel a lot of peace right now, and I don't even remember the last time I did. But the truth is, I've never really thought of God as being the answer to that. Dad never believed in an omnipotent force, and he instilled in me a pretty healthy skepticism."

Max nodded. "I can understand."

"So, you see, it isn't easy for me."

"I know, Gilly." He reached out and brushed a finger across her furrowed brow, his touch as light as a butterfly's wing. "I didn't mean to push. It's just that . . . I really care about you. I want you to be happy. You know that, don't you?"

Tears welled up in Gillian's eyes once more as she thought of the days when she had longed to hear those words from him. But even if he had said them at the time, they couldn't have been an expression of anything more than friendship. Exactly as they were now.

"I know, Max. I do." She smiled weakly. "And . . . I'll think about it. Honestly, I'm really not sure I believe what you say is true, but I think I'd like it if I found out that it was."

Max smiled, the corners of his eyes crinkling along their familiar lines, and he squeezed Gillian's hand, which she suddenly realized he still held. He looked at her tenderly, and as they lingered, her head began to spin. All at once Gillian panicked. She withdrew her hand with a jerk and began to back away.

"Look, Max . . . I've got to go. There's a whole stack of papers on my desk, and if I'm going to be any use to you at all, I think I should —"

He watched her pull back, a look of confusion deposing his previous expression of tenderness. "Gilly, *now* what's going on?" Max said in exasperation.

"Nothing!" Gillian lied, trying to regain her composure. She reached for her folder and began to make a hasty retreat. "I just —"

But Max wasn't going to let it go. "Ever since the day I got here, you've been acting like a skittish horse, rearing up and running away when I get near. Come on, don't deny it. You know what I'm talking about." He followed her to the door. "What's this all about?"

"Max, I just don't think it's appropriate

for you and me to get too close," she said, a sound of desperation creeping into her voice. Her breathing grew labored. Max was standing terribly near now. If she wanted to, she could reach out and touch the rough fabric of his shirt where the buttons met. Every instinct, every muscle in her body cried out for her to step away, but she didn't want to appear any more "skittish."

A muscle in his jaw twitched. "Because of Keith?" he said.

Gillian stared at him. His face looked so strong and masculine. A muscle twitched in his jaw. "Yes." She gladly seized the excuse. "Because of Keith. Okay?" She turned as if to head for the door, but Max moved, too, partially blocking her path. Gillian forced herself to remain where she was standing.

"And what else?"

"Max! For crying out loud!" A sigh of frustration escaped her lips. She could hear the strain in her own voice. "Why does there have to be something else?" Why did he have to keep pushing the issue? Couldn't he just leave her alone?

"Because," he insisted, "I have a lot of female friends who are married or romantically involved, and not one of them has to run away every time I come into the room!"

"That's not what I'm doing!" Drawing upon anger to save her from crying, Gillian planted two fists on her hips and squared off against him.

"It's not?" Max demanded.

"You *know* it's not!" she said hotly.

"Do I?"

"Auuuugh!" Gillian let out a small cry of frustration. Obviously sensing that he had pushed too far, Max leaned back a fraction of an inch, giving her room to breathe. "Look, can we just drop this, please? You're making me really uncomfortable, and I have to get back to work —" Gillian turned her back on him, grabbing her chance at escape.

"Gilly, come on —"

She shook her head and continued out the door.

"Gilly, wait! I'm not through talking!"

"Well, I am. Okay, Max?" She'd had enough. There was a time when she would have allowed herself to be at Max's beck and call, but those days were long gone. He was being kind to her. But that wasn't enough. She was tired of being his little buddy, his little pal. Her world didn't revolve around him, around what *he*

134

wanted. She had her own life now. One that *didn't* include Max Bishop. He wasn't in her life to stay. He never had been. "If you want to talk to someone, why don't you go call Bridget?" she said sharply.

"What? *Bridget?*" He looked at her as though she was out of her mind. "But what does Bridget have to do wi— ?"

Good grief! Where had those words come from? That wasn't what she felt, was it? "Nothing!" Gillian said quickly. "She doesn't have anything to do with this! I just . . . I mean —" She felt a sinking feeling in the pit of her stomach, but there was nothing she could do to take the words back. "Look, let's just forget it, okay? I'll talk to you later," she said firmly and closed the door behind her.

Out in the hallway, she clung to the metal doorknob, her heart welling up with regret.

At least I hope *I'll talk to you later,* she thought sadly. *The question is, are you gonna want to talk to* me?

Seven

*Friends provoked become the
bitterest of enemies.*
BALTASAR GRACIAN,
THE ART OF WORLDLY WISDOM, 1647

July 18, 1987

*I can't believe this is happening. I wish I'd
never heard of that creepy old Matt Ross or his
cousin, Chris. I wish he'd go right back to Chicago. I wish he'd never come here at all. Maybe
then I wouldn't have gotten into this mess in the
first place.*

*So here's the deal: Jenny DeWhitt, my best
friend, hates me. And I can't say that I blame
her, although I never meant to do anything to
hurt her — I swear it. In fact, the whole stupid
thing was her idea. You'd think she'd cut me a
little slack for that, but no such luck.*

*Ever since she sat next to Matt in English
last semester, Jenny's had it bad. She calls me
up all the time and tells me every little thing
about him. As a result, I am a veritable foun-
tain of Matt Ross trivia. Go ahead and test*

me. *I know that he wears a size ten and a half shoe and that his ideal woman is Daisy Duke from Hazzard County. I know that his GPA is 2.85 and that his middle name is Alfonso. I even know that he pulled a groin muscle last year at the lake while he was water-skiing. Like this is information I even* want *to know?*

Sometimes she even writes her name with his: Jenny Ross. It gets pretty sickening after a while, and I want to tell her that it makes her sound like she should be sewing an American flag or something. But I never do. I know how it feels to care about somebody, to wish more than anything that he would like you back. Jenny and I are in different boats, though. My love is one of those tragic, Shakespearean kinds that can never be fulfilled. (Except, of course, I don't plan to poison myself. But . . . you get the picture.) Jenny, on the other hand, has been working on her Matt Plan for almost a year. The Matt Plan has three phases:

Phase I: Setting the Bait. *Otherwise known as, Getting-Matt-to-Notice-I'm-Alive. This was a thoughtfully planned and carefully executed maneuver that involved countless hours of wardrobe, makeup, and hair consultation with her sister Marta and (you guessed it) yours truly.*

Phase II: The Hunt. *Once the subject's attention was captured, it was time for the* *really fun part (fun for Jenny, anyway). At this point in The Plan, basic flirtation began. This phase opened the door to endless telephone discussions that sprang from the ever-critical questions: "What-Do-You-Think-He-Meant-By . . . ?" and "Did-You-See-the-Way-He . . . ?" I was also called upon at this point to distract Matt's cousin Chris. Those two have been inseparable ever since he moved here, which hasn't made Jenny's and my work any easier, let me tell you. I accomplished the goal by sitting next to Chris at lunch and asking him questions about the football team (thereby freeing up Matt to flirt with Jenny). After the first question, all I ever had to do was mumble "Mm-hmm" every six or seven seconds. The guy is like a big talking doll . . . just wind him up and watch him go.*

Phase III: Going for the Kill. *In this the final, and most controversial, phase of The Matt Plan, Jenny had determined that we should divide and conquer. This was a problem for me. It wasn't the dividing part that I argued with. Matt's a nice enough guy, at least I thought so. Nicer than his cousin, anyway. I figured he was better off getting divided from Chris every once in a while. But I certainly didn't want to conquer Chris, myself! Jenny thinks we'd be cute together, and I'm flattered in a way. He is adorable. He's kind of* *funny, too. I sort of liked him at first. But really, he's not my type. He's not all that smart. And his interests are pretty limited. Once you get to know him, the guy is dull as a fence post, unless of course football is your religion.*

The good news is, I never really had to deal with Phase III. The bad news is, that's because The World As I Know It came to an end during Phase II.

If it hadn't been for Jenny's birthday, we might have made it through the summer just fine. But she decided to have this big ol' Birthday-fest in her parents' backyard. I'm surprised her parents agreed, but they must have felt guilty about spending all that money on their oldest daughter, 'cause they caved. Doesn't really matter, I guess, if they can afford it.

So, there we were: Jenny, Matt, Chris, and I, and about twenty or so of our closest friends. There was pizza and swimming and dancing (although nobody shook even one little booty until Jenny convinced her parents to go inside — where, of course, they watched from the living room window). I was doing my best to keep Chris busy, saying things like, "So, tell me again why you think the coach is going to play you more?" and, "How do you think the team is going to do this year?" when some wise guy held a plastic Coke bottle up over his head and started calling out a play. Naturally, Chris started yelling and ran out for the pass.

I was waiting and watching and trying to figure out this whole testosterone thing, when Matt came up and stood next to me. I didn't think much about it. We always hang out together around Jenny. I know so much about him, it would have been pretty hard not to become friends. We talked for a few minutes, and then he said he wanted to go check out the pool.

There was nothing else going on, so I followed him. But as soon as we crossed the little dance floor Jenny's dad had made, Matt slipped his arms around my waist and started moving his feet back and forth to the music. It kind of freaked me out, and I started to look all around us. "Hey, if you want to dance, I bet you Jen—"

"No, not Jenny. I want to dance with you," he said. And he said it like he really meant it.

I just stared at him. . . . I couldn't have been more surprised. At first, I started to pull away. But then I saw the look on his face, and for the first time, I realized that a boy liked me — I mean, really liked me. And just for a second, I wondered what it would be like to let him like me. I didn't really think about what

140

*it would be like to care about him — not yet
— even though Matt is pretty darn likable
himself. I just was all caught up in thinking
about how it would feel to be loved, just as I
am . . . just once. And so I relaxed, just for a
second, and leaned my head against his
shoulder, which felt really strong and warm,
and smelled good besides. . . .*

*And then he spun me around, and I saw
Jenny's face. It was greenish white and cold
looking, and I wondered in that first split
second if maybe she had eaten something that
had made her sick. And then I realized that
the thing making her sick was me.*

*I tried to talk to her after that, but she just
ran into her room and locked it. Everyone at
the party knew that* something *had happened, but they didn't know what. Her parents
begged me to tell them what was wrong, but I
didn't have the guts. I tried to get Jenny to let
me into her room, but she wouldn't even talk
to me through the door. Matt and Chris left
soon after that. Chris has a license, so they
didn't even have to wait for a ride. Pretty
soon, everyone else started going, too. I didn't
call my folks, though. I walked home instead.
It's a two-and-a-half mile walk, and even
though it was a summer night, it got to be
pretty cold. But after the kind of friend I'd
been, I figured* cold *was just what I deserved.*

Some people say that love makes the world go 'round. I doubt I'll ever find out for myself. Relationships are just too hard. I don't think I'll ever get there.

And if this is what they do to people, I'm not sure I even want to.

July 8, 1997

With slim, pale fingers, Gillian pinched the bridge of her nose and squinted her hazel eyes shut tight. Releasing her grip, she shook her head vigorously, sending her golden, shoulder-length hair flying. A moment later she opened her eyes and turned once more to the book she held in one hand. It was no use. The letters still danced across the page like ants marching to a picnic. She'd left her glasses at the office again. There would be little point in trying to read tonight.

It was a shame, too, because if there was ever a time when she needed a distraction, this was it. The day had been a complete disaster. After her fight with Max, she hadn't had a single moment of clear concentration. Originally, she planned to spend the afternoon analyzing data from other physicists who had been working on theories similar to Max's. But though she read through an entire stack of papers, the words and concepts had crossed and commingled in her mind until they formed one indistinguishable mess, just like the letters on the page now open before her. Gillian groaned. With nothing but her own miserable thoughts for company, she'd never be able to get to sleep.

"If you want to talk to someone, why don't you go call Bridget?" Where had *that* come from? What on earth had she been *thinking?* She sounded like . . . well, like a jealous shrew. But how could she be jealous? She had Keith. After failing at every other relationship she'd had over the past ten years, she had promised herself — not to mention Bridget, Pam, *and* her mother — that she was going to give this one a fair shot. Keith was sweet and kind and . . . safe. Infinitely safe. Something that Max definitely was *not*.

All right, so the thought of Max and Bridget dating was a bit disturbing. Admittedly, Gillian *had* been relieved to find out that Max had simply invited Bridget out for a cup of espresso and not dinner by candlelight. And though it would have been eternally wiser to keep her mouth shut, Gillian hadn't been able to resist the urge to warn Bridget away from the man who had stolen her own heart ten years before. But that didn't mean that she was —

All right, it did. She was jealous.

Gillian grabbed one of two overstuffed down pillows and punched it into a lumpy ball, which she placed behind her back. Settling back against the headboard, she wriggled her toes down into the deep, warm flannel sheets and squinted again at the book in her hand, a battered old copy of *Wuthering Heights*, which she now lifted close to her nose. Reading would surely help her forget her troubles.

On my re-entrance, I found Mr Heathcliff below. He and Joseph were conversing about some farming business; he gave clear, minute directions concerning the matter discussed, but

. . . but . . . but . . . but even if she was jealous, Gillian reasoned, wasn't that to be expected? Just because a person remembered her first crush fondly and harbored memories of dreams that had once lived, did that have to mean she still cared for the man? Certainly not. She forced her attention to the page, pushing back the worries that haunted her.

On my re-entrance, I found Mr. Heathcliff below.

No, no. She'd read that part already. She was still trying to find her place when she heard a solid rapping on her bedroom door.

"Ooooooooooooh," she let out a low moan. *It might be just Pam. But it could also be Bridget.* "Come in," she said warily. As the door swung open, she fought the urge to sink back against her pillows and cover her head with her old patchwork quilt.

"Hi, Gillian," Bridget said stiffly. A light cotton robe was draped over her shoulders, barely covering her long T-shirt and boxer shorts. Her short, cropped curls were tousled, as though she had just crawled out of bed.

"Hey, Bridget," Gillian laid the book down and tried to greet her roommate as if there was no rift. "What's up? Couldn't sleep?"

"Nope." Bridget fell silent. Gillian had hoped that the tension between them would eventually subside, but by the look on Bridget's face that wasn't about to happen anytime soon. "I — uh — I ran into Max during lunch today."

"Oh." Gillian fumbled for words. The

events of the day came tumbling back upon her like an avalanche. "You did." Her words and the voice with which she delivered them were equally dull.

"Yeah." Bridget's eyes flickered around the room, darting from the brightly colored rag rug to the antique-white walls to the stained pine vanity table . . . anything but Gillian's face. "And I was wondering if you could answer a question for me."

Gillian sat up straight, folded her legs Indian-style beneath the blankets and prepared for the worst. "Sure, Bridget," she said casually. "Shoot."

Bridget crammed her fists into the pockets of her robe and finally looked directly at her. "What did you say to Max about what happened between us?"

"Umm . . ." Gillian scrambled to find some way to explain. Initially, she had felt regret about the way she responded to Max simply because it was unfair and unkind to him. It was only later in the afternoon that she realized she had put her roommate in a difficult position as well. She'd been wondering how she might remedy the situation. But now, it looked like it was too late for damage control. She wished she'd said something to Max earlier in the day. But she certainly hadn't expected him to take the matter straight to Bridget!

"He knew that you and I had had some sort of fight," Bridget went on, not waiting for an answer.

Gillian tucked her comforter more tightly around her legs. "What did he say, exactly?"

"He just said that you seemed really uncomfortable when my name came up today. He wondered if something had happened between us."

"That's all he said?" Gillian couldn't believe her ears. Perhaps Max hadn't ratted on her after all.

"Yeah. What I'm wondering is, why did my name even come up in the first place?"

Again, Gillian tried to reason a way out of the question; there was no easy way to explain. But to her relief, Bridget once again pushed on without waiting for a response.

"More to the point, what *exactly* did you say to him about our fight?"

"Nothing, Bridget. Really."

"Are you sure?" Looking slightly relieved, the petite brunette sank into a slipcovered chair in the corner. "Because I'd feel ridiculous if I thought that Max knew I was interested in him." At this admission, Gillian's heart sank. But she knew better than to challenge Bridget's feelings this time. She decided to focus on the one issue she *could* handle.

"Are you kidding? What would I say to him? 'Oh, by the way, Bridget and I had a fight about you because we both like you'? No way. Not only is it *not* true, I'd look like an even bigger fool than you seem to think *you* would. Unh-unh. I didn't say a word."

"Well . . ." Bridget looked somewhat relieved, but a trace of tension still clouded her face. "Whatever. As long as you're sure you didn't say anything. But no matter what you claim, I still think you like him, Gillian."

For the briefest moment, Gillian actually considered pulling the blankets up over her head and burying her face beneath them. "Bridget, come on. Are we going to have this conversation again? I thought we worked through all of this."

The woman shook her head vigorously. "No. We didn't work through anything. How could we, Gillian?" Bridget's eyes accused her. "You're not being honest with me."

Gillian tried to shut out the bare emotion in her roommate's expression and to focus instead on her own sense of cool detachment. "Yes, I am, Bridget —"

"Gillian, please! Don't make me laugh." It didn't look like there was much chance of that. "It's so *obvious* that you're infatuated with him. I don't see why you can't just come out and say so. Don't you trust me?"

"But I *don't* like him!" The more she protested, the weaker it sounded.

"All right, all right." Bridget dragged one bare toe across the rug beneath her feet. "You've made your point. You're not admitting *anything*. I'm just saying I *know* you like the guy."

Gillian felt a renewed anger rising inside of her. Hadn't she already addressed the issue a dozen times? "Bridget, come on! I don't see why we have to fight over this."

"I'm not fighting," she protested. "*Max* was the one who seemed to think we were fighting —"

"Auuuugh!" Gillian made a face and clenched her jaw. "Bridget, don't *do* that. You do *too* know that we're fighting. We both know it. Why don't we just —"

Bridget looked at her innocently. "Yeah? Well we both know that you like Max, too. But you're not admitting *that*."

Gillian's patience was wearing thin. "That's enough, Bridget. You're putting words in my mouth."

"I'm just stating the truth," Bridget said coldly.

"Knock it *off* —" Gillian stopped herself and took a deep breath. "Please." She managed to bring her frenzied emotions back under control. "Look, it's late, and this really isn't a good time for us to be getting into this. If you want to talk about it more tomorrow, we can. But right now, I'm just too tired."

"That's fine," Bridget said, stiffly pushing herself out of the old chair. "I need to get to bed, too. I just wanted to find out if there was anything I should know about your conversation with Max. I'll get out of your hair now." As she made her way toward the door, Gillian felt a wave of regret sweep over her.

"Bridget, please. Stop. I don't want to fight over a *guy!*"

"Don't you get it, Gillian?" Bridget turned and stared at her incredulously. "We're not fighting over a guy."

Max was so clearly the issue, it was hard for Gillian not to accuse her roommate of playing emotional games. "Then, what is this about?" she asked carefully.

"It's about you being a jerk." Bridget said simply. She spoke as smoothly and easily as if she had just commented that Gillian looked good in blue.

"Excuse me?"

Bridget ignored the contortions of Gillian's face and voice. "Gillian, I *know* you're not coming clean. Either you're lying to me about your feelings, or you're not being honest with yourself. Either way, you're not being a very good friend — to yourself, or to me. The thing is, you don't have to tell me anything you don't want to." Bridget fingered the soft material at the end of one sleeve. "I just wish you'd tell me if that was the case. I thought we were closer than this, that's all. Guess I was wrong." She shrugged and turned away. A second later, she was gone.

Late that night, long after Bridget had left her alone in her room, Gillian lay still and silent in her bed, considering what had been said. It had taken her weeks to admit that she felt jealous at all, even a simple jealousy that reflected only the past. But was she kidding herself? Were the feelings she had for Max actually, as Bridget proposed, far more than a memory?

Gillian flopped over onto her side and hugged one soft pillow close under her cheek. It wasn't that the possibility of carrying a torch for Max hadn't occurred to her. As distressing as the thought was, that at least was something she had considered before. No. Perhaps most disturbing of all was Bridget's brutally honest assessment of Gillian's relationships with her friends.

To those who knew her, it was no big secret that Gillian had problems with romantic relationships. She herself admitted she was more than a little gun-shy. The romances she enjoyed most were soothing, nonconfrontational, and somewhat superficial — such as the one she had with Keith. They were based on mutual respect and shared interests, not passion. It took a long time for problems to reveal themselves under such conditions. And, by maintaining a degree of detachment, Gillian always managed to extricate herself without any significant degree of suffering.

But, if Bridget's accusations were accurate, it would seem that her *modus operandi* for friendships was alarmingly similar. While she had remained vaguely aware of her own desire to avoid the "Max issue," Gillian had never intended to deliberately deceive Bridget about her feelings. Yet their relationship had clearly suffered, perhaps irreparably. She'd known for a long time that she liked to keep people at arm's length. But she'd never before thought of herself as being a bad friend.

Burrowing her face against the soft blue-and-white flannel pillowcase, Gillian tried to identify the source of her trouble. Was it her father's neglect? The loss of Max? Her failed friendship with Jenny? Mom and Dad's divorce? Had all these situations together instilled in her an inner fear that kept her from letting anyone get close? If so, was there any hope for her future?

Without warning, Max's words came back to haunt her. *"Life is hard, Gilly. . . . I'm afraid it's harder on you than it needs to be."* She had told him that she didn't appreciate being thought of as a basket case. But she was beginning to feel more and more like one.

But God? When she thought of a divine creator, Gillian's thoughts turned toward the heavens, not toward her own petty problems. If there really was a God, she couldn't imagine that he would be concerned about her little world. Although . . . Max seemed to think that he was. And so did Mom. Maybe it wouldn't hurt to find out more about it one of these days.

As she drifted off, Gillian wondered what it would be like to *know* God. Although she hadn't come to any real conclusions about him, somehow the mere thought seemed to bring her hope, and she was not alone with her miserable memories after all. Despite her earlier fears that she would never rest, she soon fell into a peaceful, dream-filled sleep.

Eight

*Intimacy requires courage because
risk is inescapable.
We cannot know at the outset
how the relationship will affect us.*
ROLLO MAY,
THE COURAGE TO CREATE, 1975

July 20, 1987

*I've been trying to reach her for days, but Jenny
won't even come to the phone. I guess she told
her mom what happened, because Mrs. D. acts
pretty snippy toward me when I call. The next
thing you know, she'll be telling* my *mom about
the whole ugly scene. Then I'll be grounded for
sure. I haven't gotten the official green light to
go out with any guys yet. No doubt Mom would
consider this little episode a subversion of her
rules.*

*So much for dating. And . . . so much for
being in love. Jenny's bubble was pretty much
destroyed, thanks to me. And me . . . well, I
haven't seen Max in days. Dad's been spending a lot of time at his office this week, getting*

ready for some conference, so Max has been meeting him there. Not that it would make any difference if he came here to our house. No matter how much I like him, it still isn't going to happen. It's just not. I wish I could forget about him altogether. I wish I could forget about all of them. Max, Dad . . . Jenny, too.

It's just so hard, not being what they want. Max apparently wants some beautiful co-ed. And, really, who can blame him? Dad wants a little version of himself. Mom wants me to become a Christian, like her. And Jenny . . . well, Jenny just wanted me to be a good friend. Which I wasn't.

One thing's for sure. Relationships are a dangerous thing. You never know what's gonna happen. It's enough to make you think twice before getting close to anybody. I don't know what's worse — getting hurt or being the one that's done the hurting.

The other day while my mom was working at the kitchen table, she had the radio on and was listening to some program about a guy who went and lived in a cave for seven months. I don't know whether he was a monk or just a hermit. . . . I wasn't really paying attention to what was going on. But I got to thinking about it later, and I've decided that maybe the guy had the right idea. There was

156

no one to get in his way. He probably got to do whatever he wanted, whenever he wanted . . . although I suppose that doesn't mean so much when you're in a cave.

If I could do it right now, I'd go live in a cave, too. I wouldn't let anyone come see me, except Max, of course. Someone would send me supplies by mule every week. Just the basics: food and water, matches . . . and maybe Casey Kasem's Top 40 Countdown.

I could probably survive for a long time like that. Just me and Max and Casey Kasem, hangin' out in the cave and talkin' about life.

But for now, I'm stuck here in Princeton. Summer's half over already. Pretty soon I'll have to go back to Chat. Except this time, I won't have Jenny on my side. I'll have to face all the competition, the backstabbing all on my own. Oh, I have other friends, all right. But none as close as Jenny. By the time Jenny tells them what happened, they probably won't like me, either. Doesn't really matter, though. I guess I'm getting what I deserve.

I think I will miss Jenny, though. I wish she would forgive me. But it doesn't look like she's going to, and that's something I'm just going to have to live with. If I could go back in time and change it all, I would. But I can't. All I can do is try my best to keep it from happening again. No matter what it takes.

157

"That's it. No more interviews for me." Pam closed the door behind her with a re- sounding thud. "It's official," she said, drop- ping her briefcase on the floor. "I'm going to remain unemployed until the day I die."

"Alrighty," Gillian said, glancing over the top of her copy of *Sky and Telescope*. From where she lay, stretched out on the oversized camelback sofa, she could barely make out Pam's dark head. "It's nice to see that you're not being overly dramatic." She flopped her magazine down on top of the soft yellow cushions with their cheerful red rosettes.

"You think I'm kidding, Gil? It's dog- eat-dog out there." Pam stepped around the couch and into full view. Gillian studied her with a discerning eye. Dressed in a knee-length sand-colored jumper, styl- ish cotton stockings, and crisp white blouse, she looked professional and *in vogue*. If image played any factor at all, Gillian would have thought that her room- mate would get the first job she applied for. "I'm exhausted." Pam flopped down into a threadbare, pinkish red armchair that looked as though it had seen far better days. "All I want to do tonight is sink into a hot bath and soak myself until I'm one big prune," she announced, kicking off her tailored, stacked-heeled Mary Janes.

"Ooo. Sounds lovely," Gillian said sarcastically, wishing she had thought of it first.

Pam arched her eyebrows at Gillian's tone. "The part about the bath, or me being a prune?"

"It's a tough call. Seriously, though . . . save me some hot water. I could use a good soak." She reached up with one hand and began to gently rub at the bound-up muscles in her neck. That's what she needed: a long, warm, soothing retreat from the world at large. She began a mental checklist: long vanilla candles, lilac bubble bath, the soft strains of Faure's *Pelleas et Melisande*. . . .

"Pretty tense?" Pam sympathized, her deep blue eyes full of concern.

"Oh, my gosh." Gillian bit out a short laugh, but there was no humor in it. "You don't know the half of it."

"Still having a hard time with Bridget, huh?" Pam said knowingly.

"Yeah." Gillian nodded. She looked at her friend suspiciously. "Hey, maybe you *do* know the half of it. How did you hear about that? Has she talked to you?"

"As a matter-of-fact, she did, a little bit. Not that she would have had to, though, for me to notice. It's pretty obvious. You two have been moping around here like a couple of grounded teenagers."

"Yeah. Well. We've been fighting like teenagers, too," Gillian admitted guiltily. "I hate it."

"So make up, then." Pam reached forward and began to massage her aching feet.

"Wish I could," Gillian sighed. She did, too . . . if not for the sake of the friendship, then for overall morale in the house. "Unfortunately, it's not that easy."

"Ouch!" This exclamation Pam directed to her feet. She continued to knead furiously, as if she was working a loaf of bread dough. "So what's the problem?"

Gillian eyed her distrustfully. "You mean, Bridget didn't tell you?"

Pam just looked at her. "I'm asking *you*."

"Oh, it's dumb." Gillian wished they hadn't started this conversation. But Pam was waiting for an answer now, and she couldn't afford to alienate what might be her only remaining friend. She sighed. "You remember that guy in my department Bridget was interested in?"

"Yeah."

"Well, she's convinced that I like him, too, that's all. So she's mad."

"I see." Pam looked at her thoughtfully. "She's mad because she thinks you like him?"

"Uh-huh."

"Not because she thinks you aren't being honest with her?"

"No. I —" Gillian leaned one elbow against the arm of the couch. "You have been talking to Bridget," she said with a glare.

Pam dropped one aching dog to the floor and reached for its companion. "Look, Gillian. I'm not saying this to make you angry," she said, squeezing her big toe. "I promise you, Bridget isn't saying terrible things behind your back. She's just confused. She can't figure out why you won't tell her what you're really feeling."

"Maybe *I* don't know what I'm really feeling," groused Gillian.

"Maybe you don't," Pam said easily. She paused for a moment, then suggested, "And then again, maybe you do."

"You think I'm lying to Bridget?" Gillian opened her eyes wide. "And to you?"

"No." Pam shook her head calmly. "But I think you're trying pretty hard not to see something that's clear to everyone but you."

"Oh, great!" Gillian wailed. She threw her feet off the bright, overstuffed couch and planted them squarely on the almond-colored wool carpet beneath her. The subject she'd been avoiding for weeks could be put off no longer. "This is awful! What if I *do* like Max?"

"So what if you do?" Pam seemed unconcerned.

"So what? So *what?*" Gillian looked at her incredulously. "Do you have any idea what that would mean?"

Pam dropped her second foot to the floor. "Obviously not," she said dryly.

"Well, for one thing, there's *Keith.*" Gillian waited for the wide-mouth "O" of realization that would follow, but Pam's expression remained blank.

"Right," she nodded. "So, what *else?*"

"What do you mean, what else?" Gillian continued to glare at her. "He's my boy-friend, for goodness' sake."

"I guess so." Reaching around to the back of her head, Pam pulled out several bobby pins, allowing her long, black hair to fall to her shoulders. "If you want to stretch the definition of the word."

"What's that supposed to mean?" There was warning in her voice.

"Gillian." Pam addressed her in the tone

of one whose patience was being sorely tested. "You *never* talk about Keith. The two of you see each other only when it's convenient. When he goes out of town, it's like he doesn't even exist." She shook her head disapprovingly, as if that settled it. "Do you love him?"

"I don't know. . . ." With elbows on her knees, Gillian dropped her head into her hands and held it there.

"Gil? Either you do or you don't." She waited only a second for her response. "Can you honestly say that you do?"

"Well . . . no." Once it was put that way, the answer was shockingly easy to give.

Pam gave a nod of satisfaction. "And does he love you?"

"Now, that I *don't* know."

"Well," she said thoughtfully, "I'd be surprised if he felt that strongly. Most guys know how to read the signs, and you haven't exactly been giving off love vibes."

"How do you know what kind of 'vibes' I give off? You're hardly ever around us," Gillian grumbled.

"True," her roommate admitted. "I stand corrected. I don't know what makes your relationship tick. But you do."

"Meaning?"

"Come on. Help me out here. Why are

you dating Keith if you're not in love with him?"

Gillian lifted her chin from her hands. "Well . . . it's easy. There's no stress there, no pressure. Besides, I figured I might fall in love with him in time. You and Bridget seemed pretty sure that he's the one. . . ."

"Gil, no one's saying you have to marry the guy," Pam told her matter-of-factly. "He's a sweetie, that's for sure. But that's all the more reason to let him off the hook, so he can find someone who will *really* love him."

Gillian felt even more confused than before. She'd never really thought that she was in love with Keith. So why did she feel disappointed now that Pam was telling her it was okay not to marry him. "But you always said —"

"I said that you should give him a *chance*. You've done that, I think. And I'm proud of you, Gillian. But you can't force love to happen, either, if it isn't there. At some point, you have to let go and move on."

"I thought the point was *not* to walk away from relationships."

"There's a balance. You just have to find it. There are some relationships that just don't work out. And that's okay." Pam absentmindedly fingered the bobby pins she held in one hand. "There are other relationships that are worth keeping." She looked at Gillian meaningfully. "Do you understand what I'm saying?"

"You're talking about Bridget." Pam wasn't telling her something she didn't already know. It was true that she hadn't been overly close to Bridget, by most people's standards. But nonetheless, Bridget was as good a friend to Gillian as anyone. "Honestly, I hate fighting with her. I really do. I'm just having a hard time getting past it. Part of me is angry because she just kept pushing me. She wouldn't leave me alone, you know?" Pam inclined her chin in a brief acknowledgment. But although Gillian wanted to believe that her own feelings were justified, she knew that her behavior was not.

"I'm frustrated with myself, too, though," she admitted reluctantly. "I was pretty touchy about the whole subject. I wanted to pretend there wasn't a problem, but the whole time I knew there was a conflict inside me that wasn't going away. And there was Bridget, shoving the whole thing in my face. I guess I snapped. I didn't do it on purpose though. I *hate* the fact that I hurt her. Now I've got to find a way to make it up to her," she grumbled, "on top of everything else that's going on."

"You mean your feelings for Max?"

Gillian just stared at her hands.

"What *do* you feel for him, Gil?"

Gillian closed her eyes. She was tired of running, tired of hiding. Maybe it was about time she talked to *someone* about it. And Pam was perhaps the most trustworthy person she knew.

"There was a time when I absolutely adored him." She looked up with just a hint of an embarrassed smile. "I thought he was perfect. Then one day he walked out of my life, as suddenly as he had come into it." Unconsciously, one hand crept up to her mouth, and she started to gnaw nervously at one chipped nail. "I knew he hadn't done anything wrong, but I was angry with him just the same," she murmured.

"Because he left you?"

Gillian noticed the finger between her teeth and dropped her hand. "That was a big part of it," she said, blushing. "Maybe I was upset, too, because he didn't ever acknowledge how much I cared for him. On one hand, I would have felt humiliated if he knew I had a crush on him. But at the same time, I wanted him to care. He knew

I liked him well enough, I suppose. I was a terrible tagalong," she laughed. "But sometimes, I still wonder if he had any idea how *much* I liked him. He couldn't have known I would keep thinking about him, nonstop, for two whole years. But it would have been nice if he'd just said, 'I know you're going to miss me, Gilly. I'm sorry I have to go.' Is that crazy?"

Pam shook her head. "There's nothing crazy about the way your heart feels. It may not always seem logical to the head, but the heart has its own reasons for the way it responds to people."

Gillian leaned back against the soft, bright-red sofa pillows and quietly reflected on Pam's words.

"Okay, so that's how you felt about Max back then," her friend broke in. "What about *now?*"

"Well . . . most of the time, I feel uncomfortable," Gillian confessed. "Sometimes I still feel angry. Every once in a while, I snap at him, for no reason at all. I can't imagine what he must think of me." After all the years of wanting Max to like her, she certainly wasn't helping her case any now.

"Do you have any idea how he feels about you?" Pam asked softly.

167

"I guess I have a good idea." She couldn't ignore the evidence, even if she wanted to. "I think he feels sort of brotherly toward me. Last week he told me he was worried about me. He thinks I'm alone in life." Gillian grabbed a loose throw pillow and held it in her lap. "I didn't agree with him at the time. But the more I think about it, the more I wonder if maybe he's right."

"Does he have any particular remedy in mind?" Pam's blue eyes twinkled mischievously. "Like *him*, maybe?"

"Please!" Gillian rolled her eyes heavenward. "No, it's not anything like that. Max says he thinks I have sort of a spiritual hole in my life. He believes that if I had a relationship with God, I'd have more *resources* to get me through the tough times." She plucked at the fabric she held between long suntanned fingers. "Do you think he's right, Pam?"

"I don't know," she said soberly. "The truth is, I'm not sure, myself, what to believe. But I *have* known some Christians who said that same thing Max did. They were good people. People I respected. I have to admit, I was kind of intrigued."

"Yeah," Gillian said thoughtfully. "I am, too."

Pam leaned forward and peered at her intently. "It sounds like this guy really likes you, Gil, if he cared enough to worry about you like that."

"You think?" The words came out sounding more hopeful than she had intended.

"Yeah," Pam said with a knowing smirk. "*I think*. And you know what else I think?" Gillian had her suspicions, but she shook her head. "I think Bridget's right. I think you like him, too."

Out of habit, Gillian started to shake her head, then stopped herself and grinned like a fool. The truth was out. There was no hiding it.

For better or worse, she was gloriously, deliriously, and completely smitten with Max Bishop.

Again.

Nine

And the LORD *God formed the man from the dust of the ground. . . .*
GENESIS 2:7

July 27, 1987

From the first moment he met Max, my father should have realized that he had met his match. His favorite students have always been the ones who swallowed his theories whole, like seals clapping for fish. But Max isn't that easy. There are too many questions wrapped up inside him. I knew it all along. I could see it in Max's eyes. Dad could have seen it too, if he'd just been paying attention.

I've said that I wished I could forget all about Max. I don't suppose that was ever likely, but after what happened last night, there's not even a chance *of it.*

It started out as one of those rare times when Dad, Mom, and I actually were acting like a regular family. All week the weather had been pretty steamy. Mom hates being all hot and sticky, so she set up a cheap plastic sprinkler in the backyard and planted her blue-and-white patio chair just beyond the water's arc. From there she could just barely reach one scarlet-colored toenail out into the spray, or just lay back and enjoy the traces of mist that drifted by.

Well, I'm no dummy, and neither is Dad. Hot is hot, and it was pretty clear right then who was the real brain in the family. Pretty soon we had our chairs out there in a small semicircle of three, with mine smack-dab in the middle. Very "Father Knows Best."

We'd been out there for about twenty minutes when Max showed up. Dad must have been expecting him, although I hadn't heard anything about it beforehand, and I'm usually pretty good about keeping up on Max and Dad's schedule. Since the whole mess up with Jenny, though, I guess I've been pretty out of it.

Anyway, my family was gathered around the sprinkler like it was some crazy campfire or something, and Mom was telling Dad and me stories about which political candidate was under indictment for taking bribes and which was spending the summer letting his hair plugs heal. When Max got there, Dad didn't get up right away — I guess the heat was getting to him, too — and I finally got to just sit back and watch Max up close.

For a while, he and my dad chatted about critical density, special and general relativity, kinetic energy. You know, the usual stuff. After a while, Dad asked Max if he had decided on a subject for his first big paper of the fall. Max said that he had. Everything was still fine at that point. But when Max told him what he'd chosen as his topic, I thought my father was going to have some sort of fit, right there under the sprinkler.

"You propose to reconcile evidence supporting the big bang theory with the theological teachings in Genesis?" Veins bulged at the side of Dad's neck. The sprinkler wasn't much help any more. He was getting hotter by the second. "That's not science, Bishop. That's fiction!"

"I disagree, sir," Max said respectfully. "And I'm going to prove it in my paper."

My mom charged right in. "You don't actually expect to give religious credence to that . . . that theory?" I think she liked the idea of arguing science and religion without attacking my father directly — every time she disagreed with him about it, they ended up fighting. Poor Max was the lamb, and Mom was ready for the slaughter. "The Bible clearly states that God made the earth in six days," she said primly. "I understand that according to the big bang theory, it would have taken at least four-and-a-half billion years to create the earth, and maybe fifteen billion years or more to create the universe." I stared at her. She might not agree with Dad's beliefs, but at least she was listening to him. The woman knew her facts.

"That's right," Max answered cheerfully enough.

"But you're saying you plan to reconcile these two theories." She, too, looked at him as if he was crazy. "What's the compromise?"

"Oh, there's no compromise, Mrs. Spencer," Max reassured her. "The creation of the universe took ten to twenty billion years, all right. But it's also true that it took six days."

Dad sat silently, working his jaw like a cow chewing its cud. Mom didn't even blink. Max just smiled back at them, while I watched all three to see who would move first.

Mom was the one who broke the spell. After several long seconds, she sat up and peered closely at Max, like he was a magician and she was determined to figure out where he'd hidden the rabbit. Suddenly, she had an insight. You could almost see the light bulb appear over her head. "Oh, I see!" she said smugly and leaned back again in her chair. "You're not a literalist, then. You're one of those people who believes that the Genesis account is a metaphor. Each 'day' equals six

173

billion years. . . ."

"Oh no," Max broke in. "It was a literal six days. Six twenty-four-hour days," he assured her. By this time, Dad was on the edge of his rickety patio chair, veins bulging bigger with every word. Any minute, I figured, he was gonna fall right off.

"Are you trying to tell me that both explanations can be true?" Mom obviously thought Max was some kind of heretic. It didn't seem to bother him a bit.

"I believe that they not only can be . . . they are," he said confidently.

"All right, young man." Mom took it upon herself to issue the challenge. "You'd better explain. And be very careful." She threw Dad a sideways glance and laughed. "The master is watching."

"Well . . . I haven't really articulated my thoughts yet, but I have an idea of where I'm going with the subject for my paper. . . ." For a second, Max looked a little uncertain, like he wasn't quite prepared to go down that road yet. He stopped for a moment and seemed to be considering his approach. "Okay," he said finally. "Let's start with the basics. What we're looking at here are two different premises: First, the scientific theory that the universe was created over a period of ten to twenty billion years. This hypothesis is sup-

ported by measured scientific evidence, including paleontological discoveries, carbon dating, and the observed behavior of light waves. Next, there's your second theory: That the universe was created in six days by an omnipotent being. This theory is supported primarily by religious tradition and scriptural accounts inspired by divine revelation." Max held his hands out, palms upturned, presenting himself as a human scale. "Both theories pretty hard to argue with," he said diplomatically. His expression was cool, impassive. He was the very picture of objectivity.

"At first the two theories seem so mutually exclusive, it's tempting to choose one over the other or to ignore the problem completely and pretend it doesn't exist. Wouldn't you say?"

"Yeah," I agreed. Mom and Dad both turned and looked at me. I'd never expressed any interest in the subject before. But they'd never explained it this way before. Max spoke as if it was a mystery to be solved, not a battle to be won.

"So, Mrs. Spencer, let's look a little more closely at the problem." Max lowered one hand and laid it open in front of him, as if presenting evidence for examination. "The amount of time that passes during the period of creation described in the first few verses of the Bible is completely inconsistent with time

measured on earth. Does this problem occur concerning any other verses in the Bible?"

"Well . . . no. Not that I'm aware of."

"That's my understanding, too. The time discrepancy applies only to the days of creation before God rested. So we're looking at, what? Six days? What happens on the sixth day?"

"God made man," Mom supplied, ever the dutiful Bible student.

"Right." Max's head bobbed up and down. "So, is it true, would you say, that before the sixth day, there were no humans around to measure time? Just . . . God?"

Dad made a face like a man being tortured, but I could see that Mom was really getting into what Max was saying. I have to admit . . . I was, too.

"I suppose so," Mom said.

"Okay, now, Gilly. Let's pull you into this. What do you know about Einstein's special and general theories of relativity?"

The sun was going down, but I started to sweat even more. "Well, $E=mc^2$ states that the energy of a photon equals —"

"No, no. Forget the formulas. Tell me what the theories mean."

My mouth felt as dry as sand. I swallowed hard. Dad was watching me real close, and I didn't want to botch it up. "Basically, Einstein's theories state that the passage of time for an observer, traveling near the speed of light, is relative."

Max nodded. "How does this affect the passage of time?"

"Well I guess it means it's possible for two people in two different places to measure the same exact event in completely different time frames. Each frame is different, yet completely true and accurate for the person from whose perspective the event is measured."

Max beamed at me like he was the professor and I was his star pupil. Mom looked a little surprised. But, Dad . . . Dad looked like his tongue was about to drop out of his mouth. I almost laughed. He had no idea I knew all this stuff. But . . . please. I'm no dummy. I've taken physics. Besides, you can't be a kid in Dr. Joseph Spencer's house and grow up not knowing something about quantum cosmology. See, I'd been listening, too.

Max turned back to my mom. "Do you understand now, Mrs. Spencer, what I'm getting at?"

"I — I think so," she said slowly. "You're saying that it's possible for man and God to be looking at the event from two different time frames? At the same time?"

"That's what I believe."

I hadn't thought of that before. I didn't know what else to say.

"But aren't Einstein's theories just . . . well, theories?" *Mom asked timidly. With my dad nearby, she knew she was treading on dangerous ground.* "It's not as if they've been proven true."

Dad rolled his eyes and turned a darker shade of red. The veins kept bulging. But Max responded kindly to Mom, just like he always did to me.

"Actually, they have," *he explained.* "The word theory *can be a little bit misleading. Einstein's discoveries have been proven to be scientifically accurate."* Mom blushed. "Don't feel bad, though," *Max told her.* "Not everyone knows that. It's pretty common for people to 'tune out' when someone talks about Einstein's teachings. Taken as a whole, they can be pretty overwhelming. But the basic principles behind them are pretty understandable."

"And you're saying that these principles are the answer to the stand-off between religion and science?"

"I'm saying there doesn't have to be a stand-off," *Max said simply.* "What we're talking about here is a very real, scientifically proven phenomenon called relativistic time dilation — a phenomenon that completely allows for a biblical, six-day creation of the universe."

"This is ridiculous," *Dad muttered. I looked*

at him in surprise. He'd been quiet for so long, I'd almost forgotten he was there. I would have thought the debate would have stirred him up, but he didn't look like he wanted to argue, particularly. He just looked disgusted. He shook his head. "There is no scientific evidence that suggests that there is any god who made the world — either in six days or in billions of years. There are clearer, more rational explanations for how the universe began."

Okay, I decided. I'll bite. "Like what?"

Dad turned on me. "Haven't you ever heard of 'singularity'?" *I nodded. I had. But he wasn't looking at me anymore. His focus was solely on Mom now.* "Scientific study has led physicists to an understanding of singularity, a phenomenon in which matter is compressed into a single point where the gravitational field and the density of matter are infinite," *he told her.* "Today, scientists believe that the universe once existed in such a state of singularity. This highly dense, and infinitely small compressed point contained all galaxies, all radiation, all matter." *Dad was sitting up in his chaise lounge now, with his feet planted firmly on the misty ground, and his legs buckled awkwardly at either side of the chair. The expression on his face was intense. He was getting into it now, too.*

"At some time, this point exploded, sending

galaxies spinning into the outer reaches of the universe, which continued to expand — and are still expanding today," he explained, as if this were a fact known and accepted by everyone who had even a shred of intelligence. Mom looked at Max, as though she suspected she couldn't trust Dad. I think she expected Max to jump in and save her, but he just nodded. Mom looked unpleasantly surprised. She had always pooh-poohed Dad's passing comments about the big bang theory. I could tell it bothered her that Max wasn't arguing with him. For a moment or two, words escaped her.

"And you think that this negates any evidence that might point toward a creator?" She finally gave in and asked my father.

"Of course I do," Dad grumbled, as if it should be obvious.

"Sir, I respectfully disagree," Max interrupted. Dad's jaw dropped, just a fraction. My hero! I almost cheered. The day was shaping up pretty great after all.

"What about all evidence to the contrary? What about evolution?" Dad glared at him.

Max just looked right back. "I'm not convinced."

"You must be joking!" Dad was appalled. "There is clear *evidence that, over time, simple forms of life have developed into more complex forms."*

Max shook his head. "I'm not sure it's as clear as you believe."

"You can't dispute all the evidence of evolution — ?"

"Evidence of microevolution doesn't prove macroevolution," Max said evenly. "The development of various species over time doesn't justify the theory that man developed from lower forms of life. There's still no evidence of a 'missing link.' The theory you're talking about requires a greater leap of faith than that demanded of those who support a creationist theory."

"I still don't get it," I heard myself saying. I almost jumped in surprise. I hadn't intended to say a word.

"What don't you get, Gilly?" Max asked, turning his full attention on me.

"Well, you're saying that six days can equal fifteen billion years or more. But that's not the only problem, is it? In school, I learned that the building blocks needed for life started at the big bang. But the Bible says God made man from dust. Just, like, from out of thin air."

"It doesn't say anything about thin air, Gilly," Max corrected me gently but firmly. "That's just our simple human perception. Let's think about this for a minute. What if just maybe the things your mom and dad believe are both true?"

Now I was the one looking at him like he was a lunatic. "Right. How's that possible?"

"What your father believes — and correct me if I'm wrong, sir — is what many other scientists believe: that the earth is made of matter that was once supercompressed through the birth, life, death, and rebirth of countless stars. This process gave us the building blocks for life."

Dad nodded, grudgingly.

"See, that's not what the Bible says at all," I said.

"Does the Bible say exactly how God made the universe, Gilly? What the process was?"

I thought back to everything my mom had tried to teach me. "Well . . . no. Not that I know of."

"And if Einstein's teachings are true — and we know that they are — then isn't it possible that God could have pulled the material he needed for the earth from that material that once came from other stars?"

"I suppose."

"Okay, then. The Bible doesn't say exactly *how God made the universe. Or mankind. You have to form your own opinion, Gilly. But you know what I think? I think it's entirely possible that God did it exactly the way your dad says it happened. God's not an illusionist. He's* a creator. *He made us* from *something. Maybe*

even elements on earth that originally came from stars." He looked deep into my eyes. And suddenly, I wasn't thinking about how cute he was. I was thinking about how much sense he was making. And how much I wanted to be like him.

He leaned forward and whispered, as if sharing a great secret. "Maybe, Gilly, just maybe . . . you and I are both made of stardust."

And the way his eyes twinkled, just like the stars, I knew it must be true.

July 23, 1997

Warm beams of golden light poured through the white-trimmed windowpanes, teasing Gillian with just a taste of summer sun. On either side of her, at the kitchen table, piles of file folders and stacks of thick, dusty tomes obscured the cheerful blue-and-white tablecloth. Gillian stared dolefully at the mess around her. She hated working on the weekend . . . hated wasting a perfectly good Saturday morning most of all. But with her heavy load, and with her half-time class schedule, there was no avoiding it. At least she could ease the pain of the situation by curling up in her favorite corner of the old country farmhouse.

The sound of footsteps padding down the hall offered a much-needed distraction.

"Hey, Pam?" she called. "What are you doing up so early? I thought you stayed up late last night making —" Her voice broke off at the sight of the curly brown head that appeared in the doorway. She hadn't seen Bridget in several days; she hadn't even considered that it might be her approaching. "Oh, hi." Gillian tried to keep her voice friendly, but it wasn't easy. She disliked stressful situations, and this was one of the toughest she had experienced in a long time. "How's it going?"

Bridget averted her gaze and made a beeline for the refrigerator. "Okay, I guess," she said, her head disappearing behind the appliance's enormous white door.

Feeling snubbed, Gillian, in turn, buried her nose in the book that was open on the table before her. If Bridget didn't want to talk, then they wouldn't talk. Two could play at that game.

She stopped reading as the thought sank in. A game? *A game?* This wasn't supposed to be a game. She and Bridget were both grown-ups. They were friends . . . more or less. There wasn't any reason why they shouldn't be able to work through this. Especially if *someone* were to take a step forward and apologize . . .

Instinctively, Gillian knew that person had to be her. She cringed at the thought.

It isn't as though I hurt Bridget on purpose, she thought defensively. *And it's not like Bridget didn't hurt me, too. It wasn't very nice of her to push me, the way she did.* The more Gillian thought about it, the angrier she got. *It isn't anyone's business but my own who I like or don't like. If I want to keep that information to myself — or even if I'm not ready to face the situation yet — that's my prerogative. Bridget had no right — no right at all — to insist that I . . .*

"Gillian, did you eat my last egg? It was in here yesterday."

The accusation caught Gillian off guard, and she struggled to keep the cutting edge from her tone. "Nope. But I saw Pam mixing some eggs into a batch of cookie dough last night," Gillian told her. "Maybe she thought it was one of hers." Bridget stuck her nose around the refrigerator door and looked at Gillian, as though she wasn't sure whether or not to believe her. After a moment's consideration, she resumed her silent inventory of the refrigerator's contents.

Gillian fumed. *See? What is that all about? Here I am, being perfectly civil, and she automatically assumes that I'm the one who took her crummy ol' egg. That shows how much she trusts me. Probably about as much as I trust her. . . .*

Gillian laid down the volume she held in her hands and considered the matter further. It was true. She *didn't* trust Bridget. Not enough to lay herself open and ask for forgiveness . . . even though she knew full well that she had been just as insensitive as — if not *more* insensitive than — Bridget had been. It was a shame, because if one of them didn't take steps toward repairing their broken relationship — and soon — the damage to their friendship could become permanent. She really wasn't looking forward to beginning the roommate search again. Over and over, the cycle ran . . . a new roommate, some sort of conflict, time to move on. . . . If she was going to have to go through such struggles, why not go through it with Bridget and work things out?

Across the room, Bridget had abandoned her egg quest and was instead placing a filter full of coffee grounds inside her kitschy old Mr. Coffee machine. Gillian pondered the situation. Her roommate wasn't going anywhere. Bridget would have to wait for the drink to brew. There would be no better opportunity to say what she had to say.

"Umm . . . Bridget?" The words rushed quickly off her tongue before she had a chance to change her mind.

"Yeah?" Bridget put her hands behind her back and rested them against the white Formica kitchen counter, then leaned against them, appearing casual.

"I . . . uh, I've been thinking." Gillian licked her lips nervously. "About what you said the other night, and . . . well, you're right. I haven't been completely honest with you. Or myself."

Bridget opened her brown eyes wide at the confession. "You haven't." It was a confirmation, not a question.

"No. I've been examining my feelings, and I —" She took a deep breath. The words were as difficult to say as she had feared. "I think I may still feel . . . *something* for Max after all these years."

"Oh." Bridget's bright eyes clouded over. It was clear that she liked him, too. Gillian's heart went out to her. "Have you told this to Max?" Bridget asked weakly.

"No!" Shocked by the question, Gillian nearly yelped out her response. She cleared her throat and said, more evenly, "And I'm not going to, either. I don't actually want to *date* him. I just have some unresolved issues that need to be dealt with —"

Bridget turned away in disgust. "Gillian, you're doing it again." She leaned down and watched the dark liquid dripping into the pot.

"What do you mean?" Gillian protested. "All I said was —" Her eyes flickered back and forth as she analyzed her response. "Oh, all *right,*" she admitted with a groan. "Part of me really would like to date him, just like before. But that doesn't mean I'm actually *going* to." The thought was ridiculous. He didn't like her as anything but a friend. She couldn't believe they were even discussing it. "I couldn't go, even if he asked. Which he *won't.* I've got a boyfriend, you know."

"I know," Bridget said coolly. "Which reminds me . . . have you talked to *Keith* about this?" She reached up into the cupboard and withdrew her favorite blue ceramic mug.

"No, there really isn't any point."

Bridget gripped the handle of the coffeepot and began to pour into the enormous cup. "Of course there is," she said, reaching for the sugar bowl with her free hand. "You've got feelings for another man. Don't you think that will have an effect on your relationship with Keith?"

In her mind, Gillian wasn't sure that it would. "I don't know. We've never been very territorial —"

"Gillian! For goodness' sake, you two aren't wolves." Bridget made a face as she spooned the white crystals into her mug. "Do you *plan* to talk to Keith about it, at least?"

Gillian squirmed under the examination. "I . . . don't know. Not yet, anyway. Not until I know what I feel —"

"Well, *I* know what you feel, and I think Keith has a right to know, too." Bridget set her mouth in a hard line. Her spoon clattered against the countertop, where she dropped it.

"What are you saying?"

"Just that . . . maybe I'll tell Keith, if you won't."

"Bridget!" Surely she was kidding. Gillian could almost feel her blood pressure rising. "You wouldn't do that!"

"Men aren't toys, you know. You can't just play with them."

"But I'm not —"

"I'm serious, Gillian!" Bridget paced the vinyl floor. "I still see Max around the campus. He hasn't asked me out once, but he stops and talks to me about you. He's got a thing for you. You must know that."

Gillian didn't know any such thing, but it was clear that Bridget believed it.

"I know I sound jealous." Bridget's voice quivered as she spoke. "I don't mean to. But I can't help it. And I know it's selfish and mean-spirited of me, but I can't help feeling angry and well . . . sort of betrayed." The cup in her hand shook a little, and she looked as if she might cry. "It's not that you don't have a right to like Max," she said unhappily. "It's just that you acted like you were on my side, when you really weren't. You led me on, made me think you'd set me up with him. You got my hopes up, then you cut me down by telling me not to believe that he might like me. And then you lied to me about how you felt about him yourself."

Each word was like a poison dart and this time Gillian felt every sting.

"Bridget, you're right. I wasn't being a very good friend," she said awkwardly. If there was a way to make things right, she wanted to do it. At the same time, she feared promising too much. She wanted to be a good friend, but she had somehow always managed to fall short of the mark.

Bridget didn't want her to lie anymore. Was it a lie to promise that she wouldn't hurt her again? That she wouldn't fail?

"I don't know what to tell you, except that I didn't do it on purpose," she said quietly. "I thought I was okay about him coming back. I wanted *not* to like him. Then, when I realized the way things were going, I didn't know how to deal with you —" Bridget looked at her miserably, as if Gillian had just accused her of something terrible. "Oh no, Bridget! That's not what I mean. It wasn't your fault, wasn't because of anything *you'd* done. I know I'm responsible for my own feelings. It's just really hard for me to let people get close to me." She tried to think of some way to explain. "You know how we've always kidded about me losing all my boyfriends 'cause I won't give them a chance? I never saw that I was holding my friends at arm's length, too."

Her eyes cried out for Bridget to understand. "I'm sorry. Really I am. And from now on, I'm going to *try* at least to do the right thing." That, at least, seemed like a fairly safe promise.

"If you want to do the right thing, I suggest you talk with Keith." Bridget still sounded hesitant to trust her.

Gillian stared out the window at the brilliant morning light. "I suppose you're right," she said with a sigh. It was time to act responsibly. It was time to face what she'd been running from for so long. "I'm supposed to see him tomorrow night. I'll talk to him then." She turned to look out the window to her left. A cloud passed over the sun, obscuring its golden face. And suddenly the day seemed darker . . . in more ways than one.

Ten

The human heart is like a ship on a stormy sea, driven about by winds blowing from all four corners of heaven.
MARTIN LUTHER,
PREFACE TO HIS TRANSLATION
OF THE PSALMS, 1534

August 2, 1987

I was riding my bike hard today — my hair whipping in the wind like some ridiculous scarf — the way I always do when I'm upset. Mom worries about me when I'm like this, and I guess she's got a point. I don't pay a lot of attention to what's going on around me when I'm angry. I suppose that's why I didn't see the Bug until I had almost hit it.

I'm not talking about getting a bug caught in my teeth, although when I ride all wild like this, that happens, too. I'm talking about the beat-up old 1967 Volkswagen Beetle, white, except for one pitiful-looking red fender. I know *that Bug like I know my own bike, so you'd think I would have noticed. But I didn't*

193

. . . not before I was almost under it.

I was heading east on Route 518, almost to the quarry, and had just raised myself up to a standing position to push on the pedals, as hard as I could — it's a major hill. Even though I was putting all my weight into it, I could barely keep the bike moving. I grunted. I wheezed. But I refused to give up. I kept my eyes on my feet, and I guess I was looking down longer than I realized 'cause before I knew it, I had drifted over the center line and was headed into the opposite lane.

I didn't know it, though, until I heard a sick little cry that sounded like a bleating sheep that was actually the Volkswagen's horn. I looked up and there it was, heading down the hill, right at me. I gave a little scream and cranked the handlebars hard to the right, veering back over to my side and crashing along the roadside.

My arms and legs stung like anything, but I have to say it's the humiliation that hurt the worst. I untangled myself from the wreckage of my bike and looked back over my shoulder. Sure enough, he was on his way over. I was picking black, hard pieces of gravel out of my knee when he got to me.

"Gilly, what on earth? Are you okay?" Max knelt down beside me to help.

"Yeah . . ." I told him, keeping my eyes low-

ered. I'd never been so embarrassed in all my life.

"But . . . what were you doing? Don't you know you could have gotten killed?" His breath came in short gasps. "If you'd been any closer to the top of the hill, I wouldn't have had time to stop! I would have . . . I . . ." For a second, Max looked as though he was going to cry. I guess I did, too, because then he grabbed my hands and held them tight. "Kiddo . . . you scared me to death." He let go of one hand, put a finger under my chin, and turned it gently so I had no choice but to face him.

I finally met his look then, and my own eyes filled up with tears. I think my lower lip trembled, the traitor. "I'm sorry, Max. I didn't mean to. I guess I just wasn't thinking." I tried to sound natural, but my voice was all tight and strained from trying not to cry. It was too late to stop it, though. I could read the emotions on his face — concern, relief, and something else, something sort of protective. I don't remember anyone else ever looking at me like that before. It was more than I could take. Within a few seconds, I was bawling.

Max hesitated, just for a second, then placed his arms around my shaking shoulders. You'd think I would have enjoyed the moment. How long have I been dreaming about Max putting his arms around me? But all I could do was

195

sob. I was completely out of control. I felt my eyes puff up, the way they always do when I cry, and pretty soon my nose was making all sorts of disgusting noises. Max dug into his pocket and pulled out a couple of lint-covered paper napkins from some fast-food place. He laid one of them against the bloodiest of my knees. The second, he handed to me. Feeling like a fool, I put it to my nose and blew . . . hard.

Dainty, I am not. At the foghornlike sound, both Max and I laughed. "Wow," he said. "If I'd had a horn like that, maybe you could have gotten out of the way quicker."

"Unh-unh." I shook my head and wiped at the dirt that was ground into my skinned palms. "If you'd had a horn like that, you would have scared me right off my bike. I never would have had a chance."

Max laughed, a strong, hearty laugh that made me wish I laughed more, too. "Let me see that," he said, reaching for my left hand. He bent down and inspected it closely, then the right. After doing the same with my knees, he told me that he thought I would live.

"But just to be on the safe side," he said, "why don't you let me drive you home?"

"Thanks." That was a relief. The way my knees were stinging, I wasn't looking forward one bit to biking home. "Mom always warns

me not to ride when I'm mad. I guess she was right."

Max climbed to his feet, then helped me to mine. I reached for my bike, but he nudged me away, telling me to just keep the napkin pressed to my knee. In just a few minutes, he had the bike strapped to the back of the Bug and was helping me into the passenger seat.

"So . . . what's all this about you being mad?" he asked as he climbed in the driver's side. "What's on your mind?"

"Oh . . . it's nothing," I told him. I'd already humiliated myself enough. I figured he didn't really want to hear about my problems.

But apparently he did, because he kept pushing — in a nice way. "You know, when I'm having a hard time with something, it usually helps me to talk to a friend about it." He jammed his key into the ignition and cranked it, causing the Bug to sputter and shake. "I think you and I are friends, don't you, Gilly?"

I really didn't know what to say to that. Max considers me his friend? "I hope so." I tried to say it coolly, but I sounded all soft and breathless, like the lovesick teenager I am. "I mean, I'd like —"

The corners of Max's mouth crinkled up. He didn't look embarrassed at all. "So, shoot. Tell me what's on your mind."

197

I sighed. "Oh, it's just Mom and Dad. They got in a big fight this morning. Norrie's taking vacation next week, and Mom's going off to Washington. She was counting on Dad to keep an eye on me, but he just told her at the last minute that he's getting an award at some ceremony in Tucson. So now, either Mom has to cancel, or I'm going to be on my own." I turned to him and spoke very clearly, making sure he heard every word. "It's not a big deal to me. I mean, I'm sixteen years old you know." It was important that he realize I did not need a baby-sitter. "Sixteen."

"I know," he said, and let it go at that.

I leaned my head against the glass and watched the road signs pass. "I just hate it when they fight, that's all," I said. I didn't bother to tell him how often it happened. He didn't need to know what a mess my family really was.

"Well, I don't know exactly what to tell you, Gilly," he said as we turned into my driveway. My heart sank at the sight of our house and yard. Time with Max is what I live for, practically. I hated for it to be over. "I don't know the specifics of the situation," he went on, "and I don't really need to. But I do know that a lot of parents fight. You're not alone there."

Max maneuvered the Volkswagen around Mom's silver Volvo and turned the engine off.

The Bug sighed and sputtered into silence. He put one arm across the headrest behind me, but without touching me even a little bit. "I imagine you must feel really bad right now. Tell you what." I hoped maybe he'd reach out and take my hand again, like he had along the roadside, but he didn't. "I talk to a lot of friends about my problems, but one friend most of all: I talk to God when things are bothering me. If you'd like, I'll talk to him about you, too."

Coming from anyone else, it might have sounded weird. But I could tell by the look on his face that he wanted to help me, and I guess this was the nicest thing he could think of to do.

"O-okay," I said. I wasn't sure I actually wanted him to pray for me, but it was really comforting to know that someone cared. "That would be nice."

Max climbed out of the Bug, and I did the same. We spent the next few minutes examining my bike. Thank goodness, there was no major damage, only a few dings and scrapes — just like on me.

"All right, Evel Knievel," he said with a grin and then began heading back toward Dad's office. "Stay on your side of the road, now. And remember," he threw the words over his shoulder, "I'll be thinking of you."

"Yeah," I whispered, but so he couldn't hear me. "I'll be thinking of you, too."

August 2, 1997

"So then, I had to go before Judge Linwood, who, of course, I had run into that afternoon with his *girlfriend*." With a triumphant stab of his knife, Keith pierced the last bit of herbed salmon steak that lay before him. "He looked at me over the bench, our eyes met . . . and I knew I had him. There was no way he was going to risk letting his wife find out. Of course, I'd *never* get involved in something like that, but he didn't know that for sure. I could have *sneezed* my way through the entire cross-examination and still, he would have . . ."

With slow, careless strokes, Gillian dragged her fork through the mess on her plate. Once a beautiful dish of fresh, warm penne pasta, the mixture before her was now cold and unappetizing. Bits of pale salmon and dark spices peeked out at her from the heavy, quickly solidifying cream sauce. Normally she would have devoured every bite. The Peacock Inn was her favorite restaurant, and their signature dish —

lobster in a port wine sauce, served outside the shell but rearranged on the plate as a full lobster — was her favorite meal. Tonight, however, everything tasted flat. Even the water.

Across the table, Keith continued to chatter on about his day in court. Occasionally, Gillian nodded or displayed some other sign of interest, but for the most part, she let her mind wander.

"If you want to do the right thing . . . talk with Keith," Bridget had said. Ever since she'd spoken the words, Gillian had been dreading this moment. If she could have put it off any longer, she would have. But the most frustrating thing about Bridget's words was that she was horribly right. Gillian wasn't actively participating in her relationship any longer . . . and Keith had a right to know the reason why.

"Gil? Are you listening?" A lock of white-blond hair fell across Keith's eyes, making him look much younger than his thirty-three years.

"Hmm?" Gillian's fork fell to her plate with a clatter. "What? Oh, sorry, Keith. My mind was just —" She gave him a rueful grin. "Sorry."

"Are you okay?" He popped the last bit of steak into his mouth.

"Sure I am." Gillian smiled brightly and picked up her fork again. "Honest. Now, what were you saying?"

Caught with his mouth full, Keith made a face and started chewing harder. Once he had swallowed his bite, he took a long drink of lemon water before repeating himself. "I asked you if you'd be interested in heading up to New York next weekend to visit my folks. My cousin Vince is heading in from Detroit, and I promised I'd go and see him."

"Next weekend, huh?" Keith was great, but Gillian had no desire to go spend three days with his family. "I — I don't think so, Keith. I'm just so swamped. I really think I need to work."

"Even on the weekend?" He looked appalled. "You're sure working a lot these days, Gillian. Are you sure it's good for you? I don't know if it's a good idea to let this Max guy put so much pressure on you."

She shrugged it off and picked at the green beans on her plate. "Oh, it's okay, Keith. Really. I enjoy it."

"You enjoy getting pushed around?"

Gillian looked up in surprise. It wasn't like Keith to voice an opinion so strongly. That was one of the things she liked best about their relationship: he always gave her the space she needed.

"It's a great project," she said firmly, then added, "I enjoy working with Max." There. It was out. And as good a time as any to broach the subject she'd been avoiding. "Um, Keith?" Gillian tried to get his attention, but he was focused completely on their waitress, trying to flag her down with his eyes. "I was thinking about . . . that is, I've been feeling . . ." Oh, phooey. This wasn't going well at all.

"Oh, Miss?" Keith called out. The woman turned on one thin black heel and made a beeline for him. Gillian was amazed. The man drew women like flies.

He held up his cup, offering his unspoken request. Gillian watched as the woman threw Keith a flirtatious little smile, then leaned close to him as she poured his coffee. She didn't even have the decency to look apologetic when Gillian caught her eye.

"Gil?" Gillian turned to see his eyes were back on her. "You were saying?" he supplied.

She pushed all thoughts about the waitress from her mind. "Sorry. It's just that there's something that's been bothering me. I don't *want* to talk about it . . . but I feel like I *have* to."

The expression that flickered across his face could, oddly enough, almost be described as one of pleasure.

"Sure, Gillian. I'd like very much to know what's going on."

"Okay, well . . . this isn't easy to say. I don't know of any other way to do it than to just tell you." She took a deep breath and squeezed the napkin in her lap. "Remember when I told you that Max had been a student of my father's?"

Keith nodded calmly, but the look of pleasure faded slightly.

Gillian swallowed hard. "Well, at the time I had a huge crush on him. That was ten years ago. I didn't think much of it when he first came back, but after I started working with him . . . well, a lot of those old feelings came back."

Keith's eyes widened in dawning understanding. "I . . . see. You want to break up with me so you can date Max."

"No!" Normally, she was not one given to public displays of affection. But now, Gillian reached out to grab his hand and held it tight. "Oh no. That's not it at all. I don't want to break up! I just want to talk about what's going on inside. I feel like I've been hiding something from you, and

I just wanted to be truthful."

Keith listened to her words, but his hand lay still and unresponsive against hers.

Gillian's heart started beating faster. "Honest, Keith," she said a little desperately. "*Nothing* has happened between Max and me, and it's not going to. This isn't about what's happening today or tomorrow. It's about my past and the unresolved feelings I thought I'd left there." She closed her eyes and uttered a brief prayer to the God she wasn't sure she believed in. *Oh, Lord. Please help me out of this one. . . .* Why on earth had she listened to Bridget?

"Are you sure you wouldn't rather date Max?" Keith asked heavily.

"*No.* I mean — yes!" Gillian struggled to regain her composure. "That is, I'm dating *you.*"

"I realize that." The way he said the words, it didn't sound like a good thing. "Do you love him?"

"What!" Gillian's eyes narrowed. "Love Max? Are you kidding? I'm not even going out with him."

"That's not the point. I'm asking if you love him."

She scrambled for an honest answer. "Max has been like . . . like a big brother to me. Of course I love him, in *that* sense."

"But are you *in love* with him?"

"Keith, don't be silly!" Things were getting completely out of hand. "For one thing, Max barely knows I'm alive. He certainly isn't in love with me. . . ."

"I'm not asking about his feelings. I'm asking about *yours*. Come on, Gillian. Please. Answer the question."

"I —" More than anything, Gillian wanted to deny it. But the way Keith was looking at her, she knew she couldn't give him anything but the truth. "I — have a crush on him, I suppose. Just like I did as a kid. Is that what you mean? Is that love?"

"Sometimes," Keith said thoughtfully. "Sometimes not." He searched her face carefully. "I think you know in your heart what you feel for him, Gillian. Maybe you're not aware of the truth yet. But I think you owe it to yourself to find it." There was an air of finality to his tone.

"What are you saying?" Gillian suddenly felt slightly dizzy. "Is this it? Are you breaking up with me?"

Keith stared at his hands for a moment, not moving. Then he answered, "Gillian, it's not just Max. You and I have had problems for a long time."

The words stunned her. "We have?"

"Yes," Keith said evenly. "We have. The

truth is, I've been thinking a lot lately about our relationship, and I haven't been so sure that we should stick with it."

Gillian stared at him, her hazel eyes wide. "But why?"

"Because you just don't trust me, Gillian," he said simply. "We never talk about anything serious. Just our work, our shared interests . . . nothing really about what's going on inside our hearts."

"But I thought we both liked it that way!"

"No, Gillian." Keith's voice was heavy. "*You* liked it that way. You rarely show any interest in getting to know me better. And when I ask you personal questions, you change the subject before I even know what's happened. Our relationship works on a surface level, but not a deep one," he said sadly. "For a minute there, when you said you wanted to talk, I thought there might be a chance after all. But now that I think about it, I'm certain this is the right decision."

Gillian felt a sudden hollowness in her chest. "I didn't bring this up so we'd split up!" she wailed.

"I know you didn't," Keith said gently. "But I think if you search your heart, you'll agree that it's the best thing for us."

"But I don't *want* to be in love with Max!"

"Why not?"

"Because . . ."

"Yes?"

"Because . . . he hurt me."

Keith nodded. "How did he do that?"

"I don't know." Gillian sounded like a pouty child. "He just . . . left, that's all."

"Did you feel that he should have stayed?"

Her head was spinning. Was this twenty questions? "No. Of course not."

"Then, what were you angry about?"

Gillian let out a loud sigh and glared at him in frustration. "I wasn't angry at Max. I was angry at *me*," she said. "For being so dumb! For loving him. For . . . for laying my heart out there to get trampled on." Even as she spoke the words, Gillian felt a tightness growing inside her chest.

"Gillian . . ." Keith kept his voice low and calming. "Was that the first time you felt that way? Was there anyone else you loved who trampled on your heart?"

"Are you kidding?" she laughed bitterly. "I don't remember loving anyone who *didn't* trample on it."

"When was the last time you felt that way? When was the last time you lost

208

someone you truly loved?"

She thought for a moment. "I guess . . . when Max left."

Keith sat back in his chair and folded his arms. "Look, Gillian. I don't want to play amateur psychologist here," he said carefully. "Your life is your own business. But . . . I just can't help but wonder if the issue we're talking about here isn't the same one that caused problems for us."

"I don't know what you're talking about." Her voice was cool, her words measured.

"I'm talking about you not letting me in. You told me once that you liked me because I didn't push you too much," he reminded her.

"I never said that!" Gillian rushed to her own defense. "Maybe I said it was *one* of the reasons, but it wasn't the only —"

"Okay, okay!" Keith raised one hand, as if to ward off her words. "I'm not accusing you of anything. I'm just telling you what I've observed."

"And what is that?"

" '*That*,' my dear, is the fact that you won't let me get close. Maybe I'm not the only one you've done this with. Maybe you aren't letting *anyone* close. It makes perfect sense: You're afraid of what might happen if you give away too much of your heart."

"I don't think that's true," Gillian protested weakly. But, even to herself, the defense fell flat.

"I'm not telling you what to believe," Keith told her. "I'm just giving you something to think about. Maybe it'll help you someday in your next relationship." Gillian's heart sank. Keith was determined. It really was the end. "Maybe with Max," he suggested.

Gillian closed her eyes. Her world was crumbling. The thought was more than she could consider. Opening them again, she reached out and squeezed his hand one last time. "I hate this, Keith. I really do. I never meant for it to be so hard."

"I know," he said softly and returned the pressure of her fingers.

"I'm sorry about everything," she said with feeling.

"Don't be," Keith told her kindly. "Everything happens for a reason. I just know it." He flashed her the last bit of smile he held in his eyes. "No regrets . . . okay?"

"Okay." Gillian managed a weak smile of her own as she reached for her glass of water and raised it to him. "To you," she said sentimentally, feeling a warm tenderness toward Keith for the first time — too late.

"Oh no," Keith answered, confidence in his voice. "To the future."

Two crystal goblets met with a solid *clink*.

"To the future."

Eleven

It's a vice to trust all,
and equally a vice to trust none.
SENECA, *LETTERS TO LUCILIUS*

August 10, 1987

Eight days have passed since Max promised he'd be thinking about me. He said he'd be praying for me, too, but I haven't felt any different. Mom told me once that God answers prayers differently than we think he will. She says his answers are big, like he is, so they take more time than ours do. Sometimes years. She says it takes even more years for us to be able to see what he did — if we ever see it at all. I sure hope I'll be able to see it someday. Things seem pretty chaotic right now.

I went over to Jenny's this afternoon. It's the first time since the whole, ugly Matt Ross incident. I've apologized probably a dozen times, and she finally says she forgives me, but I don't think she really does. Things aren't the same anymore. I suppose we'll still be friends at school, but that's probably about it. I don't think I'll go over there again. It'll be a long summer — Jenny's the only friend who lives within biking distance. (Mom's pretty picky about how far she'll let me go.) But I'd rather be lonely than rejected.

One good thing has come out of all this, though. Without Jenny around, I've spent a lot more time by myself. I used to feel like I needed to be around someone all the time. But who have I got now? Mom? Too busy. Dad? Yeah, right. Sometimes I don't even see him for days. Actually, I don't really mind so much being on my own. I think I'm getting used to it.

I wonder if Max really has been thinking about me? He still comes by to see my dad every week, but lately he's been coming early every time. I always get a chance to talk to him then. He tells me about what he's learning in school, how much he loves the stars. I'm actually starting to love them again, too, because of him.

He asks me stuff, too, like what do I want to study in college? I told him I wanted to be an oceanographer. I don't really, but it sounded better than admitting I had no idea. He seemed pretty impressed.

It's hard for me to imagine what my life is going to be like when I'm all grown-up. It feels so far away. I'm sixteen now, almost there. But *when I think back to when I was twelve, it seems like a whole lifetime ago. I wonder what I'll be like in three years. In thirty? I wonder who I'll be. I hardly know who I am today. At the beginning of the summer, I wrote that I know who I am, but it's not true. I feel like I'm changing. And I'm a little afraid of what the future holds. It seems like there isn't anything I can count on to stay the same. Thank goodness for Max. I don't know what I'd do if I didn't have his visits to look forward to. Everyone needs hope, I'm sure of it.*

And right now, Max is all the hope I've got.

August 7, 1997

"Hey, Gilly." Max poked his curly brown head past the door of her tiny office. He held up a large manila envelope. "Merry Christmas, kiddo," he quipped. "Ed just sent over your ticket to California."

Gillian passed one hand over her weary eyes. "Huh? *Christmas?* My what?"

Max stared at her. "Your airline ticket. You know . . . Pasadena. The observatory at Palomar. Great big telescope. You. Research. For me. Next month. Does any of this ring a bell?"

"Of course . . . Max, I'm sorry." She

blinked against the light behind his head and tried to collect her thoughts. "I'm afraid my head is somewhere else today."

"Someplace fun, I hope."

Gillian snorted derisively. "I wish."

Max eyed her sympathetically. "Want to talk about it?"

"No, that's all right." She pushed her lopsided office chair away from the desk and rolled two feet over to her monstrous metal file cabinet. What would Max say if he knew her thoughts had recently been centered upon *him?* There was no way she was going to risk finding out. Some things she just had to keep to herself. "Life's just pretty confusing right now."

"Yeah. It gets that way sometimes," Max agreed. He stepped into the room and leaned his lanky body against the door frame. "I wouldn't worry too much, though," he said confidently. "Things will work out, Gilly. They always do." Gillian smiled. She was getting used to Max's little pep talks. She was even beginning to sort of like them. "Good things, too," he assured her. "Who knows? Maybe something to do with Keith?" If she wasn't so depressed, she might have laughed. Max had never seemed overly excited about her boyfriend, even after meeting him the night Keith had come by early to take her out to dinner. This wasn't just casual conversation — Max was fishing for something. And not too subtly, either.

It had been almost a week since she'd seen Keith, and so far she'd managed to keep the new status of their relationship a secret. After that terrible dinner, it had taken all her self-control *not* to call up Max and beg to see him that very night. At this point, even though she held him at arm's length, he was still the closest friend she had. Things had smoothed over a bit with Bridget, though they were still a bit awkward. But even during the best of times, Gillian hadn't known her roommates all that well. Right now, with her life in turmoil, she felt her lack of connections more deeply than ever before.

She opened one metal file drawer with a *bang* and carefully avoided making eye contact with Max. Even though she'd wanted to tell him what had happened, the whole subject felt incredibly dangerous. What if she accidentally revealed the *full* extent of her conversation with Keith? What if Max figured out that she liked him? There was no question that the feelings were one-sided, and what could make for a more awkward working situation than

216

that? She was going to have to tell him about breaking up with Keith *sometime,* though.

"Actually, I don't think it's too likely that God has something planned for Keith and me, since we broke up last week," she confessed.

"Really?" Max took a couple of steps farther into the room. *"Ohhhhhh.* Wait a minute. So, that's it. No wonder you've been moping around here all week!"

"Oh, stop it," she scolded him. "I have *not* been moping."

"Oh no? Well, what do you call this?" Max grabbed his lower lip between thumb and forefinger and gave every appearance of trying to pull it up over his nose. Hunching his shoulders, he dragged his arms at his side and began to circle the room. Gillian laughed in spite of herself. "There. See? That's better. That's what's been missing around here."

"What is?"

"Your laugh."

"Yeah, well . . ." The smile disappeared from her face. "It's been missing in a lot of places lately."

The look Max gave Gillian was one of compassion. Grabbing a stack of files from the chair opposite her, he placed them on the floor and sat down, finally managing to catch her eye. "Look, Gilly, I'm not going to push you to talk about anything you don't want to. Maybe there's more to it than you want to share. But I want you to know that if you need someone to listen —"

"Thanks, Max." Gillian managed a half-hearted smile. It wasn't his fault that she had made such a mess of things. "Really, it's not all that complicated. And not that much of a shock when I really think about it." She sighed. "It's the same problem I've had in all my relationships. I just don't want to let anyone get too close, you know?" She looked at him anxiously, hoping for a sign that he understood.

"I'm not sure I know what you mean," he said uncertainly.

Gillian closed her eyes, gathering her thoughts. What on earth had compelled her to start talking about this with him? This was the last subject she wanted to explore with Max, but there was no way out of it now. "It's just that . . . when I was younger, there were several people in my life who I really loved," she explained. "It just seemed like whatever I did, I ended up losing them. I wound up feeling crushed and alone. I always gave every bit of my-

self, and I lost every bit of myself as well."
I can predict exactly what Max will say next,
she thought. *"There's no such thing as giving
away too much love. . . ."*

"That's the thing about loving people,"
he said thoughtfully. "Sometimes they
don't love you back very well. Or at all.
People are pretty fallible creatures, Gilly.
There's a lot of risk involved." He looked
at her seriously. "Maybe the problem is,
you're giving too much of yourself. Or
maybe your expectations are a little too
high."

"What do you mean, giving too much of
myself? I've hardly been giving anything at
all." This from the man who talked so
much of God. Hadn't she heard somewhere that *God is love?*

"Maybe that's the way it is now, but it
doesn't sound like that was always the
case. What were you like when you were a
little girl? Before I knew you? What was it
like to love someone then . . . say your dad,
for example?"

"I don't know. . . . I just *loved* him."

"How did you feel when he wasn't there
for you?"

Gillian squirmed in her seat. "Well . . .
devastated, of course. He was everything to
me when I was little."

" 'Devastated' is a pretty strong word."

"Well, what do you expect?" she answered testily. "I was a little girl. Dad was *everything* to me." *Just like you were when I was a teenager.*

"I know," Max said gently. "I'm not trying to say you should have felt anything different. Your feelings are perfectly normal. I'm just trying to get to the heart of how you're responding." Gillian relaxed a tiny bit. "Children are naturally trusting," Max theorized. "But as we go through life, eventually we learn that not everyone is trustworthy. People fail each other — sometimes on purpose, sometimes without intending to. We can't open ourselves up fully to everyone we meet. It's important to hold back a bit."

"But that's what I'm doing now."

Max shook his head. "I'm not talking about shutting people out, Gilly. And I'm not suggesting that you limit the love you feel or give. I'm just saying that you need to protect yourself . . . to be careful about what you give away of yourself, and what you expect to get in return. If you give, expecting something you may not get, it can be pretty painful. But if you're able to give for the sake of giving and take whatever comes your way, it becomes much easier to love."

"It's hard for me to give *anything* these days," she said shakily.

"I know." Max's voice was gentle. "You're afraid of getting hurt again, aren't you?"

"Yeah," Gillian practically whispered. "I guess I am. It's hard for me to trust anyone anymore."

Max drew one hand roughly across his chin and gave her a thoughtful look. "I don't want to get too pushy here," he said sincerely, "but maybe there's someone in your past that you need to forgive. . . ."

Gillian looked at him in surprise. She hadn't even entertained the thought. "Why do you say that?"

"Well, it sounds as though you're still carrying around a lot of hurt from a long time ago. Forgiveness is a powerful thing, Gilly. Maybe it's time to let those things go so you can move on."

Gillian's soft brown eyebrows furrowed together as she tried to process what he was saying. She wasn't an angry person, not the type to hold grudges . . . was she?

"Sometimes people do the best they can, but they still fail to meet our expectations or needs," Max said carefully. Gillian considered this, thinking back to the way she had behaved toward Bridget and — years ago — her best friend, Jenny. She had failed them, too. Neither one of them had truly forgiven her. Would it have made an impact on her life — and theirs — if they had? She thought about her family.

"Like my dad, you mean?" she asked.

"Sure, like your dad. I could tell you guys were having problems, way back when I was coming to your house to work with him." He threw her a half-smile. "You'd come downstairs and try to act like this cool, rebellious teenager. But your eyes would always drift over to your father. No matter where he went, what he did, what he said, you were watching, waiting to take it all in. It was obvious that you loved him and wanted more from him than he was willing to give."

She hadn't thought Max had noticed, but he had. Suddenly a lump rose in her throat, and she swallowed it down hard. "And you think that's why I have problems now? Because I didn't have a good relationship with my dad?" The idea of blaming someone else was both welcoming and disturbing.

"Not your dad, specifically, although I think that relationship has had a huge impact on your life. Every relationship has an impact, really. We all need love. And when we don't get what we need, we cope the best we can. It sounds like the way you cope has definitely impacted your relationship with Keith. Maybe others."

"I'm not doing this on purpose!" Gillian wailed. "If I knew how to change, I would. But it's not that easy."

"Of course it's not." Max sounded surprised. "Change never is. We all fear change. Look at Copernicus or Galileo. They found evidence that the sun and not the earth was the center of the galaxy. But look at what these men went through — and how long the world fought against believing in the truth. Change is threatening. Everything within us resists it."

Gillian gave him a sidelong glance. She couldn't help feeling like a charity case. "Do you really think my expectations are too high?"

"I have no idea," Max told her honestly. "We've never talked about your expectations. I wonder, though, about what you're willing to accept in a relationship."

Gillian eyed him warily. "Meaning?"

"Some people set their standards too low. They settle for someone who hurts them — physically or emotionally or spiritually," he explained. "Others raise the bar too high. As a result, no one can measure up." Max leaned back in his chair and stared at the sterile, white-tiled ceiling, the way he often did when he was mulling over a favorite theory. "From what you've been saying, I wonder if maybe you're the second kind."

"I wish you wouldn't make me sound so . . . dysfunctional," she complained. "Just because I don't want to get hurt."

Max sat up again and leaned toward her. "If you're looking for relationships with people who will never hurt you, Gilly, I'd be willing to bet that you're out of luck," he said simply. "But you know, a person doesn't have to *not* hurt you, *ever*, in order to love you well. You'll have fights, you'll be inconsiderate to each other at times. That happens. That's just life."

"What if the person you love doesn't even stick around long enough to *be* inconsiderate?" Gillian thought of the long nights when there had been no one at home except her and her mother because her father had to work late. She remembered the day Max had walked out of her life. She suddenly felt a faint stinging behind her eyelids.

"Well, then you've learned something, and you won't give as much of yourself to that person the next time," he said reasonably. "But it doesn't have to have a negative impact on every other relationship that follows."

Gillian made a terrible face. "Yuck. This is no fun. Why do relationships have to be so *hard?*" she said dramatically.

Max laughed. "Oh, come on. It's not as bad as all that. You've got your whole life ahead of you, Gilly. There's plenty of reason to hope. Besides," he said grinning, "I've got just the thing to cheer you up. What are you doing Tuesday night?"

"I don't know," Gillian grumbled. "My social calendar is looking pretty open all of a sudden."

"Great!" He ignored her sullen tone. "The Perseid meteor shower will be visible this week. Tuesday's the best night. Come on. You *know* you want to go. It's the *Perseids*. Up to one hundred shooting stars per hour. Think how many wishes you could make!"

"Yeah?" That caught Gillian's attention. She sat up straight in her chair. "What time are you thinking about going?"

"Eleven at the earliest. Maybe not until midnight. The later the better. They'll be higher in the sky the longer we wait, but then you know that. Maybe we can take along a snack or something."

Gillian felt her face heating up. "I have to admit, it sounds great. The thing is . . . I'm just not sure."

Max eyed her curiously. "What's the matter, Gilly?"

By this time, she was certain her cheeks had to be bright red. "I don't know if it's a good idea for us to, you know . . . go out together." The words came out in a rush. "I mean, Keith and I just broke up a week ago, and —"

"I agree."

Gillian stopped short. "What?"

"I said, I agree," Max told her calmly but not unkindly.

"You mean you weren't —" Her hands flew to her cheeks. "Oh, my gosh. I'm so embarrassed! Max, please . . . forgive me. I didn't mean to imply that —" She climbed out of her chair and retreated to the window, trying to get as far away as possible. "You must think I'm an idiot, assuming that you would want to ask me out!"

"There's nothing idiotic about that idea," Max said in a low voice. His words only added to her confusion.

"What are you saying?" Gillian watched as he rose from his chair and came to stand beside her.

"I'm saying that I'm very attracted to you, Gilly," he said in a low voice.

"You are?" Gillian's heart started doing the rumba. "Wait. Back up. You lost me. I thought you weren't. You just said you *didn't* want to ask me out."

For once, Max seemed uncertain about what to say. "Honestly, Gilly, I'm not sure what I want," he admitted. "I mean, I *do*, in a way. I think it would be great to spend more time together, get to know each other again. But after what you've said, I'm not sure you're ready for that, or that you'd even want it. And even if you did, I don't know that it would be such a good idea for us."

Gillian's head was swimming. Were they really having this conversation? It didn't seem possible. "Why not?" Her voice sounded far away and foreign to her own ears.

"We're just in very different places spiritually." Max looked as though the words pained him. "I don't ever want you to feel ashamed for being where you're at. Your spiritual journey is your own — I can't force the issue for you," he said, and Gillian could tell that he meant it. "But, at the same time, I know how much God means to me. I couldn't pretend it was any other way. And I'd just worry about that becoming a conflict for us."

"Like it was for my parents," she said dully.

"Yeah," Max said ruefully. "Like it was for them."

Gillian nodded slowly. "My mom once told me that she and Dad had a lot of problems, but the worst was not connecting spiritually. She said that made it even harder to find common ground in other areas." A feeling of sadness gripped her heart. The thing she had wanted for so long was almost within her grasp . . . yet still far out of reach. "I think that's just one more thing I'm afraid of."

"Me, too," said Max soberly.

Gillian averted her eyes, focusing on the bright green leaves of the sugar maple outside her window. "The problem is, I don't know how I could find someone who believes the same thing I do, when I'm not even sure what *I* believe." Suddenly, she felt terribly alone.

Max reached out and squeezed her hand with gentle fingers. "I think that's a pretty important thing to know . . . regardless of *who* you decide to share your life with."

The words rang true in Gillian's mind. He was right. She had been running for too long. She turned to him to express her gratitude, but at the sight of his warm compassionate face her heart welled up and she could not find the words. If only he was the one she would spend her life with. . . .

Finally, she managed, "Max? About what you said before?"

"Yes?"

She drew in a deep breath and let it out slowly. "Do you really like me? I mean, *really?*"

Max smiled then — a smile that started at his lips and reached all the way to his eyes. "I really do."

"Yeah, well . . ." At his confession, Gillian could not keep a grin from slowly spreading across her own face. "I guess I kinda like you, too. In fact, I've always had a little crush on you."

"I know," Max said playfully and began to toy with her fingers, which he still held in his hand.

"You *know?*"

"Of course! The way you followed me around when you were a kid? It was adorable. You were the sweetest thing. . . ."

"Oh, stop. You're making me sick." She

laughed and tried to pull away, but he held her hand fast.

"I'm *serious,*" Max said. "The sad part was, you were seven years younger than me. Just a baby."

"Come on, I was *not* a *baby.* . . ." Gillian tried to protest, but she could not keep the grin from her face.

"Ah, yes you were." Max was merciless in his teasing. "But I couldn't help noticing you anyway. You had those incredible hazel eyes. And that beautiful, honey-colored hair." He reached and gently lay his free hand upon the soft golden strands at the back of her neck. "And . . ."

"And what?" she prompted breathlessly.

Max's expression grew serious. "And . . . there was just something about you that captured my heart, Gilly. Even though you were just a kid, I remember thinking how much I liked you, how I would have wanted to go out with you if I'd still been in high school, too."

She stared at him incredulously. "You're making this up."

"No," he insisted. "Really, I'm not. I'll admit, it was just a fleeting thought at the time. It never really went anywhere back then. But when I saw you again in Ed's office —" Tenderly he stroked her hair. Gillian let her eyelids fall, losing herself in the moment. And then it was gone.

Max stepped back abruptly, staring at his hand as if he'd never seen it before. "Gilly, this is crazy! We can't be talking like this. We've already said that it wouldn't be a good idea for us to date."

Gillian froze and watched him back away, feeling his withdrawal as deeply as if she were losing a part of her self. *What were you thinking, Gillian? Didn't Max just get through explaining that you need to protect your heart? You lost him once — you're not going to get to keep him this time.* "You're right," she said, carefully keeping her voice under control. There was no point in letting him see how deeply his words hurt her.

"It wouldn't be a good idea *right now,* anyway," he said thoughtfully.

"Why do you say that?" Gillian gave him a funny look as she stepped away. "You don't really expect anything to change?"

"Don't underestimate the power of God, Gilly," Max said mysteriously. "When he's involved, anything is possible."

Twelve

As a man thinketh so is he,
and as a man chooseth so is he.
EMERSON, "SPIRITUAL LAWS,"
ESSAYS: FIRST SERIES

August 13, 1987

Mom and Dad had another fight this morning. Mom wants me to start going to church with her. Dad tells her he doesn't want me getting messed up with all that religious garbage. I asked him about it once. He said it was up to me whether I wanted to go or not, but that he didn't want me to come crying to him when it turned out to be a big scam. He looked at me like I was an idiot for even considering it, and we haven't talked about it since. Mom hasn't been able to get me to go with her, either.

I don't know why I should have to decide, anyway. I'm only sixteen years old, after all. I've got plenty of time to decide what I think. I don't want to have to worry about it when there's all this pressure on me to pick which side is right. One of these days I'll figure it out for myself. In the meantime, I just want to be left alone.

Max thinks it's possible to believe in both science and God. But Dad hasn't liked Max very much since the day he said that. Poor Max pushed all of his buttons, and now Dad's really cranky with him. I've seen them arguing on Max's way out to the car. Sometimes I can even hear Dad yelling while Max is in the study with him. Max doesn't come over early very much anymore. He doesn't even like to come — I can tell by the look on his face. I sure wouldn't want to be in his shoes.

It makes me sad, though, that I don't get to see him. It's been a hard summer. Jenny hasn't been around in weeks. Mom and Dad are fighting more and more all the time. It feels like everything around me is changing.

I wish there was some kind of order to my life, but right now it seems impossible. And to tell you the truth, some days I'm afraid to find out what's going to happen next.

August 11, 1997

"I cannot *believe* I let you talk me into this!" Gillian yawned widely as she followed in Max's steps. "Are we crazy? It's almost midnight! I should have been in bed hours ago." Carefully she placed each foot on the ground, trying not to stumble as they made their way through Colonial Park's gentle darkness.

"Spoilsport," Max said fondly. In his hands he carried a massive red, plaid picnic blanket, a bag of gooey macaroons, and a bottle of sparkling water. "You must be getting old."

"I beg your pardon?" Gillian huffed. "Just because I make sure my body gets enough sleep? I don't think so. Besides, I'm only twenty-six." She eyed him critically. "And you, my friend, have no room to talk."

"I'll have you know I am a very *young* thirty-three," Max told her cheerfully, tromping on ahead.

"No kidding," Gillian muttered under her breath. "You've got the energy of a hyperactive ten-year-old." Then, more loudly, "Could we *please* slow down? I've got a rock in my shoe. Besides, I thought we were there."

"Just a little farther. Stop complaining," he laughed and led her deeper into the clearing. Gillian looked around, wondering what kind of animals might be watching them from the surrounding forest. She

234

tilted her head back and looked up at the black walnut trees, wondering if she was at that moment being observed by owls.

A sudden burst of light caught her eye. "Wait! Look!" She stopped and pointed up to the northeast, toward the Perseid's radiant, its point of origin in the sky. "Did you see it? That was a bright one!"

"Missed it. Okay, you win. Let's stop." Max handed her the Thermos and brown paper bag, then snapped the fuzzy red blanket open with a flourish and spread it out for them to sit on.

"Mmm, this is nice." Gillian sighed happily as she sat down and leaned back on one arm. As she spoke, Max settled down beside her, just a couple feet from where her hand rested. "Very peaceful. It reminds me of the times when I was a little girl and my dad used to take me out to look at the stars."

Max raised an eyebrow. "Really? Dr. Spencer did that? That sure seems awfully sentimental of him."

"Yeah, it was. Pretty out of character, huh?" Gillian made a face. "Well, don't worry. It didn't last. As I got older, Dad started acting more like a teacher than a father. I resisted, and he stopped taking me out after that."

Max looked horrified. "That must have felt *terrible*," he said sympathetically.

Gillian shrugged. She hardly thought about it any more. "It wasn't that bad."

"Maybe not anymore, but it must have been horrible at the time." He lay back against the soft cotton cover and folded both arms under his head.

Gillian frowned. It had been a long time since she'd thought about the situation, but . . . actually, Max was right. It *had* been horrible. It was so disappointing, in fact, that she had cried for a week after her dad refused to take her stargazing for the first time. He said he wouldn't take her back out if she refused to study the charts he had given her. That was when she first remembered feeling so terribly alone.

She turned to the man who lay beside her in the moonlight. Unaware that he was being watched, Max continued to stare at the sky above him, giving her the chance to examine him safely from behind the camouflage of night.

In the soft lighting, Gillian could barely make out Max's dark curls and the glint of his deep azure eyes. His rich brown corduroy, button-up shirt almost disappeared into the blackness. Only the white of his crewneck T-shirt gave her eyes an easy target to focus on.

She smiled at the shadowed figure. Everything about Max exuded a sense of peace and confidence. His presence was comfortable, reassuring. And he knew her so *well*, even though she had barely let him in. He cared about how she felt, and he wanted to know more about her. And, heaven help her — Gillian's heart started beating faster at the thought — she wanted to know his deepest thoughts and feelings, too.

Despite every protest she had uttered since the beginning of summer, Gillian had finally realized the truth: More than anything, she wanted to be with this man, to throw herself into his arms, to finally find out what it meant to love someone. *But . . . that wouldn't be right.* Gillian tried to push the thought away. Max's choice was clear. He had found a source of strength, of peace, in his God — a decision that she both respected and envied. If she had such peace, she would never do anything to jeopardize it. She couldn't expect anything less of Max.

I've got to stop thinking about this. Gillian tore her eyes from his face and scanned the sky for streaks of light. *Things aren't going to happen between Max and me,* she thought.

But a second voice whispered, *Then, why are you here?* She shook her head, as if shooing away a pesky fly.

"Did your dad ever take you out to see a meteor shower?" Max plucked a piece of meadow grass and stuck it between his teeth, the perfect picture of a preppie hill-billy.

"Sure, he did," Gillian told him. "A couple of times my mom even came along." Following Max's lead, she turned and laid her back flat against the blanket so she could see the stars better. "I remember once, she had been reading *Peter Pan* to me, and I thought the lights were fairies, flying in from Never Never Land!" As if on cue, a tiny flicker of white shot across the heavens, then disappeared. "Mom said she thought maybe the lights were angels."

Max opened his eyes wide. "*Your* mother thought that stars were angels?"

"I know, I know," Gillian laughed. "This was before she went back to church and brushed up on her facts," she explained. "But she always seemed drawn to spiritual things."

"For a minute there, I was a little bit worried about what kind of propaganda she might have been feeding you."

Gillian ignored the playful dig. "I remember one time, in particular, when Dad took me out," she said. "He must have decided that I was old enough to know the truth, because he explained all about meteors that night: the way fragments dislodge from a comet every time it passes close to the sun, and the fact that eventually these fragments separate completely from the comet, forming their own orbit around the sun."

"Whew!" Max let out a low whistle. "That's a lot of orbits."

"Tell me about it," Gillian said dryly. "It was very confusing to me as a kid. I wasn't even sure what an orbit was. Then, of course, he explained what caused meteor showers. I got scared and imagined our house being hit by flying boulders. He — oh, look! That was a good one!" She pointed toward a bright train of light directly overhead.

"So have you had nightmares about meteors ever since?" Max asked when it was gone.

"No, but I did for a while," she admitted. "One day I was looking in one of Dad's books, and I saw a picture of the meteor crater in Arizona. It was something like four thousand feet across, I think, and it looked like the surface of the moon to me. I just about came unglued." She chuckled at the memory. "But then Dad told me that most meteors, like the Perseid meteor shower, are just cometary debris. He said that the bigger, single pieces that fall to earth come from asteroid collisions, and that the odds of getting hit by one of those are too minuscule to even consider."

"Well, that's comforting," Max chuckled. "I *guess.*"

But Gillian wasn't laughing. "I really enjoyed those meteor showers," she said softly. "There was something very . . . mysterious about them, the way they just appeared out of nowhere. But then my dad explained that they were regular and predictable. That was pretty disappointing to me. I had always been so excited and proud that my daddy could guess when the falling stars were coming. It made him seem sort of godlike to me."

"I can imagine." Max had turned to watch her more closely and now rested his head on one elbow.

By this time, Gillian was so lost in her memories, she barely noticed him. "I always liked the Perseids the best," she said. "And not just because it's the biggest one. Dad told me it was named after

Perseus because all the meteors in that shower appear to come from that constellation. I always liked Perseus," she said. " 'The Hero.' I liked the legend."

Max's eyes twinkled as he watched her face light up. "You really are a romantic at heart, aren't you?" His voice was soft and low.

"Well . . . maybe a little," she admitted reluctantly, dropping her hand back to her side. "When I was a child, I dreamed that a hero, just like Perseus, would come and save me from some horrible fate."

"What kind of horrible fate?"

Gillian pursed her lips together, considering. "I don't remember, really. Monsters. Dragons, I suppose. That sort of thing." Suddenly, she realized he was staring at her. "Silly stuff." She cleared her throat nervously.

"When did you stop being a romantic?" Max asked gently.

If anyone else had asked the question, she would have been offended. But coming from Max, it sounded like an inquiry and not an accusation. "I'm not sure," Gillian answered slowly. "Life just didn't work out the way I thought it would." She thought for a moment, searching the recesses of her mind for some explanation that would

241

make sense to him . . . and to her. "I don't know what happened, really. I guess I finally just decided that I didn't need a hero, that I could take care of myself." The words were partially true. She liked being an independent woman. But somehow, her life had ended up being a lot lonelier than she had planned.

"And you're okay with that?"

"I don't know," she admitted sadly. "Sometimes it's fine. I actually like not having to depend on a man to take care of me. I like feeling strong." Her eyes followed a thin trail of white that flashed past Perseus's bright alpha star. "The problem is, I don't *always* feel strong."

Max continued to watch her carefully. "You know, even if you found your hero in this lifetime, he probably wouldn't be there for you *always*, anyway."

"Yeah . . ." Gillian sat up stiffly and wrapped her arms around her knees. The hot summer night was finally beginning to cool. Her sleeveless denim shirt left her vulnerable to the night air, and she could feel the goose bumps rising up on her skin. "It would be nice if there was someone I could count on, no matter what."

Max nodded but said nothing. The two sat together, silently, for several long minutes. "You know what I thought falling stars were, when I was a kid?" he asked finally. "I thought they were signs from God. Reminders that he's there."

"What . . . like little flares?"

"No." Max grinned. "I thought it was a symbol. Like the rainbow. My mother told me that God sent rainbows to remind us that he promised never to flood the earth again. I thought maybe he sent the stars to remind us that he's out there."

"Huh." Gillian thought about this. "Well, they certainly do get people's attention."

"Do you know what the Native Americans believed about meteors?" Max asked.

"Hunh-unh." Gillian gave a little shrug. "I suppose they thought it was some kind of sign?"

"A lot of them did. The Blackfoot thought it was a warning that illness would come to their tribe. And the Shawnee thought the meteors were beings running away from some terrible danger."

"How sad!" She looked up as a shimmering light fell to the horizon. "To think that anything so beautiful could mean something so terrible."

"The strangest belief of all was that of the Nunamiut Eskimos and some tribes in southern California and Louisiana. They believed that meteors were . . . well, the, uh . . ." Max sounded almost embarrassed. Gillian turned to look at him, but she couldn't see his face clearly in the darkness.

"What did they think they were?"

"Let's just call it, uh, star 'waste.'"

"What do you mean, 'waste'? Do you — oh! I get it!" Gillian stifled a giggle. "All right, *now* you're definitely pulling my leg." She started punching him on the arm with one small fist.

"No, really!" Max cowered, taking the beating. "I'm not making this up! I studied it in — ow!" He laughed and rolled away, out of her reach, then lay down on his stomach, facing her. "And then there's the Pawnee legend about a man named Pahokatawa." His voice dropped to a whisper, as if he were sharing a terrible ghost story.

"Forget it." Gillian waved one open palm at him, as if signaling for him to stop. "I don't believe you anymore." She folded her arms across her chest and turned away, her chin in the air.

Max was undaunted. "The Pawnees believed that after being killed by an enemy," he continued on in an eerie, singsong voice, "Pahokatawa was eaten by animals, then brought back to life by the gods. He returned in the form of a meteor and told his people that when a shower of stars fell toward earth, they did not have to be afraid because it was *not* a sign that the world was coming to an end."

She turned her head and looked back at him, interested in spite of herself.

"Years later, when the massive Leonid meteor storm fell in 1833," Max went on, "the people started to panic. But the tribal leader reminded them of what Pahokatawa had said, and they all were comforted."

Gillian planted her elbows against her knees and rested her chin in her hands. "It seems like people who look to the sky usually find something that makes them think about gods or one God," she said thoughtfully.

"It's pretty much unavoidable," Max agreed. "It would be hard to come face-to-face with the universe and not consider the nature of it. I can't imagine looking at the stars and not wondering what lies beyond them." He eyed her curiously. "Do you ever wonder about it, Gilly?"

"Yeah," she admitted quietly. "I guess I do. Probably more these days than ever before." In fact, since Max had returned and started talking about God, she'd thought about it nearly every day. It was hard not to feel like something was missing from her life after being around someone like Max, whose world seemed so complete.

"Why more now?" Max asked evenly. He gave her a look of genuine interest and concern. "What's different these days?"

"Well, you for one thing," Gillian said honestly, the words spilling out before she could stop them. Her willingness to open up surprised her. She had consumed no alcohol, but somehow she felt tipsy-drunk, perhaps on open skies and childhood memories. It had been a long time since she had felt safe enough to share her deepest feelings. There was just something about Max that made her believe he cared and would understand. "It's been a while — maybe eight years — since I've been around someone who talked about God every day. It's almost as if he's your friend," she observed. The words came out flat and matter-of-fact, almost clinical.

"He is my friend, Gilly," Max said warmly.

Gillian shook her head in astonishment. "I can't imagine what that must be like." She looked at him with interest, unable to conceal her curiosity any longer. "How does it feel? I mean, it's not like you can call him on the phone and talk to him, or go to the movies together, right? It seems like it would be hard to believe he's even there."

"Well, I don't call him on the phone," Max laughed. "But I do talk to him every day."

Gillian nodded at the obvious reference to prayer. "But he can't talk back."

"Sure he can. He does," Max said confidently.

Gillian turned and eyed him with suspicion. "Max. Please tell me you don't hear voices."

He smiled at her, his eyes dancing. "Not exactly. It's more like I feel him speaking to my heart. Sometimes it comes as a flash of insight. Sometimes a Bible verse comes to mind — one I've memorized or read recently. At other times it's just a feeling, a sense of his love, or his compassion, washing over me."

"But don't you ever feel funny, talking to someone you can't see?" she pushed. "Does it ever feel like he's — I don't know — your invisible friend or something? Like . . . what if you're being fooled?"

"Are you asking if I ever doubt God's existence?"

A sudden feeling of trepidation grabbed Gillian's heart. Was her suggestion sacrilegious? Would God punish her for asking such a thing? As the thought crossed her mind she realized, to her own amazement, that her belief in God was intact. It was, in fact, very strong, if her feelings of fear were any indication. Surely she couldn't be afraid of someone she didn't think was even there? She looked up to find Max staring at her, waiting for her response.

"Um, yeah," she said nervously.

"Well." Max thought for a moment. "Actually, there are times when I read some other physicist's interpretation of scientific facts, and I wonder if maybe my own beliefs are incorrect." As he spoke, he continued to stare up at the night sky. "During those times, I sometimes think that I might be fooling myself. But then my heart kicks in, and I relive all the tangible experiences I've had — all the times I've felt and seen God working in my life — and I focus in on what I know to be true." He propped himself up on one elbow and turned to face her.

"Then there are other times when I face troubles in life — when I'm hurt or alone, when I can't understand what God is doing, and I feel abandoned or betrayed by him." Gillian couldn't believe her ears. Max? Doubting God? It didn't seem likely. Yet here he was, confessing it with his own mouth. "Sometimes my heart feels empty," Max went on, "and it questions whether he really loves me, whether he really exists. But I know that I've made a conscious choice to follow him. My mind reminds me that I've made a rational decision, based on what I know to be true, to put my faith in him." His eyes searched hers earnestly. "Sure, I have doubts, Gilly. I suppose most people do, from time to time. But I believe that God in his grace understands our doubts. That he sees us through those times and gives us reminders that he is here. Sometimes we read those reminders with our minds and sometimes with our hearts."

"Reminders like the stars," Gilly whispered.

"Mm-hm." Max smiled. "Like little flares."

She grinned sheepishly.

"What about you, Gilly?" Max asked gently. "You told me that you're not sure what you believe. That must be hard, with your mom being a Christian and all. I'm sure she talked about God a lot. That uncertainty must be a source of real inner conflict for you."

Gillian stared at him, her eyes wide. He did understand. Better than she did, perhaps. It seemed he had intuitively sensed the truth she'd been trying to deny for years — but could not longer avoid. "Yeah, there is." She pushed back the impulse to reach out one hand and give his arm a tiny squeeze. "Mom told me about God lots of times. She said that he loved me so much, he sent his son to die for my sins."

"And where did that leave you?"

"More confused than ever, I think." She began to fiddle absently with the lace of her white sneakers. "You know, Max, it's not that I don't believe in God, or Jesus." Her tone raised in pitch as her anxiety level increased. "It's just that I got so tired of being in the middle of the Big Debate, you know? Mom said one thing, Dad another. I didn't want to have to choose, so I guess I put off thinking about it. And now . . . now I'm afraid to." Gillian's hands fell helplessly to her sides. She couldn't believe what was coming out of her mouth. She'd never talked with anyone about this before, but the words were all horribly true.

"What are you afraid of?"

Gillian looked at Max. His expression

was gentle, accepting . . . just like his heart. "Lots of things, I guess. For one, I'm afraid of believing, then finding out that it was just a pipe dream." She crossed her legs and leaned toward him, speaking in earnest. "Okay, let's say I go ahead and do what you say . . . I read my Bible. I pray. I accept that Jesus paid the price for my sins. What then, Max?" she asked. The scientist in her had taken over, but her voice sounded desperate. "What if I give my heart to him, and then it turns out he doesn't exist? What if in the end it isn't true?" She looked up at the stars, anxiously, as if she might find her answer there. "I'm afraid of choosing wrong," she said helplessly.

"Do you think that maybe there's some other god?" There was no hint of judgment in his tone, only concern.

"No, that's not it."

"Then, why do you have to be afraid of choosing wrong?"

"I'm just . . . afraid of being disappointed, Max." Gillian searched for the right words. How could she explain to him the logic that barely made sense in her own heart? "I don't dare hope, if there's a chance it might not be true. My dad was right when he said there's no absolute proof that there's a God. You said so yourself. If only it was provable, then maybe I could risk it. But the way it is . . . I just don't know if I can."

Max thought for a moment. "Remember ten years ago, when I told you I wanted to prove there was a God?" he finally said. Gillian nodded wordlessly. "Well, I never did." He sounded accepting, not bitter. "Sometimes, especially when scientists make new discoveries that support what I believe, I think that one day it will happen: we'll find definitive proof of God's existence, and then everyone will have to agree.

"But at other times — and this is most of the time — I figure the mystery is all a part of God's plan."

"But why wouldn't God just want us to know?" she asked helplessly. "Why do we have to guess?"

"It's not guessing, Gilly," Max said easily. "It's faith. There's a difference. You don't have to hold your brain in check to believe in him. There's plenty of evidence out there that supports his existence. Science and religion don't have to compete. In fact, I believe science adds to our understanding of faith and vice versa. Unfortunately, I can't offer you the absolute proof you want. All I can tell you is that everything I've learned in my studies, everything I've seen, points to him. And everything I've experienced in life has shown me that there's a void in my life that only he can fill." At the edge of the clearing, a night owl cried out from the shelter of an ancient white oak.

"You can't prove the unprovable, Gillian," Max said simply. "And for now, that's the way it is. That's the way God made it. But just because something isn't obvious doesn't mean it isn't real. Faith is a choice. Just as the men and women of the Renaissance chose to believe either that the sun revolves around the earth or that the earth revolves around the sun, you have a choice to make about God."

Gillian sat quietly, considering this. Was it really so hard to believe what Max was saying? To do what he was suggesting? After all those years of waffling, had the time come to make a decision for or against Christ? She'd always said that she would figure out what she believed about God one day. Would a better time ever come? All the evidence was in. She'd been studying the origins of the universe for years and still had no reason to believe God didn't exist. In fact, much of the evidence did — as Max suggested — support a creationist perspective. And if God was the Creator . . . then wasn't he also the father of Jesus, as the Bible stated? The truth was, she'd thought about God before, but she'd never tried to know him. Never made a choice to follow Jesus. But if what Max said was true, she had nothing to lose . . . and everything to gain. What if she just let go of her desire to know, to remain safe and in control? Perhaps it was finally time to take that leap of faith. And yet, still something held her back.

"Gilly," Max said seriously, "is the idea of walking with God at all appealing to you?"

"More than I'd like to admit," she answered softly. As she spoke, her eyes filled with tears she didn't even bother trying to hide. What would be the point? She was alone, desperate. Max knew it. He'd been watching her for weeks, and he knew she was hurting. "I know I sound pretty detached sometimes," she said sadly. "But the truth is, I'm sort of envious when you talk about your relationship with God. You say that Jesus is a friend to you. I can't even imagine such a thing. I'd give anything to have someone like that. Someone who wouldn't leave me, who accepted me just as I am . . ." Her voice trailed off as she became lost in her own thoughts.

Max reached out one cool hand and touched the warmth of her cheek. "God is like that, Gilly."

Gillian felt a tear fall from her eye and roll onto his fingers. "I want to believe it, Max," she murmured. "I really do."

"But?"

"But . . . Max, what if God doesn't even want me?" Her voice broke as she spoke.

Max's own eyes welled up with tears of compassion. "Oh, Gilly! What do you mean?" He cupped her cheek with his hand.

"I mean, look at me!" she exclaimed. "I'm twenty-six years old, and I've been running from him for almost that long. You love God, Max. I fear him. Do you know that? Sometimes, when I think about him, I become really afraid," she admitted tremulously. "I'm scared of dying. I'm afraid of what will happen to me." Her voice was barely recognizable, it was shaking so badly. "But I'm even more afraid of being alone. For the rest of my life. Forever . . ."

Max nodded somberly. "That's what hell will be like. Separation from God. The worst kind of loneliness there is."

255

At this, Gillian's body shook as she gave in to a whole new burst of tears. At any other time, she might have felt self-conscious. But the release of her long pent-up emotions was all consuming. There was no room for embarrassment; she felt only anguish.

"But, Gilly," Max said, his voice full of conviction, "it doesn't have to be this way." He took her by the shoulders and turned her to face him, forcing her to meet his eyes. "God does love you, Gilly. He wants to be a part of your life — now and forever. He wants to be a friend to you, too."

"But I don't deserve it, Max!" Gilly wailed.

"Of course you don't, honey," he said tenderly. "None of us do. But God forgives you."

"But he can't, Max. I'm . . . I'm . . ." She struggled to find the words. Gently, Max wiped away the tears that streamed from her eyes. "You're what, Gilly?"

"I'm . . . unforgivable," she said with passion. Her eyes darted about, as if searching for some way of escape.

Max looked mildly surprised but not shocked. "Why would you say that?"

Gillian shook her head helplessly. "I don't know. I just am!" She didn't understand the conviction, herself. She just knew it felt overwhelmingly true.

He put one arm around her and held her firmly as she struggled to maintain her composure. From the bag of macaroons, he pulled out two napkins which she used to wipe her eyes and nose.

"Now, let's talk about this," he said, after she had taken several deep breaths and dried her face. "Why do you feel unforgivable? Is it because you've done something you think is too terrible to forgive?"

"Well . . . I suppose." Gillian did feel unforgivably evil. Wasn't that why no one stayed in her life? She wasn't worth sticking around for. "Oh." Max loosened his hold on her shoulders and sat back. Suddenly, he was the one who looked uncomfortable. "Um . . . did you want to say what it is? I mean, I don't know if telling me — a man, I mean — is the best thing, but if you want to talk to somebody, I guess we could . . ."

Gillian stared at him. From the blush on his cheeks, it was clear that he suspected that it might be a sexual sin. She might as well set him straight on that, right away.

"No, Max. It's not what you're thinking. I've never gotten involved enough with any man to sleep with him."

Max looked both flustered and relieved. "Well, I didn't mean to imply that. I wasn't trying to say that you —"

She shook her head hard. "Don't give me so much credit. It's not a reflection on my virtue. There are reasons why I haven't gotten too close to any man, not the least of which was the fact that I couldn't be trusted."

Fresh tears began to fall. Tenderly, Max brushed them away. "I don't understand," he said quietly. His eyes urged her to go on.

Gillian sighed. "Max, I'm just a terrible person, that's all," she said heavily. "I hurt people. I disappointed my mom. Even my dad doesn't like me. And I'm a horrible friend." Before she had made a conscious decision to do so, Gillian found herself telling him all about Matt Ross and Jenny DeWhitt.

Silently and without interrupting, Max listened to the entire story. "Oh, Gilly." When she had finished, he put an arm around her shoulders and held her once again. "You're not horrible. You're just human. I'm sure your dad liked you, even if he was terrible at showing it. I know that I like you. And besides, even if we didn't, God likes you. Loves you, in fact."

"But I'm so . . . so, unworthy, Max," she protested.

Max smiled as he brushed damp tendrils of hair away from her eyes. "Unworthy people are his favorite kind, Gilly."

"What do you mean?" Despite herself, Gillian found herself looking at him hopefully, through watery eyes.

"Jesus didn't die for good people," Max explained patiently. "It says so in the Bible, over and over again. He died for the rest of us — which is all of us, incidentally — the imperfect, the flawed, the selfish, the rotten. Jenny didn't forgive you, Gillian . . . but she's not God. And your dad didn't love you well. But he's not God, either. Don't judge God by human standards. He's not like any person you know."

"Well . . . he sounds a lot like one person I know," she said with feeling. "You."

Max gave her a weak smile. "That's just because God's working in my life. It makes me happy to think he used me to demonstrate something of his love for you, Gilly — even a little bit. The truth is, though, I'm just like you. Imperfect, but loved by God."

"You really think I'm loved by God?" Gillian said tremulously.

"Yes," Max assured her. "I know you are."

Gillian pulled herself out of his embrace, sat up straight, and wiped her eyes. "Well, then I want to love him, too," she announced. Suddenly, the answer was clear to her, and she spoke with conviction. "I want to follow this Jesus of yours." She smiled timidly, relief washing over her the moment she spoke the words.

" 'We love him because he first loved us,' " Max said solemnly.

"What?"

"That's what the Bible says. 'We love him because he first loved us.' "

The words sank into Gillian's heart as she wiped at her teary eyes. "The funny thing is, I'm still afraid," she confessed. "But I want to have a relationship with God, like you do," she said wistfully. "I want him to love me the way he loves you . . . and I want to learn what it's like to love him, too."

"Oh, Gilly." Max cupped Gillian's chin in his hand and smiled into her eyes. "God already loves you far more than you know."

She smiled back at him then, and for the first time in a long time it felt like a smile that truly reflected her soul. "I'm finally starting to believe it . . . just a little bit."

"Do you want me to pray with you now?" Max offered. Gillian nodded, and he reached out and took her hands in his.

"But I don't know what to say," she said nervously.

"Just tell him what you told me — what you've decided, how you feel toward him."

"Um, okay." Gillian lowered her head, then changed her mind and stared into the darkness overhead as she had so many times before. But this time, she was looking not at the stars, but past them . . . to what lay beyond.

"Hello, God," she said, timidly at first. "Um, Jesus . . . I don't know exactly what to say. I feel kind of embarrassed, in fact." She cleared her throat nervously. "But my friend Max has been telling me all about you. My mom did, too. For years she did. Remember that? She said that you died for me. I struggled with that when I was little. I felt guilty about it . . . but Mom said that you did it because you love me, and I just want to say I'm awful grateful. I don't think I can ever do anything to deserve it. But I want to love you and to be loved by you. And I want you to be a part of my life — like you are in Max's. Thanks, God. Ummm . . ." She looked at Max, her eyes pleading with him for guidance.

"Amen," he whispered.

"Yeah. Amen," she echoed. Suddenly, it

was as if a heavy load had been lifted from her back, and she almost felt like bursting into song. Beside her, Max beamed.

"All right then. A toast!" He reached for the sparkling water and plastic cups. "This is a night to celebrate." Overhead, a ball of white fire streaked across the night sky. "Kinda like fireworks, huh?" Max grinned. "Almost like the Fourth of July."

"Except this is better."

"Yeah," Max agreed. "We're not just commemorating the past. We're celebrating your future."

Gillian raised her eyes to the heavens, which now were almost completely black. Since she and Max had arrived at the park, the Perseids' radiant had risen higher in the sky, allowing for greater visibility of the fiery rain. The stream of shooting stars was constant now.

"Is it my imagination," she wondered aloud, "or are the stars actually getting brighter?"

"Gillian," Max said, his voice thick with emotion, "after what you decided tonight, I'd say everything is getting brighter."

Thirteen

Fare thee well! and if for ever,
Still for ever, fare thee well.
LORD BYRON, *FARE THEE WELL*

August 23, 1987

When I was a little kid, I used to get scared by lots of little things. I hated bees. And fire drills. The drills upset me even when I knew they were coming. In kindergarten, Mrs. Sherman would tell us in the morning that we were scheduled to have a drill sometime that day. I wouldn't be able to concentrate until it was over. I'd chew my thumbnail, stare out the window, and wait. . . . You'd think I would have been ready for it, but whenever the bell rang, my heart would leap inside my chest. My hands would sweat. Adrenaline rushed through my veins. Even though I knew it wasn't a real emergency, I was terrified of going through the whole fire-drill experience. Of course, eleven years later, I'm not frightened anymore. Just like everybody else, I learned I could live through it.

It was the same with bees. I'd be outside,

minding my own business, when I'd hear it like a little plane in my ear. I'd jump up and run — in any direction — trying to get as far away as I could . . . as fast as I could. Getting stung by a bee was the worst thing I could imagine. Until it really happened. One day I finally got zapped by a yellow jacket . . . twice. It hurt like all get out, but Mom put some baking soda on it, and after that I was fine. Bees haven't scared me since.

But this . . . this was a different situation altogether. Exactly the opposite, in fact. I'd heard of people getting their hearts broken, but I thought it was just an exaggeration. Obviously people live through all kinds of pain. I didn't exactly look forward to getting my own heart shattered, but I never doubted that I would survive.

That was before I lost Max.

The funny thing is, it never even occurred to me that he might go away. He's a grad student at Princeton, for goodness' sake. Where's he gonna go? Other possibilities occurred to me. I imagined Angela might drug his drink and get him to propose or something. I knew he'd graduate eventually. But that was a long way off. He's got two years of school left to go. Who would have thought he'd transfer?

As it turns out, his dad has some sort of con-

nections at Harvard and had wanted Max to go there for a long time. I guess Max liked it here because he held out for a while. Things changed, though, this summer. He said God closed one door and opened another. Dad laughed when he repeated that comment to Mom and me.

I think the truth is, my dad scared him away. It's not like Max could avoid him. Dad's his academic advisor, his "mentor," Mom says. Whatever you call it, he had the power to make Max's life miserable, and I think he did. I heard them arguing a lot over the last couple of weeks. "Debating," Dad called it. At first I was just sad. Now I feel totally destroyed.

I feel angry, too, though I'm not sure at whom. My first reaction is to want to yell at Dad. I want to run into his office and scream, "It's bad enough the way you treat me, but did you have to go and ruin things with Max, too?" I'm not sure what's stopping me. Maybe it's just knowing that it wouldn't make any difference if I did it.

A lot of my anger is with me. I mean, really, how dumb can I be? Pinning all my dreams on a guy seven years older than me. Of course he's leaving, what else would he do? He's got a life, and it has nothing to do with me. Besides, I know better than to love someone too much.

265

It always hurts when you lose them. I learned that with Jenny, with Dad. Even things with Mom feel bad. The more she works, the less time for me. Not that I'm trying very hard, myself. It's easier being alone. I'm starting to like it that way.

It doesn't make a lot of sense, but I feel pretty mad at Max, too. He came over here last week, for the last time. He'd already made arrangements for the transfer. He and Dad didn't have to meet again, but he wanted to bring back some books he'd borrowed. He showed up with two of them under one arm and a long cardboard box under the other.

I was sitting on the front porch when he got out of the Bug. Normally, I can't help but grin when I see him. No poker face here. But this time, it took all my willpower not to collapse into a pile of tears.

"Hi, Gilly," Max said. He put the books and box on the porch steps and sat down next to me on the swing.

"Hey." I tried not to look at him.

Max kept his eyes straight ahead, staring at the stand of white oaks across the street, just like I was.

"I guess you've heard, huh?" He kicked his legs forward, making the swing move a little.

"I guess." I bit my lip. This time I wasn't going to let him see me cry.

"*Yeah, well.*" *And that was all he said for a while.*

"*Harvard's a good school, you know.*" *I don't know why he felt he had to say that.*

"*Sure.*" *Max kicked his legs again and got the swing moving. The silence was awkward, but it was even more noticeable to hear nothing but the springs go squeak.*

It was terrible. Awkward. Gross. I didn't know what to say, so I kept my mouth shut for once. I thought maybe Max would tell me again that he thought of me as a friend and that he was going to miss me. Part of me wanted him to say that we'd see each other again someday. "*Harvard's not that far,*" *he'd tell me.* "*It's a small world. We're sure to bump into each other again.*" *But he didn't say any of those things. He just kept pumping his legs, making that swing squeak.*

"*Is your dad around?*" *he finally asked me. I knew then that he was going to go. I shook my head; I couldn't make myself say the word. Max had called earlier — Mom gave Dad the message that he was coming, but he didn't bother to come back from the university. I guess maybe he's mad at Max, too.*

"*Well . . .*" *Max nodded toward the books.* "*Could you make sure he gets those?*" *I nodded.* "*And there's one other thing. . . .*" *He*

267

reached down, picked up the box, and handed it to me.

I figured it had to be something else belonging to my dad, so I just took it from him and held it.

"Look inside," he told me. So I did. Inside I found a cheap-looking refracting telescope. Nothing bad, really. Just nothing like the ones my dad has. I've got a pretty nice one, myself, that sits in the back of my closet. Dad bought it for me when I was way too little to use it. A lot of things have changed since then.

"I was cleaning out my dorm room, and I came across this," Max said awkwardly. "I was thinking about that time we talked with your folks about God and the stars and the beginning of the universe, and I just wondered if maybe you might . . ." He shrugged his shoulders, real casual-like. "I don't really need it anymore. I've got a newer, better one. So if you want it . . . it's yours."

I'm not even sure what I said to him after that. I didn't especially want or need a tele-scope. But it was something that had belonged to him, so of course I took it. I guess I thanked him. He said something about me being a good kid, and then he got up and crawled back into the Bug one last time and drove away. I sat and stared at the end of the driveway for a long time after that. Maybe ten minutes, *maybe an hour, maybe two. I'm not sure. I can still see it turning the corner, though.*

I really liked that red fender.

September 19, 1997

Gillian breathed a sigh of satisfaction as the gum-chewing blond waitress presented her with her order: crisp, leafy greens, juicy strips of perfectly bronzed chicken, and bright cherry tomatoes piled high on a blue china plate. "Mmmm," she mumbled happily and stabbed at an appetizing chunk of spinach and romaine.

In the days and weeks following her decision to become a Christian, Gillian's life had been transformed. The depression that was a part of her everyday life had faded. Each morning she woke up with a feeling of hope and a sense of purpose.

Perhaps most dramatic of all was the change in Gillian's attitude toward her parents. As Max had suggested soon after they began working together, there were a number of people Gillian needed to forgive — including her mom and dad.

Never before had this seemed even remotely possible — at least where her father was concerned. Though Gillian had a number of emotional issues that involved her mother, the two women remained on reasonably favorable — if not exactly intimate — terms. Gillian rarely spoke to her dad, however, and tried to keep the few conversations they had as brief as possible. Yet shortly after her conversion, she had actually initiated two different phone calls with him and had managed to be civil — even friendly — during each one.

The healing did not take place instantly. Her emotions had not changed overnight. The truth was, Gillian still felt wounded by the ways in which her parents had loved her — and failed her. Yet though the pain remained, much of the anger had subsided. Forgiveness, Gillian was learning, was not a one-time event. It was a process — one that was difficult, but that God was walking her through.

Like Max, she was beginning to see God working in her life. At first, his presence was not overwhelming to her. It took a while for her to even notice it. But before long, she realized that she didn't feel quite as alone. When she found herself struggling with a problem or with painful emotions, she was inexplicably compelled to offer up a brief prayer. With practice, those prayers were becoming more involved. Not overwhelmingly so, although it was sometimes a bit disconcerting to see how extensively her life was being affected. Still her relationship with God was growing, bit by bit.

As was her relationship with Max.

There again, the changes had been subtle. A cup of coffee here, a stroll after work there. . . . Soon she and Max were spending time together outside the office on the average of three times a week. Neither one of them referred to it as "dating," which was still a difficult thought for Gillian to entertain, and one that was more than a little threatening. If losing Max had hurt once before, how would it feel now . . . once she had *really* come to know him?

Despite their avoidance of the "D" word, however, it had become apparent that the bond they shared was based, not just on physics, but on their own, very real, personal chemistry. As always, Gillian felt a delighted little thrill whenever Max buzzed her on the phone to ask about some recent scientific finding, or sought her out in a physics department crowd, or smiled in a way that made her feel she had just experienced the first sunshine of the day.

Other things had changed, too. Like the way Max allowed his fingers to brush ever so slightly against hers as they were working side-by-side. Or the way he began to drape one arm casually around her shoulders whenever they went out walking together. He seemed to be constantly finding new and creative excuses for them to spend time together. Sometimes he talked Gillian into going with him to one of the many campus films or evening lectures. A couple of times, he had whisked her away to dinner in an attempt to foil what he called her "blatant workaholic tendencies." Tendencies notwithstanding, Gillian hadn't for one second resisted the rescues.

Eventually, Max had worked his way around to asking her out to a movie or two and even a concert. Not once did they discuss where their relationship was headed. Gillian tried not to think about it; it took all of her willpower just to relax and enjoy the ride.

The previous week, Max had told Gillian that they simply had been in the office for too long without a break, and that a long, relaxing walk would do them both good.

His choice of destination had been one of Gillian's favorite places: the beautiful, winding towpath along the Delaware-Raritan Canal. Over a century before, draft animals had beaten out the trail while pulling freight-laden barges along the slow, smooth canal that connected the Delaware and Raritan Rivers. Today, the trail attracted countless walkers, bicyclists, fishermen, boaters, canoeists, and horseback riders. Ever since she was a child, Gillian had loved the D & R State Park and had often tried to lose herself along the fifty-plus miles of paths that cut through the peaceful New Jersey countryside.

As she and Max walked alongside the gentle waters, Gillian was overcome by an unfamiliar sense of peace. The feeling was strange to her, as was the growing trust she felt for Max. Trusting did not come easily. Every day she woke up fearing that Max would not like her anymore, that something would cause him to withdraw, disappear. It was hard to let that fear go. But every day, Max would assure her in his own way that he was there to stay.

It was contentment, however, and not fear that she felt that day beside the narrow canal. It was fairly late, and a faint breeze rustled the nearby trees. Though the golden sun was low in the sky, Gillian felt warm clear through. In the gently flowing waters, a silver fish jumped, as if he, too, wanted to get a glimpse of love unfolding.

"Are you excited about going to California?" Max had asked, his words breaking the comfortable silence. For weeks, Gillian had been preparing for the trip to Palomar Mountain. She was excited about it and more than a little nervous. She would have liked it better if Max was going with her. But the university hadn't deemed it necessary — or cost-effective — to send them both. Gillian was the assistant. Collecting and processing the data was her job; analyzing it was Max's. She would have to go alone.

"Mm —" she said noncommittally.

Max laughed and wrapped his hand comfortably around hers. "What does 'Mm —' mean?"

Gillian had turned and given him a wide-eyed stare. "Silly boy, it's the sound someone makes when he or she feels a sense of pleasure," she teased. "As in, 'Mm —, this soup is good,' or 'Mm —, your hand is warm. . . .' "

"Or, 'Mm —, this is a beautiful woman'?"

Gillian stopped and stared at him again, but this time her shock was real.

"Wh-what did you say?"

Max smiled, a slow, easy smile that touched his eyes and exposed his heart.

"I said, I am looking at the most beautiful woman I have ever seen." Lightly, he

274

ran his hand up Gillian's right arm, cupping it around the elbow and gently pulling her to him.

"You are?" The fabric of his shirt was warm beneath her fingertips. Suddenly it was hard for Gillian to breathe.

"Yes, silly girl, I am," he said playfully. "Surely you know by now that I think you're adorable." The arm he held around her pulled Gillian a fraction closer.

She shook her head, unable to speak.

"Gillian!" Max reached up with his free hand and gently caressed the slope of her cheek. "You *are* beautiful, you know. And brilliant. And funny. And brave." His eyes searched hers, as if trying to look into her soul. "I'm very proud of you. You've grown so much. There's nothing I've wanted more than to see you come to the place you are today. I've thought about you for years."

"You have?" Gillian whispered. His words echoed in her ears, but she could not bring herself to believe them. "I was sure you forgot about me long ago."

"Forget you?" Max shook his head firmly. "Not likely. I'm not sure how you did it, but even then you captured my heart." He regarded her seriously. "Oh no. I never forgot. I worried about you back then. You seemed lost, not sure what to believe. I've prayed for you ever since I left." Gillian caught her breath at this. "Not every day," he admitted a bit sheepishly. "But I had you written on my list of people who I wanted to see come to the Lord. I wasn't sure if I would ever see you again, ever know what happened to you. But I always cared about you, Gillian. I think I felt something special for you, even way back then.

"Of course," he said with a grin, "it wasn't anything like *this*."

"And what is 'this'?" Gillian had to know, though she was almost afraid to ask.

"Well, this is *attraction* for one thing, that's for sure!" Max lifted one hand and ran it lovingly through the softness of her hair. Gillian closed her eyes, reveling in the sensation of being in Max's arms at last. "This is something very powerful. Something . . . kind of scary." His voice shook, ever so slightly. "And it's something that feels an awful lot like love."

At the word *love*, Gillian's head began to swim. Feeling light-headed, she finally allowed herself to relax against him, leaning in just as Max tipped his head toward hers and captured her lips in a brief, yet tender kiss.

A moment later, he pulled gently away,

gazing into her soul. The look he gave her as he stepped back was clearly one of adoration. And the hand that claimed hers said as much through its touch as if he had spoken on a loudspeaker — communicating reassurance and devotion throughout the entire walk back to campus.

As she sat at the busy sidewalk café, watching business workers and college students stroll by, Gillian smiled at the memory and chewed another forkful of salad greens. She was still replaying the scene when a rich-timbered voice broke into her musings.

"Hey there, gorgeous."

She glanced up in surprise, then broke into a huge smile. "Max! What are you doing here? I thought you had a meeting."

"I did, but it got out early, so I thought I'd join you." He reached out with lightning-quick fingers and snagged a sliver of radish from her salad, which he immediately popped into his mouth.

"You got out of a *meeting* early? Wow. I guess I *do* believe in miracles," she quipped.

Max grinned. "So do I. *You*, for one." He dropped a quick kiss onto her cheek, then settled himself across from her at the table.

"Want some?" she asked, pushing her

plate toward him.

"Nah, I'll get my own. What's good?" his eyes scanned the menu.

"Everything," Gillian assured him. The downtown restaurant was a local favorite. "Try the deep-dish chicken pot pie . . . or the sweet-and-sour pork kabobs." Ultimately, Max selected a tantalizing pine-apple-beef stir-fry. Once the waitress had taken his order, he settled back against the chair and fixed his eyes on Gillian.

"And just what are you looking at?" she asked, fork poised midair.

Max smiled. "Just looking, that's all."

"Are you going to do that the entire time I eat?"

"Probably."

Gillian shrugged. "Suit yourself." But her face flushed with a mixture of embar-rassment and pleasure.

"Thank you." Max nodded graciously. "Looking at you *does* suit me." He gave her a wink. "We're at a good place in our rela-tionship, Gillian," he assured her. "Everyone should be so lucky."

"Yeah." The thought made her nervous. She hadn't done anything to deserve this, and it still felt terribly fragile. She gave a little frown.

"Are you all packed?" he said, referring

to her trip to Palomar Observatory.

Gillian nodded. "More or less," she mumbled around a mouthful of food, then took a long drink of water. "But I don't know that I'm looking forward to it, exactly."

"Why not? Two weeks ago, you were thrilled."

"I know," Gillian mumbled unhappily. "But that was when the trip was two weeks away. Now it's here." She shuddered at the prospect of her 5:30 wake-up call the next day. "I'm looking forward to the work. It's just that . . . well, I'm finally getting used to being around you."

"Thanks." Max gave her a sarcastic smile.

"Stop it," she scolded fondly. "You know what I mean."

His expression grew serious. "No. I don't," he said soberly. "Tell me."

Gillian glanced around nervously. Tell him? *Tell him* that leaving him — even for two weeks — would be sheer torture? Tell him she was afraid that he'd realize after she was gone that he didn't really love her? Tell him that for once she was starting to feel a sense of peace, of stability, of *safety* in her life that she was terrified to disrupt?

As far back as she could remember,

Gillian had longed for more than she had . . . more attention from her father, more love, more security. Finally, she had come to a place where she was no longer consumed by her loneliness. Traveling by herself, away from Max's comfortable presence and reassuring words about her walk with God, was the most threatening thing she could imagine. Talking about those fears, however, placed a close second.

It wasn't that she didn't trust Max to be understanding. It was simply that she felt — irrationally, she realized — that if she didn't speak the words, somehow they would not come true. But as Max held her gaze with his gentle blue eyes, Gillian knew that she could not hold back the truth. If there was anyone she could trust, it was Max. And if she was ever going to learn how to let herself love someone, now was the time.

"The thing is . . ." she began timidly, "I don't really want to leave Princeton right now."

Max caught her gaze and held it. "Why?"

Gillian felt her hands begin to tremble. Carefully, she laid down her fork. "I feel safe right now," she admitted, her words soft and low. "I like the way the last few weeks have been. I've . . . I've liked spending time with you, and . . ."

"And?" Max never looked away, not even for a moment.

"And . . . I'm going to miss you." Max's eyes gleamed. Gillian breathed a deep sigh. There. She'd said it. Relief washed over her.

"I'm going to miss you, too," he said with feeling. But as he reached across the table to squeeze her fingers, the old demons of fear and doubt returned, and Gillian could not help but feel that what they were experiencing was too good to last.

She let her fingers slip from his grasp. "What are you going to do while I'm gone?" she asked brightly, forcing her attention back to the plate before her.

"We-ell," Max said slowly, a smile beginning to spread across his features. "I wasn't sure until last night, but I think I've come up with a plan to keep me busy."

"Nothing *too* fun, I hope?" Gillian said lightheartedly, but something about his words made her feel uneasy.

"Oh no. Nothing big," Max laughed. But he looked nervous, as if he was afraid she might not like what he was about to say. "I'm just going to Rome," he said casually.

Gillian's fork clattered to her plate. The world around them seemed to fade away and disappear. She could see only Max. "To . . . Rome?" She searched his eyes. He had to be kidding.

"Yeah," he said easily. "Why? What's the matter?" He smiled politely at the waitress who came and set his pineapple-beef stir-fry in front of him. Gillian waited impatiently as the woman laid out an extra set of silverware for Max. He thanked her as she turned to go, then threw a glance back at Gillian.

"What is it, Gilly? Are you bummed I didn't wait until you could come, too?" he asked kindly. "You'll have plenty of opportunity to go later. I've been thinking about heading back there at the end of the school year."

A cold chill settled over Gillian. She tried to speak, failed, then licked her dry lips and tried again. "You . . . what?" She could feel the blood rushing to her head as fear-driven adrenaline kicked in.

"Plan to go back. I have a lot of friends there that I miss." Max stuffed a huge bite of red pepper and juicy beef into his mouth. Gillian stared at him. "What?" he mumbled around the food in his mouth. "Are you really surprised? I was there for several years, you know. I miss them a lot more than I thought I would. I've been thinking about it for a while, and —"

"And just when were you going to fill me in on your little plan?" Gillian spat out bitterly. "Or maybe you weren't going to tell me at all? Maybe —"

Max froze, his mouth still full of food. "Gi— ?" He tried to speak, swallowed hard, then tried again. "Are you all right? Wha— ?"

She didn't even slow down. "I suppose you were just going to call and tell my dad and let him give me the news?"

He shook his head helplessly. "Gillian, you're going to have to give me a clue, here. I have no idea what you're —"

" 'That's right, Gilly,' " she imitated her father's booming voice. " 'Max is leaving. Oh, he didn't tell you? Hm. That's a shame.' " Max's eyes opened wide as understanding dawned on him. "Well, that's life," she continued bitterly. "Maybe you can stop by and leave me a telescope, or some old binoculars or something, before you go, and make everything okay."

"Gilly, please," Max pleaded. His face had gone white beneath his pale summer tan. "I had no idea. Really. I didn't realize that it hurt you so much when I —"

283

"Don't worry about it, Max," Gillian said coolly, trying to avoid his gaze. She stood, kicking her chair back, and grabbed her slim black purse. "I survived when you left before. I can live through it again. Go ahead and make your plans. Go back to Rome. I just wish you would have told me before I . . . before I —"

"Gillian, come on now. Stop this. Just sit down, and we'll discuss this reasonably, like two rational adults," he urged.

"No! I *won't* discuss this with you. I can't, Max. Don't you see?" She was quite hysterical now, and the other patrons in the restaurant had started staring at them. Gillian rambled on, oblivious to their looks. "I didn't want to like you again, but now I have . . . and I just can't *do this*. I don't want to hear about how you like me, but that God has opened a door for you someplace else. I don't want to pretend everything is going to be okay, that we'll visit each other — we'll write. That's not gonna happen. It's ridiculous."

"Yes," Max said heavily. He was clearly angry now. He tried once more, nodding for Gillian to reclaim her empty seat. "This is ridiculous. If you would just —"

"No, Max. Please. Just forget this ever happened, okay? For me?" She gave him a

284

pointed stare. "It's the only thing I've ever asked."

Gillian turned away, and with tears streaming from her eyes, rushed from the restaurant, onto the sidewalk, and away from the only man who had ever given her a glimpse of love.

Fourteen

Jesus looked at them and said,
"With man this is impossible, but
with God all things are possible."
MATTHEW 19:26

March 29, 1988

It's funny how things can change so fast. I re-
member when Mom gave me this diary, I didn't
think I'd have anything to write in it. It's be-
come a habit now, and I'm glad. It feels good to
get everything down on paper, though I'm not
sure it helps me make much sense of things. I
can't believe I said that nothing ever happens to
me. If only I'd known. That was almost one
year ago, but it feels more like a hundred.

Mom and I moved to D.C. during spring
break, two weeks ago today. I've talked to Dad
a couple of times on the phone. I've never
heard him sound sad before. It's a strange
thing to hear. It probably feels weird to him, to
come home at night and find no one there.
Norrie still comes by during the day and
makes little microwavable dinners for him. I

286

talked to her yesterday, too. She said she had to make Dad buy all new casserole dishes. The ones he had were just too big.

School isn't so bad, really. I'm in public school for the first time. It's kind of crazy, but I like getting lost in the crowd. I'd gotten used to being on my own back in Princeton, anyway. Jenny's got a lot of friends, and I was right when I figured people would take sides. Matt Ross made it through okay. He's dating Ginny Davis now, the head of the cheerleading squad — and if you ask me, they can have each other. His cousin Chris actually did go back to wherever he came from — Chicago, I think.

I finally broke down and told Mom what happened. Her opinion is that I made it harder on myself than it had to be. She said that in high school, everyone worries about what everyone else is thinking about them, when really those people aren't thinking any-thing at all — they're too busy wondering what everyone is thinking about them.

She tells me that if I hadn't given up, Jenny and I would have been fine. But there's no point in worrying about that: I stopped trying to smooth things over with Jenny months ago. By the time school started, we were actually avoiding each other. Maybe things would have been better if I'd given it another chance. Then again, maybe not. Maybe the other girls didn't hate me as much as I thought. I guess it doesn't matter now. I mostly keep to myself. Things are easier this way. I'm not hurting anybody, and no one's hurting me.

Mom told me last week that I have her permission to go out on dates now. She's been feeling pretty bad about dragging me away from Princeton. Apparently this is supposed to make the transition easier for me. I didn't know how to tell her I have no desire to go out with anybody.

Mom wants me to start going to church with her, too, but I think I'm gonna pass. Every time I've ever gone before, people talk about being open and involved and loving. It's very sentimental, and I just don't think I'm up to it. Back in Princeton, I thought every once in a while about ignoring Dad's grumbling and going to church. Especially after Max started talking about God. I'd never thought that Christianity was so logical before. I always thought it was antiscience.

It's not really the logic part that bothers me, though. It's just that it feels too hard to try. I don't like the way my life is right now. But at least I know how to deal with it. I'm not ready to rock that boat just yet. Mom talks about how loving everybody is at the church, but I don't want anyone to say they want to love me. Not if it isn't going to last.

Last night I unpacked my telescope and sat outside, trying to look at the stars. It's not easy here. The city lights are too bright. Stars that were clear in New Jersey are pale here, and some of them I can't even see. Draco the Dragon was almost invisible. I was able to pick out a few of my favorites, though . . . Orion and his belt; the Great Bear; Ursa Major; and of course, Betelgeuse. I still remember the look on my dad's face when I was five years old and I asked him why they named a star after bug guts.

It helps to know that the stars here are the same ones we had in Jersey, even if they aren't as bright. Sometimes it feels funny, looking into the eyepiece of Max's telescope. I never forget that it was his. Sometimes I get the funny feeling that when I look into it, I'm going to see into the past, see something he used to see. Of course, that doesn't happen. But it's fun to imagine that it could.

I've used Max's telescope a lot during the last six months. Dad looked at me real funny the first time he caught me carrying it outside. I'm sure he wondered where it came from and why I wasn't using the one he gave me. But when he opened his mouth to say something, I just gave him a really hard look, and for the first time since I can remember, he snapped his mouth shut and let me be.

Maybe arguing with Mom had taken some of the fight out of him. They argued about everything, not just Dad's work schedule and Mom's religion, during those last few months. Once the big issues became too big to handle, I guess everything else fell apart, too. I don't understand why they had to separate, though. Things have been like this for years, it's nothing new. Mom just said one day that she'd had enough, that she was moving to Washington. No one ever asked me what I thought, whether I wanted to go. It was as if there wasn't any question about me going with Mom. Dad and I haven't gotten along in years. I guess that's why it feels so odd to miss him so much.

After all these years of fighting Dad, it's strange that I'm able to look at the stars and love them again. I think about him when I do. I know that he's looking at them, too, though not in the same way. Where I see mystery and light, he sees radar readings and photometric plots. It's not the same, but it's not exactly different, either. I feel closer to Dad during those times than I have in years.

Sometimes when I'm looking up, I wonder, too, if Max is watching the same sky. It tears me up inside that I never said good-bye. But good-byes are hard. Maybe for some people the only way through them is not to say them at all.

It makes it hard for me to even want to say hello.

September 19, 1997

Gillian's hand slipped gently across the soft red leather cover of the volume she cradled in her lap. Two days after she had made her decision to follow God, Max had given her the Bible as a gift, saying simply: "I can't think of anything more worth celebrating." Inside the front cover, he had scribbled upon one of the slippery white pages:

> *To Gilly —*
> *Today is just the beginning. May God's love and mercies fill your soul from now until the ends of the earth . . . and into the eternity that lies beyond the stars.*
> > *Love,*
> > *Max*

Love . . . Max. The words blurred before her eyes, turning into nothing but a murky cloud of ink. If only she could hear him say it one more time. *"This is something very powerful. Something . . . that feels an awful lot like love."* Gillian had never known before what it felt like to be in love. She'd caught a taste of it when she was a teenager, the first time Max had stolen her heart. But that was nothing like the emotions that now filled her heart. It was different to know him, to love him as an equal and not as a child. It was different, knowing they truly *could* be together and praying that one day that dream would come true.

Never before had anyone cared so deeply for her and the state of her soul. After he had given Gillian the Bible and had watched her leaf through it helplessly, he had taken it upon himself to show her where his favorite verses were and walked her through her initial confusion concerning the book's structure, which she soon discovered was more understandable than it appeared.

At his suggestion, she had chosen to begin her studies with the Gospel accounts. Some nights, she read just a few verses. Other times, she pored over entire chapters. Before long she was meeting Christ face-to-face, discovering amazing truths about the faith she had embraced . . . truths concerning God's love for her, the plan he had for her life. It was still hard to believe it was all real, but Gillian knew that this time — even during those moments when her doubts returned — she would not walk away. She could not afford to.

Especially now.

Gillian kicked back onto the bright yellow couch and groaned. Her heart ached, her soul hurt . . . *everything* about her hurt. Even *she* was appalled at the way she had behaved that afternoon. Angry, out of control, bitter . . . she had lashed out at Max venomously. Not exactly the picture of spiritual virtue . . . or the kind of woman he would want to love. And now, she had ruined everything. Max was a gracious man, but there were limits to what even *he* could withstand. Before she stormed away from the restaurant, Gillian had seen through her tears the hard lines of Max's face, had heard the angry finality in his voice when he ordered her to sit back down and discuss the situation rationally. His tolerance level was high, but finally she had pushed Max Bishop over the top.

I didn't do it on purpose, she thought defensively. *I said what I felt.* Her response to Max's news had been a natural reaction, an instinctive move to extricate herself from the most painful situation she could imagine. Losing Max at all would be agonizing enough. Losing him *slowly* would be pure torture. She could not continue to date him, to allow herself the luxury of his company and his touch. Gillian hardly knew how she could bear to work beside him, growing to love him more with every moment, each day knowing that soon Max would leave her again.

Of course, Max had not yet expressed his decision to leave . . . although if that decision had been in question before their argument, it most certainly was settled in his heart by now. Surely Max would not want to be with her anymore. Gillian didn't even want to be with herself.

She opened the book sitting across her knees and started to flip forward to the book of Luke but paused as the pages fell open to a passage she had highlighted in Matthew 21, several weeks before.

He said to his disciples, "Why are you so afraid? Do you still have no faith?"

A knot tightened in Gillian's stomach as she read the words a second time . . . then another. Jesus might as well have been speaking to her. In the past month, her fears had subsided to a certain degree. But now, faced with the prospect of losing

Max, her feelings of panic and loneliness were quickly rising . . . and growing. She closed her eyes and prayed,

Lord, please help me. I feel like I'm losing it, here. Max told me today that he's thinking about leaving Princeton again, and I went off the deep end. I screamed and yelled, made a whole big scene. Max didn't deserve that. I'm sure you couldn't have been pleased. Her prayer was silent, but the words tumbled through her mind even faster than she could speak them.

I know you want me to have faith, God. But I am afraid. Afraid of losing Max, afraid of failing you . . . afraid of never having another relationship, of any kind, that will last longer than a month or two. . . .

Gillian wrapped her arms around herself and pulled them close, craving any tiny measure of comfort she could receive.

I'm sorry I've been so stubborn. Please help me to find some kind of peace. I want to trust you, but I can't imagine how you could make any good come out of this situation, Lord. Still, I'll be happy if you do. And I believe that you can, even if I can't see it.

She thought hard for a moment, then squinted her eyes up tight and offered up one last plea: *God, I feel like what I said to Max is true. I can't handle it if he's going to go away. I'm afraid of leaving my heart open and then losing him.* The floodgates were open now, and the words came easily. *But at the same time, I don't want to give up completely, even though that's what I've always wanted to do before. I love him, Lord. I really love him. If you have someone else for him, I guess there's nothing I can do about that. But I want you to know that I do care for him, more than I've ever cared for anyone before, even though I never told him so. I'm really glad I had him in my life, and I want to thank you for that. If I have to let him go, I'll try. I'll need your help to get through it, Lord, but I'll try. Still, I can't help but ask — because I'm finally learning that you want me to bring my dreams to you — if there's any possibility of getting one last chance, Lord, I'd be so grateful. All I ask is one more chance —*

Her lips were still moving, silently, when the front screen door swung open wide and slammed shut with a bang. Gillian opened her eyes to see Bridget stepping in from the sunshine. As usual, her eyes narrowed slightly at the sight of Gillian, but the look passed quickly, and soon her face was devoid of emotion.

"Hi, Gillian," she said casually and dropped her backpack to the floor. Gillian quickly uttered a silent *Amen* and gave her

296

roommate a curious look. Bridget's entrance at that particular moment in time was not especially remarkable. It was true that she nearly always arrived home much later in the day. But it wasn't unheard of for her to take the afternoon off. Maybe class had been canceled; perhaps she had a stomachache. Still, Gillian could not help but wonder at the timing. Hadn't she just prayed for one more chance? Of course, she had been talking about Max and was sure that God knew it. After her behavior that day, such a reprieve didn't seem likely. Perhaps God was offering her a new beginning with Bridget instead.

She cleared her throat loudly, as if she were preparing to speak before a hall of VFW veterans. "Hey, Bridget," she said brightly, addressing the woman in her warmest tone. "How'd your day go?"

Bridget gave her an odd stare. "Fine," she said quickly, but not rudely, and proceeded to make a beeline through the living room.

"Uh . . . hey, Bridget?" Gillian called after her, wondering how she could get her roommate to stop and talk.

The woman hesitated. "Yeah?" She stood with one hand on her denim-skirted hip. Her white blouse was limp and hung heavily against her skin. She looked tired. Her tone did not invite casual conversation. If Gillian wanted to talk with Bridget about the situation, she was just going to have to cut to the chase.

"Um, I feel like I really need to talk to you," Gillian said timidly. She looked into Bridget's brown doe eyes and felt a pang in her heart at the blatant mistrust she read there.

"What about?" Bridget asked uneasily.

"Well, it's about the whole Max thing," Gillian admitted, then raised one hand as Bridget opened her mouth to protest. "I know, I know, we've covered this already, but I still feel terrible about it, and I think there are some things I need to say. You may not need to go over this again, but I do, and I'd really appreciate it if you'd let me talk about it with you."

Bridget studied her warily, then cautiously moved back into the living room. She perched herself on the edge of the well-worn red armchair, as if prepared at any moment to take flight. She said nothing, simply waited for Gillian to speak.

Bridget obviously didn't want to sit around and gab, so Gillian began to speak, "I don't know exactly what to say here, Bridget," she admitted, standing awkwardly at the woman's side. "I think I've apologized, but it doesn't seem like that's enough. I know you're still mad at me, you probably hate me . . . and honestly, I understand." The longer she stood there, trying to connect with the unresponsive statue that was Bridget, the more desperate for forgiveness she felt. "I didn't at first. I couldn't see anything, really, except the fact that I was mad, too. I kind of get that way, you know? Defensive. But I know you trusted me, and I know I let you down. I don't know how to fix that."

"I don't know if you can," Bridget said honestly.

"Yeah." Gillian relaxed a bit at this first sign of real interaction. "I know. Like I said, I don't know what to tell you. My intention never was to hurt you." She tried to think of what else to say. It wasn't easy. Normally, it was her practice just to let broken relationships slip away. She hadn't extended herself in an attempt to salvage one since she was a child. "I don't know . . . I just went sort of crazy when Max got here," she tried to explain, hoping Bridget would somehow understand.

"He was . . . he was the first guy I ever felt anything for, and the last one I ever believed in. I never felt very loved by my dad, but Max at least made me feel special for a while. He treated me like I was important and valuable. After he left, I was all mixed up inside." Gillian noticed that Bridget's expression had softened slightly, and she blushed at the pity she thought she saw there. She started to turn away. "I guess this is *way* more information than you want or need about my life, so I'll just —"

"No, it's not," Bridget said clearly.

"What?" Gillian stopped and gave her a strange look. "It's not?"

"No." Bridget's short curls danced as she swung her head from side to side. "Do you realize that's the first time you told me anything personal — I mean *really* personal about your life?"

"No." Gillian stared at her. "I'm sure it's not."

"*Gillian,*" her roommate sighed in exasperation. "It is. I think you mentioned once that your parents were separated. And one time when Pam and I were grilling you about your track record with guys you mumbled something about getting burned when you were younger. That is *not* the same as sharing on a personal level."

"I guess you're right," Gillian admitted reluctantly.

"Gillian, despite what you think, I really don't hate you," Bridget said sadly, her stone-faced facade finally broken. "I never hated you. Not for a minute. I liked you a *lot*. That's why I felt so bad when I thought you'd turned on me."

"Oh, Bridget!" The sting of hot tears came to her eyes. "I never meant to turn on you. And I wasn't trying to keep Max for myself, honestly I wasn't!"

"I know," Bridget said, and she sounded as if she meant it. "But can you see why I would feel that way?"

"Of course I can. But can't you see that I —"

"Gillian." The look in Bridget's eyes was considerably less than fond. "You said you didn't know what else to do to make things better. Do you want me to tell you?"

She could see that Bridget was serious. "Yes, I do."

"If you want me to forgive you, then *ask* me to forgive you. Don't just keep on telling me your side of the story. If you know that you did something wrong, then apologize and leave it at that. I feel like you keep waiting for me to say it was okay. It *wasn't* okay. But that doesn't mean I

301

won't forgive you."

Suddenly, Gillian felt as though a massive weight had been lifted from her shoulders. Something miraculous was occurring. Bridget was actually *talking* to her. They were connecting. Perhaps — no, *unquestionably* — more than they ever had before. Here, at last, was the hope she feared she'd lost. "Bridget, I *am* sorry about what happened," she said honestly. "It doesn't matter what my intentions were. I handled things poorly. I hurt you, and I was wrong. Please," she said as meaningfully as she could, "would you forgive me?"

The emotional wall crashed to the ground. Brown eyes brimming, Bridget stood and threw her arms around Gillian's shoulders. "Of course I forgive you, Gil," she sniffed. "All you ever had to do was ask." Gillian found herself wrapping both arms around Bridget and hugging her, too. Moments later, the two collapsed side-by-side on the couch. Both were exhausted from crying, but it was a good exhaustion, and Gillian's soul felt lighter.

"You know," Bridget said after several minutes, "I really need to ask your forgiveness, too."

"You do?" Gillian looked at her in wonder. Then she felt a wave of amazement over the fact that she actually felt surprised. Up until several minutes earlier, she had been harboring a grudge against Bridget. In the process of humbling herself before her roommate, her own grievances had been forgotten.

"Yeah, I do," Bridget was saying. "I pushed you pretty hard, and there were a couple of times when I was pretty nasty. I'm sorry, Gil. I had no right to act that way."

"All's forgiven." Gillian smiled and impulsively reached out and gave her another quick hug.

"So . . ." Bridget said cheerfully, the awkward moment past, "What are you doing tonight? You wanna go grab a latté?" She interrupted herself. "No, probably not. I suppose you're going out with Max again?" Gillian's face fell. "What? What did I say?" she asked anxiously.

Before her conversion, Gillian would have brushed the question aside and left it at that. Opening up about something so personal, so close to her heart, was foreign territory to her. But something had changed in Gillian. It was as if the buds of trust were opening in her for the first time since she was sixteen. Within minutes, she had managed to explain to Bridget, through her tears, that she and Max had fought — though she did not go into detail concerning the specifics of the argument — that she was terrified of losing him, and that she had never been so miserable in all her life.

As the story unfolded, Bridget sat at Gillian's side without saying a word, patting her back and murmuring comforting phrases.

"I don't know what to tell you," Bridget confessed after she had finished. Gillian continued sniffling into a white tissue from a cardboard box on the end table. "It sounds like you have a lot to think about. I'm probably not the best person to advise you," she said honestly. "But . . . there's one thing I *can* do." She smiled eagerly, an action that caused her whole face to light up.

"What's that?" Gillian asked as she grabbed two more tissues.

At just that moment, the front door opened once more. After two steps, Pam froze just inside the threshold and stared at the two women on the couch, her eyes grazing over Gillian first, then the pile of wadded-up tissues, and finally resting on Bridget.

"Having a party?" she quipped dryly.

"*No,*" said Bridget indignantly, "but we *are* going out on the town. You, too, Pam."

"What?" Gillian turned to her, openmouthed. "We are?"

"We are?" Pam repeated, in a tone that said, "If you're going to include me in your little plans, you'd better explain yourself, missy."

"We *are,*" Bridget repeated firmly. She laid one hand on Gillian's arm. "We can't make your problems go away, but we can at least try to help you forget about them for a little while."

"But, Bridget, I don't think I can forget about anything," Gillian said heavily. "Besides, I have to get up early. I just want to go to my room and —"

"And what? Mope?" Bridget flicked her hand in the air in a dismissive gesture. "You've got two weeks to do that. You're leaving in the morning, and I want you to remember that you've got something good to come home to. *Your friends,*" she said pointedly, reaching out and patting her on the knee. "Don't worry about getting up early; we'll make sure you're not out too late."

By now, Pam was ready to jump on the bandwagon. "Why not, Gil?" she suggested, looking clearly relieved that the two had finally resolved their differences. "It's your last night home, let's go paint the town." She stepped into the living room and planted herself in the red armchair.

"Besides," Bridget jumped in, "if you're having a hard time right now, what you need is to be around your girlfriends."

Those words, more than any others, were the ones that made the decision for her. The last thing Gillian wanted was to have to spend the night being cheerful. But she'd never had friends before that she could turn to in times of crisis. It was a dangling carrot too appetizing to resist.

"Do I have to be in a good mood?" she grumbled.

"Nope," Bridget promised. "You can do anything you want. We'll let you pick the movie, the restaurant. I'll even buy you a big, sticky piece of German chocolate cake."

"I don't think I want chocolate cake," Gillian told her.

Her two roommates stared at each other in horror. "Not want chocolate?" Pam said, as if she could not believe she'd heard the words.

Bridget shook her head sadly and felt Gillian's forehead for a fever, like a sick child. "Poor thing," she sympathized. "You must be even worse off than I thought. Oh, well. More cake for me!"

Though the feelings of loss still wracked her soul, Gillian managed to muster a weak smile at the realization of how far the two of them had just come. The thought came, crazily, that Max would be proud of Gillian if he knew. . . . He would tell her she was growing, that God was working in her heart. It was at that moment that the truth behind the words Max once spoke hit Gillian with tremendous force:

"With God, all things are possible."

She smiled.

Apparently, even the impossible.

Fifteen

I will not let thee go.
I hold thee by too many bands;
Thou sayest farewell, and lo!
I have thee by the hands,
And will not let thee go.
ROBERT BRIDGES,
I WILL NOT LET THEE GO

January 7, 1989

Had a great time up in Princeton this week-end. With Dad's schedule being so busy and all, I don't get up there half as much as I'd like. Virginia and D.C. are nice, too, but it's just not the same as New Jersey. Dad had me talk to one of the guys in the admissions office. Normally, they don't work weekends, I'm sure. But Dad's still got a lot of clout. It actually felt pretty good being back on campus. As a kid, I always thought I would end up going to school there. I remember wandering around feeling like such a child. I don't feel like a child anymore.

As we left Admissions, Dad told me that he wanted to head over to his office to pick up

308

some papers he'd left there the day before. Dad's getting a little scatterbrained these days. Maybe it's age, I don't know. It could be something else. He hasn't been the same since Mom left, I've noticed. And I'm not the only one.

Mom told me last month that Dad got into a bit of trouble with the head honchos at the university. I don't know how she knew. I guess Dad must have told her. Anyway, it seems that Dad's performance has suffered a little bit over the last year. I've seen it a little in talking with him. His mind isn't as sharp, that's for sure. Apparently, his classes aren't filling up quite as quickly anymore, and I heard he got in trouble for turning in his grades late. Dad always said, if there's one thing universities take seriously, besides money, it's grades.

So Dad and I stopped by the office where we ran into Dr. Randall. I hadn't seen him in years — not since before Mom and I moved, I think. Not that I ever saw him much before. He and Dad have always been pretty competitive. Theirs is kind of a love-hate friendship. Anyway, we spent a few minutes catching up, then he asked Dad if he'd heard about the guy from Harvard.

"Who?" Dad asked.

"You know. Oh, I forget his name. Wait, it's around here somewhere. . . ." I didn't think

much about it. I don't know who the professors are over at Harvard, and I really couldn't care less. But it turned out it wasn't a teacher, after all.

"Here it is," Randall said. "Look!" He held it out to my father. Dad's face turned bright red. I looked over his shoulder.

And there it was, some scientific abstract about multidimensional theories in cosmology, written by a doctor named Zeller, or Zellum, or something. But right underneath Zeller's name, as a special honor, they had printed the name of the graduate student who assisted him in his work:

Maxwell Bishop.

Dad looked like he'd swallowed a goldfish. Ol' Randall looked pretty smug. I don't know that I felt anything at first. Crushes are strange things. The year after I met Max, I thought about him a lot. I needed to. It was a hard year, and I didn't have much else that made me feel good. Not that missing him felt good. It was agony, pure and simple. I know, I know . . . every girl obsesses about her first crush for a while. But this crush dragged on for a long time, even after he was gone.

The truth is, I still think about Max sometimes. Mostly when I'm lonely. It feels like a cruel trick, to find someone I think I could care about, no, that I actually did care about, *and to have him snatched away.*

I don't really have reason to complain, though. I have a pretty good life. I have my entire college experience ahead of me. My relationship with my parents may not be the best in the world, but at least it's improving. And of course, I've got the stars . . . and I always will.

That's right, I finally decided on a major. My counselor at school told me I had a year or more to choose one, but Dad was insistent. He was speechless when I told him I was going for astrophysics. I suppose I could have chosen math or general physics and kept my career plans to myself. But what would have been the point of that? I'm the one who would have suffered most, not Dad. Besides, I don't feel so much like punishing him anymore. After all, he is *the one who gave me a love for the stars in the first place. At least I have that to thank him for. It feels good to finally be able to say that. It took me a long time to get over blaming him for losing Max.*

I suspect I may still think about Max too much. Oh, I don't daydream about him, really. But he's always there, just under the surface of my memory . . . when I'm out on a date, when I'm thinking about the future and all that lies ahead. I remember how kind Max was to me, how compassionate and understanding. I remember the way he stood up to my dad and made his scientific theories palatable even to my mother. I remember his passion for his studies, his work, his future . . . even his God. It makes it hard to put much effort into dating guys who take me to kickboxing movies and talk about souping up their Trans-Ams. I always thought I'd get married someday, but I'm not sure I believe it anymore.

I want a family, though. Deep inside, there's a part of me that dreams about having a baby, pushing a tricycle, being a Den Mother. I picture lazy Saturday mornings filled with crossword puzzles and coffee . . . I see my husband and me painting the house together. I imagine lying out in the backyard, pointing up at the sky above, and telling my own daughter or son about the star made of bug guts. It's a "Hi, honey, I'm home" kind of dream.

I just have a hard time picturing the man who calls me "Honey."

September 20, 1997

Gillian yawned and stretched, wishing for the umpteenth time that she had taken the time to program her roommate's automatic coffeemaker the night before. Five-thirty had come all too early this morning . . . this in spite of the fact that she hadn't

312

slept a wink. She supposed she owed Bridget and Pam a debt of gratitude. If they hadn't taken her out the night before, she probably would have lain awake, staring at her plaster ceiling for more than ten hours instead of a mere six and a half.

Grumpily, she glared at the line that snaked ahead of her up to the airline ticket counter. It wouldn't be so bad, standing here, she thought, if I didn't really need a cup of coffee. She craved caffeine. Unlike Bridget, Gillian could not depend on java alone to get her going in the morning. She needed food, too. Today, she'd had neither, and as a result, she was feeling incredibly crabby.

Except . . . that wasn't exactly true, and she knew it. The cause of her distress was less physiological than it was emotional. When she'd come home last night, the first thing she'd done was check the answering machine for messages, but none were left. Clearly, Max didn't want to talk to her. But, then, why was that a surprise?

In an attempt to draw her mind away from thoughts of Max, she focused on a nearby monitor, trying to read the arrival and departure times, but there wasn't any point in that. Nothing had worked the night before, nothing was going to work now. Pam and Bridget had been real troopers, taking her out for dinner and a comedy film — "No romances allowed," Bridget had ordered as she scanned the paper's movie section — then stuffing her with air-cooked movie-theater popcorn.

Though the other two women had enjoyed the movie, Gillian hadn't let out so much as a giggle. She couldn't even remember the basic plot an hour afterward; that was how much attention she had been paying. Her roommates were understanding, though, and even sweet about it throughout the entire evening. Conversation at dinner had been light, and Pam and Bridget had carried Gillian's portion of it. Her silence at the theater was clearly noticed, but not commented upon. And after the movie, the women had taken her at her word when she said she wanted to go home. Gillian knew that they hadn't expected to actually cheer her up; they just wanted her to know that she wasn't alone. And for that, she truly was thankful.

As the line began to slither forward, Gillian grabbed her bags and moved ahead. At least they were moving. That was something.

Despite her heavy eyes, her irritation, and her growling stomach, time eventually passed, and she was able to check in with twenty-five minutes to spare before boarding. A grim-looking airline worker checked her large suitcase while a cheerful ticket agent handed Gillian her boarding pass. After a brief stop at a concourse coffee stand, she found herself sitting in one of the rows of plastic seats near the gate: carry-on bag at her feet, *café au lait* and sugar-free bran muffin in hand. As she waited, she peeled back the paper of her breakfast, which under normal circumstances would have been a treat. But this morning it tasted like sawdust.

Gillian washed the muffin down with coffee, enjoying the comforting feel of it as it eased down her throat. She needed the liquid's warmth — her short-sleeved willow-green T-shirt, loose-fitting jeans, and white canvas sneakers were perfect for a hot southern California climate but not an air-conditioned airport terminal.

She stared out the waiting-area window at the airplane that would soon carry her three thousand miles away from the man she loved. Flight attendants and pilots slipped through a door clearly designated for airport personnel. As she waited for the gate to open, feelings of regret settled over her, and her heart was filled with doubt.

Had she done the right thing in revealing her feelings to Max? It was obvious that she had handled the situation poorly, ranting like a lunatic . . . but were her feelings valid? Gillian played the argument over and over again in her mind, just as she had hundreds of times the night before. Her conclusion was the same every time. There was no way around it. There was nothing Max could have said that would have calmed her. She had been completely out of control. She couldn't justify herself by saying it had been a natural expression of emotions. The truth was, she hadn't expressed a single emotion other than anger, and even that had been communicated in a less than healthy manner. She could not expect Max to forgive her for such an outburst.

Her conversation with Bridget had had a tremendous impact on her, however. Following a full night of soul-searching, she knew she had to at least try to make peace with Max. After listening to Bridget's frank advice, Gillian understood that it was possible to work through conflicts. Max might not want to be close to her anymore, but at least she could ask him for his forgiveness. It might not bring him back, but it could at least help to soften his anger and add some closure to the whole ordeal.

She was licking dry bran crumbs from her fingers when the flight attendant informed the crowd that the boarding of their flight would begin.

"At this time we would like to begin seating all passengers with small children and those requiring special assistance," the perky brunette announced.

I wonder if that includes mental and emotional assistance, Gillian thought sarcastically. She had tipped her head back and was letting the last bit of coffee dribble into her mouth when she noticed the figure standing over her. The sight of him nearly caused her to spit the liquid out again. Gillian choked and swallowed hard and coughed once more, while he stood patiently waiting for her to compose herself.

"Max! What are you *doing* here?" she finally managed. Her heart beat heavily within her chest.

His clothes — stone-washed jeans and a crazy, navy-blue-flowered pseudo-Hawaiian shirt — were wrinkled, just as they had been the last time he'd been too preoccupied to plug in an iron. "I'm heading out to Palomar Mountain," he said simply, indicating the carry-on bag at his side.

Gillian stared at him, not understanding.

"Does this mean the school isn't sending me, after all? Do you want — ? Am I supposed to give you my ticket? Am I —" Gillian's skin turned pale as she made the connection. "Oh *no*. Does this mean I'm off the project?" She felt sickened that her tantrum might have lost her the best job she'd ever gotten. But hadn't she been thinking of the same possibility herself? If her relationship with Max was over, it would be nearly impossible to work together . . . even if it was just through the end of the school year. She had already decided that she would give Ed a call about the whole thing before she returned.

Max shook his head at her reaction. "No, of course not, silly. You're not off of anything." His face and voice still betrayed nothing.

She could not believe that he was actually standing there. "But you just said —"

"Look, we'll get to what I just said in a minute, okay?" he said firmly. "But right now, there are a few things I want to say to you."

"O-kay," she agreed. Her heart kept its wild cadence.

There was an empty seat in Gillian's row, but Max remained standing and

318

quickly began to pace. "You know, you rushed off yesterday without even giving me a chance to say a word," he said roughly, wasting no time in getting to the point.

"I know, Max," Gillian murmured unhappily. "I'm sorry." Here it was. Max's good-bye speech. She had known all along it would come to this.

"Do you have any idea what it did to me, to see you all broken up like that?" he said, his voice thick with emotion. He continued to wander the aisle erratically.

The words floated in Gillian's head, as if unsure of where to land. What was Max saying? He wasn't making any sense. She struggled to grasp some small measure of understanding.

The flight attendant's voice broke in over the loudspeaker. "Could we now have all passengers assigned to rows eighteen through —"

Max planted his feet on the carpet directly in front of Gillian and held her eyes with his own. "Gilly, I've cared about you ever since you were a girl," he said frankly. "I've been attracted to you since the minute I saw you in Ed's office. And I've loved you —" He searched for words. "I think *part* of me has loved you all along, but over the past month or so, that love has grown exponentially," he said, drawing upon his extensive mathematical background to provide the analogy. "I think about you when I wake up in the morning; I think about you when I'm working —" he gave her a hint of a smile — "which is a *major* distraction, I have to tell you, especially when you're in the next room."

His words mystified her. Gillian stared at him blankly, trying to solve the mystery of what he might be trying to say. What did any of this have to do with him being at the airport? And why was he being so nice to her? Was he trying to spare her feelings?

"Max, if you're going to yell at me, it's okay," she said quietly. "Go ahead and get it over with. I've been expecting it."

But Max gave no indication of wanting to yell at her. In fact, his voice was gentle and soothing. "Gillian," he said carefully, "when you snapped yesterday, I was shocked at first, and then, yes, very angry when you wouldn't let me explain. After you rushed out of the restaurant, part of me wanted to go after you. But part of me had to cool off. Do you understand that?"

She nodded meekly.

"The thing is," he said, keeping his eyes fixed on hers, "the more I thought about it, the more I could understand." The look he gave her was increasingly tender. "Gilly, I wasn't aware of it at the time, but I know you had a hard time that year with your parents' separation. Back then, I *did* know that you had a crush on me, but I had no idea my leaving would hurt you so badly. I thought it was just a little thing, a feeling that would fade before I was even gone. But I did care about you. That's why I —"

She nodded soberly. "The telescope."

"Yeah. The telescope," Max agreed. "I wasn't trying to buy you off, Gilly, so you wouldn't be angry. I just thought it was a little something you'd remember me by." His cheeks flushed red. "I guess it was selfish, but even then I wanted to make sure you wouldn't forget me."

Gillian's eyes grew wide. As if she could ever forget Max! But why on earth was he saying all this? He didn't want to be with her anymore. How could he?

Max continued sentimentally, "Gillian, the truth of the matter is, I love you. I've loved you for a long time. And as far as my going to Rome is concerned —"

"Max, no." Gillian stood and lay one hand gently upon his arm. "I'm sorry. I had no right to get angry with you. It's none of my business what you do. I was going to call you when I got to Pasadena and apolog—"

"*Gillian.*" The word was spoken as an admonishment, but there was amusement in his eyes. "Would you please let me finish for once?" Thoroughly chastised, she stepped back to listen. "What I'm *trying* to say," he insisted, "and what I was trying to explain *yesterday,* is that I have no intention of moving back to Rome."

Gillian shook her head. She couldn't have heard right. "You don't?"

"No, I don't. When I said I wanted to go back, I meant for a *visit.*"

She gave him a look of utter confusion. "But — but you said you were going at the end of the school year. I just assumed that the reason you wanted to go this month was to talk with them at the university about coming back. June seemed like a logical time to make a transition, to move away —"

"Do you hear yourself talking?" Max chuckled, but his laughter was not malicious. "Sweetie, I'm *not* moving away," he assured her vehemently. At the sound of the familiar endearment, Gillian felt her old fears begin to recede, ever so slightly. Slowly, a faint look of hope began to soften her features as he continued. "I'm right *here*, right now. Quite literally, in fact." He glanced around the airport terminal. Nearby, the flight crew glanced at the two of them nervously as they ushered a large group of passengers toward the plane. "And do you know why I'm here? In this airport? Getting on this plane at this unholy hour of the morning?" he asked dramatically. "Well, I'll tell you why. It's because I want to be with *you*. I'm not willing to let you go like this, and I'm willing to do whatever it takes to work through things."

"But the university said they'd only pay for one of us," Gillian protested.

"That's okay," Max assured her. "I bought the ticket myself. And I have some friends in Los Angeles I can stay with. Don't worry about any of that."

"You said you were going to Rome. . . ." she said feebly.

"Gillian, *please*." He looked offended that she thought he would even consider such a thing. "Did you actually expect me to fly halfway around the world when things are so unresolved between us?"

Gillian looked up at him helplessly, tears in her eyes. "Max, I didn't know! I thought you would hate me after the way I acted. How can you even want to *be* with me after that?"

Max reached out with one strong hand and caressed her face, tracing a line from her left temple to the delicate tip of her chin. "Because that wasn't you," he explained lovingly. "That's just a *part* of you, Gilly. The angry part. And believe it or not, I love the angry part, just like I love the rest of you. It might make *me* angry sometimes, too. But it's one dimension of who you are, so I accept it." With the stroke of his thumb, he wiped away one stray tear that had slipped from her eye and rolled down her cheek. "Besides, there's a lot more to you than just screaming and yelling."

Gillian flinched. "I *did* scream and yell, didn't I?" Her face turned scarlet, and she covered her mouth with one hand, giving him a look of chagrin. "Max, I've behaved horribly, and I completely mistrusted you. Can you ever forgive me?"

"Yes, I forgive you," he promised solemnly, brushing back a lock of golden hair that had fallen over her damp eyes. "But that brings up another issue."

Gillian stiffened and steeled herself for what he was about to say. "What issue is that?" she asked suspiciously.

"One of the most important issues of all: trust." Max told her simply. "You know, I can understand more or less why you jumped to the conclusion you did, Gilly, because I know a bit about your past. I've seen that trust is a major issue for you. But . . ." He paused and considered his words. "I have to say, I don't think most people would have jumped to the same conclusion. I think your mind twisted the words, and you believed the worst, without stopping to consider any other option." The words were harsh, but the compassion with which he spoke them softened the blow.

"Even after I tried to explain, you wouldn't hear it. It was as though there was a part of you that didn't want to believe in me, in us." He forced her to meet his eyes. "Do you think that's possible, Gilly?"

She closed her eyes and nodded wordlessly, pressing her cheek against the warmth of his hand in a gesture that expressed both a feeling of regret and a desire for comfort. Max responded to the unspoken request, untangling his fingers from her hair and enfolding her in the circle of his arms. Slowly, purposely, she allowed herself to relax within the sanctuary of his embrace.

"Gilly, I'm not ready to make you any

grand proposal. Not yet," he whispered against the soft skin at her temple. "We haven't been together long enough for that. But I *can* promise you this: I am completely, one-hundred-percent committed to being here now, and to learning to love you well." He paused for a moment, giving her a chance to let his words sink in.

"Life is about choices," he said at last, "and I'm choosing to love you. I'm choosing to see where that love will go. But that's not enough. *You* have choices, too. One of them is whether or not you want to love me."

"But, Max, I do —" He silenced her with one finger to her rosy lips.

"No, no, Gilly. I don't doubt your heart on that one. It's the other question I'm worried about. The toughest choice for you, I think, will be deciding whether or not you're going to trust in my love for you."

Gillian laid her head against the solid, comforting warmth of his chest, feeling the steady rise and fall of his breathing, pondering his words. Max was right. She hadn't believed in him . . . or in their relationship. Realizing that she had gone back to her old ways frightened her. But Max had forgiven her, and he believed in her and was willing to stick it out, to make their love grow . . . that was a truth that brought her hope.

"Gillian," he said gently, "a while back, I asked you to make the most important choice of your life, one that would affect you eternally. Now, I'm asking you to do it one more time, to make one more choice — one that will impact the rest of your natural life. I'm asking you to *believe* in me. To believe in love."

Firmly, he grasped her by the shoulders and stepped back, holding her out in front of him where he could see her entire face. "I'm not saying that I'll never fail you," he warned. "But I *am* promising to love you the very best that I can."

Gillian gave him a tremulous smile. "You know, a month ago, I wouldn't have been sure how to answer you," she answered a bit unsteadily. "Two months ago, I'm pretty certain I would have run away. In the past few weeks, though, and even in the past few days, I've learned what it means to let myself be led by God." As she spoke she gathered confidence. Finally, she could meet Max's eyes without feeling a sense of shame. She was healing. She was on her way.

"When I see how much he's changed me

already, how he's surprised me in every area of my life, I can believe that there is reason to hope, no matter what lies ahead." Impatiently, she wiped the tears from her eyes, wanting nothing to blur her vision of the man she adored.

"I love you, too, Max!" she said passionately. "I want to learn what it means to know you, and to let you know me. I know there's a risk. But I think . . . no, I *know* I'm ready. And I'm willing to trust that no matter what happens, God will be with us, helping us through."

With those final words, the last of the questions were answered, the last of the walls torn down. His eyes brimming with tears, Max placed one hand on either side of Gillian's face and stepped in close, so their bodies were almost — but not quite — touching. With breathless anticipation, Gillian watched, wide-eyed, as his face drew ever nearer, anticipating the gentle sweetness of his lips on hers. . . .

"THIS IS THE *LAST* CALL FOR FLIGHT NUMBER FOUR SIX TWO," the once-perky flight attendant announced meaningfully, staring pointedly at the tickets in Gillian's and Max's hands.

Gillian jumped. Max laughed and planted an off-center kiss on the side of

328

her nose, diffusing her look of disappointment by whispering, "Later, my love."

"And now, I believe that's our boarding call." He grinned and waved cheerfully at the airline attendant, indicating that they were on their way. "I don't know about you," he told Gillian confidently, "but I'm looking forward to spending some quality time at the telescope together." Carry-on bags shouldered, they headed for the gate.

Gillian smiled up at the man who had so completely captured her heart, her earlier suffering forgotten. "I'm so glad you're coming, Max!"

He returned the grin. "Me, too. I have a funny feeling you and I may very well be spending the rest of our lives together, gazing at stars," he said. "And I can't wait to begin."

Gillian shook her head seriously and reached up to bestow one more kiss on his cheek before boarding. "Oh no, Max," she told him, her heart brimming with the promise of love. "We've already begun."

Epilogue

Surely he has done great things.
JOEL 2:20
*Praise the LORD, O my soul, and forget
not all his benefits — who . . .
crowns you with love and compassion,
who satisfies your desires with good things. . . .*
PSALM 103:2-5

One spring morning

"Honey, you up? Gilly? Hon?"

Moaning softly, Gillian withdrew one hand from under the thick down comforter and swatted halfheartedly at the warm breath tickling her ear. "Unnh. Go 'way." She fumbled with the tangerine plaid bedspread, hoping — but failing — to pull it up over her ears before the next attack.

"Hooooooooo-ney," Max softly blew on a tendril of honey-colored hair at her temple, then ended the teasing once and for all with a solid kiss to her ear. "Come on, lazybones. Get up. You've slept half the morning. It's time to wake up and smell the coffee."

Gillian rolled over to face the man sitting beside her on the feather bed, holding a steaming mug of fragrant French roast. She issued a blank stare through sleepy eyes, somehow managing to keep her laughter in check. "You've just been *dying* for me to wake up so you could say that, haven't you?" she asked groggily.

Max grinned and waggled his eyebrows. "*Maaaay*-be. Then again, maybe I've just been dying for you to wake up so I could give you this. . . ." Carefully holding the coffee out to one side of the bed, he leaned in once more — this time seeking out her lips and planting them with a kiss that was gentle, yet held a tantalizing hint of promise.

"Mmm," Gillian said a moment later, smacking her lips. "Tastes like you've already had your coffee."

"That's right," Max agreed, watching her playfully. He began to inch forward once more. "And now I'm going to get some sugar. . . ."

Gillian laughed and squealed and rolled slowly out of reach, watching Max struggle to balance the coffee as the mattress moved under her weight.

"Watcha doin', Mama?" a sweet voice called from the doorway. Gillian sat up and smiled. In her pale-yellow footie pajamas and halo of golden curls, the child resembled a small sun.

"Come here, angel," Gillian said lovingly, and sat up in bed, making room for her daughter's flannel-covered body. She fluffed up two plump pillows and positioned them behind her back. "Oh, not there, sweetie," she said gently, as Emily wriggled up into her lap, poking one tiny elbow against her slightly burgeoning belly.

"Did I hurt the baby?" Emmie asked, moving over slightly but staying within the warm circle of her mother's arms. Her tiny features pinched together in a serious expression.

"No, no. It's okay, Em," Gillian assured her, running her fingers through the child's unruly curls. "I've got quite a bit of padding down there." She laughed and rolled her eyes at Max, who had placed the coffee on the nightstand and was settling down beside them to cuddle with "his girls." "Maybe a little *too* much padding," she complained wryly.

"Now, now. That's just silly." Max leaned down to plant a kiss on the stomach in question. "The doctor said you're right on schedule weight-wise. Besides . . . you're beautiful."

"Hmm." Gillian pretended not to believe him, but her face was flushed with pleasure.

"Mama?"

"Mmm, yes, sweetheart?"

Emily turned her head and looked up at Gillian with wide eyes the same shade of blue as the sky. "I want to ride my bike," she announced, referring to the cherry-red tricycle she had received for her third birthday. To Emmie, every two- or three-wheeled vehicle was a "bike."

"I think we can do that today," Gillian told her. Across the top of Emmie's head, her eyes met Max's and caught the look of love in them. A soft smile teased her lips and spread across her face as she looked at her beautiful child and then her adoring husband.

Gillian reveled in the feeling of contentment. If only she could have known as a teenager, and as a young woman, what God had in store for her. If only she could have trusted, could have believed. How different her life might have been! How much more joyous. . . .

Such thoughts still came to her as she struggled to come to terms with the life she had once lived. And yet, the realization had recently dawned on her that it was this same life — the life filled with loneliness, anger, and fear — that led her to make the life choices that had placed her in the path of Max: the man who would lead her to the Lord and one day become her husband.

The feeling of sadness was fleeting, her heart surged with delight once again. Perhaps this was yet another manifestation of God's mercy: the realization that all things in life — all choices, all emotions, all failures, all weaknesses — are redeemable by God. The aspects of her life she hated most were the very ones that had ultimately drawn her to God's arms. It was true: all things *did* work to the glory of God for those who loved him. Even for people like her.

"No, Mama," Emily insisted, interrupting her thoughts. "I wanna ride my bike *now*."

Max grinned. Gillian smiled ruefully. Their little girl certainly was a handful. But she was a lovable handful, a precious handful, and Emmie's parents treasured every minute with her.

"Breakfast first," she informed the child.

"But, Mama —"

"No 'buts,'" Gillian insisted. "And you've got to get dressed and brush your teeth before you can go outside."

"Slave driver," Max whispered in her ear.

Gillian's lips twitched in amusement. "Your father will help you," she said.

Max laughed and kissed Gillian once more — this time on the forehead, for good measure — then scooped up his giggling little girl and swung her around the sun-drenched room before heading off to satisfy Gillian's list of demands.

As Gillian watched them go, a feeling of contentment welled up inside her. The Lord who was able to accomplish great and mighty things had outdone himself when it came to her life. Great were his blessings. Mighty was his grace.

And the words Max had written in her Bible six years ago were true.

It was just the beginning.